THE
STORYTELLER
OF
AUSCHWITZ

BOOKS BY SIOBHAN CURHAM

An American in Paris

Beyond This Broken Sky

The Paris Network

The Secret Keeper

The Scene Stealers

Frankie Says Relapse

Sweet FA

Non-Fiction

Something More: A Spiritual Misfit's Search for Meaning

Dare to Write a Novel

Dare to Dream

Antenatal & Postnatal Depression

THE
STORYTELLER
OF
AUSCHWITZ

SIOBHAN CURHAM

bookouture

Published by Bookouture in 2023

An imprint of Storyfire Ltd.
Carmelite House
50 Victoria Embankment
London EC4Y 0DZ

www.bookouture.com

ISBN: 978-1-83790-248-4
eBook ISBN: 978-1-83790-249-1

A camp needs a poet, one who experiences life there, even there, as a bard and is able to sing about it... Let me be the thinking heart of these barracks.
Etty Hillesum

PROLOGUE

Every story worth its salt brings its protagonist to his or her knees in the end. As a professional storyteller, I know this – I have *done* this in every novel I've written. And then, of course, the hero finds a strength they didn't know they possessed, which helps them rise up one last time and slay the metaphorical dragon. As I lay on my bunk in that godforsaken place at the end of the railway line, at the end of humanity, listening to the guards outside screaming the words I'd come to detest – *'Raus! Schnell!'* – I knew I'd reached that moment in my life story. The latest shocking twist, the new depths their cruelty had plumbed, had brought me to my knees – but I didn't want to rise up again. I wanted to lie there until what was left of my skin and bones disintegrated and fell like dust between the slats of the bunk and into the ground. There was nothing, *nothing*, left there for me. No reason to search my hidden depths for a strength I didn't know I possessed. And yet...

As I contemplated giving up, Tomasz's words echoed back through time to me: 'When this is all over, you will be able to tell the world what they did to us. You could write it in a book.' When he had said that to me at the beginning of the war, I had no idea what this would come to mean – what they would do to us, what they would do to the people I loved. And now something began to kindle inside of me. A spark of anger at the injustice of it all. Why should they get away with it?

In the distance, I heard a child cry and instantly I was taken back to that terrible moment when my world had collapsed and I was brought crashing to my knees. But why should my story end there? The Germans had already ended so many stories way too soon. Another thought occurred to me: can a person truly die if their story lives on? Their body may be gone, but their spirit is transmuted into folklore, to be brought back to life every time their tale is told.

I felt a cold hard knot of determination tighten in the pit of my stomach. If I lived to tell the story of what happened, I wouldn't just be letting the world know what those monsters did to us, I'd be bringing the people I loved back to life. All of their wisdom and complexities and passions and love would live on. I looked down at my frail body, at the jutting bones and the paper-thin, flea-bitten skin. And in a moment of absolute clarity, I realised that my story couldn't end there. I had to survive. I had to tell their stories so that they might live on. I had to share the incredible gifts they'd given me so that others might benefit too. Wincing from the gnawing pain in my hip, I slowly sat up.

1

OCTOBER 1940, PARIS

I knew something was wrong the instant I arrived at Café de la Paix and saw my publisher, 'the indomitable Anton Janvier' (as he was frequently described in the *Paris Journal*), scrutinising the menu with the intensity of a detective searching for clues. Anton had been dining at la Paix most of his adult life; some days he'd even been known to take breakfast, lunch *and* supper there. He knew the menu upside down and inside out and *never* needed to look before placing an order.

Other signs that all was not well were the dark shadows beneath his eyes and his hair, which, usually slicked back, flapped in wispy grey strands in the breeze. Normally when I met Anton for lunch, I'd find him at his favourite table outside, halfway down a bottle of Beaujolais, admiring the view of the opera house across the plaza. I glanced across Place de l'Opéra and suppressed a shudder at the sight of German soldiers marching past, their polished jackboots gleaming in the pale gold of the autumn sun. Was it any wonder that Anton's shoulders were hunched and his forehead creased? Ever since the Nazis had occupied our beloved city in June, every Parisian

must have gained an extra frown line or two. Maybe the reason
Anton looked so uneasy was nothing to do with me. Hopefully...
But even if it was, I still had my Plan B up my sleeve. And it was
a most excellent plan, even if I do say so myself.

I took a breath, patted down my freshly rolled hair and
arranged my face into what I hoped was a defiant expression of
optimism against the odds.

'Good day, dear friend!' I cried in our customary greeting as
I approached the table.

Anton put the menu down and rose to greet me, but I
noticed his frown intensify before he forced a smile.
'Claudette!' he exclaimed, kissing me on both cheeks.

The apprehension inside me grew. He hadn't called me by
my full name for years. As soon as my debut novel, *The Adventures of Aurelie*, became a bestseller, Anton and I had become
the firmest of friends, and he had referred to me by my childhood nickname, Etty. That was seven years ago and I'd since
penned four more novels about Aurelie, each of them building
on the success of the previous books. The women of France had
taken my feisty dance-hall heroine into their hearts and become
invested in her adventures. But that was before the Germans
had arrived and started banning certain books by certain
authors.

'How are you?' Anton asked as we sat down. The bottle of
wine in front of him was almost empty.

'I'm OK,' I replied. 'How are you?'

'Ah, so-so, you know.' He shrugged and I noticed that his
plum-coloured velvet jacket was looser on his shoulders. Even a
bon vivant like Anton, who could still afford to dine in restau-
rants, had been affected by the food rationing introduced in
September. The Germans had ruled that we French could only
order one hors d'oeuvre, one main course and one piece of
cheese when dining out. 'One piece of cheese! I am a man, not a

mouse!' Anton had bellowed upon hearing this news, seemingly unable to comprehend a future that didn't involve the twice daily consumption of a cheeseboard.

A waiter appeared at our table and Anton ordered the sausage cassoulet – his old favourite veal blanquette having been another casualty of the occupation. I ordered my favourite onion soup, onions having thankfully so far escaped the cull.

'I have good news,' I said cheerily.

'Oh yes?' He leaned forward and lowered his voice. 'Are you getting out of Paris?'

'What? No!' When the Germans had begun their march on Paris, many people had fled the city, including my beloved neighbour Levi, who lived in the apartment above mine. He had begged me to go with him, but I'd refused. I'd worked so hard for my apartment on the Left Bank of the Seine, I wasn't about to give it up for anyone, least of all Hitler and his cronies.

'Oh.' Anton slumped back in his chair, looking disappointed.

'I've finished the first draft of Book Five. I finally figured out what to do with Aurelie's annoying pursuer...' I paused for dramatic effect. 'He meets a sticky end in a vat of porridge in the Ritz Hotel kitchen.' I was hoping this might prompt one of Anton's hearty guffaws, but his expression saddened.

'I-I have some news,' he stammered, picking up the bottle and filling my glass with what was left of the wine.

'Oh yes?' My gut clenched. Judging by his grave expression, it wasn't the kind of news I was accustomed to hearing from him, usually about book sales exceeding all expectations.

Once again he leaned forward, glancing left and right before continuing. 'It's about the new statute the government have brought in – Le Statut des Juifs,' he whispered.

The hairs on the back of my neck prickled. Ever since I'd learned about the cursed statute banning Jews from working in certain professions, dread had taken root inside of me. Could my worst nightmare be about to come true?

Don't forget Plan B, my inner voice reminded me. *Don't forget the enterprising spirit that brought you here – from the slums of Marseille to the heart of literary Paris. That same spirit can easily outwit our treacherous government!*

'I'm so sorry,' he continued, looking down at the table. 'We... we're no longer allowed to publish you.'

I fought the urge to gulp. When Anton had given me my first publishing deal, it changed everything. Becoming an author was like being given the keys to a magical kingdom light years away from the world I'd grown up in. And ever since my debut novel was published, my life had run parallel to that of my fictional heroine, Aurelie, in a wonderful example of life imitating art, or art imitating life – it was impossible to know which, our fates had become so intertwined. The thought of having that snatched away from me was almost too much to comprehend. I wouldn't just be losing my career; I'd be losing my identity.

'I'm so sorry,' he said again. Finally, he met my gaze and I saw that his brown eyes were shiny with tears.

'It's all right,' I replied breezily. 'I'd anticipated that their stupid laws might create a problem, so I've come up with a cunning plan...' I paused and silently prayed that my plan would meet with approval. 'From now until the Germans are defeated, I shall write under a pen name. I was thinking of Edith London. Edith as a tribute to my favourite singer, the Little Sparrow, obviously, and London because, well, I've always wanted to go there.' I forced a smile onto my face. 'I dream of taking afternoon tea at Fortnum and Mason, and riding in one of those black taxicabs. Not to mention hearing a bona fide Londoner say, "All right, my old Dutch."' I was aware that I was wittering but afraid to stop for fear that Anton might pooh-pooh my idea. 'It's a term of endearment,' I added, noting his confused expression.

'What is?'

'My old Dutch. It's what Londoners call their wives.'

'You want to marry a Londoner?'

'No! I just want to hear them speak.' I began fiddling with the edge of my napkin, frustrated that we'd ended up taking this conversational wrong turn. 'So, er, what do you think of my idea – about the pen name?'

As I awaited his response I hardly dared breathe. Writing under another name had been the only solution I'd been able to think of when I'd anticipated this happening. If he said no, I didn't know what I'd do.

To my horror, he shook his head. 'How would we explain the Aurelie books suddenly being written by a different person?'

'We could put the series on hold until the war is over,' I replied, trying not to think of all the work I'd put into my recently completed first draft of the fifth book. I'd anticipated him saying this when I came up with my plan, so as much as it pained me, I was willing to put the series on hold. I was willing to do anything as long as it meant I could keep writing. 'I could write something completely new.' I looked at him hopefully. 'Please?'

'I'm sorry, it's just too dangerous.' He placed his hands upon mine on the table. His nails had been bitten down to the quick. 'You have to forget about writing for now, Claudette. You need to get out of here. I know people. I can help you escape to the free zone.'

I couldn't help snorting at this. The unoccupied parts of France might be free from direct Nazi rule – for now at least – but there was no denying our new Prime Minister, Marshal Pétain, was Hitler's puppet. After all, wasn't he the one who'd devised the statute against the French Jews?

'But I don't want to run away.' I pulled my hands from Anton's and took a gulp of wine. It tasted as sour as vinegar and burned the back of my throat.

'Things are only going to get worse,' he whispered. 'Please, let me help you.'

'But what about the Jewish people who aren't able to escape?' I stared at him defiantly. 'I'm not going to turn my back on my people.' The truth was, I hadn't set foot in a synagogue for years, not since the last time my father beat me and I ran away to Paris. Ever since that day, I'd done everything I could to forget my roots, no longer observing the traditions and rituals, but now that I was being persecuted for my background I felt a fierce sense of loyalty forming inside of me.

Anton gestured to a waiter for more wine. 'I had a feeling you might be stubborn about it.'

'It's not about being stubborn, it's...' I broke off. How could I explain to him what running away from everything I'd built would do to me? Anton came from a wealthy family, and the success of his publishing house had only increased his fortune. He didn't know what it was like to come from nothing. He didn't know what it was like to be haunted by the fear that you might one day end up back there. Then a terrible thought occurred to me. 'If you're not going to publish the fifth book, will you want me to return my advance?'

To my relief, he shook his head. 'No, of course not.'

That was something at least. Thankfully, I hadn't frittered all of the money away, and the good thing about coming from nothing is that you surely know how to make a franc stretch.

We sat in silence for a moment and I stared over at the opera house. According to Anton, who was an expert in literary folklore, Oscar Wilde, who used to love frequenting Café de la Paix, once thought he saw the apparition of an angel while sitting on this very same terrace. It turned out to be the reflection of one of the golden statues perched on the top of the ornate building. Wilde may have also indulged in one too many glasses of absinthe. When Anton had first told me that story, I'd thought it hilarious, and I'd been thrilled that I was walking in the footsteps – or drinking in the glass-prints – of such a literary great, but now the memory left me feeling cold. It seemed symbolic somehow of what had happened to this great city. Nothing was as it seemed anymore; any signs of our former lives were merely an apparition.

A waiter arrived with our food and a fresh bottle of wine. I picked up my spoon and prodded at the bread floating on top of the soup. An oily sheen glimmered on the cheese, making my feeling of nausea grow.

'I'm still here for you if you need anything,' Anton said, tucking his napkin into his shirt collar.

'Thanks,' I muttered, taking a sip of soup. It might have been my sudden foul mood souring things, but it didn't taste nearly as rich or meaty as normal. I felt tears burning at the corners of my eyes. 'Actually, I'm not hungry,' I said, pushing the bowl away. 'I think I should go.'

'Etty, please.' Anton looked at me imploringly.

'It tastes horrible,' I said lamely. 'There's no beef stock in it, I can tell.'

He stared at me, bewildered, as anger burned through the fog of my shock. Why had he invited me here to break the news? Now the café that had been the scene of so many happy memories would forever be remembered as the place where my hopes and dreams came crashing to an end. He should have got me to come to the office – unless... Maybe he didn't want a Jew to be seen entering the premises. The words from the posters that had been springing up all over Paris like mould came back to taunt me: *Our enemy is the Jew.*

'It's disgusting,' I spat, getting to my feet.

'Etty.' He stood up, taking his napkin from his collar. 'I don't know what to say.'

I looked across the table at my old friend, my mentor, the one person I'd thought I could trust to take care of my writing career. 'It just isn't the same without the beef stock,' I stammered, then turned and fled as tears spilled down my cheeks.

2

OCTOBER 1940, PARIS

I somehow managed to pull myself back together long enough to make it home. My apartment by the river with its long sash windows and high ceilings was the first place I'd ever truly felt at home. Just like Café de la Paix, it was like a museum of lovingly curated memories – everywhere I looked, I was reminded of wonderful conversations, laughter-filled dinner parties and passionate encounters. Over the five years I'd been there, I'd turned it into the kind of home I'd always dreamed of having as a child, full of books and interesting artefacts and antiques, and radios in every room so I always had music to dance to. Above all, I'd created a safe haven from the world – the perfect antidote to the house of horrors I'd grown up in.

As I climbed the wide stone staircase to the second floor, I felt my fear grow. How would I afford to stay here without my publishing deal? There was only so far my latest advance payment would stretch, even with my expertise in budgeting. I let myself in and went straight to the living room and my favourite thinking spot – the window seat overlooking the river. I sat down and hugged one of the velvet cushions to me. Had my neighbour Levi been right to leave when he did? Oh, how I missed the soft pad of his footsteps crossing the ceiling. Oh, how I missed the tinkle of his piano drifting through the open window on the breeze.

I turned my gaze back to the living room and for a moment I could hear the ghostly echo of the chatter, laughter and music of parties past. I glanced at my typewriter, set up on a desk in the other window. The manuscript for the fifth Aurelie book was placed neatly beside it. As I thought of all the work that had gone into those pages – all of the plotting and replotting and trying to make her latest love interest roguish yet loveable – I felt despair building inside of me.

I strode over and picked up the manuscript, flicking through the pages, staring forlornly at the thousands upon thousands of carefully typed words. As a child, I would lose myself in wonder at how just the right letters arranged into just the right words had the power to create whole new worlds. But now my words seemed no more than meaningless marks and squiggles that no one would ever get to read.

A sudden commotion broke the silence and I heard men's voices in the hallway downstairs. My blood turned to ice at the sharp clip of what I'd come to know as jackboots marching up the stairs. German soldiers. Were they coming for me? To tell me that I could no longer work as a writer because I'd committed the crime of being born Jewish?

But the feet continued marching past my front door and up to the top floor. I winced at the sound of a loud bang above and heard the boots clomping their way across the ceiling. I looked up, trying to imagine what they might be doing in Levi's flat. After a few minutes, I heard some of them singing a German song as they went back downstairs.

I pressed myself to the wall beside the window and peered outside. An army truck had been parked by our building and a soldier was hauling one of Levi's paintings into the back. My throat tightened. Levi's art collection was his pride and joy. The first time he had invited me up to his place for a cocktail, he'd introduced them to me with all the fondness of a father introducing his children. 'I never married,' he'd told me before taking a sip of his kir royale. 'My piano is my one true love.' He had then regaled me with wonderful tales of his life touring the world as a concert pianist, buying a treasured piece of artwork in every city he visited. I'd found the backstories even more compelling than the paintings themselves – especially when he'd told me how he'd bartered a private piano recital for a Rembrandt. And now those Nazi pigs were helping themselves without a care in the world. I winced as one of them slung another painting inside the truck, with no regard for the fact that it could have been by a master.

But it turned out it wasn't just Levi's art the Germans were after. For the next couple of hours, I watched as they filled the truck with all his worldly goods, even his bed linen and saucepans. It was when I saw them fling his beloved rocking chair onto the back that I almost cracked and had to fight the urge to run down and launch myself at them. Whatever they were doing wasn't just motivated by greed; it was as if they were trying to erase all proof that Levi ever existed.

As the truck finally pulled away, I looked around the living room at my own possessions. Just like Levi's paintings, every-thing in the room had a story attached to it. The battered, one-eared bust of Mozart I'd taken pity on in a flea market, the antique sewing machine I used as a hanger for my necklaces, the gramophone that had been the focal point for so many parties, my beloved 1920s Art Deco radio. Then my gaze fell upon the Aurelie doll, clad in a red sequinned costume, stand-ing, arms wide open, on the mantelpiece. Anton had her made for me when my third novel became an instant bestseller. Up until now, the doll had been a fun symbol of all I'd achieved, but her painted-on grin seemed to be taunting me, reminding me of all that had been stolen from me. In a blind fury, I hurried over and grabbed the doll, then ran downstairs and outside.

The sun had disappeared behind a swollen bank of grey cloud and the still air smelled of imminent rain. I felt a wild energy coursing through my veins, the like of which I hadn't experienced since the day I'd run away from home. How dare the Nazis swarm into our country and plunder our belongings? How dare they tell us where we could and could not work? Why, oh why, couldn't Anton have agreed with my plan? Why couldn't he let me carry on writing under a pen name?

I had to stop thinking about him. I had to stop thinking about Aurelie. I could no longer rely upon either of them.

I marched over to the bridge and, without a second thought, flung the doll into the dark water.

As soon as I heard the splash, I regretted it. How could I be so heartless to my own literary creation? How could I send her to a watery grave? It wasn't her fault this was happening. She'd saved me from poverty and hardship and this was how I repaid her? I was no better than a heartless German.

'Oh, Aurelie, I'm so sorry,' I cried, clambering onto the side of the bridge. I caught a glimpse of her bright auburn hair floating below, but before I could dive in to save her, I heard footsteps running towards me. Let it be a German soldier. I no longer cared.

'What are you doing?' a man's voice called in French with an accent I couldn't place. I felt a strong pair of hands grip my arms from behind.

I glanced over my shoulder to see a man smartly dressed in a black suit. But his dark cropped hair and the jagged lightning bolt of a scar on his cheek suggested that he would be more comfortable in less formal attire.

'I need to save her,' I yelped, struggling to free myself from his grasp.

'Shit!' He peered down into the water. 'Is she in the river?'

'Yes,' I gasped.

He let go of me and tore off his jacket.

'What are you— No, you don't understand...' I stammered as he leapt onto the side of the bridge with the ease of an athlete.

'Don't worry, I'll get her,' he said, before plunging down into the water.

'No!' I cried.

'I can't see anyone. Is she a child?' he called up to me, his voice echoing eerily beneath the bridge.

'No, er, she's a doll,' I called back, grimacing as I awaited his response.

There was a terrible silence and finally he swam back into view.

'A doll?' he yelled.

'Yes, I'm sorry, you didn't give me enough time to explain.'

I heard a muttered curse and some splashing about and he started swimming for the bank.

Picking up his jacket from the floor, I hurried over to meet him.

'A doll!' the man muttered as he waded out of the water. His now sodden shirt clung to his body, revealing broad shoulders and muscular arms. He was holding a very bedraggled Aurelie in his hand. 'Is this her?'

I nodded, my face flushing. 'But she's not just any old doll,' I said as I took her from him, desperate to redeem myself.

'Oh really?' He wiped some dirt from his eye. 'So, what kind of doll is she then?'

I pulled a handkerchief from my pocket and offered it to him. 'Here – to dry yourself. Well, your face at least.'

'Thanks,' he muttered, scowling at the dainty scrap of fabric.

'I'm an author,' I said. 'I write a series of books called *The Adventures of Aurelie*. You might have heard of them?'

He shook his head.

'Oh, well, your wife or sister probably have.'

'I don't have a wife, or a sister,' he growled, wiping his face with the hankie and streaking the white cotton brown.

'Oh, OK. Well, anyway, the doll was made for me by my publisher,' I said, desperately trying to salvage the situation, and what was left of my dignity.

'How nice,' he replied drily.

'Yes,' I agreed, deciding to ignore his sarcasm. 'But I've had a really bad day and I ended up throwing her in the river.'

'You *threw* her in?' He stared at me as if I'd just escaped from an asylum for the mentally infirm.

'Yes, but I instantly regretted it, which was why I was about to jump in and save her, before you beat me to it.'

He gave a long sigh. Clearly, I was the most pitiful human he'd ever had the misfortune to cross paths with.

'I'm very sorry,' I said forlornly.

What a truly terrible day it had been. But my bad luck wasn't over yet. The screech of a car came echoing up the road. The only cars that populated the Paris streets these days tended to be the black Mercedes cabriolets driven by the Germans.

'Shit!' the man exclaimed.

'It's OK, it's not curfew yet,' I reassured him.

'I can't let them see me,' he said, looking around frantically as if searching for a hiding place.

'Quick.' I pulled on his sodden sleeve and we ran across the road and into my apartment building. 'Come with me,' I said, leading him up the stairs.

Outside, I heard the car screech to a halt and my heart skipped a beat. Had they seen us? I opened the door to my apartment with trembling hands and gestured at the man to follow me inside.

'You live here?' he murmured, gazing at the chandelier hanging from the hall ceiling.

'Yes – well, for now at least.'

I hurried into the living room and peered outside. Some men in German uniform had got out of the car and were looking up and down the street.

'Are they... are they looking for you specifically?' I asked, quickly shutting the curtains.

'No, but if they find me, I'll be in a lot of trouble,' he replied, standing in the living-room doorway. 'They're looking for all non-French Jews. They're rounding us up and sending us to a camp by the Pyrenees.'

'You're Jewish?'

He nodded, then instantly looked defensive. 'Don't worry, I'll be out of here as soon as they've gone.'

'It's OK, I-I'm Jewish too.' It felt strange saying those words out loud after eight years of trying to forget my heritage.

'You are?' He glanced around the room as if trying to find proof and his gaze fell upon the silver Shabbat candlesticks on the dining table: the only remnants of my former life. They'd belonged to old Madame Bellamy, my childhood neighbour, who I'd loved dearly. She'd left them to me when she died. It had been a long time since I'd lit the candles on a Friday evening, though. The man looked back at the window. 'Are they still there?'

I peered outside and saw the men getting into their car. 'Yes, but I think they might be leaving.' I waited a few seconds, but the car stayed put. 'Or maybe not.'

'Great,' he muttered.

'It's OK, you can stay as long as you need. I'm not sure it would be safe going out like that anyway; you'll hardly blend in.' I gestured at him, dripping dirty water onto the carpet. 'You can clean yourself up in the bathroom if you like. I'll see if I have anything you could change into. I did go through a phase of wearing men's suits a couple of years ago, although I have a feeling they might be a little on the small side.' I glanced at his huge shoulders and felt a flicker of apprehension. Should I really be telling a strange man, who was clearly as strong as an ox, to go and get undressed in my bathroom? 'I ought to let you know that I am an expert in the fighting system known as Krav Maga,' I added, hoping he wouldn't see through my blatant lie. The closest I'd come to the hand-to-hand combat developed in Slovakia to help Jews protect themselves from anti-Semitic attacks was learning about it from Levi.

'You are?' For the first time since our paths had crossed, the man smiled, instantly transforming his face from grim to boyish. There was a cleft in his chin, so deep it looked as if it had been chiselled in. I felt the familiar instinct to reach for one of the many notebooks I had dotted about the place for whenever inspiration struck. He could form the perfect basis for an intriguing stranger in Aurelie's next adventure. Almost instantly a wave of grief went crashing through me. There would be no next adventure for Aurelie.

'Yes, so anyway, why don't I show you where the bathroom is before you turn the carpet brown.' I hurried past him into the hallway.

'I'm a fighter too,' he said as he followed me.

My heart sank. 'Oh, really?'

'Yes, a boxer.'

'Oh.'

'Tomasz Zolanvari, you might have heard of me?' His grin broadened. He was clearly teasing me about my earlier comment, but his smile was warm rather than mocking.

'No, I'm sorry. Boxing isn't really my thing.'

'Oh, I thought it would be, what with you being an expert in hand-to-hand combat.'

'Yes, well, I prefer taking part rather than being a spectator,' I muttered, walking into the bathroom and turning the bath taps on, praying my burning cheeks would cool down. I was a hopeless liar. My face always gave me away instantly.

'Whoa, this is almost the same size as my entire place!' he exclaimed, turning in a circle to take in the room.

'Yes, well, why don't you go ahead and have a bath,' I said, flustered, 'and perhaps you could wash your clothes in the sink? I'll go and look for something for you to change into.'

He nodded. 'OK. Thank you.'

I shut the door behind him and took a moment to compose myself before hurrying through to my bedroom to search the racks of clothes in my closet for something – *anything* – vaguely suitable. The only thing I could find that would hopefully be large enough was a pink satin robe with roses embroidered on the breast. It would look ridiculous, but at least he wouldn't be naked. I took it back to the bathroom.

'I've found something for you to wear while your clothes dry,' I called through the shut door. 'I've left it outside.'

'OK, thank you,' he replied and I heard a splash of bathwater.

What a crazy day it had been.

I went back into the living room and peered outside. Dusk was gathering now, spilling along the street below in long dark shadows. The car had gone, but I could see a patrol of soldiers making their way along the pavement beside the river.

I picked up the bedraggled Aurelie doll from the table. 'I'm so sorry,' I whispered, holding her to my chest. I'd made many friends since coming to Paris, but Aurelie had been my constant companion, like a child's imaginary friend, living inside my head. 'I'm going to miss you,' I whispered.

'Why? I'll still be here inside your mind,' I imagined her whispering back. *'And not even Hitler himself can remove me.'*

3

OCTOBER 1940, PARIS

To take my mind off the Nazis patrolling outside my apartment and the naked stranger in my bathroom, I decided to go to the kitchen and put the kettle on the stove. While I waited for it to boil, I turned the radio on. As the room filled with music, I felt my tension ease a little. *'Elle fréquentait la rue Pigalle'* by Edith Piaf was playing – one of my favourite songs from the previous year. I loved the way the lyrics told a story, and I loved that the story was about a woman from Pigalle – one of my favourite neighbourhoods in Paris. I loved the gritty buzz of its bars and dance halls and artistic community so much I'd made it Aurelie's fictional home. I could also relate to the woman in the song being from the wrong side of the tracks. After all, wasn't that exactly what I was, if you scratched beneath the surface glamour of my book deals and Left Bank apartment? It's why I loved Edith Piaf too. I felt as if the Little Sparrow and I were kindred spirits.

I was twirling round the kitchen, singing into a pestle microphone, when Tomasz appeared in the doorway clad in my robe, the pink satin straining to contain his shoulders. He was holding his wet clothes in a bundle in front of him.

'I was thinking of making something to eat. Are you hungry?' I asked, hurriedly placing the pestle back in its mortar.

'I'm famished,' he replied. 'But...' He looked around the kitchen, as if searching for food.

'It's OK, I have some things in the pantry.'

'No, I wasn't looking for food, I was looking for a clock.'

'A clock?' I stared at him, confused.

'Yes, do you know what the time is?'

'Why, are you about to turn into a pumpkin?'

Now it was his turn to look confused and the awkwardness of the situation grew.

'It was a joke,' I muttered. 'You know, like Cinderella needing to leave the ball before midnight? I thought perhaps you had to eat by a certain time.'

'I do – today,' he replied. 'The seudah hamafseket – it has to be eaten before sunset.'

'Oh, yes of course,' I said hastily, realising that it must be the eve of Yom Kippur. 'Don't worry, we still have time. It's not even five o'clock yet.'

'Excellent.'

We exchanged awkward smiles while I tried desperately to remember the Erev Yom Kippur rituals.

'But before that, let me take these to dry by the fire.' I took the wet clothes from him.

'You still have coal?' he asked, following me back into the living room.

'No, but I have a lot of kindling.' I took my manuscript from my desk and placed it in the grate.

'That doesn't look like kindling.'

'No, but it's all it's good for,' I muttered.

'What is it?' he asked as I fetched a book of matches from the mantelpiece.

'It is – *was* – my latest novel.'

'What?' He grabbed my hand to stop me. 'You can't set fire to your work just to dry my clothes. Do you have another copy?'

I shook my head. 'No, but I no longer have a writing career, so what does it matter?'

'What do you mean? Why not?'

'Le Statut des Juifs,' I replied glumly. 'Thanks to our government kowtowing to the Nazis, I'm no longer able to earn a living writing books.'

He frowned, a sight made slightly less menacing by the rose pink robe. 'Is that why you flung your doll in the river?'

'Yes. I thought it would make me feel better not having the constant reminder of what they've taken from me grinning down from the mantelpiece.'

'You could have just put her in a cupboard.'

I shook my head. 'That wouldn't have been nearly dramatic enough.'

He laughed. 'Well, you certainly created a drama.'

'Yes, I'm sorry.' I set the wooden clothes horse by the fireplace.

'So, how many books have you written?' Tomasz asked as he hung his trousers on the frame.

'This would have been my fifth.' I nodded at the manuscript.

He leaned past me and took it from the hearth. 'They'll never be able to stop you from being a writer, not if you don't let them.'

'You don't understand. My publisher isn't allowed to publish my books anymore. The Nazis are banning books by Jewish authors from being sold.'

'Yes, they did that in my homeland, Poland, too. They even set fire to books by Jews.'

I felt sick at the mere thought.

'And here you are, about to set fire to your own book,' he said softly.

I grabbed the manuscript from him and held it to me tightly. 'I don't know what's wrong with me today. I just feel so... so helpless.'

He nodded. 'I understand, believe me, but you can't let them win.'

'They already have,' I sighed. 'They've taken my career from me.'

'How do you write your stories?' he asked.

'Over there, on that typewriter.' I pointed to the desk in the window.

'No, before you use the typewriter, how do you come up with them?'

'Oh, I see – in my head.'

'Exactly. And are there any Nazis in your head?'

'Only when I think of them.'

'So, don't think of them. Keep making up your stories. And one day when this is over and we've beaten them, you'll be able to take your stories out of your head and put them on the page again.'

'That's what she just told me!' I exclaimed, pointing to my bedraggled Aurelie doll on the table.

'The doll talked to you?' He frowned.

'Not out loud, in my head.' I laughed. 'Don't look so worried. All of my characters talk to me. How else would I be able to tell their stories?'

He shrugged and gave me a bemused grin.

'I don't really think you're in any position to mock me.' I looked pointedly at the satin robe.

'This is true.' And now it was his turn to blush.

There was a beat of silence.

'I'll go and prepare our feast then,' I said, to try to break the growing embarrassment. 'Well, as much of a feast as the rationing will allow.'

'Are you sure?' He looked concerned. 'I'm happy to start my fast now if you don't have enough.'

'No, it's fine. You stay here, make yourself comfortable.'

I hurried back to the kitchen, hoping he wouldn't follow me so I'd have a moment to regroup. There wasn't enough time to make matzah balls before sundown, but I was pretty sure I could scrape together the ingredients for Madame Bellamy's chicken soup – minus the chicken. I took my last two carrots and onion from the pantry.

Last year, Levi had invited me to dinner at his apartment on Erev Yom Kippur and we'd feasted on chicken and potatoes and fresh challah. Then, after lighting the yahrtzeit candles in remembrance of the dead, he'd gone to synagogue and I'd come back to my apartment, where I'd written a chapter about Aurelie dancing at the Moulin Rouge and tried with all my might not to remember my father, who I'd learned had passed away the year before.

It had been a while since I'd longed for a proper, loving family. The friends I'd made since moving to Paris had become a carefully curated family of choice. But since the Germans had arrived, they'd scattered on the wind, most of them moving to the unoccupied zone, or even fleeing the country. How much easier would this strange new world be if I had loving parents who were still alive, or a sibling or two, or even a distant cousin? As I started chopping the onion, my eyes filled with tears. What was I going to do? How would I survive this by myself?

'Can I do anything to help?' The sound of Tomasz's voice made me jump. I turned to see him standing in the doorway and I quickly wiped my eyes.

'Stupid onion making me cry,' I muttered. 'I'm afraid there isn't time to make matzah balls, but perhaps you could help me make some chicken soup – without the chicken.'

'Chicken soup without the chicken?' he echoed, raising an eyebrow.

'Yes, it's the very latest in cursed rationed cuisine.'

'Ah, I'm familiar with that cuisine,' he said as I handed him a couple of carrots.

As he set about chopping the carrots, I pictured Aurelie in her kitchen in Pigalle, imagining that she'd met a boxer at one of her shows and he'd offered to cook her dinner. He wouldn't be dressed in a pink satin robe, though. I envisioned a character based on Tomasz, clad in slacks and short sleeves, the muscles in his arms rippling as he chopped vegetables. *Stop thinking about Aurelie!* I silently scolded myself.

'So, you're from Poland then?' I asked as I put a pan on the stove.

'Yes. But I came to France when I was eighteen. My parents sent me to join my uncle, who is – was – a tailor in the Pletzl – the Marais,' he added, as if I might not be familiar with the Yiddish nickname for the Jewish quarter in the fourth arrondissement.

'Ah yes,' I replied knowingly, although, to be truthful, I'd only ventured to the Pletzl once before – to research a scene for one of my novels, where Aurelie went on a hunt for chicken soup after a vicious bout of influenza. 'So how long have you been here?' I asked, in part to find out his age.

'Seven years. The irony is, my parents sent me here to escape the growing anti-Semitism in Poland.'

'That is very ironic.' I added the chopped vegetables to the pan. So he was twenty-five, the same age as me. 'Was it bad over there?'

'Very.' He gave a pensive smile. 'It wasn't all bad, though. It inspired me to become a boxer.'

'How?'

'Growing up, seeing my people being brutalised just for being Jewish, it made me want to defend myself – and others. But you should know all about that, being an expert in Krav Maga.'

I cursed my earlier lie – I should have known it would come back to haunt me.

'It's why Imi Lichtenfeld developed it,' he continued, 'so the Jewish could defend themselves against the fascists in Bratislava.'

'I know,' I said defiantly.

'You'll have to show me some of your moves,' he said with a grin.

'I don't think that would be appropriate tonight. We're supposed to be atoning and forgiving.'

'Fair enough.' But his knowing smile implied that he'd seen right through me.

Once we'd made the soup, we took it through to the dining table in steaming bowls. The aroma of the onion caused my stomach to gurgle in hunger. Thanks to my dramatic exit at Café de la Paix earlier, I hadn't eaten a morsel since breakfast.

'Don't you have any family in Paris to spend Yom Kippur with?' Tomasz asked, once we were seated.

'I don't have any family,' I replied.

He paused, spoon midway to his mouth. 'What do you mean? Everyone has family.'

'My mother died when I was an infant and my father died a couple of years ago. They were both only children and my grandparents are all gone too.'

'I'm sorry.'

'Don't be. I'm not.' But my bravado belied the little pit of loneliness I felt at the very core of me. 'The closest thing I had to family was my neighbour Levi, who lives – *lived* – upstairs, but he fled when he knew the Germans were on their way.'

'You weren't tempted to go too?'

'No! Why should I? And where would I go? Vichy France is no freer than occupied France.'

He nodded.

'And besides, I worked really hard for this.' I gestured at the apartment. 'Why should I let the Germans have it?'

'You paid for this yourself?'

'Of course. How else do you think I got it?'

'I don't know. I'd assumed you'd come from a wealthy family – or married a wealthy man.'

'I decided long ago never to marry,' I replied defiantly.

'Oh really?' He arched one of his eyebrows and I made a mental note that this made for an attractive character detail, if I was ever able to write fiction again.

'Yes.'

'Dare I ask why?'

'I never want to be in a position where a man controls me.'

'Interesting.' He nodded thoughtfully. 'But what if you met a man who didn't want to control you?'

'I'd rather not take the risk. Anyway, I'm proud to say that I paid for this all by myself.'

Something about the way he was looking at me changed. As if he no longer saw me as some foolish woman who talked to imaginary characters and flung dolls into the river on a whim. It was a look of curiosity and respect.

'You are a very interesting woman, Claudette Weil.'

'Thank you – wait – how do you know my full name?'

'I took a quick look at your bookshelf while you were in the kitchen.'

'Ah, I see.'

'I admire you for staying,' he said, his expression deadly serious.

'You do?' Even though I didn't know Tomasz at all, his admiration sparked a flicker of hope inside of me.

'Yes, especially as you are a writer.'

'What do you mean?' I instantly felt defensive. Was he

suggesting that artistic types wouldn't be courageous enough to confront the Nazis?

'You have a real purpose for staying.'

I put my spoon down. 'I do?'

'Of course. Forget about your stories about a dancer from Pigalle...' Clearly he'd read the blurb on my book covers too. 'When this is all over, you will be able to tell the world what they did to us. You could write it in a book.'

'Oh – yes, I suppose I could.' I thought about the fact that I'd deliberately made Aurelie Catholic rather than Jewish and felt a twinge of guilt. As a child, I'd always found the Catholic Church so melodramatic and compelling. All of that incense and talk of guilt and sin, and the notion of spilling my darkest secrets to an unseen priest in a confessional was so thrilling. 'She isn't Jewish, though.' I pointed my spoon at the Aurelie doll, who was now propped up against the candlesticks in the centre of the table.

'So?' Tomasz looked at me, confused.

'Oh, do you mean I should write non-fiction?'

'I don't know. I don't suppose it matters – as long as you let the world know what happened here.'

We finished our soup in silence, then Tomasz glanced at the clock on the mantelpiece.

'It must be almost sundown. Shall we light the candles?'

'Yes, of course.' I cast my mind back to Levi's last year. He lit three candles in total – one in remembrance of the dead and two to celebrate the holiday. If only I could remember the blessings. I fetched the matches and a candle in a glass holder. 'I'll light them and you say the blessings.'

'Sure.' Tomasz cleared the dishes to one side.

I lit the candle in the glass holder first, muttering what I could remember of the kaddish, while trying to push any remembrance of my father from my mind. Then I moved

Aurelie out of the way and lit two of the candles in the candlesticks.

'*Barukh ata adonai eloheinu melech ha-olam asher kiddishanu b'mitzvotav v'tzivanu l'hadlik ner shel shabbat v'shel yom ha-kippurim,*' Tomasz recited as I lit them. His voice was deep and melodic, like a cello – another very pleasant character detail, I noted, before batting the thought away. 'Shall we recite Shehechiyanu?' he asked.

'Oh yes, absolutely,' I replied, praying I could still remember it.

'*Barukh ata adonai eloheinu melech ha-olam shehechiyanu, v'kiyimanu, v'higiyanu la-zman ha-zeh.*'

I repeated every word he said a fraction of a second after he said it, to make it look as if I was still fluent.

'I guess we won't be going to synagogue for Kol Nidre,' Tomasz said with a sad smile.

'No,' I replied, relieved to have escaped another potential source of embarrassment at not being able to remember the words of the prayer.

'I could sing it now, though,' he continued.

I fought the urge to frown. If Tomasz ever wanted to turn his back on boxing, becoming a rabbi could certainly be a viable alternative vocation.

'Yes, absolutely. That would be lovely.' I sat bolt upright in my chair, suddenly struck by the inappropriate urge to laugh at the bizarreness of the situation. A strange man was sitting at my table in my pink satin robe about to chant the prayer that introduced Yom Kippur. But I knew I mustn't laugh at any cost. Kol Nidre was so serious, it would be completely inappropriate.

'Could I use your tablecloth?' Tomasz asked.

I stared at him, confused. 'What for?'

'As a tallit. It's white,' he added, by way of explanation.

Just when I thought things couldn't get any more surreal.

'Yes, of course.'

We moved the dishes and I picked up the candleholder so he could take the tablecloth and drape it around his shoulders like a prayer shawl.

'Feel free to put something white on too,' he said, nodding at my emerald green dress. 'And if you have anything I could use as a kippah...'

'Oh, absolutely.' I scrambled to my feet. 'I'll be right back.'

I raced into my bedroom, where half the contents of my wardrobe were still cast on the floor from my earlier search. The only thing I possessed that was white was a shirt I'd used as an overall when I was going through a brief painting phase following an encounter with Pablo Picasso in Café de Flore. I'd been unable to wash out the splatters of crimson and blue, but hopefully it was white enough to pass the test. But what could I give him to use as a kippah? My gaze fell upon the lace doily Madame Bellamy had made me, sitting on my dresser. It was embroidered with daisies, but it was round at least.

I put the shirt on over my dress and returned to the living room. Tomasz was now standing at the head of the table in my robe and tablecloth and I had to disguise an errant laugh with a cough.

'Are you all right?' he asked.

'Yes, yes, absolutely,' I spluttered. I'd never thought it would be possible to find anything funny on this most terrible of days, so for that I was truly grateful. 'Would this be all right – for a kippah?' I handed him the doily. 'Hopefully you can overlook the daisies.' Again, I had to fight the urge to laugh.

'I like daisies,' he replied gruffly.

'Oh, me too!' I exclaimed as he placed the doily on his head.

'Shall I begin?' he asked, looking suddenly shy.

'Yes, please do.' I stood awkwardly at the other end of the table, the candles flickering between us.

But as soon as he started to sing, all of my awkwardness and desire to laugh instantly faded away. His singing voice was even more cello-like and I was instantly transfixed. The words were so laden with emotion, you could hear his voice cracking in places. It was more moving and beautiful than any cantor I'd ever heard in my childhood.

I closed my eyes and suddenly I was back there, in my home city, Marseilles, surrounded by adults all singing these same words in Hebrew. The Kol Nidre had originally been written in medieval times, when Jews had been persecuted and forced to convert to other religions. It was about absolving people of any vows to other faiths they may have made under pain of death. When I was younger, it had seemed a bit irrelevant and confusing, but as Tomasz's voice filled the room, the words felt painfully apt. Were the Nazis going to make us renounce our faith? To join with them in their worship of the so-called 'master race'? Indignation began building inside of me, in tandem with the crescendo in Tomasz's voice. I thought of Jews throughout the ages singing Kol Nidre, and for the first time, I felt a tugging inside, a deep sense of connection and loyalty to my people. When Tomasz reached the part where the congregation join in, I instinctively chanted along. The sound of our voices blending in harmony and defiance was so bittersweet, so moving, my face became slick with tears.

Once he'd sung the prayer the customary three times, I no longer saw the ridiculous pink robe, or the tablecloth shawl; all I could see was his gaze meeting mine through the flickering candlelight, and all I could feel was a presence far greater between us, as if he'd conjured God himself with the fire and passion of his voice.

Tomasz cleared his throat and looked away, as if suddenly embarrassed. 'Well,' he said, 'that was quite something.'

I wiped the tears from my face. What had happened had been so raw and so real, I felt the sudden desire to strip away all pretence. 'I have a confession to make.'

'Really?' He looked at me curiously. 'Well, if you can't atone on Yom Kippur, when can you?'

We both laughed as we sat back down.

'True, but the thing is...' I broke off.

'Yes?' he said softly.

'I haven't been to synagogue for many years.'

'How many?'

'Not since I ran away – left home. Eight years ago.'

'Oh.'

'I haven't really practised at all since then. I was trying to...'

He looked at me questioningly.

'I was trying to forget.'

'Forget about God?'

'No, yes, no. I don't know.'

He laughed at my indecisiveness.

'I was trying to forget about my father really, but in my mind he was so closely connected to God, to going to synagogue, I couldn't separate the two.'

'I understand,' he replied.

I looked at him hopefully. 'You do?'

'Yes.' He gazed into the flickering candlelight. 'There are things I'd like to forget too. Did it work, though? Were you able to forget him?'

I had a flashback to one of my most frequent nightmares. My father bearing down on me, screaming at me for being such a colossal inconvenience and the biggest mistake he'd ever made. Me cowering in the corner, covering my head with my arms. 'Mostly,' I muttered.

'I'm sorry,' Tomasz said, looking awkward.

'What for?'

'For making you light the candles. For singing Kol Nidre. I didn't—'

'No, it's fine,' I interrupted. 'It was beautiful. So moving. I felt...' I paused, struggling to express how I felt.

'What?'

'I felt as if I'd come back home, but not to my family home, a deeper home, here in my heart. Oh, it's so hard to put into words!'

'And you're a writer,' he joked.

'Yes... well, I was.' I shrugged.

'You *are*.' His smile faded. 'I'm glad I helped you feel like that. Our faith is more important now than ever before. It's not just a source of strength; it's another way we don't let the Germans win. We don't let them erase our identity.'

I nodded thoughtfully. For so long, I'd seen Judaism as being my father's identity. But in the Nazis' eyes, and in my own government's eyes, I was Jewish. Perhaps it was time to reclaim my faith and wear it as a badge of honour. 'You know, if the boxing doesn't work out for you, you should really consider a career as a rabbi, or a cantor.'

Tomasz's expression remained grim. 'Oh no, there's no chance of that.'

'Why not?' I asked, instantly intrigued.

'Let's just say I've done things a rabbi would never do.'

'Oh, I see.' I shifted in my chair. From the gravity of his tone he was clearly referring to more than working on the Sabbath or eating leavened bread during Passover.

'It's all right, you're safe, but I have a lot of atoning to do.'

'Haven't we all,' I quipped, trying to keep things light-hearted. 'But I'm sure that nothing you've done could be anywhere near as bad as what the Nazis are doing.'

To my surprise, he shook his head.

'Is there any way you can apologise for whatever you did?' I asked, thinking of the meaning of teshuva. 'Are you able to ask the person concerned for their forgiveness?'

'I can't.'

'I know how hard it can be to apologise. Last year, I had to apologise to a *boulanger* for yelling at him because a cake I'd ordered for a party tasted of garlic. I hadn't realised at the time that I hadn't washed the knife I'd used to cut the cake after chopping some vegetables. Then, when I did remember, I felt awful, and I felt compelled to put it right, but it was so difficult apologising to him in his shop, in front of so many customers, especially as he was clearly revelling in my discomfort. But afterwards I felt so much better, so much lighter. If a person chooses to be ungracious in the face of your apology, that's their issue. As long as you—'

'I can't apologise to them,' Tomasz cut in, his voice strained. 'Because I killed them.'

4

OCTOBER 1940, PARIS

I instinctively drew back in my chair. 'You killed them?'

Tomasz stood up and walked to the other side of the table, looking distraught. 'What am I doing, telling you this?'

'Was it... was it during one of your boxing matches?' I asked, hoping to somehow lessen the severity of his confession.

'No.'

The apprehension inside of me grew. Was he about to confess to a cold-blooded murder, and would he then need to kill me too, as the only living witness? The instinct to reach for my nearest notebook mingled with my fear. Aurelie meeting a murderer would certainly give the series a darker, spicier edge.

There isn't going to be another Aurelie book, and your own life could now be in danger! my inner voice yelled.

'Would you like a cup of tea?' I blurted out, anxious to both change the subject and leave the room.

There was a beat of silence, during which my question seemed increasingly ridiculous. Tomasz had just told me that he'd killed someone and I'd suggested I put the kettle on. Our eyes met and we both started to laugh. The kind of laughter that has a slightly hysterical edge – on my part at least.

'I'm sorry. I don't know why I told you that,' he said, looking embarrassed.

'It's OK. Forget it ever happened. I certainly have. And I will never speak of it to anyone, ever, obviously.' I crossed my fingers beneath the table, hoping this would be enough to appease him.

He looked at me anxiously. 'Oh no, you mustn't worry. I wouldn't do anything to hurt you.'

'I didn't think for a moment that you would,' I lied.

'I'm not... It wasn't...' He broke off and tightened the belt on my satin robe.

I waited for him to continue, half of me still anxious at his revelation, the other half hoping he might offer up some more information. I'd never met a killer before, or at least not that I knew of. And, like a magpie, I was always on the lookout for shiny details with which to feather my books. But Tomasz remained silent. He looked so crestfallen and he'd been so kind, it was hard to imagine he would do me any harm.

'Well, I really didn't expect my day to end like this,' he said eventually, looking sheepishly at the satin robe and tablecloth shawl.

'Me neither, but I have to say, this is the most interesting day I've had in a very long time.'

Tomasz laughed, took off the tablecloth and hung it on the back of one of the chairs. 'Same here.' He smiled at me. 'I'm glad you threw your doll in the river,' he said softly.

'So am I.' We both looked at poor Aurelie, her red hair now dried to a frizz.

Tomasz and I spent the next few hours telling each other a potted history of our lives up until that point. I shared some of the less brutal anecdotes from my childhood, and some entertaining tales about the French literary scene. And I learned all about his childhood passion for fishing and the mentor who had taught him how to box. I didn't learn any more about his blurted confession, though. And the more I got to know him and warmed to his mixture of worldly wisdom and boyish humour, the more curious I became.

Eventually, at around midnight, I was unable to fight the tiredness consuming me and let out a huge yawn.

'I should let you get some sleep,' Tomasz said instantly.

'OK. Will you... will you be all right, sleeping here on the chaise longue?' It was now long past curfew so there really was no alternative.

'Of course,' he readily agreed.

I went and fetched him some blankets and pillows.

'Thank you for everything,' he said as he arranged them into a makeshift bed.

'No, thank *you*,' I replied and I felt a wave of sadness that this strange yet magical evening was coming to an end. 'I'll see you in the morning.'

'Yes. Goodnight.'

As I left the room, I glanced back over my shoulder and saw Tomasz standing silhouetted in the candlelight, looking lost in thought.

As soon as I got into my bedroom, I opened the top drawer of my nightstand and took out the notebook I kept there for whenever nocturnal inspiration struck. I turned to a fresh page and wrote *Tomasz Zolanvari* at the top, underlining it for emphasis.

The next morning, I woke to the tinkle of a woman's laughter drifting up from the street below. For a blissful moment, it was just like any other morning before the occupation, as I drifted like a feather on the breeze in that hazy state between sleep and waking. Then the events from the day before began creeping back into my consciousness. Anton had let me go. I no longer had a publisher. I was no longer a writer. I had thrown poor Aurelie into the river. Tomas Zolanvari had saved her...

Tomas Zolanvari.

I hastily got out of bed, pulled a shawl over my nightdress and hurried from the room. The living-room door was open. Maybe Tomasz was up already. I went in to check and my heart sank. The blankets were neatly folded on top of the pillows at the end of the chaise, along with my pink satin robe. The clothes horse by the fire was empty. All that remained of our magical night were the burned-out stubs of the candles, molten wax trickling like veins down the silver holder. Then I saw a piece of paper at the end of the table, propped against the Aurelie doll. As I drew closer, I saw that it was the cover page from my manuscript.

Thank you for everything, Tomasz had written, in small neat script. *And never forget, you will always be a writer, and now you are needed more than ever. You have to tell the story of what they are doing to us. Tomasz.* He'd left no address or invitation to see him again, which left me feeling more disappointed than I'd have cared to admit.

I read the note several times over, as if trying to prolong my connection with him. Then I looked at Aurelie and felt a stab of concern. Would I return to the depression Tomasz had found me in, upon the bridge, now that our time together was over and I had no distraction from my harsh new reality? But, to my relief, I felt a seed of determination planting itself in my heart.

I picked up Aurelie and returned her to her place on the mantelpiece. I liked the fact that she now looked bedraggled and world-weary; it seemed symbolic somehow. She'd come close to a watery grave but survived, and I was going to capture some of that same spirit. I might not be able to write about Aurelie for the foreseeable future, but my meeting with Tomasz had given me a new-found purpose. And perhaps the stories I would end up telling would turn out to be far more important than those of my dance-hall heroine.

Once I'd got dressed and had a breakfast of leftover soup, I headed downstairs to fetch my beloved bicycle from the cupboard in the hall. As soon as I was outside and pedalling away, my new-found determination burst into bloom. Ever since I was a child, cycling was the one thing guaranteed to make me feel better – aside from escaping into a book. When I was about eight years old, I'd found an abandoned old bike in an alleyway by my house, which I quickly claimed as my own. It was rusty and too big for me, but I didn't care. Riding around town made me feel free as a bird. And with my vivid imagination, that bike was transformed into so many things – an automobile, a plane, a horse, or even, at times, a dragon. The possibilities were endless and I never felt freer than I did when I was pedalling away from home, the wind in my hair and a song on my lips. If only I could keep pedalling now, far, far away from the war. But like an insidious fog, the Nazis had crept their way across Europe, shrouding everything in their wake with terror and pain. Britain was the only place they hadn't yet reached, but even with my vivid imagination, I wasn't going to be able to cycle across water.

I sped along, my mind abuzz with memories from the night before: the candles, the singing, the heartfelt conversation. And then, most bizarre of all, Tomasz's confession that he'd killed someone. But who? And how? And why?

Who? How? Why? Where? And *what?* The five questions that formed the starting point of any story. But Tomasz had left me with all questions and barely any answers. I did know the answer to who he was, though. I knew his name, and his profession. The trouble was I knew nothing about boxing, so I couldn't verify if what Tomasz had told me was true. I knew a man who could, though. I screeched to a halt and did a U-turn, heading back towards the Latin Quarter.

'Tomasz Zolanvari?' Bruno said, nodding enthusiastically. 'Of course I've heard of Tomasz Zolanvari.'

Bruno was the owner of a bistro called Once Upon a Time in the heart of the Latin Quarter. It was the name that had first drawn me in there one sultry August night, several years previously. I figured that any bistro named after the beginning of a fairy tale would surely be an interesting experience, just as anyone who chose to name their bistro Once Upon a Time would be an intriguing character. And I hadn't been disappointed; Bruno and I instantly hit it off. He was passionate about the works of Albert Camus and one of those people who was in a perpetual state of wonder at the world, which I found infectious. He was also passionate about sport.

'So he is a boxer then?' I asked.

'Yes, of course. He won the French middleweight title a couple of years ago, but then he withdrew from fighting.' Bruno ran his hand through his black curly hair. 'Shame. He had the talent to go all the way. Coffee?' He picked up a pot from behind the bar. 'It's the real thing,' he whispered. 'I got some on the black market.'

'You did? Yes please!' My eyes widened at the prospect of real coffee. Since the Germans had inflicted their punitive rationing upon us, we'd been reduced to drinking a flavourless substitute that was rumoured to be made from acorns. I'd always been a great fan of oak trees, but as a source of coffee, they were a terrible disappointment.

Bruno filled a white china cup with the thick dark liquid and passed it to me.

I was unable to stop myself from moaning with pleasure as I took the first sip. 'Oh coffee, how I have missed you!' One silver lining of the occupation was that the simple pleasures taken for granted before could now bring about a state of ecstatic bliss.

Bruno chuckled as he poured himself a cup.

'So you don't know why Zolanvari withdrew from fighting?' I asked, once I'd stopped swooning.

Bruno shook his head. 'No. Why do you ask?'

Thankfully, I'd had time to come up with an excuse on the cycle over. 'I'm doing some research for a writing project.'

'Ah, I see. The new *statut* hasn't affected your work then? I was worried about you when I heard the news.'

My coffee-induced buzz began to fade. 'It has affected me, yes. I'm no longer allowed to write my novels.'

'No!' He thumped one of his meaty hands on the bar and I was touched by how genuinely sorry he looked, especially as *The Adventures of Aurelie* were hardly his literary preference. Then he frowned in confusion. 'So now you are writing about boxers?'

'Not exactly.' I sighed. 'To be truthful, I don't know what I'm going to write, I only know that I must write. I can't let them take away my identity.'

'That's the spirit.' Bruno glanced left and right before leaning across the bar towards me and lowering his voice. 'The other day I heard about something you might be able to write for.'

'What is it?' I stared at him hopefully.

'It's for the Resistance,' he whispered.

'The Resistance?' I whispered back, a shiver of excitement running up my spine.

'Yes, the people of Paris are waking from their dazed stupor; they're starting to fight back against the Nazi scum.'

'Oh, thank God!' I'd seen signs that people might be on the turn, but it had mainly been defaced German posters.

'I could put you in touch with them if you're interested?' Bruno continued. 'It would be very dangerous, though.'

'I don't care,' I replied defiantly. And the truth was, I didn't. I truly felt as if I had nothing left to lose. As far as I was concerned, the chance to write again was well worth any risk.

'All right. Leave it with me, and meet me back here on Monday, but you must be really careful. The Germans have spies and collaborators everywhere. When you come here, you must make sure you aren't followed, and if you see anyone suspicious lurking outside, you must go around to the back and knock three times on the kitchen door.'

I raised my eyebrows. This kind of cloak-and-dagger behaviour belonged in a spy novel, surely. It felt like a surreal dream that this should be happening in real life, in Paris, yet Bruno continued looking at me earnestly. 'Of course.' I downed the rest of my coffee, then stood to leave, planting a kiss on his stubbly cheek. 'Thank you.'

I cycled back home, feeling joyful as a lark, my veins coursing with caffeine and excitement. Anton might have abandoned me, but thanks to Tomasz and Bruno, I might still be able to write. And the prospect of writing for some kind of resistance movement filled me with hope.

5

NOVEMBER 1940, PARIS

I am here for the meeting of Les amis d'Alain-Fournier, I repeated over and over in my head as I cycled along the Avenue de New York towards Jardins du Trocadéro. It had been four weeks since Bruno had made his enticing offer and now, finally, I had instructions to go to a meeting. Intriguingly, the meeting was taking place in Le Musée de l'Homme, where I'd spent a couple of afternoons before the war, browsing through their cabinets of curiosities, wondering at the intriguing artefacts sourced from all five continents of the world. Back then, the museum had seemed like a celebration of humanity. As I'd gasped in awe at the tribal masks from the plains of Africa and the ancient pots excavated from the deserts of Asia, I could never have guessed at the dark twist waiting for humanity just around the corner, the scourge of Europe now threatening civilisation.

I am here for the meeting of Les amis d'Alain-Fournier, I mentally rehearsed again, as I locked my bicycle outside the museum. I assumed that the meeting of a literary society in honour of one of France's greatest writers was just a cover story. Or maybe it was some kind of elaborate test to see if was up to the task, whatever the task happened to be. Thankfully, I was a huge fan of Alain-Fournier's novel *Le Grand Meaulnes* and could talk about the twists and turns in Augustin's love for Yvonne for hours if need be.

Don't talk too much, I cautioned myself as I walked up the steps to the formidable white stone building, trying not to look at the Eiffel Tower in the distance. The tower used to be such a symbol of freedom to me, back when I dreamed of running away to Paris. But ever since the Nazis had arrived and hoisted their terrible swastika onto it, the mere sight of the iron lattice frame made my heart constrict. Now Koechlin and Nouguier's feat of engineering felt like a symbol of oppression.

But you could be about to learn how you can help fight the oppression, I reminded myself.

'I am here for the meeting of *Les amis d'Alain-Fournier*,' I said to the woman on the reception desk.

She looked me up and down as if she was sizing up a lamb chop in the butcher's and for an awful moment I thought she was going to deem me unsatisfactory and send me away. The hope that I might be able to write again was all that had kept me going for the last few weeks – that and daydreaming up stories about the mysterious Tomasz Zolanvari. After what felt like an eternity, she gave me a curt nod and said, 'Wait a moment please.' Then she picked up her telephone receiver and muttered something so quietly, it was impossible to hear what. She replaced the receiver and nodded again. 'The literary society are meeting down in the basement. In room 213. You may take the lift.' She pointed across the lobby.

'Thank you very much.' I hurried away before she could change her mind.

In contrast to the light airy spaces of the museum above, emerging into the basement was like entering a rabbit warren. A labyrinth of cold, dark corridors, smelling of musty old books, all of which only added to the air of subterfuge.

I finally found room 213 and knocked on the door. The murmur of voices inside abruptly stopped.

The door opened and a man peered out. He looked strangely familiar, but I couldn't quite place him.

'Hello, I'm here for the meeting of *Les amis d'Alain-Fournier*,' I parroted before lowering my voice. 'I'm Claudette. Our mutual friend Bruno put me in touch with you.'

'Ah, yes.' The man nodded and opened the door wider. Two women and another man were sitting at a table inside. 'Do come in.'

I stepped into the room, aware of all eyes upon me.

'Bruno tells me you are a novelist,' the man said, gesturing at me to sit in one of the empty seats.

'Yes – or at least I was. My publisher is no longer allowed to produce my books, thanks to the Germans,' I said, keen to show my resistance credentials. 'I write a series called *The Adventures of Aurelie*.' The man looked blank, but I was gratified to see one of the women present nod in recognition. 'But the statute means I'm no longer allowed to write – officially,' I added, again wanting to make my intentions clear.

'It's terrible,' the woman muttered and I smiled at her gratefully.

'Bruno tells me that you would still like to write,' the man said, sitting down in his seat across the circle from me.

'Yes, absolutely.' It was starting to feel a little like a game of poker, but who was going to show their hand first? 'Especially if I could write something that would make a positive difference.' I lowered my voice. 'Against our occupiers.'

The man looked around at the others as if for approval, and one by one they nodded.

'I am Jean Cassou,' he said.

'What, *the* Jean Cassou?' I replied, instantly forgetting my desire to be taken seriously and gaping at the famous novelist, poet and art critic like an awestruck kid. No wonder he'd seemed familiar. I cringed as I thought of how I'd expected him to have heard of Aurelie. In spite of my books' huge success, I still felt a bit of a fraud in the presence of literary writers, afraid that they'd resent this young upstart from Marseilles invading their world with her tales of dance-hall adventures and other frivolity. And now here I was face to face with a bona fide belletrist.

Cassou chuckled. 'I am the writer Jean Cassou, yes.'

'It-it's a pleasure to meet you,' I stammered before looking around at the rest of the group, trying to identify any other literary greats.

'And I'm Yvonne Oddon,' the woman said. 'I'm the head librarian here at the museum. And this is the art historian Agnès Humbert.' She gestured to the woman next to her and we exchanged smiles. 'And this is Boris Vildé,' Yvonne continued. 'He's an ethnographer here at the museum.'

'Very nice to meet you,' Vildé said in what sounded like a Russian accent.

'And you too,' I replied, my heart swelling.

'Bruno speaks very highly of you,' Cassou said with a smile.

'I speak very highly of him too!' I blurted out in my excitement. 'And of his coffee.'

Why did you say that? my inner voice wailed. *You sound like a blabbering idiot.*

'His coffee?' Cassou raised an eyebrow.

'Yes, he serves the most delicious coffee – or at least he did,' I added, unsure Bruno would want people knowing about his black-market stash, even if they were fellow members of the Resistance.

To my relief, Cassou smiled. I might have written several bestselling novels, but in the presence of a literary great I could still easily be reduced to a quivering wreck.

'He gives me his word that you can be trusted,' Cassou continued.

'Of course!' I exclaimed. 'I can't bear what's happening here in France. What they're doing to the Jewish people. I feel I'll go mad if I don't do something to fight back.'

'That's exactly what I said to Jean,' the art historian, Agnès, said.

Cassou nodded and they both smiled at me warmly. I felt a wave of relief, as if I'd just passed an important test.

'Have you ever written any journalism?' Cassou asked.

'No.' My heart sank; could I have failed after all? 'But I taught myself how to write novels, so I'm sure I'd be able to. I'm a very fast learner.'

'I like your enthusiasm.' Cassou looked thoughtful for a moment. 'Perhaps you could write something about the plight of the Jewish people living in Paris. Anonymously, of course.'

'Of course,' I echoed, my spine tingling.

'Shall we tell her what we're doing?' Yvonne asked.

To my relief, the rest of the group nodded.

'We are starting a newspaper,' Cassou told me. 'A clandestine newspaper, against the fascists who have invaded our city.'

My skin erupted in goosebumps. The idea of a clandestine newspaper, and of me being a part of it, was a like a shot of adrenaline straight to my heart. All of the impotence I'd been feeling began to dissipate.

'We will be able to use the printing press here at the museum,' Yvonne explained.

'But obviously it is very risky,' Vildé added, 'so you mustn't breathe a word of it to anyone.'

'Of course.'

'Perhaps you could write me five hundred words on the Jewish experience in Paris,' Cassou said to me, 'and if it's up to snuff, we'll include it in the first edition.'

'I-I don't know what to say,' I stammered. I hadn't known what to expect from this mystery meeting, but this was exceeding all of my expectations. Then, to my complete embarrassment, I began to cry.

'Oh no, what's wrong?' Agnès said, placing a hand on my shoulder.

'Nothing is wrong; everything is right,' I replied. 'These are happy tears, I promise. It just feels so good to be of some use again. I don't think I'd realised how much it had hurt to have the thing I feel I was born to do stolen from me and to be dropped by my publisher. To be thrown on the scrap heap and made to feel like a second-class citizen in my own country.'

'Write about it then, in your article,' Cassou said softly. 'People need to know. They need to be brought to their senses. In my experience, personal stories are one of the most powerful ways of winning people's support.'

'I will. Thank you.' I took a handkerchief from my pocket and blew my nose. 'How will I get it to you?'

'Give it to Bruno. Is a week enough time?'

'Of course. These days, I sadly have little else to do.'

'Thank you.' Cassou stood up and I realised it was my cue to leave.

I quickly got to my feet and we shook hands.

'It was so nice to meet you.' I looked at the others gratefully.

'And you,' Yvonne said, and the others nodded in agreement.

I left the museum, my spirits soaring like the final rousing movement of a symphony. The notion that these people should have come together like this to try to resist the German occupation in the basement of the Museum of Humanity had rather poetically restored my faith in humanity. I was on such a high, I decided to do something I'd been toying with for the past few weeks – to cycle into the Pletzl in the fourth arrondissement to see if I could find Tomasz.

Just like my literary creation, Aurelie, I was not the kind of woman to go chasing – or indeed, cycling – after a man, but Tomasz had had such an impact on my life in the few hours we'd spent together, I felt a craving for more. And now I had the perfect excuse for trying to find him – I could thank him for making me see that I could use my writing as a weapon against the Germans.

As I cycled off along the road, I could practically hear Aurelie tsking at me. '*A fully realised woman has no need to pursue a man*' – one of her most popular and quoted lines came back to haunt me. '*A fully realised woman is too busy pursuing her passions and creating her own adventures.*'

'Stop being such a smarty-pants,' I muttered under my breath, half wishing I'd created the kind of bosom-clutching, sappy heroine with no mind of her own who featured in most romance novels. The trouble with characters who live in your head is that there's no escape from them, especially when they're as truculent as Aurelie. I started humming '*La Marseillaise*' to try to distract myself.

When I reached the Place Saint-Paul, I got off my bicycle and secured it to a lamp post. The word Pletzl is Yiddish for 'little place', and as I made my way along one of the narrow streets off the square, it felt as if the city had folded in on itself. The grimy walls of the five-storey buildings either side of me seemed to lean in slightly, causing the pale winter sunlight to dim.

The Stars of David in the windows of the butchers' and the bakers' made me simultaneously grateful and uneasy. It was comforting to be surrounded by so many signs of people who wouldn't judge me, but I was equally worried for these people. Compared to my opulent, leafy street by the river, there was evidence of poverty everywhere here, from the hollowed-out faces of the people passing by, to the clothes hanging loosely from their frames. At least where I lived I could blend in. These people were sitting targets for the Germans.

Which is why you must write about them in your article, a voice inside my mind calmly stated.

I looked down at my fur-trimmed coat, painfully aware and slightly ashamed of my comparative wealth. No wonder Tomasz had been shocked at the prospect of me living all alone in my spacious apartment, if this was what he was used to.

The sight of a bookshop stopped me in my tracks. A lot of the books on display in the window were in Hebrew and clearly religious texts. But when I tried the door, it was locked. Of course it was. If I'd been forbidden from writing for being Jewish, there was no way our new hateful government would allow Jewish books to be sold.

'May I help you?' a reedy voice called from somewhere above, causing me to jump.

I looked up to see a man with the white pointed beard of a pixie leaning out of a window on the third floor. A pair of wire-framed glasses on a chain around his neck dangled in the air.

'Oh, I was just wondering if I could buy a book, but I see that the shop's closed,' I replied.

'That's where you're wrong,' the man called down. 'The shop isn't closed, the door is.'

'Oh – I see.' I couldn't help grinning. 'I don't suppose you know how I could get the door to open, do you?' I half expected him to announce that I needed to say the secret password.

'One moment,' he said, disappearing from view, the window slamming shut behind him.

More than a minute went by and I was starting to wonder if I'd been the victim of a prank when the man appeared from an alleyway at the side of the shop. He was even more pixie-like up close, stick-thin with stooped shoulders that made him barely five feet tall. His dark, beady eyes darted this way and that before his gaze alighted on me.

'Good day, and who might you be?'

'I'm Claudette Weil,' I replied, offering him my hand. He showed no recognition at my name but I wasn't expecting him to. His store did not look like the kind to stock my books.

He took my hand and gave it a brisk shake. His grip was surprisingly strong for one so small. 'Very nice to meet you. I'm Solomon Finkelstein.'

'Very nice to meet you too. Are you the proprietor of this store?'

To my confusion, he shook his head as he produced a large bunch of keys from his trouser pocket. 'No, I am the Guardian of the Books, the Keeper of the Stories, the Host of the Poems.' He grinned at me over his shoulder as he unlocked the door. 'I think that sounds far more exciting than bookstore proprietor, don't you?'

'Oh – yes, absolutely!' I chuckled as I followed him inside. I'd only been in his company for a few seconds, but I already liked him immensely. I felt as if I was in the presence of a true kindred spirit.

'Were you looking for anything in particular?' he asked before locking the door behind me. 'Just to keep any undesirables out,' he said by way of explanation.

'I understand.' My skin tingled. After this morning's meeting at the museum, it felt great to witness another small act of rebellion. 'I'd just like to have a browse, if I may,' I said, too embarrassed to admit that I was eager for texts to help me rediscover my heritage. Ever since Tomasz had talked about the need to stop the Germans from erasing the Jewish identity and the magical feeling I'd experienced when he sang Kol Nidre, I'd felt a growing need inside of me to reconnect with my childhood faith. 'Oh, and also, I was wondering if you knew a man by the name of Tomasz Zolanvari?'

'Is he a writer?' Solomon asked.

'No, he's a boxer, or he was until a couple of years ago, and I believe he lives here in the Pletzl.' I looked at him hopefully.

Solomon thought for a moment, then shook his head. 'I'm afraid I don't.'

'Never mind,' I replied breezily to try to disguise my disappointment. 'I'll look for a book then.'

'Browse away! If you need me, I'll be over there' – he pointed to an armchair by the counter – 'smoking my pipe.'

'But of course,' I replied with a smile.

Steering clear of the books in Hebrew as I knew I wouldn't be able to understand them, I opened a French prayer book and brought it to my nose, inhaling the earthy scent. I heard Solomon chuckle and turned to see him watching me through a cloud of pipe smoke.

'The actions of a true bibliophile,' he commented.

I laughed. 'Yes indeed. I've always loved the smell, ever since I was a kid. To me, it's the smell of stories.'

'Yes!' he exclaimed, clapping his gnarled hands together. 'And there is nothing more important than stories – as long as the story is transformative, that is.'

'What do you mean?'

'Are you familiar with the Baal Shem Tov?'

I shook my head.

'He was an eighteenth-century rabbi from my home country of Poland, and the founder of Hasidic Judaism.'

I nodded.

'One of his disciples, an elderly man so lame he could barely move, was once asked to tell a story about his teacher. So he told a tale about how the Baal Shem used to jump and dance around while he prayed.'

I couldn't help smiling at this image. Dancing while you prayed made it seem much more fun.

'The old man got so immersed in the story he was telling

that he leapt to his feet and began dancing about to demonstrate. And in an instant he was cured of his lameness.'

'Wow.'

'Exactly.' Solomon took another puff on his pipe. 'Every story should have the power to transform both the recipient and the teller.'

I thought of how my Aurelie novels had transformed me, giving me the courage to be as fearless as my heroine. And from the letters I'd received from readers, it seemed she'd transformed the lives of many of her readers too. 'I've never thought of it like that before. I love it,' I said, bringing the book over to pay for it. 'How much do I owe you?' I fetched my pocketbook from my purse.

'Not a single franc,' he replied.

'What? But I have to pay something.'

He shook his head. 'It is my good deed for the day.'

'But—'

'I insist,' he interrupted. 'Are you aware of the concept of tikkun olam?'

'Yes,' I frowned, trying to recall the definition. 'It means "repair of the world".'

'That's right.'

'Through prayer,' I continued as the memory came back to me.

'And good deeds,' Solomon added.

'Oh.' I didn't remember that part and he must have noticed my confusion because, quick as a trice, he was up and out of his chair and searching one of the bookshelves.

'Where are you?' he called in a sing-song voice, shoving his wire glasses onto the end of his nose.

Again, I stifled the urge to giggle. A man who talked to books was definitely my kind of person.

'There!' He returned and triumphantly placed a book on

the counter in front of me. It was a collection of Hasidic tales. 'Do you have time for another very short story?' he asked.

'I *always* have time for a story,' I replied.

'Excellent!' His eyes lit up. 'Once upon a time – at the very beginning of time – when the Creator was busy creating the world, He momentarily lost control of the process.'

'God lost control?' I asked, finding the concept of an accident-prone God strangely comforting.

'Yes, and sparks of His being spilled down into the physical world, where they became trapped, and so His power was diminished somewhat, leaving the world vulnerable to chaos and evil.'

'Like the Nazis?' I asked and Solomon nodded. One question that had plagued me since the Germans had begun their persecution of the Jewish people was how God could allow such cruelty. A weakened God certainly made sense. 'So there's no hope for us?' I added, only half joking.

'Oh, but there is!' he replied triumphantly. 'We can right the wrong and heal the world.'

'How?'

'Through tikkun olam. Every time we perform an act of religious contemplation, like prayer or through doing a good deed for another, one of the sparks of light is released and able to return to God, and the goodness in the world is strengthened.' He nodded to the book of Hasidic tales and smiled at me. 'And that way, spark by spark, the world will be repaired and harmony restored.'

I pictured sparks showering down like shooting stars, embedding themselves in the world, waiting to be released, and as Solomon passed me the books, I imagined a spark of light flying free from the pages and spiralling upwards. 'I love that story,' I murmured.

'Me too. It helps me stay sane in the face of all the madness.'

I nodded. What he was saying made perfect sense.

'Let me wrap these for you,' he said, producing a roll of brown paper from under the counter. 'Just in case you are stopped and searched.'

The fact that carrying a couple of harmless books could now get me into trouble in Paris – one of the literary hubs of the world – was instantly sobering. 'Thank you. But please, you have to let me repay you somehow.'

'Promise me you will keep releasing the sparks of light, every day, no matter what. That is surely the best gift you could give to me – and the world.' He looked up from wrapping the books.

'Yes, yes of course.'

He passed me the books and smiled at me. His brown eyes were milky with age, but I could imagine that when he was younger they must have twinkled like stars. 'It was a pleasure to meet you, Claudette.'

'All my friends call me Etty,' I said.

'And all my friends call me Solly, Etty,' he replied.

'Goodbye, Solly. I hope our paths cross again someday.'

'Goodbye, Etty. I hope so too.'

I stepped out onto the street feeling moved by such a beautiful and poignant encounter. And, once again, I had Tomasz Zolanvari to thank. Crossing paths with him was feeling more and more like something fated, and it made my desire to see him again even stronger.

I spied a boulangerie on the corner at the end of the street and made a beeline for it. A mosaic of tiny blue and white chequered tiles framed the door and a handful of small round tables had been arranged outside. I decided to get something to eat and watch the world go by. It was obviously a really long shot to expect that I might see Tomasz, the kind of thing I'd never put in a novel as it would be way too clichéd and unbelievable, but still. Real life frequently had a habit of being stranger than fiction, and I couldn't shake the feeling that he and I had been meant to meet that day.

As soon as I stepped inside, my nose was flooded with a smell that took me straight back to my childhood, as I stood and waited impatiently while Madame Bellamy stirred her famous chicken soup at the stove, tugging on her apron and wheedling over and over again, 'Is it ready yet?'

A thin woman with greying hair stood behind the counter, arranging a tray full of freshly baked bagels. She looked up and smiled at me. 'Shalom.'

'Shalom,' I replied. The word felt strange coming from my mouth. Strange, but not unpleasant. 'Is that chicken soup I can smell?' I asked, practically drooling.

'Yes, kind of. I had to use turnips instead of chicken.' She looked at me and raised her eyebrows as if to say, *What can you do?*

'Could I have some please, and a bagel.'

'Of course.'

As she prepared my food, I opened my pocketbook.

'I don't think I've seen you here before,' she said without looking up.

'No, I'm just passing through. Well, I'm looking for someone actually.'

'Oh yes?' She glanced up.

'Tomasz Zolanvari. He lives here, in the Pletzl. I don't suppose you know him.'

A brief look of recognition flickered across her face, but then she shook her head firmly. 'No, never heard of him.'

I couldn't blame her for being suspicious given the climate of fear. 'He's a friend of mine.'

'And you don't know where he lives?' She frowned, holding the bowl of soup as if unsure whether I could be trusted to have it.

'Not exactly, no. I know that his uncle was a tailor here,' I said, producing the one other clue I possessed to his identity.

The woman shrugged. 'I'm sorry. I don't know.'

I took my soup and bagel and went and sat at one of the tables outside. She did know Tomasz, I was certain of it. But why did she clam up at the mention of his name? Did she suspect I might be a Nazi collaborator, or was there some other reason the mysterious Tomasz Zolanvari didn't want to be found? I shivered and pulled up the collar on my coat as the words from his Erev Yom Kippur confession echoed through my mind: 'I can't apologise to them... because I killed them.' Who was this mysterious Tomasz Zolanvari who'd had such an impact upon my life, and who had he killed?

6

FEBRUARY 1941, PARIS

Once upon a time, there was a rabbi named Yaakov Rabi-
nowicz who lived in Poland in the eighteenth century. One
day he was out walking when he came across an upturned hay
wagon. The wagon was so huge, it was blocking the whole road
and bales of hay had been cast everywhere. A Christian
peasant was standing next to the wagon looking distraught.

'Please, sir, would you help me right my wagon,' he
pleaded.

The rabbi knew that it would be a mitzvah to help the
peasant, and that with every act of kindness, the light in the
world is increased, but he felt certain that he wasn't strong
enough to lift the wagon and so he shook his head.

'I'm really sorry,' he replied, 'but I can't.'

'You mean you won't,' the peasant replied. 'You aren't
willing to help me.'

His accusation pierced the rabbi to the core and he
instantly hurried over and together the men came up with the
idea of using some wooden boards to insert beneath the wagon
to lever it upright. Then they placed the bales of hay back on

the wagon and the peasant thanked him before preparing to continue on his way.

'Could I walk with you a while?' the rabbi asked.

'Of course, my brother,' the Christian replied and they set off in companionable silence.

After a while, the rabbi asked the question that had been burning in his mind. 'Why did you say I wasn't willing to help you when I told you that I didn't think I was able?'

'No one knows whether they are able to do something until they have actually tried to do it,' the Christian replied.

'But what made you think I'd be able to lift the wagon?' the rabbi asked.

'Because you happened to appear in just the place and exactly the time that I needed help,' the Christian replied with a smile.

The rabbi laughed. 'Next you'll be telling me that I was meant to be here to help you.'

'But of course, brother.' The Christian chuckled.

Today, as I walk the streets of my beloved Paris, as a Jew, I feel as if the hay wagon of my life has been upturned. Everywhere I go, I see posters declaring hatred for me. My own government have decreed that I can no longer make a living in my profession. Friends and acquaintances have had to flee for their lives. I've been urged to do the same. But why should I give up the life and home I've worked so hard for? And where would I go anyway? Where is safe anymore for the Jewish in Europe?

Now more than ever I need a Christian brother or sister to come to my aid. If you're reading this and you feel you wouldn't be able to do anything to help, please take inspiration from this old Hasidic tale. How do you know whether you're able to help someone until you try? Think of the love and hope the kindness of your action might release. What if your life has

led you to this moment, here in Paris, precisely so that you
might help a brother or sister in need?

As I read my article in the third issue of *Resistance*, the
clandestine paper set up by Cassou and his friends, I felt a thrill
pass through me more powerful than any excitement I'd felt
upon seeing my books for the first time. The thought that my
piece, inspired by one of the tales in the book Solly had gifted
me, might in turn inspire Parisians to rise up in our hour of need
filled me with joy and hope, and once again I thought of
Tomasz. Our paths had only crossed for a matter of hours, and
several months previously, but I was still feeling the positive
ripple effect from our encounter. Surely, like the rabbi and
Christian in the tale, we had met on the bridge that day for a
reason. I might have been no closer to finding him but he had
led me to this moment.

I traced my fingertips over the typewritten page. With its
stencilled banner and smudged ink, *Resistance* looked as if it
had been handmade in someone's basement, precisely because
it had. My breath caught in my throat as I thought of the
bravery of the men and women in the basement of the museum
risking everything to try to kindle a flame of resistance in this
city.

After reading the entire thing three times, I hid my copy of
Resistance under a floorboard beneath my bathtub. I'd put
Madame Bellamy's Shabbat candlesticks and her wedding ring
– my most precious possessions – there too, just in case the
soldiers raided my apartment the way they'd raided Levi's
upstairs. Then I applied a dash of lipstick and brushed my hair.
It was time to take my latest article to Bruno.

I fetched it from where it sat, freshly written on the typewriter, and folded the page smaller and smaller until I was able

to tuck it inside my bra. I'd become accustomed to such cloak-and-dagger behaviour over the past couple of months, but every so often the insanity of the situation would strike me and I'd be filled with indignation all over again. How had it come to this? How had my beloved France fallen victim to this infestation of hatred and oppression? Still, at least I was writing for an audience again, even if they could never know that I was the author.

As I set off for Bruno's bistro, I pondered the fact that once, not so long ago, I'd loved that I was a published author and the way in which my readers had taken me into their hearts. Being an author had gone a long way to erasing years of my father chipping away at my self-esteem with his steady stream of insults. Writing for *Resistance* had made me realise that I no longer needed that personal acclaim. Solly, who I now met up with every week, had made me see that releasing more light into the world was all that mattered, especially in these dark days. And I had learned the vital lesson that whenever you release light, you can't fail to benefit from its glow.

By the time I reached the Latin Quarter, I was positively humming with optimism, thinking about my new role. I scanned the street in front of the bistro. A man was leaning against the wall beside it smoking a cigarette. The collar on his coat was pulled up and his hat was pulled down, obscuring his face. Could he be a spy for the Germans? A shiver ran up my spine as he turned his head to look at me.

I couldn't afford to take the risk, so I strolled past him, heart pounding, to the end of the block. Once I'd turned the corner, I stared into a milliner's window as if fascinated by the hats on display, and waited to see if the man was following me. The folded-up article inside my bra seemed to slice into my skin. Who knew what punishment awaited me if I was caught with it in my possession. It was an intensely sobering thought.

I walked around the block, stopping every now and then to check I wasn't being followed, until I reached the alleyway leading to the back of the bistro. I hurried down and knocked three times on the door. The air smelled sour from the row of bins and in the distance I could hear the sharp clip of German soldiers' boots.

Hurry up! I silently implored. *Open the door!*

After what felt like forever but was probably only half a minute, the door opened a crack and a teenage boy in kitchen overalls peered out.

'I'm here to see Bruno,' I said quietly. 'He's expecting me.'

The boy glanced beyond me into the yard, then opened the door just wide enough for me to slip through. 'Go to the office,' he hissed, nodding to a door at the other end of the kitchen.

I hurried past a chef stirring a pot at the stove and into a darkened corridor. I caught a waft of Bruno's cigar smoke and followed it to a slightly open door at the other end of the corridor. I found Bruno hunched over his desk, a deep frown etched upon his face.

'Something terrible has happened,' he whispered as soon as he saw me, beckoning me inside.

My stomach clenched. 'Tell me.'

Bruno shut the door behind me. 'They've been arrested.'

'Who?' I asked numbly, not really wanting to hear.

'The founders of *Resistance*. Someone who works at the museum denounced them.'

'No!' I felt sick as I thought back to my visit there. I hadn't seen any of the museum group since our first meeting – they'd thought it would be safer for me to stay away – but their bravery had made a huge impression upon me, and the thought of Jean Cassou, Yvonne, Agnès and Boris languishing in jail, facing a potential death sentence, was devastating.

Bruno ran his hand through his coarse, dark hair. 'I'm so sorry. You'd better get out of here, and steer clear for a while, just in case the Germans find out about my involvement.'

'Oh Bruno!' I grabbed his arm, as if by clinging on to him I could somehow stop everything from unravelling. The thought of the Germans arresting one of the few people I could still trust in Paris was too much to bear. 'What should I do with my latest article?'

'You need to destroy it.' He went over to his desk and picked up a book of matches. 'I'll do it for you now.'

I turned away and fished the piece of paper from my bra and handed it to him. He took it over to the grate and set it alight. As the paper curled and glowed and my words went up in smoke, I had to fight the urge to cry.

'You must destroy any other evidence of your work for *Resistance* too,' he said, turning to face me.

I thought of the copies I'd hidden under my bathtub. I'd been so proud of them, so proud of doing something to fight back. I blinked back the onset of tears.

Bruno wrapped his bulky arms around me and hugged me tight. 'I'm so sorry, Etty.'

I inhaled the scent of garlic and cigars woven into the fabric of his shirt, trying to commit it, and him, to memory. Then he ushered me back through the kitchen. As the back door slammed shut behind me, it was as if someone had clamped a vice to my heart and was squeezing out every last drop of my new-found hope. I looked down the dingy alleyway and felt loneliness creeping up to meet me like a freezing fog. I couldn't bear the thought of going home, so I set off in the direction of the fourth arrondissement and the Pletzl.

When I reached Solly's store, I slipped down the passageway beside the building and knocked on the door that led to his apartment above the shop. We'd taken to having our weekly meetings up there as it was safer than risking being seen in the shop. Just as with Bruno, we had devised a coded knock so that Solly would know it was me.

For a horrible moment, I thought he wasn't in, or even worse, had been spirited off by the police or the Germans, but then I heard his footsteps on the stairs and the door creaked open.

'Etty, my dear,' he greeted me in his wavering voice, beckoning me inside.

'Oh Solly, something terrible has happened. Again!'

'Dear, dear, dear, if I had a franc for every time I heard those words...' he muttered as we made our way up the stairs.

Solly's living room had essentially been taken over by books, with a couple of holes burrowed out, at one end of the sofa and on one of the armchairs, for people to sit. I perched on the sofa next to a pile of leather-bound poetry collections and clasped my hands together.

'The people I've been writing for have been arrested. Someone denounced them.' I hadn't told Solly any details about my work for *Resistance*, other than I was using my writing to help free France.

'Oh no. I'm so sorry to hear that.' His cloudy eyes widened in alarm. 'Are you in danger? Do you need somewhere to hide?'

'I don't know. I hope not.' No one knew I wrote for *Resistance* apart from Bruno and Cassou and the others and I felt certain they wouldn't denounce me. But what if they were tortured?

My concern must have shown because Solly instantly patted me on my shoulder. 'You can always stay here if you need to. Although I'm not sure we'll be safe here for much longer.'

'Thank you, but unless I can shrink myself down to the size of a bookmark, I'm not sure I'd fit,' I joked, trying, and failing, to lighten the mood. I sniffed the air. In spite of there being no sign of any food, I could smell something peppery. 'Can I smell mustard?' I asked.

'It's my feet,' Solly replied, hitching his trousers up. He was so thin now, they were slipping down over his hips in spite of his old leather belt being buckled to the tightest notch.

'What do you mean?' I stared at him, baffled.

'There's mustard on my feet.'

'Why?'

'To try to keep them warm. All of the most stylish Parisians are doing it this winter, you know.' He chuckled.

But I wanted to cry. I looked down at my fur coat and felt ashamed. What was I thinking, coming to see him flaunting such wealth? I wriggled out of the coat and held it out to him. 'I want you to have this.'

'I'm not sure it goes with my frocks,' he quipped, raising his snowy white eyebrows.

'I don't mean to wear – at least, not outside. But you could use it as a blanket.'

He frowned. 'But what would you wear?'

'I have other coats,' I said with a shrug.

'But on your way home today? It's so cold.'

'I'll be fine. I'm a fast walker; I'll be warm enough.'

Solly looked at the fur in my hand.

'Surely you're not going to deprive me of releasing a spark of God's light,' I said, revealing what I hoped was my trump card.

He laughed and took the coat. 'I think I've trained you too well.' He went over to his old threadbare armchair, which had become perfectly moulded to fit the curve of his spine. As he sat, he tucked the coat around his legs and his face broke into a relieved smile. The grateful glint in his eyes seemed to send sparks of light spiralling into the room. Then I remembered what had happened to the founders of *Resistance* and my heart instantly sank.

'I hate the Germans; I hate what they're doing to us. And I hate our police and government for going along with them.'

I was expecting Solly to nod in agreement, but to my

surprise he shook his head. 'We mustn't hate,' he said softly. I knew Solly well enough by then to know that he always spoke words of wisdom – the kind of utterances that you find yourself pondering on and drawing great solace from, weeks or even months later, but still...

'But the Germans are so full of hate.'

'Exactly, and that's why we need to love them.'

'Love them?' I was barely able to spit the words out.

'Yes, to compensate for the lack of love they bring to the world.'

'Are you being serious?'

'Completely. It was one of the main teachings of the Great Rabbi Pinchas of Koretz.'

'I'm sorry, but there's no way I can love those...' I somehow managed to stop myself from cursing. 'I can't.' I thought of the brave souls behind *Resistance* and what horrors now awaited them. The notion that I should love their captors and the snake who'd denounced them seemed ludicrous to me.

Solly looked at me and chuckled. 'I was like you once upon a time, so full of fire and righteous indignation...' As Solly had fast become one of my favourite people, my heart glowed at the comparison. 'But then I got well,' he continued.

I stared at him indignantly, 'Are you saying I'm ill?'

Again he chuckled. 'In a way, yes.' He leaned forward. 'Tell me, how does your hatred for them make you feel?'

'Angry,' I replied.

'And?'

I pictured the hatred inside of me, sour and curdling in the pit of my stomach. 'Bitter.'

'And do you think that bitterness is good for you?'

'No. But we can't let them get away with what they're doing.'

He leaned back in his chair. 'Who said anything about letting them get away with it?'

'I don't understand.'

'We can still fight against injustice. But if you fight from a place of love, you don't end up poisoning yourself too.'

I looked at him blankly.

'Can I tell you a story?'

My spirits lifted a little. I'd come to love Solly's stories. 'Of course.' I settled back on the sofa, causing the pile of poetry books beside me to spill into my lap.

Solly took his pipe from the table next to his chair and lit it. 'Once upon a time, there was a wise sage named Hillel who was renowned for never losing his temper and remaining calm at all times.'

I instinctively closed my eyes, memories of Madame Bellamy reading me bedtime stories rushing back to me – small pockets of warmth and love from my childhood that I treasured.

'Hillel was so well known for being patient that one day a local man bet his friend four hundred zuzim that he could make him lose his temper,' Solly said.

'Zuzim?' I looked at him questioningly.

'Ancient Hebrew coins made of silver.' Solly took another puff on his pipe before continuing. 'So the man called at Hillel's house on a Friday right before Sabbath when he knew he'd be bathing. He knocked on the door and waited while Hillel dried off and put on a robe before going out to see him. Trying to test his patience, the man asked what he knew was a ridiculous question: "Why do the Babylonians have round heads?"

'But instead of becoming impatient, Hillel praised the man for asking such a great question and answered it as best he could. Then he returned to his bath and the man waited just long enough for him to start washing his hair when he called out that he had another question. Once again, Hillel had to go through the inconvenience of getting out of the bath, putting on a robe and wrapping a towel around his hair. And, once again, the man asked him a ludicrous question. Hillel thanked him for the question, answered it calmly and returned to his bath. And even when the man interrupted his bathing with a third nonsensical question, he remained unruffled.'

'Seriously?' I stared at Solly incredulously. If someone interrupted me three times with ludicrous questions when I was washing my hair, I'd probably throw a bucket of bathwater over them.

'Yes, indeed. And when the man angrily informed Hillel that, thanks to his unshakeable patience, he'd lost a bet of four hundred zuzim, Hillel urged him to be careful with his temperament and told him that it was better that he should lose eight hundred zuzim than get Hillel or anyone else to lose their temper.' Solly took a puff on his pipe.

'Is that it?' I frowned at such a dissatisfying ending. If I'd written that story, the smug Hillel would have been made to drink his own bathwater.

'Yes.'

'But what if you haven't been born with the patience of Hillel?'

'I don't think even Hillel was born with that kind of patience,' Solly replied. 'He chose to cultivate it. And he chose to define situations in ways that wouldn't make him angry. Instead of seeing the man as an annoyance, he saw him as someone eager to learn, and he embraced the opportunity to teach.'

'Right. If only the Nazis were asking us Jews annoying questions while we washed our hair, rather than persecuting us and blaming us for all the ills of the world.'

'But don't you see?' Solly gazed at me intently. 'The same principle applies.'

'How?'

'We can see them as hated oppressors or we can see them as people who've chosen evil over love and whose souls have been corrupted.'

'But...'

'"That which is hateful to you, do not do to your fellow. That is the entire Torah and the rest is commentary." Hillel's greatest teaching,' Solly added by way of explanation.

I wished I could have the patience of Hillel and the wisdom of Solly, but every time I thought about what had happened to Cassou and the others, I felt sick with rage and despair. I looked at the old clock ticking away on the mantelpiece. If I wanted to get home before curfew, I ought to leave now.

'I should go,' I said, getting to my feet.

'Are you sure?' Solly looked at me, concerned.

'Yes. Thank you for the story.'

'Some stories take a while to take effect,' he told me, wincing as he stood up. 'In fact, I would say the best stories are slow to take effect.'

'Yes, well, I hope it works before I end up throttling a German,' I muttered as he accompanied me to the door.

'I'll be praying for you,' Solly said and I forced myself to smile, not wishing to appear ungrateful. 'Are you sure you'll be all right without your coat?' he asked with a shiver as he opened the door and a sharp breeze blew in.

'Of course.' I turned and planted a kiss on his cheek. '*Bonne chance*, Solly.'

'*Bonne chance*, my dear Etty.'

As I made my way back out onto the street, I heard Solly locking and bolting his door behind me and there was something about the sound that filled me with sorrow. The fact that an old man should have to live like this, putting mustard on his feet to try to keep warm, forbidden from opening his beloved bookshop, and living in constant fear, filled me with outrage. How could I not want to do to the Nazis what they were doing to us? How could I ever show them love?

A driving rain was falling now, each drop nipping at my face and causing me to shiver. Everything felt so hard, so hopeless. I headed down the narrow street in the direction of the river. Up ahead, I could hear chatter coming from a bar, the only sound around. The noise increased as the door opened and a figure emerged on a cloud of cigarette smoke. I only ever smoked when I was drunk, which was hardly ever, especially these days, but all of a sudden I was filled with the longing for wine to warm my empty belly and numb my fearful thoughts. Before I had enough time to reconsider, I pushed the door open and walked in.

The bar was tiny, and seemed even more claustrophobic once everyone turned to stare at me. Following the scent of wine like a bloodhound, I made my way to the bar at the back, where a tall thin man was standing watching me as he dried a glass.

'Red wine please,' I said and, thankfully, people began resuming their conversations.

As the man poured me a glass, I glanced around. This was exactly the kind of place I imagined Tomasz coming to. Perhaps the barkeeper knew him.

'I'm looking for someone,' I told him as I paid for my wine. 'Tomasz Zolanvari.'

I wasn't sure if it was coincidence, but the two men at the bar next to me instantly stopped talking.

'Never heard of him,' the barman said quickly, perhaps a little too quickly.

I cursed my stupidity. The city was now crawling with traitors and denouncers; was it any wonder that people in the Jewish quarter might be suspicious of newcomers? I took my wine and sat at a table in the corner. The man who'd been standing next to me at the bar said something to his companion, then left, but not before shooting me a searching stare.

I'm not the enemy, I'm one of you! I wanted to yell, but the truth was, I didn't feel I belonged anywhere anymore. And now I didn't even have the sense of community I'd got from writing for *Resistance*. The loneliness I'd been trying to escape through books and bike rides and endless daydreams swelled inside of me, until I was barely able to breathe. What if I never got my old life back again? What if I was destined to spend the rest of my days isolated and alone, with no outlet for my imagination and passions?

I took a large gulp of wine, wanting to get out of there and back home as soon as possible. I'd have to run at least part of the way now to make it back before curfew.

As soon as I finished my wine, I hurried outside. The cold wind stung my face like a slap, and the alcohol on my empty stomach made me feel woozy. As I made my way along the street, I heard footsteps behind me, gaining on me. I stopped to let whoever was in such a rush go past, but instead I felt an arm around my waist and before I could react, I was being pulled back into a darkened shop doorway.

7

MARCH 1941, PARIS

I tried to elbow my assailant in the ribs, but their grip was too strong and I was unable to move.

'Why are you asking about Tomasz Zolanvari?' a man's voice growled in my ear. 'What do you want with him? Who sent you?'

'I sent myself,' I replied.

His grip loosened slightly and I slammed my elbow back with all the force I could muster.

'Ow!' the man yelped, but rather than being rendered helpless as I had hoped, he tightened his grip. 'Who are you?' he asked.

'Claudette Weil,' I replied. 'And I'll have you know Tomasz is a very good friend of mine.'

'Is that so?' The man spun me round to face him. His coat collar was pulled up and his flat cap pulled right down, but I could just make out the bottom of a jagged scar on his cheek and a cleft in his chin.

'Oh.'

'What's wrong? Aren't you pleased to see your very good friend?' Tomasz asked, letting go of me.

'I've seen you in my pink satin bathrobe. I think that constitutes a certain level of intimacy,' I retorted, and to my relief he grinned. For months I'd dreamed of finding Tomasz again, but now he was standing right in front of me, I didn't know what to do or say.

'What are you doing here? Why are you looking for me?' he asked.

My daydreams of us being reunited had not gone like this. In my dreams, he was always delighted to see me, not bewildered.

'I-I wanted to thank you,' I stammered. For so long I'd wanted to thank him, but that was when I was still writing for *Resistance* – before they'd been betrayed.

'What for?'

I lowered my voice. 'I did what you suggested. I started writing about what's going on in Paris. About what's happening to the Jews.'

'You have? But what about the Statut?'

'I was writing for a clandestine newspaper,' I whispered. 'For the Resistance.'

'That's fantastic,' he replied, but he looked distracted.

'It was – until the people I was writing for were arrested.'

'No!' He glanced up and down the street anxiously as if worried he too might get arrested by being seen with me.

A deep disappointment filled me. I felt so stupid for daydreaming our meeting into something fated and momentous, for investing so much hope in a happy outcome. 'I should go,' I muttered. 'It's almost curfew.'

'Will you get back in time?' He looked at me, concerned. 'And aren't you cold without a coat?'

'Yes. No. I'm fine.'

'Do you want me to walk with you?'

'No. It's fine. I'll be fine.' *Fine, fine, fine, fine!* The word seemed to echo back at me in the darkness like a taunt. I was anything but fine. My stupid imagination and its capacity to entice me with impossibly happy endings would be the death of me.

I started walking away so he wouldn't see the tears building in my eyes.

'I'm going to walk with you,' Tomasz said, running to catch up. 'It's not safe for you to be out on your own – in spite of your prowess in Krav Maga. Talking of which, I'm surprised you weren't able to evade my grip just then.'

'I would under normal circumstances,' I replied stiffly, grateful for this slight thaw in his mood. 'You took me by surprise.'

'Hmm, surely a fighter like you would be trained to deal with the element of surprise.' He grinned down at me.

But before I could respond, there was a commotion from further along the street and a man's voice yelled, 'Come out, you Jewish swine!'

'Shit!' Tomasz cursed. 'It's the police.' He grabbed my arm and pulled me down an alleyway next to a boulangerie.

'What are they doing?' I whispered.

'Harassing us. It's their new favourite sport,' he hissed in response.

We ran to the end of the passageway and Tomasz peered out to check the coast was clear. More banging and shouting rang out.

'Quick,' he said, leading me along another narrow street. He stopped about halfway down and unlocked a door next to what had once been a jeweller's but was now boarded up. 'Come in.' He beckoned me to follow him inside.

The door opened directly onto a steep flight of steps similar to Solly's. I followed him to the top, where he unlocked another door.

'Welcome to paradise,' he said drily as he ushered me inside.

The only thing I could make out in the darkness was teetering piles of crates and boxes. The cold air smelled musty and damp.

'What is this place?' I whispered.

'It's my home,' Tomasz replied.

I heard the sound of a match being struck and the room filed with the flickering amber glow of a lamp. I looked around and saw that the two windows had been boarded up from the inside.

'You live here?' I said, unable to disguise my shock.

'Yes, sorry there aren't any chandeliers or gold-tapped bathtubs.'

'No, sorry, I didn't mean it like that, I was just... surprised. Where do you sleep?'

'You want to see my bed?' He took off his cap and looked at me quizzically. His hair was slightly longer than before and his jaw was shaded with dark stubble.

I instantly blushed. 'No... I-I just... It doesn't look like there's much room.' I nodded at the boxes.

'There's enough room for me and the rats.' He looked at me defiantly, as if wanting to prompt some kind of hysterical reaction. Little did he know I'd adopted several pet rats as a child.

'Ah, that's nice,' I replied. 'In my experience, rats make excellent companions. I was always glad of their company as a child.'

He frowned at me. 'You lived with rats as a child?'

'Yes, well, they lived beneath the floorboards in my home. My favourite was my good friend, Rat-a-tat-tat. I haven't always lived in a world of gold bath-taps and chandeliers, you know,' I added, feeling the need to earn his respect and prove for once and for all that I wasn't some kind of spoiled princess.

He started to laugh. 'You are full of surprises.'

'Pleasant ones, I hope?' I looked at him and he nodded before turning away.

'Well, it looks as if it's my turn to be the host. Would you like a drink?'

'Yes please.'

He disappeared behind a wall of boxes in the corner and re-emerged holding a bottle of wine and two tin cups. 'Here...' He gestured at me to follow him through a corridor of crates to the opposite corner of the room, where a single mattress lay on the floor. A book and a watch had been placed next to the head of the makeshift bed. I instinctively wondered what the book was. I know you probably shouldn't judge a person by their books, just as you shouldn't judge a book by its cover, but we all do, or at least I do, but it was too dark to make out the title. 'I'm sorry,' he said, looking slightly awkward, 'but this is the only place to sit.'

'It's fine.' I couldn't find any other words as I perched down on the end of the mattress. The faint aroma of sweat drifted up from the bedclothes. It wasn't unpleasant, though. Finally, things seemed to be looking up. This might not be anything like the reunion I'd daydreamed of, but it was certainly becoming interesting.

Tomasz sat at the other end of the mattress and poured us both a drink. Then he set the bottle on top of his book and passed me one of the cups. 'Mazel tov,' he said drily, raising his cup.

'What are we toasting?' I asked, clinking my cup against his.

'Old friends.' He smiled shyly.

'Do you mean me?' I blurted out, too happy at this development to be coy.

'Of course,' he replied, and his smile faded. He looked down into his lap. 'I've thought about you a lot since Yom Kippur.'

'I've thought about you a lot too!' I exclaimed.

'Really?'

As our gazes met, I felt something stirring deep in the pit of my stomach. 'Yes, as I was trying to explain to you earlier, I've been so grateful to you.'

'For encouraging you to continue writing?' he asked.

'Not just that.'

'For saving your doll?'

'No! I mean, I am grateful you saved her from a watery grave, but you've done way more than that. Meeting you changed everything for the better.'

I took a gulp of wine for courage before telling him all about how he'd inadvertently helped me find a new friend in Solly, which in turn had given my life a deeper purpose.

'You have made me feel so much better,' I finished, hoping I hadn't overdone it and caused him to feel awkward. In my experience, men preferred women who played their emotional cards close to their chest. Certainly, my literary heroine Aurelie would never be so gushing and forthcoming in a situation like this. But these were unprecedented times. It had been so hard to find Tomasz, and who knew if I'd see him again after tonight. I didn't have the luxury of being able to play games. I glanced at him and saw to my surprise that he was wiping his eyes. 'Are you crying?'

'No!' he exclaimed, but he wouldn't meet my gaze.

'I really hope I didn't upset you; it's just that with things the way they are, I can't see any point in not being honest with people, especially when you have something nice to say.'

He nodded. 'It's been a long time since...'

'What?' I asked softly.

'Since anyone said something that nice about me.' His voice was barely more than a whisper.

'Well, I meant every word,' I replied.

The chill air between us suddenly seemed to warm. It felt so good to finally find him again, to be able to thank him, and to see him look so moved. I imagined a spark of God's goodness being kindled and released between us.

'Thank you,' he murmured, shifting slightly so he was facing me.

'You're welcome.'

The warmth between us intensified and I felt a longing deep inside of me. I don't even think it was sexual, although I certainly found him handsome. All I wanted in that moment was to be held. I'd been staving off the forces of loneliness and fear for so long; I'd been trying to stay strong for so long. The desire to be held, to absorb some of his strength, was overwhelming.

He placed his hand on the bed between us and I instinctively moved mine so it was right beside it. He inched towards me and our fingertips touched, sending what felt like showers of tiny shooting stars fizzing through me.

'Etty,' he whispered and the sound of my name in his mouth, and the urgency with which he said it, made me lose all sense of reason. Clearly something similar was happening to him.

Our hands came together and our fingers entwined and I heard him gasp. Then our bodies were pressing together, our mouths finding each other, expressing with a kiss what we were unable to say with words.

In every one of Aurelie's books, I'd written her passionate love scenes as a form of wishful thinking. I'd had some very nice romantic encounters since arriving in Paris but never once experienced the kind of electrifying attraction I was now feeling. I'd started to think it only existed in fiction or poetry or the movies.

The stubble on Tomasz's chin felt coarse against my skin, but it only added to the intensity of the moment. He wrapped his arms around me, pulling me closer and closer until we toppled down on the mattress.

'Oh Etty,' he whispered again, running his hand through my hair.

I placed my hand on his chest and could feel his heart beating. This was what I'd been missing, what I'd been craving. This closeness with another human being. The sense that no matter what horrors might be ahead, we'd be OK because we had each other.

'I'm so happy,' I whispered, moving my hand up to stroke his cheek. And in an instant, everything changed. He pulled back as if I'd slapped him.

'I'm sorry. I don't know what...' He sat up abruptly. 'I didn't invite you here to...'

I lay there stunned. What had happened to cause such a change in him? Had I done something wrong?

Tomasz looked past me at the book beside the mattress and I noticed the top of a photograph sticking out of it. 'I should never have... I'm sorry,' he muttered, scrambling from the bed. Seeing him look so mortified made me squirm. This certainly never happened in the movies.

He murmured something about going to the bathroom before disappearing off through the boxes.

I sat up and smoothed down my hair, then I picked up the book and studied the cover. It was a copy of the Torah. I flicked it open to look at the photograph and what I saw made my stomach lurch. It was Tomasz and a woman. She had her arms draped around his shoulders and was gazing at him lovingly. He was laughing into the camera. He looked so happy and carefree, and so in love, it was like looking at a different person.

I dropped the book like it was a hot coal, a sticky mixture of shame and anger creeping through me. What a fool I'd been, gushing about what Tomasz had meant to me! What a fool I'd been daydreaming of a happy ending for us, when all along he was clearly in love with this other woman. He obviously hadn't wanted to see me again; he knew where I lived, after all. He could have returned to find me any time he liked, but he hadn't. My loneliness and fear had turned me into a desperate fool and he'd almost taken advantage of my vulnerability. But not anymore.

I got up from the mattress and hurried through the labyrinth of boxes. There was no sign of Tomasz, thankfully. Quiet as a mouse, I let myself out and tiptoed down the stairs and back out into the cold, dark evening. It would be past curfew by now, but I didn't care. I'd rather take my chances with the police and the Germans than face the embarrassment of more time with Tomasz and the woman tucked like a secret into his book.

8

SEPTEMBER 1941, PARIS

I made it home safely from the Pletzl, clinging to the dark corners of the streets like a shadow, and I spent the next few months trying to forget all about Tomasz Zolanvari and the look of mortification on his face after he'd kissed me. In desperate need of some kind of routine and without the purpose of *Resistance*, I started spending my mornings at the library and my afternoons at Café de Flore, which had mercifully been left alone by the Germans and was still a hotbed of writers, artists and philosophers. It was nice being in the company of the few writer friends who'd remained in Paris, even though some days jealousy would bubble hot as lava inside me when they talked about the publication of their new books.

Every Friday, I would visit Solly for a pre-curfew Shabbat and more spiritual inspiration. It hadn't taken long for my embarrassment at what happened with Tomasz to harden into anger and every time I visited the Pletzl, part of me wanted to bump into him so I could give him a piece of my mind for treating me so shabbily. But clearly it wasn't fated to be and I never saw him again.

One day when I was coming home from Café de Flore

along rue Saint-Benoît, I had stopped outside the building
where Madame d'Aulnoy had lived and hosted her infamous
literary salon back in the seventeenth century. Madame
d'Aulnoy had always been a literary heroine of mine; as a child,
I'd adored her book of fairy tales, *Les Contes des Fées*, and
when, as an adult, I learned about her extraordinary life, my
love for her had only grown. She'd been married off to a baron
thirty years older than her when she was just thirteen. By all
accounts, the baron was a nasty character, so much so that when
she was eighteen, Madame d'Aulnoy conspired to implicate him
in a crime of high treason that would be punishable by death.
Her plan was foiled and she was briefly imprisoned, but then
pardoned for lack of proof about her role. She eventually
returned to Paris, buying her house on rue Saint-Benoît, where
she set up her salon and became the first writer to establish the
literary fairy tale as a genre. The thing I loved most about her
fairy tales were her feisty and fearless heroines. As I'd stared at
up at the building where Madame d'Aulnoy had cooked up her
tales, I vowed to re-read them all for inspiration, and when I got
home, I'd dusted off my copy of *Les Contes des Fées* and famil-
iarised myself with my old childhood friends.

Then summer had arrived like another long-lost friend, and,
inspired by the dazzling sunshine, I added an early-morning
cycle to my daily routine as soon as curfew ended at five o'clock.
It felt wonderful to be out before the city had roused itself from
sleep and I retreated once more into my childhood flights of
fancy, pretending my bike was anything from a wild stallion to a
winged chariot. Of course, I should have known that with the
Germans' game of cat and mouse, my pretend freedom would
be short-lived.

In May, there'd been a round-up of thousands of Jews
following raids in the eleventh arrondissement. They'd been
taken to a new internment camp in a suburb of Paris called
Drancy – which had been created from a half-built apartment

complex that was supposed to have been a model for modern living – the first American-style high-rise buildings in France. The complex had previously been nicknamed La Cité de la Muette, the Silent City, which had a far more sinister ring to it now that the government were spiriting people away there.

At the end of August, a raft of new laws was introduced, with the sole purpose, it seemed, of crushing the Jewish people's spirit. The first was the confiscation of our radios. I'd sold my gramophone back in May to raise some money and was beside myself at the thought of a life without music, and the companionship the radio offered me living alone. The prospect of only having my increasingly frantic thoughts for company was not a good one.

I spent more and more time cycling the streets of Paris, but no matter how fast I pedalled, or how creative my flights of fancy, I couldn't quite escape my fears.

Then, one morning in September, I was cycling along the boulevard des Italiens, when I saw a sight that both horrified and infuriated me. A huge banner had been hung along the side of the Palais Berlitz, advertising an exhibition titled 'LE JUIF ET LA FRANCE' – the Jew and France. The image beneath showed an old man with a huge hooked nose and claw-like hands grasping at a globe. The Germans hated us so, they were holding an exhibition to proclaim it boldly. The sight so sickened me, I almost crashed into a man crossing the road.

'Look where you're going, you stupid bitch,' he snapped at me.

It was as if hatred was oozing from every crevice of the city that had once welcomed and celebrated me.

I pedalled on, my vision blurry with tears. All the way along the boulevard, I saw posters advertising the exhibition stuck to lamp posts and buildings. How had this happened? How had we allowed it? The further I cycled and the more posters I saw, my sorrow started calcifying into anger. How could people be so weak? So sheep-like? I understood that they were afraid, but how could they welcome the very people who'd just killed so many French soldiers in the Battle of France – and imprisoned hundreds of thousands more?

As soon as I got home, I opened a book of Hasidic tales Solly had gifted me and flicked it open to a random page, in need of some inspiration.

A man should be like a vessel that willingly receives what its owner pours into it, whether it be wine or vinegar. I pictured the Nazis pouring their sourness inside of me. Why should I willingly receive this? Why should any of us? It didn't make sense to me. I flung the book to the floor in frustration.

After a pitiful lunch of half a stale baguette, I went back out on my bike. I longed to return to the Palais Berlitz and rip down those posters, yell at anyone who might be queuing to see the exhibition. But instead I made myself cycle in the opposite direction. I would pretend that I was Madame d'Aulnoy's famous character Belle-Belle riding her talking horse, Comrade, off to do battle with the dragon, a favourite daydream from childhood.

I was racing along the road, a warm breeze rushing through my hair, when I saw two policemen standing on the corner ahead of me.

'Halt!' the older one called, holding up his hand. His face was red and shiny with sweat.

Reluctantly, I squeezed the brakes and came to a stop.

'Papers please,' he barked at me, while the other, younger one looked on.

I took my identity papers from my pocket and passed them to him, trying to fight the surge of indignation at having an excellent daydream so rudely interrupted.

'Ah, Jewish,' the policeman said, seeing the letter J stamped on the papers.

My hackles raised. This was definitely not the day for him to test my tolerance.

'Bicycle please, mademoiselle,' the other policeman said, taking a step closer and extending his hand.

'What do you mean?' I frowned.

'Jews are no longer allowed to own bicycles,' the sweaty gendarme stated, raising his voice as if he were giving me a sermon.

'What?' I stared at him, horrified.

'I'm sorry,' the younger one said, at least having the good grace to shift awkwardly from foot to foot.

'But you don't understand; I need my bicycle,' I pleaded.

And then I heard my old friend Aurelie come to life inside my mind. *'Tell him to go to hell and just ride away,'* she urged. That was certainly what she would do. But this wasn't a novel where I could write myself a safe escape.

'Hand it over, now,' Sweaty Face commanded without displaying a shred of remorse.

I stared at him, incredulous. Just a couple of years ago, these men would never have spoken to me like this. They would have seen it as their duty to protect citizens like me. How had Hitler managed to poison so many minds so quickly?

'Get off the bike!' Sweaty Face yelled, and before I had time to react, he cuffed me across the cheek.

Somehow I managed to keep my balance and as the dizziness faded, I heard Aurelie yelling, *'Don't let him win! Don't let him take it!'*

'Go to hell!' I yelped before getting back on the bike and pedalling furiously.

I heard their footsteps running down the street behind me. I imagined that I was the fearless Belle-Belle on Comrade. They weren't going to capture me. I cycled faster and faster and the sound of their footsteps became fainter. I was doing it. I was going to escape! They might have taken my radios, but they were never going to get their hands on my bike.

But then, seemingly out of nowhere, a gleaming black shape lurched into the periphery of my vision. A car was speeding towards me out of a side street. I heard the screech of brakes as the car clipped my front wheel, and I was sent flying onto the ground, bicycle on top of me, the front wheel still spinning. The footsteps of the police became louder again. I heard the car door open, and a man yelling something in German. The older policeman, sweatier than ever, reached me.

'She's a Jew,' he spluttered, out of breath from the chase.

Hands grabbed at me, pulling me to my feet, and I found myself face to face with a German soldier. My arm was grazed and the side of my hip ached.

'We were trying to confiscate her bicycle and she rode away,' the gendarme whined like a petulant child.

The German soldier looked me straight in the eyes. 'You no longer allowed bicycles,' he said in broken French. 'You understand?'

I nodded, feeling winded from the shock.

'Shall I arrest her?' the older gendarme asked, with the eagerness of a hound scenting blood. Meanwhile, the younger one was picking up my precious steed from the road.

The German thought for a moment, then shook his head. 'No, just her bike take.' He looked back at me, completely expressionless. 'Now get back home before you break curfew.'

I trudged away, dizzy, and in pain my earlier spirit of defiance disappeared without trace. If they'd taken my radios and bicycle, surely it wouldn't be long until they came for everything else. And then what would I do?

9

MAY 1942, PARIS

As the months passed, the rules against the Jewish people became ever more punitive. By the end of 1941, our curfew had been extended by an hour, starting at eight in the evening rather than nine, not that it really mattered as we were no longer allowed to go to public places. It was the strangest thing, walking past the music halls, theatres, cafés and parks I used to frequent but was now banned from entering. It was like having died and returned as a ghost, drifting around my old haunts, completely invisible to those who used to welcome me with open arms. *I'm still here! I'm still alive!* I wanted to cry.

Thankfully, I had my weekly visits with Solly to help keep my flame of hope burning. Every week, he would ask me how I'd helped to reveal more light in the world, which meant that every week I was on a mission to gather examples to share with him. After a while, it became second nature, and I found myself instinctively wishing passers-by on the street a cheery 'good day!' and writing words of encouragement on scraps of paper and leaving them all over the city for people to discover – things like, ALWAYS REMEMBER TO LOVE and YOU ARE BRAVER THAN YOU THINK, tucked into benches or hidden beneath stones. The joy I felt imagining someone finding just the right words at just the right time lit me up from the inside too.

In the late spring of 1942, I began volunteering at a charity for Jewish children, whose parents had either been killed or spirited off by the Germans to Drancy or to prison. Although my job there was to help serve the meals, it wasn't long before I found an outlet for my storytelling. Inspired by Madame d'Aulnoy, every day after lunch I would gather the children in a circle and tell them fairy tales I'd created especially for them. Most of them featured incredibly brave children defeating monsters with German-sounding names. And so my days took on a new rhythm, creating stories at home at night, then walking across the city the following day to tell them to my 'literary salon' of wide-eyed small people. I loved their enthusiasm, and how they'd get so involved in the tales: the way they'd gasp in horror and laugh with delight at every twist and turn, causing showers of light to fill the room.

On my weekly visits to Solly, I'd tell him tales *about* my storytelling, and he grew to love those children too, even though he'd never met them. One day, he told me a Hasidic proverb: 'When a child walks down the road, a company of angels goes before him proclaiming, "Make way for the image of the Holy One." I would say the same about you, Etty. What you are doing, the way you are helping, it is in the image of God.'

'Oh, I wouldn't go that far,' I joked, but deep inside I felt joy unfurl in my chest like the brightest yellow rose. All through my childhood, I'd longed for the slightest crumb of approval from my father, but all I'd received was disdain and derision. To experience Solly's pride in me felt like a healing balm to my soul and I was truly grateful.

But then – yet again – the Germans struck us a bitter blow, ordering us to sew a yellow star with the word *JUIF* on the left breast of our coats.

'I refuse to wear it!' I declared to Solly, the Friday after the regulation came into effect. 'I won't be labelled like a piece of meat.'

I expected him to heartily agree, but as he placed the challah on the table, he smiled at me and shook his head and I knew I had another of his nuggets of wisdom coming. 'What if you didn't choose to see it that way?'

I sat down and sighed. 'How on earth should I see it then? Surely not even you can see a silver lining to the wretched thing!'

He continued to smile. 'What if you saw the star as a shield? After all, isn't that what the Star of David is – the *Magen David* – a symbol of protection?' He handed me a book of matches so I could light the candles. Due to the curfew, we had to start Shabbat before sundown in the summer months.

'But I don't feel it's going to protect me,' I argued. 'It feels more like wearing a target on my chest.'

'If you choose to see it that way,' he said softly.

I sighed, as I frequently did after one of Solly's sermons, but I knew by now not to dismiss it out of hand.

And, sure enough, the following Monday, when volunteering at the charity, I found a very good use for his wisdom. Several of the children were anxious and confused about having to wear the star and at my post-lunch literary salon, they were full of questions about it. Not wanting to add to their distress, I told them the story of a young king named David, who, before going to battle, made a round shield for himself, with two interlocking triangles attached to the back. The battle was so fierce that the triangles fused together, forming a star shape, and young David was victorious. 'From that day forth, the star formed by the two triangles was known as *Magen David*, or David's shield,' I told the children, 'and it is a symbol of great strength in the face of adversity.' I said a silent prayer of thanks to Solly as I looked around at their relieved faces.

Grudgingly, I sewed a star to my jacket – how could I not wear it now, after what I'd told the children? Initially, I was heartened by the responses I got from my fellow Parisians. Many people made a point of looking at the star and then giving me a smile as if in solidarity. One man even stopped me and said he was thoroughly sick of what was happening and reassured me in hushed tones that there were plenty of French who were desperate to rid our country of the Germans. But every day came more tales of arrests and deportations.

One sweltering afternoon in early July, I arrived in the Pletzl after my stint at the charity eager to regale Solly with the latest tales from my junior literary salon. But as I turned onto his street, I saw a sight that turned my blood to ice. A group of policemen had gathered outside his shop. The window had been smashed and the pavement around their feet was covered in shards of glass, glimmering like diamonds in the sunshine – a terrible, sickening beauty.

I stopped, rooted to the spot, and watched as some German soldiers inside the shop began throwing his books out onto the pavement. *Oh Solly, please be safe. Please be OK*, I silently prayed, looking up at the darkened windows of his apartment.

I heard a man yell something in German and then I saw two policemen appear from the doorway to the apartment. *Oh no! No!* I fought the urge to scream as I saw Solly being frogmarched out behind them, holding a battered suitcase. When Solly saw his beloved books scattered all over the ground, he stopped walking and I heard him say something. One of the policemen holding him yelled at him to get moving. Solly continued to speak, his voice a low hum. He was praying. Even in this moment of utter darkness, he was somehow able to focus on the light.

Finally recovering the use of my legs, I strode down the street towards them. I had to do something. I had to stop them taking him. But what? How?

As I drew closer, Solly looked up and our eyes met. He quickly and almost imperceptibly shook his head and looked away. The policemen shoved him into the back of their car. More books came flying out of the store and onto the street, landing at my feet.

'Move!' one of the policemen yelled at me.

Somehow I made my legs carry on walking, past Solly and away, although every fibre in my being yearned to fling myself into that car after him. Broken glass crunched beneath my feet, as splintered and shattered as my heart.

10

JULY 1942, PARIS

The following day, after barely any sleep and with a belly aching with hunger, I reached for the book of Hasidic tales Solly had gifted me. 'Please, tell me what I should do,' I whispered before flicking it open to a random page. *Everyone should carefully observe which way his heart draws him*, I read, *and then choose that way with all his strength*. In that moment, my heart felt drawn to finding Solly like the most powerful of forces. The prospect of a world without his wisdom and light was too depressing to comprehend.

'Right!' I said out loud, as if to motivate myself. 'I am going to find him.'

As Drancy was the most likely place he'd been sent to, I decided to start there. It broke my heart to think of Solly being taken there. The other staff at the charity were full of stories about how brutal the conditions were, the straw for bedding and the lack of food. He was so old, so frail. How would he survive? How had it come to this? The world had gone insane.

The husband of one of the women who volunteered at the children's charity had been taken to Drancy a month ago and I knew that the inmates there were able to write to their loved ones and allowed to receive parcels. If I could establish that he was there, at least I could write to him, and he could write back if he wanted. I sat down at my desk and hastily wrote Solly a letter, giving him my address, and asking him to write to me asking for anything he needed and I'd be happy to send it to him. As soon as I'd signed the letter and put it in an envelope, I felt marginally better. At least I was doing something.

I called in to the charity en route, explaining that I had an emergency to deal with and would be back the following day. I'd been avoiding going anywhere on the Metro since the government had implemented their new law consigning Jews to the last carriage of the train, but today I had no choice. Drancy was about six miles outside of the city and without my bike I didn't feel I had the energy to walk there and back. I was too weak from the constant hunger.

The air underground was sticky and hot and smelled of stale sweat. As I made my way to the end of the platform, I fought to suppress my indignation. Why must we travel in our own separate carriage as if we were infected? What were people so afraid of? If I dwelled on the injustice of it all for too long, I felt I would lose my mind. So I lost myself in Madame d'Aulnoy's fairy tale *The Blue Bird*. It was hard to concentrate, though, and every so often, I'd lift my gaze from the page to glance at my fellow passengers and see their haunted looks above their yellow stars.

I arrived in Drancy feeling sick with nerves. What if I'd come on a wild goose chase? What if Solly wasn't here after all? And what if I ended up being taken into custody? Wasn't marching up to Drancy with a yellow star on my chest just like entering the lion's den with a sign saying, *Please eat me!* '*Don't be so cowardly,*' I heard Aurelie hiss in my mind. '*I wouldn't run away and you mustn't either.*' And so I walked on and into the den.

Having heard so much about a place, it was strange finally

seeing the internment camp for the first time. The fact that it was originally intended to be a residential complex was even more poignant, seeing it in the flesh, with the high barbed-wire fences and watchtowers, and the guards stationed at the front. Once again I was left despairing that the French government and police were able to do such a thing to their own citizens.

Don't focus on that; focus on Solly, I urged myself, thinking of the letter in my pocket. If I had any hope of finding out if he was in the camp and getting the letter to him, I would have to be courteous to the guards in order that they might help me. Summoning my courage, I approached the gate.

'Yes?' The guard looked me up and down dismissively before focusing in on the yellow star on my chest.

'Good day, I think someone I know has been brought here. Would it be possible to check?'

He sighed as if this was the very last thing he needed, and once again I felt my indignation bubbling to the surface.

'Don't be hot-headed; you need to outsmart him,' Aurelie whispered.

'I know it's an inconvenience and I'm terribly sorry, but my great-uncle is in poor health. He never really recovered since the lion bit him, to be honest, and I'd love to be able to get his medicine to him.'

'He was bitten by a lion?' Finally the guard looked at me with something approaching interest.

'Yes, but thankfully he saved the child who'd fallen into the enclosure, so that was something. He was a zookeeper, you see.' I had no idea where this yarn was coming from, but I had the guard's attention and that was all that mattered.

'What is the name of this uncle of yours?' he asked.

'*Great*-uncle. His name is Solomon Finkelstein.'

'Right, and you are?'

'Etty Weil.'

The guard went back into his hut by the gate and I crossed

my fingers and waited. The complex was like a three-sided square and from my position I was able to see through to a courtyard in the middle. Every so often, someone would stroll into my line of vision. I glanced up at what would have been the apartment blocks. Sure enough, there was no glass in the windows. I shuddered as I thought of what that would mean in the cold winter months.

'Yes, your great-uncle is here,' the guard said, returning.

'He is? Oh that's wonderful!' I exclaimed. I took the letter from my coat pocket. 'Please, could you give him this?'

To my horror, he took it from me and tore open the envelope, and began to read the letter. Thankfully I'd had the foresight to anticipate the letters might be checked, but still, he could have had the decency to wait until I'd left.

I bit on my lip and waited, heart pounding. I'd been really careful not to write anything at all incriminating, but the way things were going, Jews might soon be banned from writing words as harmless as 'the' or 'because'! After what felt like forever, the gendarme stuffed the letter back in the envelope and nodded.

'Thank you so much, monsieur!' I gushed, feeling sick at myself.

I turned and trudged back to the station, clinging to the hope that the guard would stay true to his word and give Solly the letter.

When I got back to Paris, I got off the Metro at an earlier stop, eager to escape the soup-thick air. It wasn't much better above ground. Even though the sky was sheet white with no sign of the sun, the humidity pressed down like a lid upon the earth. As I walked past Notre-Dame, I tried so hard to find a blessing to focus on, but it was like trying to spy a fleck of dust. And then, just as I thought despair and hunger might bring me to my knees, a butterfly fluttered down in front of me and landed on my arm. I was so astounded, I stopped in my tracks. We remained motionless for a few seconds, the butterfly and I, and it spread its gossamer-thin wings wide, as if wanting to remind me that beauty still existed. Its wings were a kaleidoscope of orange, brown and cream, with the most intricate design I'd ever seen. *Don't give up*, it seemed to be saying. *This is what's possible. This is the kind of magic life is capable of creating.* And then it took off again.

I followed, entranced, not wanting the moment of enchantment to end. It flew in a loop in front of me as if beckoning me onwards. I dreamed of it leading me home, living with me in my apartment. I'd call it Hope, and every day it would swirl in great loops around me, weaving a magical trail of joy and wonder. I laughed as it flew higher and followed as it led me on, finally landing on a bush in front of me. Careful not to startle it, I slowly leaned closer.

'Hey, you!' A man's voice tore me from my reverie. 'Jew!' he yelled, causing my heart to plummet.

I turned to see a gendarme scowling at me.

'You're not allowed in here,' he called, marching over.

At first, I was confused, then I realised that the butterfly had led me into the small public garden behind the cathedral. I'd been in this garden many times before. How could it suddenly be such a crime for me to be there? A young couple sitting on a bench nearby were staring at me.

'You need to leave,' the policeman said as he reached me. His eyes were small and mean, too closely set above a bulbous nose.

'I was just looking at the butterfly,' I said weakly.

As if coming to my defence, the butterfly fluttered down from the bush, landing on the path beside me. The gendarme smirked, then before I could do a thing, he raised his foot and stamped his boot down hard, grinding the butterfly into the ground.

'No!' I cried, and before I could think better of it, I was pummelling my hands on his barrel-like chest. 'How could you?'

'Get out of the park!' he yelled, pushing me off hm.

'No!' I yelled back.

For a terrible moment, we stood in silence, staring at each other. One day, I told myself, one day, when this was all over, I would write a novel featuring a character based on this brute, and I would devise a grisly death for him to avenge the butterfly. Being stamped on by an elephant, perhaps.

'I won't warn you again,' he said, his voice low and tight. 'Get out of the park now, filthy Jew.'

I'm not sure if it was the heat or the hunger, or the months and months of fear and frustration, but in that moment I no longer cared anymore. I was so sick of being treated like this. 'Does it make you feel more of a man, picking on a woman half your size and a poor helpless butterfly?' I responded.

The couple on the bench were leaning forward now, mouths open, as if the movie they were watching had reached its gripping denouement.

'And all because I have this stupid badge on my chest,' I continued. I grabbed at the star and tugged. Thankfully I was terrible at sewing, so it came off easily. I threw it on the floor and trod on it the way he'd trodden on the butterfly. 'And now, I am free to do as I please,' I cried, feeling giddy from the adrenaline. I turned and started walking along the path, whistling gaily. As I drew level with the bench, I saw the couple's eyes widen with horror at something behind me and felt a hand grab my collar and yank me backwards.

'You're coming with me,' the gendarme growled.

It was the strangest sensation. For months I'd been terrified of being rounded up or arrested, but, in a moment of crystal clarity, I realised that I honestly had nothing left to lose. Their taking Solly was the final straw. What did I have left for me now in Paris?

'Do you see this?' I called to the couple on the bench. 'Arrested for taking a walk in a garden. Is this the France you want to live in?'

They both looked away and I saw that I'd conveniently become invisible to them, just as I'd become invisible when I walked past the bars and cafés I used to frequent. In that moment, I hated them more than the gendarme for their cowardice. Just a couple of years ago, the woman might have been queuing up in a bookshop for a signed copy of one of my novels. Now she couldn't even look me in the eye.

The policeman marched me through the garden, past the remains of the butterfly, now a rust-coloured stain on the footpath. That was how easy it was to snuff out such beauty – it seemed horribly symbolic somehow. When we got outside, he led me over to another couple of gendarmes, who were standing talking by the cathedral.

'I've arrested this Jew for being in the garden,' the butterfly killer informed them. I wondered if one of them might have a shred of conscience and tell him that perhaps he was overreacting, but no, they simply nodded.

'We'd have probably got her by the end of the week anyway,' one of them said.

'What do you mean?' I asked.

'Never you mind,' my captor snarled, tightening his grip on my arm.

My skin prickled with goosebumps. Rumours of more round-ups had been swirling for weeks now. Is this what he meant? Did they have more planned? Were the French planning to rid the country of all of their Jewish people? To stamp us all out until nothing remained, just like the butterfly.

11

JULY 1942, PARIS

After a cursory and quite frankly ludicrous interrogation at the police station, where the butterfly killer claimed that I – a woman not even half his size – had 'physically assaulted' him, and an interminable wait in a cell, I was bundled into the back of a van with another woman and a teenage girl, who I assumed must be a mother and daughter as they both had the same heart-shaped faces and lustrous manes of auburn hair. They looked so alike, they reminded me of those Russian dolls that slot one inside the other. I wondered if my mother and I would have been the same had she still been alive.

'Why did you have to tell that policeman to go to hell?' the girl muttered sullenly as the van pulled off.

'Because that's where vermin like him belong,' the woman replied tersely before offering me a weak smile.

'They do indeed,' I said, nodding in solidarity.

The girl huffed and stared down into her lap. From what I could tell, they were both expensively dressed. The girl was in a pretty summer dress dotted with pale blue forget-me-nots and the woman was wearing a simple but classically cut shift dress.

In spite of the gloom in the back of the van, a diamond wedding band sparkled on her ring finger.

'I'm Marguerite,' she said, leaning forward and offering me her hand.

'Etty,' I replied, shaking her hand firmly, thankful for their company.

'And this is my daughter, Danielle,' she continued, nodding at the girl, who carried on staring sulkily into her lap.

'Hello, Danielle,' I said, to no response.

'Danielle, where are your manners?' Marguerite said, looking embarrassed.

'I no longer have any, as there's absolutely no point,' the girl replied theatrically and I had to bite my lip to stop from smiling. I couldn't help agreeing with her. At this stage, good manners seemed futile indeed.

'I'm sorry,' Marguerite said with a sigh.

'It's fine,' I replied. 'I seem to have lost my manners too recently, especially where the police are concerned.'

I noticed a slight flicker of interest on the girl's face before she closed her eyes.

'Have we met before?' Marguerite stared at me. 'You look familiar.'

'I don't think so, unless...' I broke off. This was the last place I wanted to come across as a boastful author.

'Unless?' the woman asked.

'Well, I used to be a writer.' *'You're still a writer, I still exist!'* Aurelie bellowed inside my head. 'Maybe you once saw a photo of me in a newspaper or magazine,' I added.

I noticed Danielle open her eyes and give me a sideways glance.

'That's it!' the woman exclaimed. 'You're Claudette Weil! You wrote the Aurelie books.'

I nodded, feeling embarrassed. Being an author seemed so trivial in the face of our current circumstances.

'I love those books. But why haven't you written one for so long?'

'I'm no longer allowed,' I replied glumly.

'Why not?' Danielle asked, her foul mood clearly temporarily abandoned.

'Because I'm Jewish.'

'Are you?' Marguerite looked surprised. 'I had no idea.'

'Yes, well, I-I never really mentioned it in interviews,' I stammered, feeling slightly ashamed. Now that I'd reconnected with my Jewish faith and gained so much solace from the teachings and prayers Solly had shared with me, I felt guilty for ever having turned my back on it.

'I hate the Germans,' Danielle muttered. 'And I hate our government. And I hate being Jewish.'

'Danielle!' her mother exclaimed.

'What?' Danielle stared at her defiantly. 'If we weren't Jewish, none of this would have happened. We wouldn't be being sent to prison' – she gestured in my direction – 'and if she wasn't Jewish, she'd still be able to write her books.'

'We're not being sent to prison,' Marguerite replied weakly.

'Oh really?' Danielle scowled. 'Then where are they taking us? On holiday?'

While I liked the girl's spirit, I couldn't help feeling sorry for her mother. Raising Danielle must be a bit like trying to break in a wild colt.

Danielle turned to me. 'Where do you think they're taking us?'

I shrugged. 'To Drancy maybe?'

'I told you!' Danielle cried, looking back at her mother.

Marguerite visibly shuddered. I wished there was something I could say, something to make our situation seem in some way better. What would I have made Aurelie do if this were a scene in one of my books?

'This is what us authors call a character-defining situation,' I said.

'What do you mean?' Danielle asked with a frown.

'Well, when I write my novels, I always like to put my main character, Aurelie, in taxing situations.'

'Why?' Danielle looked at me like I was mad.

'To give her a chance to shine.'

Marguerite nodded. 'Like the time she got kidnapped by the sailor?'

'Exactly. And the time she finally confronted her abusive father.'

'Sounds like so much fun,' Danielle said sarcastically.

'Claudette's novels are wonderful.' Marguerite instantly leapt to my defence. 'Reading about Aurelie gave me the confidence to do many things in my own life. She taught me that being a woman is a powerful thing – in spite of what our great leader Pétain might think, telling us that we should be chained to the kitchen sink, having babies,' she scoffed.

'Thank you!' Her words fuelled my confidence and I looked back at Danielle. 'Imagine if you were a character in a novel—'

'I don't read novels,' she said dismissively.

'Danielle!' Marguerite shook her head, seemingly in despair.

'What? I don't!'

'Do you watch movies then?' I asked, determined not to be beaten by this teenage spitfire.

'Yes,' she muttered.

'Well, imagine you are the heroine of the latest movie to come out of Hollywood. Audiences everywhere shall be watching your story. They're watching now as you've been put into the back of this van to be taken who knows where.'

'I thought you said we were going to Drancy?' she retorted.

'Well, we don't know that for sure yet.' *Stay patient*, I told myself, somehow managing to remain smiling sweetly. 'What kind of heroine do you want to be? Brave and dignified or...' I broke off, wanting to say *spoiled and petulant* but not wanting to incur even more of her wrath.

Danielle huffed and looked back into her lap.

'Thank you,' Marguerite mouthed silently to me.

By the time we reached our destination, I'd learned that Marguerite and Danielle had lived in the affluent Avenue Foch, until the Gestapo had taken over their apartment building. They'd since been living with Marguerite's sister in the sixth arrondissement. Marguerite's husband, Danielle's father, had been killed in the Battle of France. It was hardly surprising that Danielle was a little on the sullen side; she'd been through a lot in her fourteen years. Marguerite had been arrested for defacing an anti-Jewish poster earlier that day, and when the police had discovered that her parents were from Austria, she and Danielle had been taken to the same police station as me.

The van came to a halt and as the engine cut out, we fell silent. The fear I'd managed to keep at bay by talking to Marguerite came rushing back, causing my throat to constrict. I heard footsteps outside and the van door was flung open. It was now dark outside, but I knew instantly that we were at Drancy. I recognised the silhouette of the buildings against the light from the watchtower. It was hard to imagine that I'd been there just hours before, searching for Solly. The one silver lining in this whole situation was that I might now be able to find him. Slightly cheered by this prospect, I got out of the van, to be greeted by three French guards. As Danielle scrambled out behind me, I could see that she was trembling. I gave her an encouraging smile, but she stared at me blankly, clearly full of fear.

We were taken into a room, harshly lit by a bare bulb. One of the guards took our names and another asked us to hand over any valuables we had in our possession. Thankfully, the string of pearls I was wearing was an imitation bought from a street hawker I used to know in Montmartre, so I handed them over without any anguish. Danielle, however, began to sob, clutching her wrist, trying to hide the gold watch she was wearing.

'Papa bought me this,' she cried.

'Don't fuss, you'll get them back,' one of the guards said. 'Make sure you don't lose this, though,' he added, handing her a voucher in exchange for the watch.

I noticed a smirk pass between the two other guards, as if they knew full well the voucher was meaningless.

'Please, can I keep my wedding ring?' Marguerite pleaded. The diamonds in the band shone even brighter in the light of the bare bulb.

'I'm sorry, no,' the younger guard said. 'But you will get it back as long as you keep this safe.' He handed her a voucher.

'But it's the only thing I have left of my husband,' Marguerite cried.

'Hand over the ring,' one of the older guards barked.

'He was killed fighting for France. He was a hero!' Marguerite responded, tugging the ring from her finger and slamming it into the guard's outstretched palm. 'Unlike you traitors!'

'Maman!' Danielle cried, grabbing her mother's arm, but I wanted to cheer at Marguerite's bravery. These puppets for Hitler *were* traitors to France.

The men issued us with yellow stars and registration numbers and then we were taken into the main complex and one of the would-be apartment buildings.

'Come,' the younger guard said, ushering us into a long room.

It was too dark to see anything much, but I noticed the smell instantly, a mixture of stale sweat and urine. Danielle clearly noticed it too, judging by her horrified gasp.

'It's all right, my love,' Marguerite whispered and I felt a wistful pang. My mother dying when I was less than a year old meant that I had no memories of maternal love, but I'd learned long ago that it's entirely possible to miss something you've never had.

'You're to sleep here,' the guard said gruffly, leading us over to a set of wooden bunks. The sound of snoring rumbled like distant thunder from all corners of the room.

Our bunks were beside an open window and a pale finger of moonlight shone through, onto what looked like straw spread across the wooden slats. Again, Danielle gasped in horror. For so long I'd seen my poverty-stricken childhood as a bad thing and something to forget about at all costs, but upon arrival in Drancy, I started to see how it might also have been a blessing: preparation for the hardships to come.

I took the top bunk and Marguerite and Danielle took the bottom. As I tried to settle on the hard wooden slats, the straw pricked my skin. So this was what it had come to. The final humiliation, forcing us to sleep on straw like animals. But who were the animals really? Us, or our captors for treating us like this?

I heard Danielle sniffling below me in the dark and prayed she would find the strength to toughen up. She needed to. Perhaps I could help her. But who would help me? I closed my eyes tightly. *You have to become like a dandelion seed*, a voice whispered through my mind. It seemed so different to my normal inner voice, or that of Aurelie, that I had to open my eyes and check someone hadn't snuck into my bunk in the darkness. But there was no one there.

I closed my eyes and pictured a dandelion seed, drifting weightlessly on the breeze. When I was little, I thought they were fairies with their magical star-like fronds. *Let life blow you where it needs to...* the voice whispered again. Could I really be needed here, in this terrible place? Could any of us? The notion seemed insane to me.

. . .

Almost as soon as I'd finally drifted into a light sleep, I was woken by dazzling sunshine streaming through the shutterless holes in the walls where the windows were supposed to be. All around me on the bunks, women began stirring. As I sat up, a tall thin woman with angry red sores at the corners of her mouth came over.

'Newcomers,' she said by way of greeting. 'Where are you from?'

'Paris,' I murmured, rubbing my eyes and shifting onto my side.

'What's it like out there?' another woman called from across the room. 'Is it true they're rounding up more Jews?'

'That's certainly the rumour,' I replied. 'I'm Etty,' I said to the woman by my bunk. 'How long have you been here?'

'I'm Valerie. I've been here three months,' she replied. 'So I can tell you the routine.'

'Yes please.' I straightened up, the straw digging through my cotton dress into my legs.

'Reveille at seven, roll call at eight,' Valerie said officiously. 'From eight until ten, callisthenics outside. At eleven thirty, soup. At five thirty, soup.'

'What do we do in between all the soup?' I asked.

'Die of boredom,' a wag called from a bunk across the room.

'Or play bridge,' another called.

'Same thing,' said another, causing a few dry laughs.

My apprehension eased a little. At least my fellow inmates seemed friendly and had a sense of humour.

'Maman, I don't want to be here,' Danielle murmured from the bunk below.

'Who does?' someone called in response.

'Will we be able to see the men when we go outside for exercise?' I asked, immediately thinking of Solly.

'Please don't tell me you're looking to find love,' Valerie retorted with a frown.

'If I was looking to find love, I'd buy a dog,' I replied, raising a chuckle from the bunk next to mine. 'I'm looking for a very dear friend who I believe is here.'

'How long ago was he brought here?' Valerie asked. 'He could have already been shipped out.'

'Shipped out?'

'Taken east,' she said in a more sombre tone.

'Oh!' Danielle wailed from below.

'It's all right, *ma chérie*,' Marguerite consoled.

'But east is Poland; east is Germany,' Danielle cried.

'He was only brought here two days ago,' I said, trying to remain positive.

'In that case, he's probably still here – for now...' Valerie turned and walked away and a chill passed right through me.

'I need the toilet,' Danielle wailed.

'Did they show you where the latrines are?' Valerie called.

I shook my head.

'OK, come with me.'

Marguerite, Danielle and I clambered from our bunks and followed Valerie outside. The sun was already beating down and the grass plot in the centre of the courtyard had been bleached pale brown. The sound of men's voices drifted out through the window holes of the apartment buildings on the other side. Was one of them Solly's? Was he in there some-where? I clung to the hope to keep me strong.

'Here we are,' Valerie called almost gaily as we approached a slightly raised wooden platform containing a row of holes in the corner of the yard. There were no partitions between the holes and a couple of men were squatting down, relieving themselves.

'No!' Danielle gasped, clutching Marguerite's arm in horror. 'I can't go there, with everyone watching.'

'It's all right,' I said, fighting to suppress my own horror at the situation. 'We can stand around you, form a screen.'

'I can't, it's horrible!' Danielle cried.

'Well, the only other option is the bucket in the dorm,' Valerie replied, causing even more anguish in Danielle.

My bladder now burning, I decided to lead by example and marched over to one of the holes, pulled down my underwear and took a seat.

'Good day!' I called merrily to the men further along the row. 'Lovely morning, isn't it?'

They chuckled, but unfortunately my plan seemed to backfire and rather than being reassured, Danielle buried her face in her mother's chest. 'I'd rather go in the bucket than make a show of myself like her!' she cried.

Marguerite looked at me apologetically before bustling her daughter off.

'I don't suppose there's any toilet paper?' I said to Valerie.

She shook her head.

I sighed and took the voucher I'd been given for my fake pearls from my pocket. Wiping my derrière with it was probably all it was good for anyway.

I pulled up my underwear and marched down from the latrines. 'Have a good day,' I called to the men over my shoulder, determined they wouldn't see through my false bravado.

By eight o'clock that morning, I was more than ready to escape the dormitory again. Clearly traumatised by having to go to the toilet in a bucket, Danielle wouldn't stop crying, and much as I sympathised, her distress was beginning to set my nerves on edge. As soon as I got outside, I scanned the courtyard. A group of men were doing press-ups in their vests and trousers in a corner, and others were clustered around talking, but there was no sign of Solly's long white beard or stooped frame. Panic bubbled up inside of me. What if he'd already been sent from here? What if I never saw him again?

A wiry woman named Beatrice led the women's exercise routine.

'It's so important that we stay strong,' she called as about twenty of us gathered around her. 'A strong body makes for a strong mind.'

I'd never been one for organised exercise, far preferring the sense of freedom that walking or cycling gave me, but as Beatrice put us through our paces, getting us to squat up and down, up and down, like rows of bobbing dolls, I quite enjoyed the release it gave me. It was as if with every squat I expelled a little of the tension I'd been carrying since my arrest, and eased the stiffness from sleeping on the wooden slats of my bunk. It also felt good to have a set of instructions to distract me from thinking too much.

Beatrice had just told us to lie on our backs on the dusty ground in preparation for a set of sit-ups when a hullabaloo erupted on the other side of the courtyard. I sat up to try to see what was causing the commotion. A group of men had gathered in a circle, shouting and cheering excitedly.

'What's going on?' I asked.

'Oh, it's nothing,' Beatrice replied nonchalantly. 'One of the prisoners here used to be a professional boxer and the guards get him to fight for their entertainment and in exchange for certain privileges.'

My skin prickled with goosebumps. Surely it couldn't be... 'I'll be back in a minute,' I muttered, scrambling to my feet and making my way across the courtyard. As I got closer, I could hear the sound of thwacking and panting in between the men's cheers. I pushed my way through the crowd to see a ring of guards at the front. One of them blew a whistle and called, 'End of round!' I peered between two of them – and found myself face to face with a panting, sweating Tomasz.

12

JULY 1942, PARIS

'You!' he gasped, breathless.

'How lovely to see you again,' I replied drily.

'What are you doing here?' one of the guards shouted at me. 'Get back to the other women.'

'She's a friend of mine,' Tomasz said quickly.

'No, she is not,' I muttered, but only loud enough for Tomasz to hear. 'So, I hear you've become their plaything. I should have known you'd have no principles.'

'What?' Tomasz frowned.

The guard blew his whistle. 'Round two!'

'I hope the privileges you get for being their boxing puppet are worth it,' I hissed before turning on my heel and marching off. All of the anger that had been building inside of me suddenly had a focus and I felt a hatred for Tomasz so great it practically winded me.

I marched back past the exercising women and into the dormitory. I had no appetite for exercise now; I felt thoroughly sick. Back in the bunks, Danielle was still crying and Marguerite was still fussing over her like a mother hen. *For God's sake, pull yourself together!* I wanted to yell at the girl.

Marguerite's show of maternal love now made me feel bitter rather than wistful. I hated myself for being so hateful. If only I could find Solly. I'd never been more in need of his soothing wisdom.

'Are you all right?' Marguerite asked as I clambered up onto my bunk.

'I think I need more sleep,' I replied tersely.

But it was impossible to sleep with the sun now burning straight through the hole in the wall upon me.

I thought of the wise voice I'd heard whispering to me the night before, urging me to be like a dandelion seed. Why, oh why, did life have to keep blowing that rat Tomasz in the same direction as me? It had been bad enough when he'd acted as if kissing me had been akin to swallowing poison, but to see him entertaining the guards here to try to save his skin make me sick to my stomach.

What did you expect? my inner voice chided. *He told you himself that he'd once killed someone. He's clearly a horrible person. It's your fault for imagining him into some kind of romantic hero. Think of something else.*

But as soon as I wiped my mind clean of Tomasz, I thought of what Valerie had said earlier about people being deported from Drancy. Where were they being sent? And would we be next? I'd managed to put on a show of bravado at the latrines, but how long could I maintain it if sleeping on straw and shitting in holes was to be our future?

My spirits sank even further when we were given our first soup of the day. It was a watery cabbage affair and, according to Valerie, guaranteed to give you diarrhoea. It might seem ridiculous, but as a consummate food lover, being fed slops felt like the worst insult of all.

Afterwards, I sat on my bunk staring blankly out of the window. It was hard to imagine that on the other side of the barbed-wire fence our fellow Parisians were walking around

freely, getting on with their day, completely oblivious to what
was happening in here, or choosing to appear so.

In the afternoon, Marguerite, Danielle and I sewed our stars to
our clothes and were told we could write a letter to a friend or
family member. I wrote to my boss at the children's charity,
telling her I was now in Drancy. It broke my heart to think of
my junior literary salon. Why had I been so hot-headed? The
children had got so much from my stories. Who would show
them how to see themselves as heroes now?

At some point, the heat got too much and I drifted into a
fitful sleep, dreaming of delicious, rich onion soup. I was just
about to take a mouthful when I was rudely awoken by one of
my roommates.

'They've rounded up thousands of Jews!' she cried from the
doorway.

'Who have?' someone called.

'The police. Hundreds of them are arriving now. The others
have been taken to the Vélodrome d'Hiver.'

'The velodrome?' I muttered to myself in shock. The
thought of the stadium that was home to the hugely popular six-
day cycling races now being used to imprison people made my
blood run cold.

The sound of chatter outside started growing. I peered out
of the window to see a stream of dazed-looking people pouring
into the courtyard, some of them clutching suitcases, others just
in the clothes they stood up in.

'Where are they going to go?' I asked no one in particular.
And no one replied. The camp was already crowded. How
could they house hundreds more here? I thought of what
Valerie had said about people being deported east, and again I
felt awash with dread. Would we be deported to make way for
this new intake? And where exactly would we be sent?

It didn't take long before a group of frightened-looking women were being ushered into our dormitory. Thankfully, Danielle had stopped crying and was now sitting in stunned silence. We watched as Valerie did her introductory spiel and then the women were peppered with questions: mainly different variations on what was happening in Paris and were the rumours about the velodrome true? It was impossible to imagine that a stadium that had been built for sport, for fun, should be used in this way, but then, hadn't our camp here in Drancy been intended to be the very latest in suburban living? I could feel a hardness growing in my heart and again I longed for Solly.

While the women talked, I slipped out and back downstairs. More of the new intake were filing into the courtyard. I saw an old man limping in, leaning on a cane and clutching a battered brown leather suitcase. One of the guards yelled at him and he stopped, looking around, bewildered. The guard kicked the old man's stick from his grasp and another guard who'd been watching started laughing. The hardness growing inside me erupted into a burst of anger and before I knew it, I was over there, picking up the cane.

'Leave it!' the guard who'd kicked it yelled.

I spun round to face him, brandishing the stick as if it were a truncheon. 'What is wrong with you people?' I yelled. 'Where's your humanity?'

In an instant, the guard grabbed me by the shoulders. As we stood, eyeball to eyeball, I heard the old man murmur something behind me, and then, just like that, the guard started to laugh as if he had tired of his game tormenting us. He pushed me away and flung the stick at the man.

'Get back inside,' he said to me.

I turned and saw Danielle standing motionless in the doorway. I was expecting her to burst into tears again, but to my surprise she gave me the thinnest of smiles.

'That was very brave,' she murmured as I reached her. Her face was pale and her beautiful auburn hair hung in lacklustre clumps either side of her face.

'I never want to be guilty of turning a blind eye to cruelty,' I said, thinking of the couple in the garden by Notre-Dame who'd watched me get arrested without saying a word. 'Too many people are doing that in this country.'

'Can you...' She broke off and looked down at the dusty ground.

'Can I what?' I replied, my voice softening.

'Can you teach me how to be brave?' Her own voice was barely more than a mouse's squeak.

I was blindsided by the question but thrilled to have had this breakthrough with her. I wasn't exactly sure if I had the required credentials to teach bravery, but I knew an opportunity to release a spark of light when I saw one, thanks to Solly's expert tuition. I just had to work out how. 'I can try. Come...'

I led her back upstairs and into our room. Most of the women, including Marguerite, had gathered at one end of the room, talking in hushed tones. I led Danielle to our bunks at the opposite end. Thankfully, on the way back to the dorm, I'd come up with a way to hopefully fulfil her request.

'I'm going to tell you a story,' I said, sitting beside her on her bunk.

Instantly she pulled a face, like she was way too old and worldly-wise for such childish things.

'A story about you,' I continued, hoping to appeal to her vanity.

'But you don't know me,' she said.

'Not yet,' I replied. 'But if you answer five simple questions, I'll be able to tell you the story of your destiny.'

'No you won't!' she exclaimed, but she looked interested.

'Well, if you don't want to know...' I stood up.

'OK, what are the questions?' she said quickly and I sat back down.

'The first question is, what is something you're proud of achieving?'

She thought for a moment. 'Being voted prettiest girl in my class – two years running,' she added with gravitas.

I internally groaned but forced a smile onto my face. 'Wonderful, well done. And what would you say is your best trait?'

'My hair,' she answered instantly.

'I was thinking more of a personality trait,' I said and she looked dejected. 'But that's OK. You do have very lovely hair.'

She nodded in agreement.

'So what would you say is your best characteristic?'

'My hair.'

'No, you've already said your hair, something more to do with your—'

'My eyes,' she answered before I could steer her away from physical attributes.

'Wonderful,' I gushed, trying not to panic. These were the questions I always asked of new characters when they were taking shape in my mind, to try to give them more depth. Sadly, it didn't seem to be working quite so well with Danielle. 'What subject do you most excel at in school?' I asked, trying a different tack.

She frowned. 'I find school very boring.'

'What do you most love to do in life then?' Once again, I could feel my patience being stretched taut as a drum-skin. If she said she loved to gaze at her hair and eyes in the mirror, I would have to admit defeat.

I waited as she thought for a moment.

'I love to dance,' she said finally, a dreamy expression coming over her face.

'Excellent,' I exclaimed in relief. Now I had something to work with. 'What kind of dance?'

'Ballet.'

'And what do you most hate?'

'The Germans,' she said instantly.

'Why?'

She looked at me as if I was mad. 'Because of what they're doing to us.'

'What are they doing?' I probed, trying to get her to say more.

'Persecuting us, of course.'

'So you hate bullies?'

'Yes.'

'What do you most admire in other people?'

'Beauty – and talent,' she added as an afterthought. She sighed and I could sense I was losing her. Sadly, I was going to have to begin my story with a rather one-dimensional main character.

'Once upon a time, there was a very beautiful young woman named Danielle Très Belle...' I began, and the faintest trace of a smile appeared on her lips. 'Everywhere she went, people commented on her beauty, and in particular her eyes, which were likened to the rarest of emeralds, and her lustrous red hair.'

'Auburn,' she interrupted.

'Her lustrous *auburn* hair. Now, Danielle wasn't just beautiful, she was extremely talented...' I closed my eyes and pictured Danielle in a dance studio, clad in a pale pink tutu, standing en pointe at the barre. 'She was a primo ballerina—'

'Prima,' Danielle corrected.

'Indeed.' I fought the urge to give my fictional Danielle an unfortunate accident involving an over-extended arabesque. 'Now, sadly, being both extremely talented and beautiful made Danielle the target for unhappy, cowardly people who hated themselves and their lives – in other words, bullies,' I continued.

Danielle nodded enthusiastically, as if this had indeed been her experience.

'And one of those bullies was a girl named... Tomaszetta.'

'That's a strange name,' Danielle remarked.

'Tomaszetta was a strange girl. She lied and she was mean and she was given to fits of violence.'

'What did she look like?' Danielle asked.

A bizarre image of a female Tomasz began forming in my mind. 'She was muscular with broad shoulders and dark cropped hair.'

Danielle looked suitably horrified.

'Tomaszetta so badly wanted to play the lead in the production of *Swan Lake*, but Danielle excelled during the audition, and besides, no one would believe in a swan that looked more like a bulldog.'

For the first time since we'd met, Danielle laughed. A sight and sound that made me irrationally happy.

I quickly continued, not wanting to lose my audience's good favour. 'Tomaszetta was furious when she learned that Danielle had landed the coveted role and, to add insult to injury, she had been cast as the evil von Rothbart.'

Cue another snort of laughter from Danielle. Victory was in my sights; I was winning her over!

Emboldened, my imagination began to flow, and I continued to spin a yarn about the increasingly desperate ways in which Tomaszetta tried to sabotage the *très belle* Danielle's performance. 'But sadly, unlike Danielle, Tomaszetta had not been blessed with intelligence,' I said with an internal smirk. This story wasn't just cheering my audience up, it was proving hugely therapeutic for the teller too. I smiled as I remembered the first lesson Solly ever taught me, about how a story needs to be transformative for the teller as well as the listener. 'And unlike Tomaszetta,' I continued, 'Danielle was the proud possessor of fabulosity, strength and wit in abundance.'

At some point, Marguerite returned to our bunk, but Danielle instantly told her to hush. It wasn't until I reached the exciting denouement of my tale, during which Tomaszetta tried to sabotage Danielle's performance on opening night by smearing mustard inside her costume, that I heard laughter coming from the surrounding bunks and realised that some of the other women had been listening too. I ended the story with Danielle giving the ballet performance of her life, in spite of sweating profusely and smelling like creamy mustard chicken – to a hearty round of applause from my dorm-mates, and the best prize of all, a beaming smile from Danielle. It was incredible how much more beautiful she looked when she wasn't scowling. It was as if she'd been lit up from the inside, and seeing the transformation in her lit me up too as it reminded me of the power of storytelling.

'That was wonderful,' Marguerite exclaimed. 'So funny!'

'She made it up just for me,' Danielle informed her proudly.

'You certainly have a vivid imagination,' one of the other women called.

'She ought to; she's the writer Claudette Weil,' Marguerite announced proudly, 'author of the Aurelie novels.'

As soon as she said it, I winced, but to my relief the women seemed genuinely happy at this revelation.

'I love those books,' one of them said.

'Aurelie is my hero,' said another, grinning across the room at me. 'If only I could be as strong as her. God knows, I need some of her feistiness now.' This brought a chorus of murmured agreements.

'We can all be Aurelie,' I found myself saying.

'What do you mean?' Marguerite asked.

'I mean, we all have the opportunity to triumph over adversity.'

'As long as we use our fabulosity, strength and wit,' Danielle said, parroting the line from her story.

'Yes, exactly!' I exclaimed, happy that it had left a mark.

'Can you make up one of your stories for Maman?' Danielle asked, snuggling up to Marguerite. 'Please!'

'Yes, please, tell us another story,' the woman on the next bunk pleaded. 'It will help to relieve the boredom.'

'Well, if you insist...'

'We insist,' Danielle and Marguerite chorused.

'She has to ask you some questions first,' Danielle informed her mother, clearly taking on the role of my personal assistant. 'Character-defining questions,' she added importantly.

'How intriguing,' Marguerite replied, giving me a grateful smile and mouthing 'thank you' to me over her daughter's head.

Little did she realise that I was the one with a heart full of gratitude. Somehow, in this grotty room, stripped down to stone and straw, I felt my old storytelling self sparking back into life. It felt like being reunited with a long-lost, and much-loved, friend.

13

JULY 1942, PARIS

For the next couple of days, a new feature was added to the daily Drancy routine and my sadly fruitless searching for Solly – every afternoon and evening, the women in our dorm would gather around my bunk and I would choose one to ask my character-defining questions to, then create a story about them. I soon saw these questions as an opportunity to remind my roommates who they were outside of this place, adding 'What is your greatest dream?' and 'What are you curious about?' into the mix.

Some of the women were a little reticent at first. Fear seemed to have taken their dreams and curiosities into a chokehold. But then my newfound assistant, Danielle, would come to my aid, gently prompting them, or offering her own suggested questions. I would then weave a story from their answers, a story that made them a heroine cut from the same cloth as Aurelie – full of fabulosity, strength and wit.

Before I began, I always experienced the fear that inspiration might desert me when I most needed it, but I trusted in the process. And, just as I'd experienced when I was writing about Aurelie, it felt as if the stories already existed and I was merely a channel for them. I found it a welcome distraction from all that was happening too. With more and more people arriving following the round-up, two questions hung in the air and echoed around the courtyard: *When will they move some of us on? And where to?*

Rumours were rife about where the previous Drancy detainees had been sent. Some people, usually the older ones, liked to say that the Third Reich had created a homeland for Jews in Eastern Europe. I, for one, didn't believe this for a second. Hitler and his Nazis had made it clear what they thought of us; there was no way they would go to the trouble of creating us a homeland. Another rumour was that they'd been sent to labour camps. This, I was far more inclined to believe. The third rumour, which I tried to block from my mind, was that they'd been sent to their deaths. While I was certain the Germans had no qualms about killing us, I couldn't see how this was possible. How would they be able to kill so many of us at once?

And then, one morning at the end of July, our worst fear became a reality. At roll call, we were told that some of us had been chosen to be 'resettled'. A stunned silence fell upon the courtyard, broken only by the sound of a laughing child some-where outside of the camp, drifting through the hot still air. A painful reminder that on the other side of the barbed wire, life was continuing as normal. I felt Danielle tremble beside me and instinctively linked my little finger through hers. She squeezed it tightly in response.

I listened numbly as hundreds of names were called, waiting and wondering if I would hear mine, every muscle in my body clenched. And then I heard it: Claudette Weil. Danielle's grip on my finger increased. And then came her name and Marguerite's. So we would remain together at least. Not that it gave me much relief. I would much rather they remain in France, as surely that had to be safer.

The rest of roll call passed by in a haze. Those who had been chosen for the transit were instructed to go and get our things, then gather in an area cordoned off by barbed wire.

Back in our dormitory, there was none of the usual morning chatter. All were ashen-faced, even those who hadn't been chosen, for we knew it was probably a question of when, not if, we would all be deported and that being kept behind for now was just prolonging the agony.

I looked at Danielle, worried that this latest development would trigger a return to her tearful self, but she returned my gaze stoically, biting on her bottom lip.

'Are you all right?' I whispered.

She nodded. Then shook her head. 'I'm scared,' she whispered.

'It's all right to be scared, as long as you remember that you are Danielle Très Belle, full of fabulosity, strength and wit,' I replied.

'I will,' she replied firmly and I gave her a hug.

Marguerite, who had been packing their meagre belongings into their case, took hold of my hand. 'We three must stay together,' she said.

'Absolutely. Like the Three Musketeers,' I replied.

'As long as I can be D'Artagnan,' Danielle said.

'Of course,' I replied, only too glad to give up my coveted role of swashbuckling hero to keep her happy.

We said our goodbyes to the women who were staying behind. I'd tried not to think about Tomasz since our encounter in the courtyard, but I couldn't help wondering if he'd be safe from selection as the guards' plaything. At least our paths wouldn't cross again if that was the case, I thought to myself bitterly.

Once outside, we were ushered into the penned-off area, the guards barking orders at us, first to move faster and then to stand still. Overseeing the operation was a grey cluster of

German soldiers, watching from a distance. It made me sick to see the French guards jabbing at us with their rifle butts, clearly putting on a display for their Nazi overlords, as if to say, *See, we can be just as hateful as you.*

I glanced around at my fellow deportees. Some of the older people present had clearly dressed in their finest clothes. Baggy suits hung from the men's gaunt frames, and the women wore hats and smart, if crumpled, dresses. Some had even gone to the effort of applying lipstick. I wondered if old age naturally made a person more optimistic, or perhaps they were unable to believe that the world had become such a horrifying place. There was still no sign of Solly and I hoped against hope that if he was still there he'd escaped having his name called.

I saw a row of old buses and army trucks with grey-green camouflage tops parked on the road outside the front of the camp. So that was how we'd be leaving this place. I looked up at the guard on the nearest watchtower and was again struck by the nightmarish quality of what I was seeing. How could the local people of Drancy just walk on by such a spectacle? How could they tolerate this happening on their doorstep? Did they hate us this much? Or was it just cowardice? Perhaps it was a mixture of both.

My blood was beginning to boil at the injustice of it all when I saw a sight that caused a bolt of hope to surge right through me. An old man standing a few yards in front of me, with his back to me, leaning on a cane. There was something familiar about the curve of his shoulders, but was it...? Could it be...?

I sidled forwards through the crowd.

'Solly?'

The man didn't move.

'Solly?' I called again, louder this time, and I saw him start. As he slowly turned to face me, I saw that long white beard and I cried out in joy. 'Solly!'

'Etty!' he called back, his voice wavering. 'Etty, oh my dear!'

A second later I was hugging him tightly. Then I held him back from me and studied his face. He didn't look much frailer than when I'd last seen him, thankfully.

'Oh, I am so happy and so sorry to see you!' he exclaimed.

'Likewise,' I replied. 'I began looking for you as soon as I learned you'd been taken. I came here, before I was brought here, I mean. I wrote a letter to you.'

'Oh yes, I received it.' He smiled. 'It gave me a lot of explaining to do.'

'What do you mean?' I asked, alarmed that I might have got him into trouble.

'About my lion-keeping past.'

'Oh!' I laughed. With everything that had happened since, I'd forgotten all about my creative attempt at capturing the guard's attention.

Marguerite and Danielle made their way over to us and I introduced them to Solly. Oh, if only it weren't under such dire circumstances. I loved the thought of them growing to know and love Solly the way I had. Especially Danielle. She could certainly benefit from his worldly wisdom.

'We must stick together,' I said, linking my arm through Solly's. 'Now I've found you, there's no way we're being separated again.'

'We'll see,' he said in that enigmatic way of his. 'But whatever happens, it too will be for the best.'

I stared at him, wondering how he could be so hopeful at a time like this. How could anything about this situation be for the best?

'Get a move on, you dirty kikes!' a guard yelled, clearly playing to the German gallery.

I focused on keeping Solly upright in the crush that ensued, while Marguerite put a protective arm around Danielle.

To my relief, the four of us were herded onto the same

truck. I was so happy to have found Solly, I didn't even care that we were crammed in so tightly, there was no room to sit, or indeed that I had no idea where we were heading.

'You can lean on me if you need,' I told him.

'Thank you, my dear.'

As the truck juddered off down the street, I peered through a crack in the side and saw a woman in a headscarf hurrying along, a basket on her arm. A little boy was running along beside her, holding her hand. He pointed to the truck and said something to the woman. She shook her head curtly and kept her gaze fixed straight ahead. There was something about this vignette that sent an icy chill deep into my bones. To our fellow Parisians and their fear of being targeted by the Germans, we hadn't just become invisible. It was as if we'd never existed.

After a few minutes, someone attempted to start a rousing rendition of '*La Marseillaise*'. As more voices joined in, I felt a sliver of hope. Perhaps if we made enough noise, the residents of Drancy wouldn't be able to ignore us. Perhaps it would rouse them to their senses.

'Grab your weapons, citizens.' I joined in at the top of my voice. 'Form your battalions! Let us march! Let us march!'

But, of course, nothing happened. The truck kept on going and our voices faded. I don't think I've ever heard a silence more full of dread than the one that followed.

A few minutes later, we arrived at Bourget-Drancy, a small, nondescript station with only one train waiting – a freight train made up of cattle trucks.

'Surely they're not making us travel on that,' a woman said from somewhere behind me and I heard someone else begin to cry.

I turned to look at Danielle and saw that she was staring straight ahead, a look of grim determination upon her face. I gave her arm a quick squeeze and she smiled at me gratefully.

'Where do you think they're taking us?' Marguerite whispered.

'Pitchipoi,' someone replied.

'What is Pitchipoi?' I asked. It sounded like a fantastical place, like something out of a children's fairy tale.

'It's an imaginary name invented by Polish Jews,' Solly explained.

'An imaginary name for what?' I asked, confused.

'For whatever place they're sending us to,' he replied.

My heart sank. The word Pitchipoi sounded way too cheery for whatever the Germans had in store for us. Maybe that was the point. To sound reassuring.

'We have to stick together,' I said again, linking one arm through Solly's and the other through Danielle's.

A heavily pregnant woman in front of us began to wail as she was jostled off the truck.

'Shut up!' a guard yelled at her. Then, when she continued to cry, he whacked her across the stomach with his rifle butt.

'No!' I cried, stepping forward, but Solly pulled me back. 'But I have to do something,' I hissed.

'And get beaten too – or worse?' he replied.

I could feel myself beginning to spiral from the mixture of fear, anger and dread forming inside me, sucking me down into a deep despair.

'Remember what I told you,' Solly whispered. 'About the teaching of Rabbi Pinchas of Koretz. We have to make up for their lack of love.'

I remained silent for a moment. 'All right, but if one of those brutes lays a finger on you, I'm afraid I won't be responsible for my actions.'

He chuckled and, to my surprise, I saw that his eyes were glassy with tears. 'I'm so glad we found each other again, Etty. You are like a daughter to me. Or perhaps a granddaughter would be more accurate, given my senior years.'

'No! I want to be your daughter,' I blurted out, my own eyes filling. 'Thank you.'

Once we were all off the transport, the guards started herding us into groups of a hundred. Thankfully, we four musketeers were able to cling together, but further down the platform, a commotion broke out when what appeared to be a husband and wife were separated.

'Please!' the woman begged, falling to her knees. 'Please let me travel with him.'

But instead of taking pity on her, one of the guards mimicked her wailing before prodding at her with his boot to get up. When she refused, he cocked his rifle and there was a collective intake of breath.

'Get on the train or I'll kill you, Jewish swine,' the guard yelled.

Trying to take Solly's advice, I turned away to look at Danielle. Her bottom lip was quivering. 'Fabulosity, strength and wit, remember,' I whispered to her and she nodded.

Thankfully, the woman did as the guard said, but a terrible silence fell upon the platform as we all contemplated what could have happened, and what could still happen to any one of us.

We were each given a piece of dry, grey bread and then each group was jostled onto one of the cattle trucks. As we lined up to get on, Marguerite took hold of my hand. 'If anything happens to me,' she said quietly into my ear, 'please take care of Danielle.'

'Nothing is going to happen to you,' I said, far more assertively than I felt. 'Not while I have anything to do with it, and besides, you are Marguerite the Magnificent,' I added, reminding her of the story I'd created for her back at Drancy.

Marguerite gave me a weak smile and we clambered onto the truck. It took a moment for my eyes to adjust to the darkness after the bright sunshine outside. It was just as cramped as the lorry that had brought us to the station, if not more so. Even though we had no idea where we were being taken, I knew it was out of France. Could we really survive a long journey like this?

A guard slung a bucket onto the truck behind us. 'The latrine,' he called with a snigger.

'Oh no,' Danielle murmured.

'It's all right. It'll be all right,' I replied, as much for myself as for her.

As my eyes adjusted, I glanced around. The only light came from two small windows – one at the front of the car on the right-hand side, the other at the back on the left. Both had horizontal iron bars running across them.

'I feel like I can't breathe,' Danielle gasped.

Thankfully, the four of us had ended up next to the right-hand wall of the car. I spied a crack in the wood and showed it to Danielle. 'Keep looking outside,' I told her, hoping it would take her mind off the horrors on the inside.

'Where is God?' someone cried as the door was slammed shut behind us and we heard the sound of a bolt being slid across. 'How could He allow this to happen to us?'

I instinctively looked to Solly.

'God did not do this,' he whispered to me. 'Men did.'

Now the car had been shut and locked, the heat of the midday sun started to become unbearable.

'Water, we need water!' people began to cry, but to no avail.

When the train finally juddered into life, I almost felt relieved. At least once we were moving, we'd get some kind of breeze coming in through the two small windows.

'I think I need to sit for a while,' Solly said. I helped him slide onto the floor with his back against the wall and I crouched down beside him. 'Oh, Etty, I almost forgot,' he added, his eyes lighting up. 'I met that man you were looking for.'

'What man?' I looked at him blankly.

'The fighter. Tomasz. Do you remember, you asked me about him the first time we met?'

'Oh, yes.' My heart sank.

'What's wrong?' Solly asked, clearly noticing the expression on my face.

'Let's just say I'm no longer interested in finding him.'

His bushy white eyebrows knotted together in a frown. 'Why not?'

'Because he's a despicable person.'

Solly shook his head. 'Maybe I have the wrong person. Tomasz Zolanvari?'

'Yes, that's him. Where did you meet him?'

'In Drancy. I thought he was a very good man.'

'A very good man?' I felt a stab of childish jealousy. How could someone as wise as Solly be taken in by Tomasz? 'You obviously didn't know about the arrangement he had with the guards there, fighting in exchange for privileges.'

'Oh, I knew.' Solly nodded.

'And you still think he's a good man?' I stared at him incredulously.

'Of course.'

'But doesn't that make him selfish? Doesn't it make him a traitor to the rest of us?'

Now it was Solly's turn to look bewildered. 'But he didn't use those privileges for himself,' he replied.

'What do you mean?'

'He used them to help others. And he used them to save me.'

14

JULY 1942, FRANCE

'What do you mean, he used them to save you?' I asked as the cattle truck rocked from side to side.

'He saved my life, shortly after I arrived at Drancy,' Solly replied. 'I'd challenged one of the guards who was beating a woman. He took his pistol out and was about to shoot me, when Tomasz stepped in.'

'How?'

'He told the guard to stop, and he did. I found out later that he was a well-known fighter and that this gave him a certain influence. And from then on, he took me under his wing. The guards gave him extra food in exchange for fighting, but he always passed it on to me and a couple of the other older gentlemen in our dormitory.'

I stared down into my lap, the heat and the rocking of the train making me feel sick. 'I didn't realise,' I murmured. 'When I found out he was receiving privileges, I lost my temper. I said some terrible things to him.'

'Oh dear.' Solly shook his head. 'He was so happy to hear that I knew you. He asked me lots about you.'

I frowned. If Tomasz was so interested in hearing about me,

why had he acted so horribly after we'd kissed? It didn't make sense.

'I bet he didn't tell you that he'd once killed someone,' I blurted out. I knew it was churlish to bring it up, but I couldn't help it; I was angry and confused.

Solly looked shocked. 'No, no he didn't.'

'Yes, well, he did.' My face flushed. 'I just didn't want you thinking he was some kind of perfect hero, that's all,' I added, trying to sound less petulant.

'Who is?' Solly gave a wistful smile. 'Nothing and no one is ever as straightforward as that. It's like the story of the farmer and the horses.'

'What story?' I asked, instantly eager for an opportunity to escape into one of Solly's wise tales. Over on the other side of the car, an argument had broken out over someone taking up too much room. I tugged on Marguerite and Danielle's skirts, gesturing at them to join us sitting down. 'Solly is about to tell one of his stories,' I told them, once they were hunched down beside us, knees pressed into their chests.

'Are they as good as yours?' Marguerite asked.

'Far better,' I replied. 'Far wiser.'

'Oh, I don't know about that.' Solly gave a bashful smile before clearing his throat. 'Once upon a time, there was a farmer who owned just one horse, but then, one day, that horse ran away. "What bad news," the farmer's neighbour said, upon hearing what had happened. "Good news, bad news, who knows?" the farmer replied.'

'That's exactly the kind of thing you would say!' I said to Solly.

He smiled. 'Thank you. Anyway, the following day, the farmer's horse returned, bringing with it a beautiful wild stallion. "Now you have two horses, what good news!" the neighbour exclaimed. "Good news, bad news, who knows?" the farmer replied. Soon after, the farmer's son was out riding the wild horse when it bucked and threw him to the floor, breaking his leg. "What bad news," the neighbour said when he found out.'

'Don't tell me,' I interrupted, 'and the farmer said, "Good news, bad news, who knows."'

'That's uncanny, how did you guess?' Solly joked, bringing a smile to Danielle's face. 'But then a war broke out,' he continued, 'and because of his broken leg, the farmer's son avoided being conscripted.'

'That's lucky,' Danielle said.

'Good luck, bad luck, who knows?' Solly and I chorused, and all four of us laughed.

'So, you see,' Solly said, 'we can never tell how something – or someone' – he looked at me pointedly – 'is going to turn out to be. I could have thought that it was very bad news indeed to have to leave Drancy today. But then I was reunited with my beloved Etty, and now I have three wonderful women listening to me tell a story, so I would say that was very good news indeed.'

Completely unexpectedly, my eyes filled with tears. 'I love you, Solly,' I whispered, leaning into him.

He grasped my hand in his. 'And I love you too, my dear.'

I came to rely on Solly's story more and more as our journey progressed. As the heat increased, so did the stench from the bucket that was our toilet and the chatter in the cattle truck faded. *Good news, bad news, who knows?* I repeated in my head over and over in time with the clatter of the train in the tracks. *But how can anything good possibly come from this?* my inner voice of doubt instantly piped up.

Every so often, I would stand in order to stretch my legs and ease the cramping and I would gaze through the bars on the window at the small patch of blue sky beyond. I thought of what Solly had told me about Tomasz. It didn't change the fact that he'd been rude and hurtful to me when we'd kissed, but I was filled with regret over what I'd said to him at Drancy. If only I hadn't gone in search of him in the Pletzl. If only I'd left it to our first encounter, he would have forever remained as a treasured memory. But now any thought of him would always come tinged with bitterness.

Why are you even thinking about him at all? I scolded myself. *There are far more pressing issues at hand. Like will we even survive this journey?* It had been hours since we'd last had anything to drink and I kept fantasising about crystal-clear streams and wild gushing waterfalls. The one good thing about the dehydration I was now experiencing was that I had no desire to go to the toilet. Not that I'd be able to. The bucket was now full and the contents slopping over the sides with every jerk of the train.

'I feel sick,' Danielle murmured, surely voicing all of our thoughts. The stench of sweat, excrement and urine was becoming overpowering. Almost as soon as she said it, I heard someone vomit on the other side of the car, causing a collective gasp of horror.

'You've been sick on my dress!' a woman wailed and another bout of bickering ensued. It was interesting to see how quickly our camaraderie faded in such trying circumstances. Interesting, and depressing.

'Do you think they're going to kill us?' an old woman asked.

'*Ribono shel olom, ribono shel olom...*' a man with a long dark beard started praying, reaching his arms upward as if trying to pull God down from the heavens to come and save us.

Good news, bad news, who knows? I repeated silently yet again.

Finally, twilight began to gather outside, bringing a welcome drop in the temperature. Silence fell too, as exhaustion took over. I nibbled at what was left of my bread, but it only left my mouth drier. Then the train began to slow down.

'Are we stopping?' someone asked.

'Are we in Germany already?' another called.

The train came to a standstill and I heard the sound of German men's voices outside. We waited and waited, but nothing happened. People started crying out for water. Then I heard a scream from the next truck to ours and a woman's voice calling, 'She's dead!' Who was dead?

Marguerite, Danielle and I exchanged anxious glances, then we all looked at Solly, as if he might have an answer, or some words of consolation at least. But he just closed his eyes. In the gathering darkness, his crinkled skin gave off a waxy pallor, and for a horrible moment it looked as if he, too, had passed away. A terrible thought occurred to me. What if there were no labour camps? What if we'd been herded into these cattle cars to be kept here until we all starved to death?

Don't be so ridiculous! I scolded myself. *How would they dispose of so many bodies?*

After what felt like an eternity, we heard the sound of the bolt sliding across and the doors opened.

'Oh thank God,' a man called from somewhere in the gloom.

'We need water,' someone else gasped.

A guard yelled something at us in German. I didn't know what he was saying, but I could tell from the aggression in his tone that it wasn't good. To my relief, however, we were allowed off, most of us moaning in pain and rubbing our limbs after being cramped up for so long. Poor Solly needed Marguerite and me to help hoist him to his feet.

I glanced around. We were in a tiny, two-platform station in what appeared to be the middle of nowhere. One of the German soldiers slammed a bucket of water on the ground in front of us and handed out a couple of tin cups. When people began scrambling for the cups, he started to laugh. Hatred filled my mind, dark and thick as tar.

Putting an arm around Solly to try to protect him from the scrum, we finally made it to the bucket. There was hardly any water left, but I managed to scoop up half a cupful, which I passed to him. He took a sip and passed it straight back.

'Have some more,' I insisted.

'No, you have it. I'm OK.' He didn't look OK, though. He looked like a plant that had been left in the sun for too long and had begun to wilt.

Thankfully, a soldier arrived with another bucket of water and we were both able to drink a cupful each, but the fact that he'd been so willing to sacrifice his drink for me touched me deeply. In the middle of such darkness, Solly had still managed to release a spark of goodness and love. It was inspiring to me and I vowed to try harder not to let hate get the better of me.

In no time at all, we were being herded back onto our truck. After breathing the fresh evening air, the stench of vomit and excrement was even more unbearable and I had to fight the urge to retch. Thankfully, my group of four musketeers were able to return to the relative comfort of a place by the front of the truck, even closer to the window. As we took our positions, Danielle turned to me, her eyes wide with despair.

'How long do you think this journey will last?' she asked.

'I don't know,' I replied, finding her hand and giving it a squeeze. 'But we'll be OK. We've got each other.'

An old woman cried out behind me. 'My legs are so tired; my knee is so sore,' she sobbed.

'Please, take my space,' I said, offering her the spot next to Solly against the wall. Then it dawned on me that even in this chaos, we might be able to come up with some way of helping each other. 'Why don't we give the older people the places by the walls so they can sit,' I called.

I half expected to be greeted by moans of dissent, or silence, but to my delight there were murmurs of agreement, and slowly but surely, we shuffled our way into some kind of order, with the elderly and infirm sitting against the walls, and us younger folk standing in the middle. I managed to get a spot where I could still see Solly and the look of pride he gave me helped me ignore my aching legs.

Once the train had resumed its journey, a man suggested that we younger ones take it in turns to stand, as there was room for half of us to sit at a time, and so a shift system was introduced: two hours of sitting, followed by two hours of standing, increased to three hours throughout the night. As the train rattled onwards, it warmed my heart that in spite of everything, we'd found a way to maintain our dignity and take care of each other.

Sadly, by the time we'd been travelling for two days, tempers started to fray. We'd gained an extra bucket for our 'latrine', but pretty soon both were overflowing. Poor Danielle, who was standing next to me, had held on for so long, she ended up wetting herself.

'It's all right, it's only urine,' I whispered, trying to console her, but I could tell her spirit was close to breaking and it worried me. I ended up telling her a fantastical tale about our destination, Pitchipoi, a land full of castles, unicorns and dragons, featuring a fearless warrior princess named Danielle Courageux. Thankfully, it kept her distracted. I only hoped I wasn't lulling her into a false sense of security. I had the horrible feeling that in reality, Pitchipoi would be full of nothing but monsters.

Our journey lasted for three days and three nights in the end. We didn't have another break for water and we weren't given any more food. By the end of the second day, I'd started to believe that the train was going to keep on going until we all died. By the time it did come to a screeching, juddering halt, sending those of us who were standing flying forwards, we were all in a dazed stupor, badly dehydrated and weak from hunger.

'Are we in Pitchipoi?' Danielle called, her voice cracking.

'I don't know,' I replied, not wanting to get her hopes up.

'I hope so,' Marguerite whispered.

I turned to see her face illuminated by a shaft of sunlight coming through the bars of the small window. She looked so pale and drawn, it was like looking at a ghost.

Solly was sitting with his eyes closed, murmuring the words of a prayer.

A man standing by us peered through a crack in the side of the truck. 'What is this place?' he gasped.

I heard a dog snarling and my stomach lurched. We all jumped as something banged against the side of our truck, as if someone was hitting it with a metal pole. Then the bolt slid across and the door was flung open and bright sunlight flooded in. I blinked as my eyes struggled to adjust after hours and hours of gloom. As my vision cleared, I saw a German soldier in a black SS uniform, recoiling, his hand clamped to his mouth, no doubt from the stench he'd unleashed. Another guard, holding a snarling dog, yelled at us in German. Again, I couldn't understand what he was saying, but it was clear he wanted us to get off the train. Holding hands with Danielle and Marguerite, we made our way over to Solly.

'Are you all right?' I asked, helping him to his feet.

'Yes, my dear, I'm fine.' He smiled at me. But when he saw our yelling, snarling reception committee, his smile faded. 'So this is Pitchipoi.'

'We have to stay together. We can't be separated,' I said, my voice wavering as I fought to contain my growing feeling of panic.

'Etty, we will always be together.' Solly raised his gnarled, arthritic hand to his chest. 'That's what love does. It unites us, even in death.'

'Don't say that,' I cried, but he continued to smile that calm, knowing smile of his.

'Love isn't measured by a clock, Etty; it's measured by the heart. Always remember that.'

I was too dazed to give what he said much thought.

We slowly made our way to the door, our limbs stiff, our eyes dazzled by the bright sunlight. I'd been expecting the train to have arrived at a station, but we'd stopped on a single track in the middle of nowhere.

'You have arrived at your destination, Arbeitslager Auschwitz,' one of the guards called through a loudhailer in French with a German accent. 'Leave all of your luggage in the wagon; you will receive it later in the camp.'

'But what if we don't get it back?' Danielle whispered as Marguerite put their case down. 'All of my clothes are in there. And I need to get changed.' She looked down at the dried urine stain on her dress.

'I'm sure we will,' Marguerite replied. 'After all, they're not going to want to have to clothe us, are they?'

Danielle nodded.

'Is there anything valuable in there that you could keep in your pocket?' I asked Solly as he put his own case down.

He shook his head. 'The only thing I have of any value is you.'

It was such a beautiful thing for him to say, and for me to hear, and once again I pictured a spark of love spiralling up in the air between us.

'Thank you. And the same to you,' I whispered in response.

'Get into rows of five!' the guard shouted through his loud-hailer as we stumbled from the train.

I breathed a sigh of relief. Hopefully we four musketeers would be able to stay together.

'Men on the right, women on the left,' the guard continued.

I clutched Solly's frail hand tighter, unable to bear the thought of us being separated and him being all alone in this place.

A man wearing what looked like blue and white striped pyjamas and a matching hat made his way through the crowd towards us and onto the truck we'd just got off. Who was he? And why was he wearing dirty pyjamas? He started slinging the cases out of the truck. Marguerite winced as hers came crashing onto the ground.

'Men on the right and women and children on the left, in rows of five,' the guard repeated.

Another man wearing the strange pyjamas appeared and shouted something at Solly in German. I noticed a green triangle sewn to the front of his shirt, and a number printed on a strip of white cloth above.

'Stop!' I cried as the man tried to shove Solly over to the right.

'Shh,' Solly whispered to me. 'It's all right. We're together in here, remember.' He tapped his chest.

I nodded. But as he shuffled away to join the men, I had to bite my lip to stop myself from crying out.

More guards appeared, holding dogs snapping and snarling and straining on the leash. Where had they brought us? What was this place? I looked around, but it was hard to tell; all I could see was the train and hordes of dazed people trying to form themselves into rows.

Marguerite and I stood either side of Danielle, who now looked close to passing out. The woman with the sore knee who'd sat next to Solly joined us, along with a younger pregnant woman I hadn't seen before. She gave me a frightened smile and

I couldn't help shuddering at the thought of being pregnant in this place.

A young man wearing the pyjama outfit streaked with dirt walked past us, then stopped and took a step back.

'How old are you?' he asked Danielle quietly in French.

'Fourteen,' she replied.

'If anyone asks, say you're eighteen,' he muttered, before joining his colleagues taking the luggage from the train.

'Why should I say I'm eighteen?' Danielle asked.

'I don't know, but I think you should do as he said,' I replied. 'He seemed as if he was trying to help.'

'OK,' Danielle replied, but she looked unconvinced.

Slowly, we began shuffling forwards, as instructed by our captors. I peered through the rows in front of us and saw a line of guards, male and female, pointing people to the left or to the right. From what I could make out, it seemed to be mainly women and children to the left, where a line of lorries were waiting, and men to the right. I guessed they must be taking us to separate living quarters. But when Solly's row reached the front just ahead of us, one of the guards pulled him out and instructed him to go left with the women. Perhaps we would be together after all. But then I saw a couple of young women ahead of us being told to go to the right with the men.

As we reached the front, I tried to keep my head held high under the guards' scrutiny in spite of the fact that I knew I looked like hell and probably stank like it too. The guards were the animals here, not us, I reminded myself.

A female guard came over and looked our row up and down.

'How old are you?' she asked Danielle.

I held my breath; what would she say, and would her answer lead to us being separated?

'Eight-eighteen,' Danielle stammered.

The guard frowned for a moment as if she didn't believe

her.

'She was born in June 1925,' Marguerite piped up.

'And who are you?' the guard asked, looking her up and down.

'Her mother,' Marguerite replied eagerly.

'Right. You to the left.' The guard gestured to Marguerite before turning her icy gaze on Danielle. 'And you to the right.'

'To the right,' a male guard said to me. 'And you two to the left,' he said to the pregnant woman and the elderly woman.

'No,' Danielle cried. 'I want to go with my *maman*.'

'It's all right,' I said, linking my arm through hers. 'I'm sure we'll be back together again soon.' I gave Marguerite a reassuring smile. 'It's OK. I'll take care of her until we're reunited.'

'Thank you,' Marguerite replied before shuffling off to the left. At least she'd be able to take care of Solly. *'Good news, bad news!'* I imagined him saying.

'But I don't want to leave Maman.' Danielle's bottom lip began to quiver.

'To the right!' the guard barked, prodding Danielle with her truncheon.

'Shh!' I whispered. 'We need to do what they say. It's going to be OK. They're taking the older and weaker people on those lorries, that's all.' I knew I should be reassured that they were being taken care of, but I couldn't help feeling an inner dread at being separated.

I looked over to the left, desperate for a last glimpse of Solly, and saw his stooped figure shuffling towards the lorries. *Please turn around,* I silently willed. *Please.* I needed to see his reassuring smile again.

As if he were able to hear my thoughts, he looked over his shoulder and he smiled back at me.

You will see him again, I told myself as he was lifted by two guards onto the back of a lorry. *Of course you will.* But in spite of the oppressive heat, I felt a chill pass right through me.

15

AUGUST 1942, AUSCHWITZ

Those of us who had been instructed to go right half marched, half stumbled on for what felt like forever, until finally a sprawling red-brick structure came into view. As we drew closer to the gate at the entrance, I saw an inscription in wrought-iron letters across the top – *Arbeit Macht Frei*. I didn't know the meaning of those words then, of course. If I had, I would have been struck by the bitter irony of the proclamation: 'Work makes one free', surrounded by armed watchtowers and barbed-wire fences for miles.

'What is this place?' Danielle whispered as we approached the gate.

I heard the sound of classical music and saw the strangest sight. A band, all clad in those shabby striped pyjamas and arranged in a semicircle, were playing a rousing piece as we marched towards them. The presence of yet more SS guards scowling at us told me that the music wasn't meant to be taken as a warm welcome. A horrible smell filled the air, worse even than the smell on the train, growing stronger and stronger as we approached. It was impossible to tell what it was.

'First, you will go and have a shower,' one of the guards said in French as we walked in through the gate.

Danielle and I exchanged relieved smiles. The prospect of washing the stench and the stress of the last three days from my body was hugely appealing and propelled my weary legs onwards. We marched past rows of long, low buildings, and were herded into a large square yard, where we were once again told to stay in our rows of five. Danielle held my hand so tightly, I could feel her nails digging into my palm. Another man in pyjamas with a green triangle badge on his chest and an armband saying 'Kapo' ran over and hit our hands apart with his truncheon.

'Ow!' Danielle cried.

He shouted something at her in German, then pointed to a large chimney looming over the buildings beside us. It was belching thick smoke into the air. I heard someone behind me gasp and I wondered what the man had said to prompt this reaction. One thing was becoming instantly apparent; I would need to learn some German and fast if I was to survive in this place.

One of the SS guards came and addressed us all, again in German. Then the men and women were led over to separate buildings.

'We must be about to have our showers,' I murmured to Danielle, hoping to cheer her up. My mouth was so parched, all I could think of was opening it beneath the stream of water and gulping down every drop I could. But as soon as we got inside the building, my heart sank. A female guard brandishing a whip was screaming at those already inside as they began removing their clothes.

'Where are the showers?' Danielle asked, looking around frantically. 'Why are they getting undressed?'

'I think we all have to get undressed first,' I replied.

'But—'

'We have to,' I said tersely. I hated having to speak to her like that, but I really didn't like the look of the brute with the whip.

Numb with shock, I started unbuttoning my dress and kicked off my shoes. Reluctantly, Danielle followed suit. I'd been hoping we'd be able to keep our underwear on, but another female guard, this one in the striped pyjamas, tore a woman's slip from her body, laughing as she cowered, trying to cover her breasts. Some male guards came into the room and started sneering and yelling at us, laughing every time someone cried.

Clad only in my underwear, I gripped Danielle's arms and stared into her eyes. 'Pretend you're somewhere else,' I hissed through gritted teeth. 'Pretend you're in a Danielle Très Belle story. Draw upon your strength.' I didn't know what else to say to her. She really needed her mother at a time like this. I looked around frantically, hoping to see Marguerite, but there was no sign of her.

Danielle took off her skirt and blouse, her hands trembling violently. Why had I insisted she lie about her age? If I hadn't, she'd still be with her mother. I smiled at her encouragingly and took off my bra. One of the men smirked and called something to me, but I pretended not to hear. I thought of a scene I once wrote where Aurelie was changing backstage for a show at Le Moulin Rouge and a peeping Tom was hiding behind her screen, watching while she got changed. Aurelie retaliated by keeping her cool and demanding that he strip off too. He was so shocked, he fled the scene. There was no way that would work in this situation, but I could still call upon some of my heroine's chutzpah. I took off my underwear and stood, arms folded across my chest. I nodded encouragingly to Danielle and she timidly followed suit. The thought of her, a fourteen-year-old girl, being made to stand naked in front of a room full of strangers, some of them men, was abhorrent, but it was as if I could hear Solly in my mind, urging me to remain calm.

We were jostled over to the end of the room, where a line of short-haired women in pyjamas were standing holding scissors. I heard Danielle gasp as they began hacking at the hair of the women at the front of the queue. 'Etty, please,' she begged.

'Don't worry, it will grow back,' I muttered. It was the best I could come up with; my head was beginning to spin from a lethal combination of shock, exhaustion and hunger.

A guard grabbed me and shoved me onto one of the chairs. Behind me, a woman began hacking off handfuls of my hair. I watched numbly as the dark locks started littering the floor. I couldn't let them break my spirit, as much for Danielle as for me.

'*Très chic!*' I declared once she'd finished, patting my bristly head.

A couple of the other women gave tearful smiles, but Danielle's expression remained horrified.

A male guard came over and made me stand up, forcing my legs apart with his truncheon. All of my bravado disappeared in an instant. What were they going to do to me? A woman with a razor crouched down in front of me and set upon removing my pubic hair, nicking at my skin. Flinching, I tried thinking of Solly's story about the farmer, but there was no way I could see how what was happening could be deemed 'good news'. Another woman appeared with an old rag smelling of petrol and she daubed at my now bald pubic area. The thought that Danielle was watching all of this, waiting for her turn, made me feel sick. Whatever I did, I mustn't show any sign of weakness. But when I turned back to give her a look of encouragement, she was staring blankly into space, clearly catatonic from shock.

Once we'd been shorn, we were ushered into another room, where we instinctively pressed ourselves against the walls, as naked and hairless as a dress shop's mannequins. All that remained of Danielle's beautiful auburn hair were a few rust-coloured tufts sprouting from her scalp. I tried desperately to think of something rousing to say, praying that my good friend Aurelie would channel through me.

'Your hair will grow back,' I said, taking hold of her hand. 'But those monsters will never be able to grow back their humanity.'

A woman on the other side of me murmured in agreement and started humming '*La Marseillaise*' under her breath. I noticed a brown, franc-sized birthmark on her stomach. How strange it was to be naked in front of a complete stranger.

'And besides,' I added, turning back to Danielle, 'now you have such short hair, we're all able to see your incredible cheekbones.'

'Really?' The slightest flicker of hope sparked some life back into her eyes.

'Absolutely! I'd give anything to have such a heart-shaped face. I fear that now I'm bald, I must look like an egg on legs.'

Danielle gave me a weak smile. 'You don't look like an egg at all, and your eyes look bigger than ever.'

'Are you saying I look like a frog?'

My heart warmed as her smile grew, and I pictured a spark of light being released on her laughter and spiralling up to the ceiling.

'This is what we must do,' I whispered. 'We must keep supporting each other, no matter how hard it gets.'

Danielle nodded.

A couple of male guards came into the room and started laughing at us, pointing at some of the women and making comments in German.

Don't lose your temper. Stay calm, I urged myself. I thought of the story Solly told me about Hillel, the man who never, ever lost his temper. I wondered what he would do in this situation. It was one thing being asked annoying questions when you were trying to wash your hair, but the provocation we now faced was on a completely different level.

'*We have to compensate for the lack of love they bring the world,*' I heard Solly whispering inside my head. '*Keep your focus on Danielle.*' I linked my little finger in hers and squeezed tightly.

A female guard came in and barked something at us in German.

'We're being taken for our showers,' the woman with the birthmark said, noting my blank expression. 'I won't tell you what else she said.'

'Thank you. I think I can guess,' I replied as the female guard continued yelling what was undoubtedly a torrent of abuse.

We were jostled into another room and, without warning, water started trickling down upon us. I opened my parched mouth and almost cried out with relief. But within seconds, the water stopped and the shower was over.

'*Raus! Raus!*' the female guard screamed from the door. I made a mental note that '*raus*' must mean 'hurry' or 'get out'.

We were led outside, still completely naked, where the heat from the sun soon dried our damp skin. Then we were marched single file into yet another room, where a row of men and women clad in the strange dirty pyjamas were sitting waiting. This time, I happened to be at the front of the queue, with Danielle right behind me. I was ordered to go over to one of the men, who had a red triangle sewn to his breast with the letter P in the centre. Having to sit completely naked in front of him made my skin crawl and I was unable to meet his gaze. He picked up a metal implement and took hold of my left arm. As he brought the implement to my arm, it began to buzz and I felt a strange burning sensation.

'What are you doing?' I asked, trying not to flinch.

He said something to me in a foreign language I was pretty

sure was Polish. Unlike the other people I'd encountered at the camp so far, his tone was gentle and his grip on my arm was soft. When he'd finished, I saw a number in black now etched into my skin.

'This number – this you now,' he said to me in broken French. 'This your identity.'

I stared at him in shock before hearing Danielle cry out in pain as another man began tattooing her arm. So, having been transported in cattle cars and shorn like sheep, we were now being branded like livestock. *The Germans are the animals for behaving like this*, I reminded myself, but it was becoming increasingly difficult not to feel overwhelmed by fear and despair. How was this happening? How had this been allowed to happen?

Hopefully, we would soon be reunited with Marguerite and Solly. That would be something at least. I guessed that, as they'd been brought to the camp in the lorries, they'd probably already been through the humiliation of this registration process. I tried not to think of poor Solly having to cower naked, for fear that it might make me apoplectic.

Next, we were taken into yet another room, where a line of more pyjama people, as I'd come to think of them, were waiting by piles of what looked like rags on the floor. A strange, stale smell filled the air. It soon became apparent that the piles of rags were in fact our new clothes and the source of the smell. We were each given a huge pair of saggy underpants that came down to the knees, a vest, a scarf, a dress and a jacket, which bore the now familiar blue and white stripes. My dress was damp and smelled of mould and as I put on my jacket, I noticed a splatter of what looked like dried blood on the front. We were each issued with a pair of crudely made wooden clogs. Mine had a strip of leather going across the top that cut into my skin as they were slightly too small. But this was no Parisian boutique and the guards soon made it clear there was no way of changing anything. Poor Danielle was dwarfed by her jacket, which was several sizes too big.

Finally, we were taken into a room where we were instructed to sew yellow Stars of David to the front of our jackets, along with a white strip bearing the number that had been branded on our arms. As I said '*Merci*' to the woman who issued me with a needle and thread, she gave me a sad smile.

'You have come from France?' she whispered in French.

'Yes. How long have you been here?'

'A couple of months, I think.'

'Two friends that came with me were brought here from the train on lorries.' I glanced over my shoulder to make sure no truncheon-wielding guard was watching. 'Do you know where they might have been taken, and when we will see them again?'

Her smile faded and she visibly paled. 'I'm so sorry,' she whispered.

'What for?'

'You won't see them again.'

'What do you mean?' I desperately tried to maintain my composure.

'They are on their way to heaven.'

'To heaven?' I stared at her in shock. 'But how?'

'The chimneys,' she whispered, before turning to issue someone else with a needle and thread.

I fought the urge to shake her and demand more of an explanation, but I was acutely aware of Danielle just a few feet away, sewing the Star of David onto her huge jacket. Surely Marguerite and Solly couldn't have been killed. It didn't make sense. I thought back to the selection process, trying to remember who else had been sent to the left. It had mostly been middle-aged women and the elderly and the children who had been transported with us. My throat tightened as if caught in a noose. Surely they wouldn't have killed innocent children.

I thought of the chimney towering over the camp belching

out the thick smoke and the strange vile smell that hung over the place. I'd assumed it had been part of some kind of factory. If my stomach hadn't been so empty, I'm sure I would have been sick as the horror of the realisation hit me.

'Oh Solly!' I silently cried, my heart splintering in two.

16

AUGUST 1942, AUSCHWITZ

Somehow, I managed to stop myself from wailing out loud. Now more than ever, I had to stay strong for Danielle, and besides, the woman could have been mistaken. I had no proof that the people on the lorries had been killed. There had been so many of them. Surely it was impossible for them to have been killed so quickly. Surely we would have heard the gunshots before they were taken to the crematorium – if that's what the strange chimney was. Wouldn't we?

Back outside, we were once again arranged into rows of five by some of the pyjama people with the word 'kapo' on their arms. The fact that we wore the same clothes – although their pyjamas all fitted well and were smarter and cleaner – would indicate that they too were prisoners here but had somehow managed to achieve positions of power. It must be something to do with the badge system as they mostly seemed to be wearing green triangles. The acrid smell in the air seemed even worse, but I wasn't sure if it was because the smoke was thicker or because I was more aware of it now after what I'd been told.

They can't be dead, I told myself, over and over. *They can't be.*

After what seemed like hours, we were marched through the camp, past seemingly endless straight lines of long, low buildings. Every so often, one of us would stumble or cry out in exhaustion, only to be met with yells from the kapo people and the threat of their truncheons. At some point along the journey, we encountered a procession of men in the striped uniform, so painfully thin and pale it was like watching a procession of skeletal puppets being held up by invisible strings. A terrible thought occurred to me. What if this wasn't a labour camp at all, but some kind of starvation camp? After all, we hadn't been offered a morsel since we'd got here.

Finally, we arrived outside one of the long wooden buildings and one of the kapos, a short, squat woman with closely set eyes, clad in a much cleaner version of the striped uniform, appeared in the doorway and began barking out instructions in French with a strong German accent.

'I am your *Blockalteste*, your block leader. I am in charge of this barracks – your new home. From now on, you will eat, sleep and live here.'

At the mention of the word 'eat', I felt a surge of relief and my stomach let out a plaintive gurgle.

'In a moment, you will be issued with your spoon and *Schüssel*,' the *Blockalteste* continued. 'As you are all dirty Jewish thieves, there is a high chance these will be stolen from you, and if they are, you will receive no replacement. So if I were you, I would tie the *Schüssel* to your waist and keep the spoon in your pocket. Do you understand?'

There were nods and murmurs of agreement. I understood all right. If we lost our bowl, we wouldn't get any food. By this point, I was almost hallucinating from hunger so just the mere thought was unbearable and I knew I would guard that bowl with my life.

As we were ushered inside the building, my first impression was that it was like a stable, with its wooden framework and beams. The only light came from a row of narrow windows at the very top of the walls. As my eyes adjusted to the gloom, I saw a knee-high cement bank running down the centre of the room, with rows of triple-tiered wooden bunkbeds either side. Some of the bunks already had inhabitants, staring at us blankly. Just like the men we'd encountered, their faces were hollow.

'Go to your bunks. Food will be served shortly,' the *Block-alteste* yelled. Clearly, her position of authority meant extra rations as her face was far from thin.

We shuffled down the narrow passageways either side of the central concrete bank. A woman on one of the top bunks gestured at us to keep going to the far end, where we found some empty beds. There weren't enough for us to have a bunk each, so it was going to be a tight squeeze.

'Come, we'll take this one,' I said to Danielle, heading for a bottom bunk at the back.

'What about Maman?' she said as we perched down. There was only a couple of feet between the bottom and middle bunk above us, so we had to hunch right over in order to sit. 'Where will she go? When will she get here?'

'She can share with us. I'm sure she'll be here soon,' I replied, jaw clenched, praying that what I'd heard wasn't true and that at any minute now Marguerite would walk through the door.

A cry rang out from halfway down the hut, as anguished and piercing as a dying animal. Danielle instantly cowered and I put my arm around her.

'Say it isn't true,' a woman called, as another started chanting Kaddish.

'What's wrong?' asked the woman with the birthmark on her stomach, who'd taken the bunk above ours.

'They're saying that our family members have been killed,' someone replied. 'The ones who rode in the lorries. They were taken away to be killed. That's what the smell is. They're burning their bodies.'

'No!' Danielle gasped. 'No! No! No!'

The *Blockalteste* burst into the hut wielding her truncheon. 'What is going on?' she yelled. 'Silence!'

Everyone fell silent, apart from the woman saying Kaddish, who kept chanting away quietly.

'He who creates peace in His heavens, may He make peace for us and all Israel,' she chanted, 'and say amen.'

'Amen.' A chorus rang out around the hut. It felt so good to say the word out loud: one small act of defiance.

The *Blockalteste* marched over and yanked the praying woman from her bunk by the collar of her striped jacket, and she smashed her truncheon into her head. The woman collapsed to the floor, moaning.

'Take her away,' the *Blockalteste* ordered two kapos wearing green triangles, who'd appeared in the door behind her. Danielle began to quietly sob.

The kapos picked up the woman and dragged her from the building. Her eyes were shut and blood trickled down the side of her face. I looked down at the blood on my jacket. Was that how it had got there? Had the previous owner been beaten over the head by these prisoners with all the power? Was I wearing the clothes of a dead woman? Were Solly and Marguerite really dead? Desperate questions clamoured for attention inside my head.

'Is it true?' Danielle sobbed. 'Is Maman dead?'

'Shh!' someone hissed. 'If you want to survive, you won't ask any more questions.'

I pulled Danielle closer to me, kissing her shorn head, trying to hug her into silence. How could Solly be dead? And after we'd just been reunited. If only I could get our time on the truck back again, so I could tell him I loved him. Had I told him I loved him? Everything was starting to blur. *Love isn't measured by a clock, Etty; it's measured by the heart.* As I remembered his words, they did little to soothe me. The thought that Solly and Marguerite might no longer be living was too horrific to comprehend.

'How can God allow this?' someone muttered.

'There is no God. The Germans have proved that,' another woman replied.

I thought of what Solly had told me about God losing control when He was creating the world, leaving it vulnerable to chaos and evil. Was it just an old fairy tale? Or was it true? And was tikkun olam even more important now we appeared to have descended into hell?

'It's all right, we've still got each other,' I whispered in Danielle's ear.

'But I don't want you, I want Maman!' she spat, pulling herself from my arms. 'If you hadn't told me to lie about my age, I'd still be with her.' She rolled away from me onto her side, sobbing loudly.

I lay on my back, staring up at the wooden slats of the bunk above, tears spilling from my eyes. I was so dehydrated, I stuck my tongue out to try to catch them to moisten my cracked lips. I felt overwhelmed with guilt at encouraging Danielle to lie about her age. For all I knew Marguerite could be somewhere safe and warm now and Danielle could have been with her and spared from this trauma. It all felt so impossible.

'You can't give up. Don't give up,' I heard Aurelie calling to me in my mind, but her voice was fading, as if I was losing her, or losing consciousness. What was the point in trying to carry on if Marguerite and Solly were gone, and Danielle was blaming me for separating her from her mother? Maybe it would have been better to have gone on the lorries. At least we would have all stayed together.

'Are you all right?' The woman with the birthmark peered down at me from the middle bunk.

I quickly wiped my face. 'I don't know. How about you?'

'Well, I've stayed in better hotels,' she quipped and I couldn't help smiling. 'I'm Madeleine,' she said. Her brown eyes were almond-shaped and flecked with amber and there was a sprinkling of freckles across her nose.

'I'm Etty,' I replied.

'That's a lovely name. I hate Madeleine.'

'Why?'

'Because it's like being named after a cake. Still, now we've all been renamed as numbers, it's making me see Madeleine in a far fonder light.' She looked morosely at the number tattooed on her arm. 'I'd rather be called Macaroon than a number.'

'Well, I'd be happy to call you Macaroon,' I joked back, grateful for this unexpected moment of light in the darkness.

'Thank you. But only if I can call you Galette – that way, you can still shorten it to Etty.' Her eyes widened. 'Or is that why you shortened your name? Were you named after a cake too?'

'I wasn't,' I replied. 'My real name is Claudette, but for now I'm happy to be renamed Galette.' I noticed that Danielle had stopped crying, perhaps distracted by our nonsensical cake talk. 'I think it might help raise our spirits to be renamed after our favourite cakes,' I continued. 'What do you think, Danielle? We could call you Gateau.'

'I'm not a stupid cake!' she snapped, trying to move away from me.

'Are you two related?' Macaroon asked.

'No, we are not!' Danielle retorted.

'She was separated from her mother,' I whispered, 'when we arrived here.'

'Oh!' Macaroon gave me a horrified look.

'Because of you!' Danielle muttered.

I wanted to point out that it wasn't solely due to me, and that actually it had been the French man who'd told her to lie about her age, and Marguerite had also told the guard that Danielle was eighteen. We'd all been complicit in this terrible turn of events, but highlighting that fact would no doubt make Danielle feel even worse, so I kept my mouth shut.

The door opened and the *Blockalteste*'s two kapo henchwomen came back in, an appearance made all the more ominous by the flickering candlelight at that end of the hut. One was holding a stack of bowls and a container of spoons and the other, a large metal pot. The one with the bowls barked something at us in German.

'They want us to line up for our food,' Macaroon said, clambering down from her bunk.

At the mention of food, I was up and out of my own bunk in a trice. 'They've brought something to eat, Danielle,' I said, touching her tentatively on her shoulder.

'I'm not hungry,' she muttered, shaking my hand off.

'Really? Not even for a bowl of soup or a freshly baked baguette,' I wheedled, causing myself to drool.

'You are so annoying!' she muttered, but she rolled over and got out of the bunk.

I gestured at her to join the queue after Macaroon and in front of me, so I could keep an eye on her and make sure she didn't get into trouble with our surly waiting staff. Now the women had all left their bunks, there was barely room to move in the narrow passageways.

'Apparently, when you get to the front, you have to tell them your number,' Macaroon conveyed to us over her shoulder.

'OK, thank you,' I replied. 'Did you hear that?' I whispered to Danielle.

'Of course I did. I'm not deaf, I'm angry.'

'Oh, OK.' *'Let her be angry,'* I imagined Solly advising me. *'She needs somewhere to direct it. Far better that it's at you than at the Germans.'*

Macaroon reached the front of the queue and read out her number. She was given a red enamel bowl and a spoon and instructed to go over to the kapo standing by the iron pot. Whatever was inside smelled vaguely of vegetables, but it definitely wasn't anywhere near as aromatic as French onion soup.

I held my breath as Danielle took her turn, murmuring her number. The kapo with the bowls – a mean-looking woman with cropped dark hair and a pinched face – yelled at her.

'I think she wants you to speak louder,' I whispered in her ear.

Danielle raised her voice slightly as she repeated her number.

The kapo mimicked her in a squeaky little voice. I felt my hackles rise and this time there was no voice of Solly to caution me – or, if there was, I couldn't hear it for the blood pumping in my ears. I stepped forward and barked out the number on Danielle's jacket.

The kapo stared at me and I stared back, and I felt an old part of me sparking back into the life. The part that grew up on the roughest streets of Marseilles and encountered bullies like her every day of the week. She raised her truncheon and whacked me across the face. Danielle gasped as I went reeling to the side. I tasted the metallic tang of blood on my tongue and wondered for a moment if I'd lost a tooth. Thankfully, they gave Danielle her bowl and spoon and she stepped forward to get her soup.

I regained my balance and stood in front of the ferret-faced woman who'd hit me, calmly reciting my number. As she gave me my bowl, she leaned forward and spat in it. Oh how I longed to smash the bowl in her face, wipe that smirk off it. But the image of the belching chimney loomed into my mind. Danielle might now hate me, but if anything happened to me, she'd have no one looking out for her. *Thank you for the seasoning*, I imagined saying to the kapo, just as I'd have Aurelie say if I'd been writing this scene for her. It made me feel marginally better as I stepped across to the other kapo, to be given a ladle of what looked like dirty pond water with the odd potato peeling floating in it.

I returned to our bunk, my face stinging but determined not to show any sign of weakness. Danielle was hunched over her bowl, gulping down the soup. I'd been hoping that seeing me get hit would have softened her feelings towards me, but she still refused to make eye contact and as soon as she'd finished, she lay back down. At least she'd eaten so that was something.

I sat on the edge of the bunk, staring into the murky contents of my bowl. Obviously, I would never have normally eaten something someone had spat in, but I was so hungry now I felt I had no choice. I took a spoonful of the tepid liquid. It tasted vile, but my hunger now overrode everything, including my pride. I began guzzling it down, hating myself more with every mouthful and hating the monsters in this place even more.

17

AUGUST 1942, AUSCHWITZ

Unlike our dormitory in Drancy, that first night in Auschwitz, there was no chatter as we settled down for sleep. We were all too shell-shocked and exhausted. Heeding the warning from the *Blockalteste*, I put my spoon in my pocket and tucked my bowl beneath the thin straw pillow. The one good thing about being so bone-tired was that I didn't even notice the unforgiving wooden slats beneath the paper-thin mattress. As I was pulled down into a deep sleep, I welcomed the escape.

At some point, I began dreaming of Solly. He was calling to me in the dark, but I couldn't find him. Then the dream cut to our arrival at the camp and the moment when we'd been told to take off our clothes. One of the male guards started pointing and laughing at me, then he removed his hat to reveal that he was in fact Tomasz. 'I knew you weren't to be trusted!' I cried. He just laughed.

I woke with a start to the sound of someone getting out of their bunk. I listened to the pad of their footsteps as they made their way up the hut, then heard the tinkle of liquid against metal. We'd been told before going to sleep that we wouldn't be allowed out to use the latrines in the night – not that this was any terrible hardship; they were even worse than the ones in Drancy – so we were back to using a bucket. The sound of someone relieving themselves made my own bladder start to ache. I really didn't want to have to get out of the bunk, but the need to go to the toilet was becoming more acute by the second. I waited until whoever it was had returned to their bunk, then slid out of mine, being careful not to wake Danielle.

I tiptoed down the hut until I reached the end where the night guard or *Nachtwache* – a prisoner with a red triangle on her chest – was sitting. A lamp flickered on the stand beside her seat. I pointed to the bucket, and she nodded. As soon as I sat down, I felt the urge to defecate, too strong to be able to fight. Aware of the night guard's stare, I felt my cheeks flush with embarrassment.

She's the one who ought to be ashamed, not you, I tried consoling myself as the sound of me emptying my bowels echoed through the silence. I looked around on the floor beside the bucket for anything I might use to wipe myself.

'Is there any paper?' I whispered, forgetting for a moment that she might not speak French.

The woman shook her head and I grimaced. I was about to stand up when she reached under her chair and threw what looked like a rag at me. I picked it up and saw that it was a saggy pair of men's underpants.

'To wipe yourself,' she whispered.

'Thank you,' I whispered back. I quickly wiped myself. 'What should I do with it?' I asked, holding the dirty pants out to her.

'I don't want them back,' she whispered. 'Keep them so you can use them again.'

I'm not sure I've ever been given a more unsavoury gift, although with time I would come to realise that in Auschwitz having a rag to wipe oneself was to be treasured indeed.

I nodded my thanks and returned to the other end of the

hut, where I stuffed the underpants beneath our bunk, hoping they didn't smell too much. As I lay back down, I prayed for sleep to come and take me, but after the embarrassment on the bucket, I was now wide awake, heart pounding. How were we ever going to survive this hell we'd been brought to? This degradation and humiliation.

I thought back to Drancy and how my storytelling had helped the others. But, back then, we'd still been in France, and there'd still been a glimmer of hope that we might one day return to our homes and our lives. But now we'd literally reached the end of the line. How could I possibly create stories here that would offer hope? Surely they'd just bring despair, a reminder of all that had been lost.

I felt Danielle stir beside me. I had to stay positive, not just for my sake but for hers. I'd promised her mother I'd take care of her. A mother I'd helped separate her from. If only she could find it in her heart to forgive me.

I heard some movement at the far end of the building and someone started banging on the bunks and yelling one word over and over – '*Aufstehen! Aufstehen!*'

People started stumbling out of bed and into the narrow passageways beside the rows of bunks.

I gave Danielle a nudge. 'I think we have to get up.'

She groaned and rolled away from me.

'Danielle, please.'

'It's still night,' she murmured.

'Good day, Galette,' Macaroon said, swinging her long legs down from her bunk.

'Good day, Macaroon,' I replied. 'Come on, Gateau, we have to get up.' I shook Danielle's arm again.

'I'm not a cake!' she exclaimed again grumpily, but she got up at least.

The kapo who'd hit me the day before was back, this time holding a whip. As she yelled more instructions, I watched the women who clearly understood German fumble for their clothes in the dark. The passageway between the bunks was becoming so crowded, it was difficult to move without jostling each other.

'We need to get dressed,' I said to Danielle. 'Don't forget to put your spoon in your pocket, and do this with your bowl.' I showed her how to attach her bowl to her rope belt. I turned to Macaroon, who was watching curiously. 'It's the latest design from Coco Chanel, don't you know,' I said, eager to try to lift her spirits.

'Then I simply must wear my bowl as an accessory too,' she replied with a laugh and followed suit.

The ferret-faced kapo led us out into the pitch dark, prodding at us with her whip.

'What time is it?' I whispered.

'Way too early to be getting up,' Macaroon replied.

Why were they making us get up in the middle of the night? My pulse began to race. Were we being taken somewhere to be killed?

We filed round the side of the building, where we were led to the open latrine with one solitary tap behind it. The ghostly white light from the electric wire fence illuminated the surreal scene as some women relieved themselves and others gathered in the line for the tap. One by one, we took it in turn to fill our bowls with water. Some were so thirsty, they drank it straight down. Others used the water to wash, or to make a token gesture at washing at least. Still feeling filthy from the journey, I used mine to wash my hands and face. Macaroon and Danielle did the same.

The pinch-faced kapo started yelling and cracking her whip on the ground by our feet. I decided to take advantage of the fact that I didn't understand what she was saying and pretended she was crying pleasantries like, 'You look so beautiful!' and 'I

love Jews!' It was a silly thing, but it kept my spirit from
breaking.

We were herded back into the hut, where the *Blockalteste*
was waiting with her other kapo helper and some food, a sight
that flooded me with relief. We were each given a slice of black
bread bearing the ghostliest trace of margarine, and some ersatz
coffee, which turned out to be even more flavourless than the
one we had back in Paris. But in that moment I didn't care. It
was liquid for my parched mouth and I guzzled it down eagerly.

Once we'd finished eating, we were ordered back to our
bunks and my favourite kapo came marching over. For a terrible
moment, I thought she was going to attack me again, but instead
she pointed her truncheon at our bunk. As she began barking
out instructions in German about something called *'Betten
bauen'*, Macaroon whispered a translation in my ear.

'She's showing us how we have to make our beds each
morning.'

The kapo folded the blanket into a neat square and placed it
over my thin straw pillow. Then she adjusted the mattress until it
was ruler straight. I was feeling relieved that I wouldn't have to make
my own bed when she messed it all up again with her truncheon,
smirking at me before saying something else and tapping her watch.

'What did she just say?' I asked Macaroon as the kapo
turned on her heel and marched away.

'We've got five minutes to make our beds as neatly as she
did,' Macaroon replied. 'But how can I do mine without
messing yours up? I need to stand on your bunk to be able to
straighten my mattress.'

'It's OK, you go first,' I said, hoping she wouldn't take too
long. Every second she took was a second less for me and I
didn't want to see what Ferret Face would do to anyone who
took longer than five minutes.

Danielle was able to start work on her side as it was out of reach of Macaroon's feet. The seconds seemed to tick by faster and faster as I waited. Finally, Macaroon was done and I set to work. I'd never been a stickler for such detail before, and the more I tried to straighten the mattress on one side, the more it seemed to become uneven on the other. Realising I was running out of time, I set to work folding my blanket and placed it on the pillow just as the kapo called halt.

The three of us stood beside our bunks, my heart pounding as if I'd just run a race. Slowly, the kapo began making her way down the room towards us, every so often delivering a stinging slap across someone's face, prompting a yelp of pain. I felt Danielle tense beside me. Finally, the kapo reached our bunk, checking Macaroon's first and giving her a curt nod of approval. Then she peered into the bottom bunk. She examined my bed first and to my relief I saw her nod. Then she looked at Danielle's and pointed at the blanket on the pillow and yelled something.

'She's saying the blanket isn't straight,' Macaroon whispered in my ear.

The kapo looked at Danielle and shouted something else.

'She wants to know which of you is sleeping there,' Macaroon explained.

I glanced at Danielle and before she could say anything, I said, 'I am.'

The kapo's eyes seemed to gleam with delight at the prospect of being able to hit me again. But although it stung, the slap wasn't nearly as bad as the blow with the truncheon.

'Oh, Galette,' Macaroon said, squeezing my hand sympathetically as the kapo strode off.

'Clearly she has a thing about hitting me,' I murmured. Then I felt something icy in my other hand and looked down to see that Danielle had taken hold of it.

'Thank you,' she whispered, and just hearing those words

and seeing her tearful smile made all the pain in the world worthwhile.

Once the bunks had all been inspected, we were made to file outside and stand in rows of five again. Women from the surrounding barracks were filing out too. Rows and rows of us standing like endless bowling pins in the dark. The sight made my breath catch in my throat. How had they managed to spirit so many of us away to this place? And what did they plan to do with us? I pictured German soldiers arriving and shooting us all down with their rifles. But none appeared. Any time anyone moved out of line or staggered from exhaustion, you'd hear the crack of a kapo's whip.

I gazed up into the sky and saw a star shining brighter than I'd ever seen before. I might have been hallucinating from exhaustion, but it seemed to be winking at me. It struck me as being the perfect symbol of reassurance – that even on the darkest of nights, it's possible to find a bright light to focus on. I kept my gaze fixed on the star as the kapos prowled around us like tigers scenting a kill, cracking their whips and yelling their insults.

'*The world needs us to compensate for the lack of love they bring,*' I imagined Solly whispering in my ear. '*Keep finding the goodness. Keep releasing the sparks of light.*'

I glanced at Danielle standing to the right of me, her head slumped. *Stay strong*, I silently willed her. *Please stay strong.*

Finally the *Blockalteste* appeared and started doing a roll call. After what seemed like forever and we'd all been accounted for, we were allowed back inside. I'd assumed that we'd been put through this rigmarole because it was our first day in the camp – but one of the women who'd been there a while informed us that it was a daily form of torture.

Back inside the barracks, our grim-faced *Blockalteste* told us that it was time for work. We were made to line up and marched off through the camp. The sun was coming up now, pale fingers of light creeping through the gaps between the endless rows of buildings. I'd never seen a more dispiriting sunrise. There was no landscape here in this hellish place, no nature, no variety, just miles and miles of barbed-wire fence, broken every so often by a watchtower, and rows and rows of low, nondescript buildings. Once again, I was horrified by the scale of the place, so much so that I ended up retreating into my trusty imagination and pretending that I was walking through the streets of Paris. Instead of watchtowers, I'd imagine the Eiffel Tower – before the swastika – and instead of dull flat barracks, I'd picture tree-lined boulevards and beautiful apart-ment buildings. It brought scant relief, however, only reminding me of all I had lost. All that had been stolen.

A line of SS guards was waiting by the gate, most of them holding snarling, fang-baring dogs. Some of the guards peeled away to join us and we were marched out of the camp and across more dull, flat land. Any energy I'd gained from our breakfast was soon gone and my legs became weary and heavy. There was no chance of stopping for a rest, though; the kapos with their whips and the guards with their dogs, shouting, '*Links! Zwei! Drei!*' over and over, made sure of that. Once again, I wondered if we were being marched to our deaths. But why would they have gone to the trouble of clothing and feeding us and making such a fuss about how we made our beds if we were going to be killed? I tried reassuring myself.

At some point along the journey, we passed a procession of male prisoners just like the one we'd seen the day before. They were so thin, their frames seemed to be folding in on them-selves. Was this what was to become of us? A premonition of our future? By the time we reached our destination, a swampy field in the middle of nowhere, my feet were torn and bleeding from my poorly fitting clogs. I glanced at Danielle beside me, hoping to give her an encouraging smile, but her vacant gaze remained fixed on the ground. The guards barked instructions and the kapos gave us all spades and hods and told us we had to fill wheel-less barrows with stones and mud, which then had to be dumped into a ditch at the end of the field.

As the sun climbed higher, the weight of our hods seemed to become heavier and heavier. There was no shade and no respite. Sweat clung to my skin in a sticky film and the palms of my hands became raw. Was *this* how the Germans planned on killing us? I wondered, as I dug and carried – slowly and painfully through a carefully devised programme of over-work and underfeeding.

I thought of Solly and Marguerite, wondering yet again what had become of them. If they had been killed as soon as they arrived, had they actually been spared an even worse fate – one which now befell Danielle and me? I glanced at her, wan-faced, digging away beside me. There was no way Solly's frail body would have been able to withstand such physically gruelling labour. It sickened me that it should have come to this, that I should feel some relief that he'd died quickly. The worst thing was, I had no idea if the rest of the world knew about this hellish place at the end of the line. If they did, surely they would bring an end to it.

I had a sudden flashback to the day I first met Tomasz on Erev Yom Kippur, and how he'd urged me to use my storytelling skills to inform people of what was happening. Never in my wildest dreams could I have imagined having to write about a horror such as this. But I realised with a piercing clarity that the greater the horror, the greater the need to inform the world. As I brought my shovel plunging down into the mud, I made a silent vow to do everything in my power to try to stay alive, so that I might protect Danielle, and live to tell this very worst of tales.

18

SEPTEMBER 1942, AUSCHWITZ

The next few weeks passed in a haze of hunger and exhaustion. Macaroon, Danielle and I formed a tight knot, a family of sorts, and no matter what horrors we encountered during the day in the Valley of Death, as Macaroon called the camp, at night in our bunks we were able to regroup. Macaroon and I shared stories from our lives – it turned out that Macaroon had been the owner of an art gallery in Montparnasse and she'd been arrested when the French police discovered she'd still been hosting private viewings in spite of the ban on Jewish people owning businesses. We both spoke of our teenage years in an attempt to draw Danielle from the shell she'd retreated into since her mother's disappearance. Sadly, she wouldn't take the bait – not even when I shared the hilarious tale of how I'd sprained *both* my ankles wearing a pair of high-heeled Mary Janes at the age of thirteen, trying, and hopelessly failing, to impress a boy – and remained largely silent, but I hoped that our tales would give her some solace and distraction at least. Although how I could distract her from the ever-present chimneys belching their hideous smoke over the camp was beyond me.

Every day, I gave thanks that fate had caused Macaroon and I to cross paths. She was like the wise-cracking big sister I'd always longed to have and her dry sense of humour and warm heart were such a tonic. I loved the way we were able to spark off each other.

But then one humid day in August, Macaroon lost her spark. From the moment we were yelled at for roll call, she seemed flat. Of course, I didn't think too much of it at first – being wrenched from sleep at 3.30 every morning is hardly a recipe for feeling chipper. But when Macaroon barely uttered a word on the way to our work detail, I got the first hint that something was amiss. Normally, we would engage in a sarcastic commentary en route, muttering things like, 'I hear the architecture around here is known as barracks chic, such an improvement on Art Deco,' and 'Isn't it kind of our hosts to protect us from their watchtowers.' It was as much for Danielle's benefit as our own, but that day I couldn't get a peep from Macaroon. Every time I asked her if she was all right, she nodded, but from the way she was biting her bottom lip, it seemed she was fighting back tears. It wasn't until we were back in our bunks at the end of the day that I was able to question her properly.

'Macaroon, please tell me what's wrong; I'm worried about you,' I called up to the bunk above. Although Danielle didn't say a word, I could tell from her anxious expression that she was concerned too.

'What if we never get out of this place?' Macaroon replied. 'What if we never get the chance to...' She broke off.

I slipped from my bunk and stood beside her. 'To what?' I asked softly.

'To make amends,' she replied.

The two women who shared her bunk, Michelle and Hannah, propped themselves onto their elbows, and looked at me hopefully, as if they too needed the answer to this problem.

'To make amends for what?' I asked.

'For the things we regret,' she murmured, and a tear rolled from her eye and down her face.

'Oh Macaroon.' I reached out and stroked her thin arm. Like the rest of us, her skin was now rough and bumpy from bites.

'It's Yom Kippur soon and we won't be able to atone,' she sobbed. 'We won't be able to change anything; we can't say sorry to the people we've hurt.'

Michelle and Hannah nodded sorrowfully.

'Is there someone in particular you have in mind?' I asked.

Macaroon nodded. 'My friend Paulette. My very best friend. I was horrible to her the last time I saw her, before I was arrested. I didn't realise it would be the last time I ever saw her. If I did, I never would have said what I did. And I never would have thrown green paint on her mink coat!'

I stared at her, startled. 'You threw green paint on her coat?'

'Yes, in the middle of the gallery too,' she cried. 'And in front of a nun!'

I glanced down at Danielle in the bottom bunk. Her eyes were saucer-wide in surprise.

'But... but why?' I stammered.

Michelle and Hannah stared at Macaroon, clearly equally riveted by this unexpected plot twist.

Macaroon closed her eyes and sighed. 'Because I was jealous.'

'Well, at least the green paint was in keeping with the theme,' I quipped.

'What do you mean?' Hannah asked.

'Green with envy,' I muttered, instantly regretting making light of Macaroon's distress. I wanted to kick myself for being so insensitive.

She opened her eyes and stared at me, then, to my huge relief, she began to laugh. 'Oh, Galette, thank you!'

Hannah and Michelle started to giggle and when I looked

into the bottom bunk, I saw that Danielle was grinning too. It was a sight and sound that filled my heart with joy.

Not so for the night-watch, unfortunately. Hearing the laughter, she yelled down the hut at me to get into my bunk.

'Why don't you tell us the story of you and Paulette,' I said to Macaroon as I slipped back beside Danielle. 'The story of how you became friends.'

'Yes, I'd like to hear it too,' Danielle said.

Hannah and Michelle murmured their agreement.

'Are you sure?' Macaroon asked.

'Yes. Let's hear about your happier times together,' I replied.

And so Macaroon told the story of how she and Paulette first met at art college at the age of eighteen. The further she got into her story, the lighter her tone became, especially when she regaled us with some colourful tales from their twenties, when they shared an apartment in the shadow of Sacré-Coeur in Montmartre. The Paulette she painted was a warm and funny woman, the kind of friend who would drop everything to be there if you needed her, which made what Macaroon had said about the paint and the fur coat all the more intriguing. How had they gone from being women who shared everything – clothes, jewellery, deepest secrets – to having such a dramatic and public spat? Macaroon ended her story by telling us how she'd given Paulette a job in her art gallery two years ago, after Paulette's husband ran off with a flower seller from Saint-Germain.

'It sounds like the perfect friendship,' Danielle said.

'It is – *was*,' Macaroon replied forlornly.

Determined that she shouldn't sink back into her gloom, I reached up to her bunk and gave her hand a squeeze. 'Do you mind telling us how the green paint incident happened?'

Macaroon cleared her throat. 'It was right before the Statut was passed banning the Jewish from owning businesses. We all knew it was coming. We'd seen what they'd done to the Jews in

Austria and Germany and I was going out of my mind with worry and anger. I poured my heart and soul into that gallery – it was my life's work, my life's passion. I couldn't understand how it could be taken from me just like that. It was so unfair.'

I thought of how I'd felt that terrible day Anton had told me he could no longer publish my books. 'I understand,' I said. 'It's completely unjust.'

'At around about the same time, Paulette had fallen head over heels in love...' Macaroon paused, 'with a policeman.'

'Oh.' My heart sank as I thought of the implications this must have had for their friendship.

'So while I was going out of my mind with worry, she was on cloud nine, drunk on love.'

'So that's why you were jealous of her?' Hannah asked. 'Because she'd found love.'

'No. No, I was jealous because she wasn't Jewish,' Macaroon replied. 'I was jealous that she was free to fall in love. I was jealous that she was still able to see the police as her protectors rather than the enemy. And I was jealous that...' She broke off, looking pained.

'Yes?' I asked gently.

'The day of the green paint incident, she'd turned up at the gallery in a new fur coat her policeman lover had bought her and she told me she'd had an excellent idea. Why didn't I transfer the ownership of the gallery to her – that way she'd be able to keep it open.'

Ah. I guessed how this must have felt for Macaroon. It would be like someone asking if I would write books to be published in their name. It didn't feel pleasant.

'So I told her no,' Macaroon continued, 'and she told me I was being pig-headed – which I was, I see that now – but at the time I was blinded by the injustice of it all. Why should she get to have everything, including my precious gallery, while I – we – were having everything taken away?'

'I think you were right to feel as you did,' I said and Danielle murmured her agreement.

'Maybe, but I wasn't right to throw the paint at her.'

'How exactly did that happen?' I asked. 'And how did a nun get to witness it?'

'Sister Maria was a regular visitor to the gallery and she happened to be having a browse when Paulette arrived,' Macaroon explained. 'I'd been painting one of the gallery walls green to try to take my mind off things – I've always found green to be such a soothing colour – but then, when everything got heated, I lost control and I picked up the paint pot and flung it in Paulette's direction in frustration. I didn't mean for it to go all over her coat.'

'Then what happened?' Danielle asked, clearly riveted.

'Then Paulette ran from the gallery crying.' Macaroon's voice began to waver. 'And the worst thing is, I didn't go after her, and I didn't reach out to her afterwards. I never apologised. And now I might never be able to.'

I thought for a moment. If I was writing the story of Macaroon and Paulette, I would definitely want to give them a happy ending. After all of those years of friendship, it would be tragic if they didn't get to resolve things.

'I just wish I could relive that day.' Macaroon sighed. 'I wish I could have done things differently.'

An idea began forming in my mind. 'Perhaps you can.'

I heard the creak of the wooden slats as Macaroon shifted on the bunk above. 'How?'

'Yes, how?' Danielle whispered.

'Why don't we recreate the scene right now,' I suggested. 'I'll be Paulette and you be you.'

'Can I be the nun?' Danielle asked.

'I don't see why not.'

I waited anxiously for Macaroon's response, hoping she wouldn't think I was making light of her troubles.

'What's the point in recreating it here?' Macaroon asked, but I could hear her sitting up, so I clearly had her attention.

'Sometimes, when we aren't able to control the events in our life story, it can be helpful to rewrite them in our imagination,' I replied, thinking of the countless times I'd recreated scenes from my childhood in which my father didn't drink and abuse me and my mother had lived and we'd been kindred spirits. 'Trust me, I've done it a lot.'

'OK,' Macaroon said, sounding doubtful.

'So, you're painting the gallery wall and the nun is browsing,' I said, setting the scene.

'Yes,' Macaroon replied.

'Oh, sweet Jesus, how I love these pictures,' Danielle exclaimed.

'Pardon?' I stared at her, confused.

'I'm being the nun!' she hissed.

'Ah yes, of course.' I coughed to try to stop myself from laughing. 'And then I – Paulette – come through the door.' I imagined Paulette having a sing-song, girly voice. 'Hello, dear friend,' I trilled, 'do you like my new coat? Officer Traitor-head bought it for me.'

I heard a snort of laughter from the bunk above.

'It's real mink, don't you know. Oh my goodness, I'm so in love. I'm so happy. My life is so wonderful.'

'Did she really speak like that?' Danielle said with a frown.

'Actually, Galette isn't too far from the truth,' Macaroon replied with a new lightness in her voice.

Emboldened, I continued, warming to my role of slightly insensitive, love-drunk friend. 'Anyway, as well as falling head over heels in love, I've had the most incredible idea.'

'Oh yes?' Macaroon replied.

'Yes. Why don't you sign all of your life's work over to me? That way, the Germans won't be able to close the gallery. Of course, you'll have to deal with the minor irritation of watching me take over your life. Not to mention hearing me witter on about how lucky and in love I am with a puppet for the Germans who will be actively oppressing people like you, but, hey, *c'est la vie!*'

I heard Hannah and Michelle giggling.

'I think I would have thrown the paint at her too, to be honest,' Michelle said.

'Really?' Macaroon asked hopefully.

'Yes. I mean, I know people can go slightly nuts when they first fall in love, but she could have been more sensitive.'

I sent a silent prayer of thanks to the bunk above.

'Thank you,' Macaroon replied.

'Now, let's pretend that Paulette didn't run from the gallery,' I said. 'Let's pretend that she – *I* – stayed.' I cleared my throat. 'Why did you do that?' I asked in my high-pitched Paulette voice. 'Why did you throw paint at me?'

'Don't worry, my child, I shall pray for your sinner's soul,' Danielle piped up.

'Pardon me?' I said, glancing at her, confused again.

'I'm being Sister Maria!' she exclaimed impatiently. 'I'm helping Macaroon repent of her sins.'

I heard a snort of laughter from Macaroon. 'Thank you, Sister Maria,' she called down.

'You're very welcome, my child.' Danielle grinned at me. 'Please continue.'

'Thank you,' I muttered before slipping back into my role as Paulette. 'Why did you throw paint at me?'

'I'm sorry, I was just really frustrated.' Macaroon paused for a moment. 'And I'm really afraid.'

I felt a lump begin to grow in my throat. 'Afraid of what?' I asked in my normal voice.

'Of losing everything, and... and when I see you so happy, it makes me...' She fell silent.

'I'm so sorry,' I said, and I'm not sure if I was replying as myself or Paulette or both.

'So am I,' Macaroon said softly.

Danielle wiped away a tear.

'You don't need to apologise,' I continued. 'I should never have been so insensitive. You're my best friend. I love you. And I would never deliberately want to hurt you.'

I heard a choked sob from the bunk above. 'I would never want to hurt you either.'

'A friendship like ours doesn't end over a silly spat,' I said, thinking about my final lunch with Anton and the onion soup. 'A friendship like ours is so much deeper than that. We don't even need to be together to know that, because we'll always be in each other's hearts.' Now it was my voice that was trembling. Danielle took hold of my hand beneath our thin blanket, giving me the strength to continue. 'So we can say we're sorry and we can forgive each other even when we're miles apart, and we'll still feel it, in our hearts.' I gulped, unprepared for how emotional this exercise was making me.

'Do you really think she'll feel it?' Macaroon asked. 'Do you really think she'll know how sorry I am?'

'Absolutely,' I replied. 'And hopefully you'll be able to feel how sorry she is too. How could she not be?'

'Yes, I agree,' Hannah said. 'I imagine she's feeling so sorry.'

'Thank you so much,' Macaroon said, and suddenly she appeared, leaning down from her bunk. Her upside-down face was shiny with tears, but she was smiling.

'You are so welcome.' I reached out and stroked her damp cheek.

'Etty,' Michelle called, sounding hesitant.

'Yes.'

'I was wondering if maybe you could do something similar for me. I really regret how I left things with my husband.'

'I'd really like a turn too,' Hannah said. 'I'd love to make amends for the way I spoke to my next-door neighbour when I was rounded up. I thought he'd denounced me, but now I'm sure I was mistaken, and was overreacting out of fear.'

'I would be honoured to help you,' I replied, shifting into a seated position, all of my weariness gone. The Germans might have imprisoned my body, but my spirit and sense of purpose felt stronger and freer than ever.

And so the five of us spent the next couple of hours helping each other retell our stories, and transmuting pain and regret into love and atonement.

19

YOM KIPPUR, SEPTEMBER 1942, AUSCHWITZ

As Yom Kippur approached, a new topic for debate preoccupied the Jews in the barracks – whether or not we should observe the fast.

'Every day in this place is Yom Kippur,' Macaroon remarked drily, looking at her breakfast, a shrivelled piece of black bread. 'I really don't think God would expect us to observe the fast in here. We've been fasting for weeks already.'

'But don't you think that would make it mean even more?' I said before taking a sip of the lukewarm slop the Germans called coffee. 'To fast when we're already half-starved shows real commitment.'

'Or real stupidity,' Danielle muttered. 'Why should we starve ourselves any more for God after what He's done to us?'

'But God hasn't done this to us, *people* have,' I said gently, thinking of Solly with a wistful pang.

'But God's allowed it,' Danielle responded, her voice rising.

I remained silent, not wanting to upset her further, but in my mind a plan was hatching: a way of fighting back against our oppressors. They'd taken so much from us, they had so much control over us, but refusing to eat their paltry offerings for a day was a choice I *could* make, a declaration of my pride in being Jewish, and a way of connecting to Solly and Marguerite and all the others whose lives had been taken because of their faith. The thought of doing teshuva in spite of it being forbidden brought a spark of life back to my weary, aching body.

On Erev Yom Kippur, I ate my meagre dinner ration, pretending it was the pre-fast feast and then I lay in my bunk remembering how Tomasz had chanted Kol Nidre that night we first met, and how magical it had been in spite of the fact that he'd been wearing a tablecloth and my pink satin gown. We'd proved that you could find God anywhere, not just at the synagogue. And now I was going to test this theory to its limits by attempting to find God in this Valley of Death.

'Can you tell me a story?' Danielle whispered, rolling over to face me.

'Of course.' And I told her the story that had been replaying itself in my mind – the story of how Tomasz and I met, and how we'd spent Erev Yom Kippur together, omitting his confession to having killed someone. When I reached the end of my tale, I saw to my surprise that for the first time since we'd got to the camp, Danielle's eyes were bright with curiosity.

'What happened next?' she asked, wincing as she pushed herself up onto her elbow. It pained me to see her looking so thin and frail.

'Nothing,' I replied, far too mortified to tell her about the second time Tomasz and I met.

'You never saw him again?'

I shook my head.

'But didn't you want to?' she asked, wide-eyed.

'Yes, but some encounters are best left as short stories rather than stretched into novels.'

'Why?'

Much as I was happy to see Danielle interested in something, I couldn't help wishing it was over something less personally humiliating.

'Because if they're left as short stories, they have a happy ending,' I replied.

'I think that's a sad ending, though.' Danielle lay back down and sighed. 'I wanted you to fall in love.'

'Yes well, sadly I wasn't writing this story.'

'If I was writing it, I'd have made him turn up at your apartment and declare his undying love for you,' Danielle continued.

I thought of what had actually happened when Tomasz and I had met again and squirmed, but Danielle wasn't giving up.

'He would say, "My darling Etty, ever since saving your doll from a watery grave, I cannot stop thinking about you!"'

'Hmm, I don't think being made to dive into the Seine to rescue a doll is much of an incentive to fall in love,' I retorted.

'Shh! Now I'm telling the story,' Danielle said crossly.

'Very well, if you insist.' I closed my eyes and smiled as her words began painting scenes across my mind as if it were a movie screen. Tomasz and I going for romantic walks along the Seine and having candlelit dinners. Tomasz presenting me with endless gifts. Danielle's version of Tomasz was certainly a lot less rough around the edges and he spoke like a seventeenth-century English lord, but that only made it more entertaining. And the further her version got from the reality, the less painful and embarrassing I found it. It was actually quite fun to be able to escape into the world of someone else's imagination.

'And then tragedy strikes,' Danielle announced dramatically. 'You are arrested and brought to Drancy. And when you don't turn up for your dinner date, Tomasz thinks you've jilted him.'

'Oh no!' I couldn't help exclaiming, having been swept up into the saga.

'He walks the streets of Paris, a wounded soul, howling at the moon in despair,' she continued.

I thought of Tomasz howling at the moon like a wolf and tried not to laugh.

'But you have no way of telling him where you are.'

'Couldn't I have written to him from Drancy?'

'Shh! This is my story.' She glared at me.

'Sorry.'

'You want to write to him, but you can't remember his address.'

'OK.'

'And then you are sent to this place, where you are made to work every day, digging mud and hauling stones.'

'I really hope this story has a happy ending,' I muttered.

'It does...' She paused. 'I just have to work out what it is.'

The writer in me was desperate to jump in with potential ideas, but I kept my lips zipped. This was the most Danielle had talked since we got here and the most enthused I'd seen her. I didn't want to do anything to stop it. I knew only too well the joy to be had in letting your imagination run wild. She remained deep in thought for a few moments before continuing.

'Then, one day, while you're working, you see a figure on the other side of the fence. He's dressed in a German soldier's uniform, so you just assume it's one of the guards. When he beckons you over, your heart sinks. "Oh please God, say it isn't so!" you silently wail,' she whispered melodramatically. '"My poor feeble body can withstand no further punishment."'

I frowned at her in the gloom. There's no way I'd ever speak like that – or think like that, but again I stopped myself from saying anything, not wanting to interrupt Danielle's flow.

'But you drag yourself over to the fence, and you drag your gaze up to meet his...' Danielle paused.

'And?' I urged, eager to discover where she'd go next.

'And you see a scar shaped like a lightning bolt upon his cheek. And you think to yourself, "Forsooth! It is he!"'

'Very Shakespearean,' I replied.

'Shh! Do you want me to tell you what happens next or not?'

'Yes!'

'"My darling Etty,"' she continued, '"ever since I found out what happened to you, I have been searching high and low, trying to find you."'

'How did he find out I was here?' I whispered.

'Er – um – a friend in the French police told him,' she improvised.

'OK.' I decided to ignore the glaring plot holes this opened up. All l cared about was encouraging this new enthused Danielle.

'"But we must make haste; we have no time to lose," Tomasz continues in his deep, masculine voice. "Come, my love, climb over the fence."'

'But it's electric,' I whispered. 'Is he trying to kill me?'

'No! He... he's found a part that isn't,' she hissed back, clearly exasperated.

'I see.' *Oh if only*, I thought wistfully, picturing the scene.

'So you climb up the fence and drop down on the other side, into his strong, manly arms.'

I thought of the last time I was in Tomasz's arms, before it all went so horribly wrong, and how safe and protected I'd felt, and I felt a pang of longing deep inside.

'"Etty, my darling one," Tomasz says, falling to one knee. "Will you do me the great honour of being my wife? Will you marry me?"'

My eyes sprang open. 'He proposes to me here?'

'Yes.' Danielle gave a sigh. 'Isn't it romantic?'

'I suppose so,' I said, although personally I couldn't think of a worse place to be proposed to. Plus all this dilly-dallying around by the perimeter fence would surely have got us shot, a thought that was instantly sobering. 'But how do we escape?'

'Tomasz has a car waiting nearby.'

'Wouldn't I stand out like a sore thumb in my delightful striped outfit?'

Danielle gave another impatient sigh. 'He's brought a change of clothes for you – the latest design by Coco Chanel, a beautiful black dress and a fur stole, and comfortable shoes.'

'Oh,' I couldn't help moaning with delight at the thought of no more painful wooden clogs. In that moment, comfortable shoes felt more appealing than a strong-armed Shakespearean suitor bearing a proposal of marriage – to my poor worn-out feet at least.

'So you get changed and he looks at you with tears in his eyes,' Danielle continued. '"Etty, my darling girl, you are the most beautiful, exquisite creature I have ever seen," he gasps.'

I bit my lip to stop myself from laughing. I hadn't seen my reflection since arriving here, but I was willing to hazard a guess I looked far from beautiful or exquisite, and the thought of Tomasz talking like this was comical, to say the least.

'And you drive off together to a life of full of love, happiness and freedom. The end,' Danielle announced. 'What did you think?' she asked eagerly, her eyes shining.

'I think you're a wonderful storyteller.'

'Really?' There was such hope in her voice, it was both uplifting and heartbreaking.

'Absolutely. You did what every good storyteller must do – you transported me into the world of the story with your words. You made me forget myself for a moment – even though the story was about me. Thank you.'

'You're welcome.' She lay on her back and gazed up at the bunk above, where Macaroon's soft snores rumbled away. I thought maybe Danielle had talked herself into exhaustion, but then she rolled over to face me. 'I've decided to observe Yom Kippur too,' she whispered.

'That's wonderful,' I whispered back. I felt for her hand and laced my fingers between hers.

'Could we pretend that we've lit the yahrtzeit candle?' she asked.

'Of course,' I replied, my skin prickling. Could she want to perform the act of remembrance for her mother? Had she finally accepted that Marguerite had gone? I felt a fresh pang of despair at all the poor girl had had to endure. 'Here, I'm lighting it now,' I whispered, mimicking striking a match. 'Blessed are You, Lord our God, Ruler of the Universe, who has made us holy with commandments and commanded us to kindle the lights of Yom Kippur,' I said. 'I'm going to say a prayer of remembrance for Solly...' I braced myself, waiting for her response.

'OK,' she said so quietly I barely heard.

'Dear God, I hope Solly is with you now and his soul is at peace,' I whispered. 'Thank you for the gift of his friendship and his love. Thank you for keeping him in my heart always, and for the way he watches over me still.' I fell silent, my eyes growing warm with tears. I hoped that Danielle might take comfort from my prayer, and that it made her think of her mother in a similar way.

'Dear Maman,' she whispered, causing a shiver to run up my spine. 'I miss you so much, but I hope you're at peace, and I hope you're watching over me now, like an angel...' Her voice wavered. I took hold of her hand again and held it tightly. 'Dear God, please look after my *maman*. And thank you for Etty.'

At first, I thought I'd misheard, but she gave my hand a squeeze before continuing.

'Thank you for sending her to take care of me.'

I leaned closer and planted a kiss on her forehead.

'I love you, Etty,' Danielle whispered, before snuggling into me.

'I love you too,' I replied, the lump in my throat growing so big I could barely breathe.

That night, for the first time since arriving in Auschwitz, I had a pleasant dream rather than a nightmare. Food featured of course, as it now seemed to feature in all of our dreams, but instead of being deprived of things to eat, Danielle, Marguerite, Solly and I were enjoying the Erev Yom Kippur feast. The table we sat at was laden with freshly baked challah and soup full of tender pieces of chicken and potatoes and other vegetables. After the soup, Solly gave us all slices of the sweetest honey cake and wished us well over our fast. In my dream, he seemed younger somehow, no longer stooped and his knuckles no longer swollen from arthritis. I was about to wish him well too when there was a sound of clanging and banging and my dream faded to black.

I opened my eyes. I seemed to be awake, but I could still smell the soup. 'Can you smell food?' I whispered to Danielle as she stirred from sleep.

'Yes,' she replied, sniffing the air. 'It smells delicious.'

Murmurs of surprise began filling the room and Macaroon stumbled down from her bunk above, rubbing her eyes. 'What's that smell?'

'Good morning,' the *Blockalteste* called, in an unfamiliarly friendly tone. I'd picked up quite a few German words and phrases by that point, but I couldn't understand what she said next.

'She's saying that she understands that today is a special day for us Jews,' Macaroon explained. 'So they've prepared a special breakfast for us.'

'But we're supposed to fast on Yom Kippur,' I replied.

'Maybe she's got the days confused and she thinks today is Erev Yom Kippur.' If this was the case, it really would be the most bitter of ironies.

The smell from the soup grew stronger and more delicious, causing my mouth to water. The *Blockalteste* said something else, a horrible smirk upon her face.

Macaroon sighed and shook her head. 'She hasn't got the days confused; they're doing this deliberately, to test us. Anyone who doesn't eat their breakfast will receive a lashing.'

Danielle looked at me, her eyes wide with terror.

'It's all right,' I whispered. 'I think you should eat. I think God would want you to keep up your strength.'

'But what are you going to do?' she asked.

What *was* I going to do? As we queued for our breakfast, I wracked my brains. I was so determined to make a stand for what I believed in, but how could I get away with it without incurring a beating – or worse?

It became even harder to think once I'd been served. For once, the soup wasn't an insipid watery liquid. It was thick with vegetables and smelled divine. Maybe I should just eat it? But one look at the *Blockalteste*'s smirking face hardened my resolve. I took my soup and followed Danielle back to our bunk. As she guzzled hers down, I mimicked eating, but from an empty spoon. Then, as soon as the guards were looking the other way, I turned my back to them and gestured at Danielle to come closer. Before she could say anything, I tipped the contents of my bowl into hers.

'Etty!' she exclaimed.

'Shh, just eat,' I whispered.

She didn't need any further encouragement. When we were given the murky brown water that was supposed to be coffee, I lifted my straw mattress and poured it through the wooden slats of my bunk onto the ground below. It was so disgusting I knew Danielle wouldn't want my share. Thankfully, it had no aroma, so I felt confident I could get away with it. I carried on miming drinking, feeling especially emboldened that I had helped feed Danielle *and* do teshuva and observe my fast right under the Germans' noses.

I kept returning to that thought as we made the long trek to the marshes for our day of labour, to power me through the light-headedness of my hunger. I saw sparks of God's light being released with every step I took, leaving golden footprints in the mud, and I pictured Solly smiling down on me, urging me on.

At lunchtime, we were given more of the delicious-smelling soup.

'Anyone who does not eat will be beaten,' one of the guards yelled.

I met Danielle's gaze and nodded and she began to eat. This time, I hid my bowl behind a pile of rocks and stones. They always kept us working past sundown, so my plan was to eat it as soon as it got dark and we were allowed to break our fast. My plan worked, and even though the soup had spoiled slightly from the heat of the afternoon sun, I didn't care. I wolfed it down and in that moment it was the most delicious thing I'd ever tasted.

I returned to the barracks with a spring in my step. I'd managed to get one over on the Germans, not once, but twice. This was a very good day indeed. But when we reached our hut, the *Blockalteste* was standing in the entrance, her whip in one hand and a German shepherd straining on the leash in the other. She muttered something to the ferret-faced kapo, who came marching down the line, stopping by Danielle and me. The *Blockalteste* barked out our numbers and the kapo pulled us out of the line by our collars. The *Blockalteste* yelled something in German I didn't understand, but I saw Macaroon flinch.

'She says that one of you didn't drink your coffee,' the kapo snarled, causing my heart to race. 'Which one of you was it?'

With a sinking heart, I stepped forward.

20

SEPTEMBER 1942, AUSCHWITZ

The kapo marched me over to the *Blockalteste*, who was yelling so savagely now, saliva was forming in the corners of her mouth.

'She wants to know why you didn't drink your coffee,' the kapo barked in my ear.

Because it tastes like piss, I felt like replying, but bit my lip.

'Tell her! Why!' the kapo yelled, slapping the side of my face.

'I wasn't thirsty,' I replied. I couldn't say I was fasting because then they'd want to know what had happened to my soup.

The kapo relayed what I'd said to the *Blockalteste*, prompting another torrent of what was undoubtedly abuse. As if feeding on her anger, the dog began growling ferociously. As a child, I remember being told that animals can sense our fear, which makes us more vulnerable to becoming their prey. *Show no fear, show no fear*, I started repeating in my mind, an old mantra I'd often used with my father too.

'She wants to know what you did with your soup,' the kapo said.

A terrible silence fell. I so badly wanted to tell her that I'd given it away, that I'd been fasting for Yom Kippur, that I was proud to be Jewish and to have found a way to get closer to God in this hellhole. But if I told the truth, she'd want to know where my soup had disappeared to and then Danielle could get in trouble too. *What does it matter what she thinks?* I imagined Solly advising me. *You and God know the truth; that's all that counts.*

'I ate it,' I replied, staring at the *Blockalteste* defiantly.

She glared at me for a moment, then barked something to both her kapos and in an instant they set upon me like wild beasts, tearing my clothes off until I was naked in front of everyone. Then I was marched into the centre of the yard.

'You will be punished for your insolence,' Ferret Face informed me. 'And as you are not thirsty, you are to have nothing to drink tomorrow.'

I heard a gasp from behind me and willed Danielle to stay quiet.

The *Blockalteste* marched over and stood behind me and drew back her whip. The first few cracks stung like hell and made my eyes smart. I was determined not to cry, though. As the whipping continued, I became half delirious with pain, but I didn't break. I remembered what I used to do whenever I heard the sound of my father unbuckling his belt prior to a beating and I mentally left my body, knowing I needed to lose myself in a story. Danielle's tale from the night before instantly came to mind and I pictured Tomasz appearing at the fence. But this time he didn't speak like a Shakespearean character. This time, all he said was, 'I'm sorry. Please forgive me.' 'I'm sorry too,' I pictured myself saying. 'I shouldn't have been so quick to judge you.' And when I realised that I was asking for atonement in true Yom Kippur style, I felt a new-found surge of strength. *You might be able to beat my body, but you'll never be able to break my spirit,* I yelled to the *Blockalteste* inside my head. It was an important and liberating realisation.

Finally, the whipping stopped and I heard quiet sobs coming from the line of prisoners who'd been forced to watch. It sounded as if several of them were crying. I opened my eyes and saw Danielle and Macaroon at one end of the line. Danielle's shoulders were quivering and I was comforted to see Macaroon reach for her hand.

'Silence!' Ferret Face yelled at them before turning back to me. 'You are to stay here and stay standing until morning or you'll be shot.'

Show no fear, show no fear, show no fear, I reminded myself as the others were all led back into the hut.

I saw a rat scurrying across the floor. In stark contrast to us prisoners, its body was positively rotund. I tried not to think about what it may have been feeding on. The hum from the electric fence seemed to grow louder and louder, a reminder that death was ever-present and could catch me at any moment. My body ached and my back burned from the lashing, but somehow I remained standing. A sudden breeze danced around me, cooling my wounds. I looked up just as the moon came out from behind a cloud. It was glowing bright orange – the harvest moon, I remember old Madame Bellamy telling me as a child. I'd never seen it quite this orange before, though. It was glowing like the brightest piece of amber. As I gazed up in awe, a wonderful thought occurred to me. I was supposed to be being punished, but actually the *Blockalteste* and her henchwomen had inadvertently treated me to a display of beauty the like of which I hadn't seen in months. And then another irony struck me – thanks to the curfews implemented by the Germans as soon as they occupied France, this would be the first time I'd been out all night in over two years. Admittedly, I wasn't meandering back along the Seine after a night on the tiles with a head buzzing from music, laughter and conversation, but still... what an unexpected gift, and I was determined to appreciate every second of it.

As more time passed, the lights went out in the barracks, making the moon appear even brighter. Every time my legs started to buckle, I felt the moon pulling on me, the way it pulls on the tides, keeping me upright. But then I heard the sound of male voices and instantly tensed. The silhouettes of two German soldiers appeared in the pool of light beneath the watchtower, and they were walking in my direction. I closed my eyes the way a young child does, trying to make herself invisible. *Please, don't see me*, I silently implored.

Their conversation grew louder and louder and then it stopped suddenly – as if they'd noticed something, as if they'd noticed me.

Please, please, please, keep walking.

I heard their footsteps resume, growing louder and closer. I opened my eyes and gazed up at the moon as if hoping to drink in some of her fiery orange strength. The men came and stood right in front of me and looked my naked body up and down. I could smell stale liquor oozing from their breath. I tried to mentally escape into a story; I tried to imagine Tomasz from Danielle's story leaping over the fence and putting all of his boxing skills into action, pummelling these Nazi animals into the ground. But it was no good. The moon disappeared behind a cloud as if she couldn't bear to watch what was going to happen next.

One of the men said something to the other, prompting him to snigger and then, to my horror, he unbuttoned the fly on his trousers. The other quickly followed suit. He spat a word at me that was clearly an insult, but as I didn't know its meaning I pictured it falling to the floor, unable to touch me, although in that moment, words were the last of my worries. All of the exhaustion I'd been feeling vanished as adrenaline coursed through my body. It was one thing being beaten, or starved or

deprived of water, but to be raped was my very worst nightmare, and nothing in my life had prepared me for what was
about to happen.

One of the men stepped towards me and I saw his limp
penis in his hand. Part of me wanted to beg them to have mercy,
but I knew that would only give these pigs greater satisfaction. I
closed my eyes and prayed for strength instead. Then I heard
the sound of liquid and felt something warm splash against my
bare legs. I opened my eyes to see that they were pissing on me.
On and on it went – clearly they weren't being deprived of
things to drink – then finally the stream faded to a trickle and
they buttoned their trousers up again.

Don't show any emotion; don't move, I willed myself.

One of them said something and the other one laughed.
Then they took it in turns to stand right in front of me and spit
in my face.

Don't flinch. I stared blankly ahead, and then finally they
bored of me and went on their way, leaving the smell of their
urine clinging to me like a curse.

I looked up at the sky, willing the moon to reappear, but she
remained hidden, and I didn't blame her. I wouldn't want to
look down at the horrors taking place on earth if I had the
choice. I'd tried so hard to remain strong and defiant, but the
contempt with which the men had treated me left far deeper
scars than the *Blockalteste*'s whipping, and they'd reopened old
wounds.

I remembered Madame Bellamy once trying to explain my
father's anger towards me. 'It is as if he has a disease,' she'd said,
holding a cold compress to my swollen eye, 'a disease of the
mind. That is why you must never take it personally, no matter
what he says. When he tells you that you are to blame for your
mother's death, it's his illness talking, not him.' I always found it
hard to understand this theory – whenever my father launched
one of his tirades about how my birth had caused the health

problems that ultimately led to Maman's death, he might have been drunk, but he was very convincing. And, after all, it was the truth.

A stabbing pain pierced my heart as I thought of the mother I'd only known from a handful of old sepia photographs. If she hadn't fallen pregnant with me, she would still be alive. Just like Tomasz, I'd been responsible for taking another life. Maybe not intentionally, but I had been to blame for her death.

The sour smell of the guards' urine filled my nostrils and clung to the back of my throat. I'd tried so hard to escape my past, to literally write myself into a new and happy future, but here I was again, the subject of insults and abuse. I felt my knees begin to weaken and a tear trickled down my face. Maybe it would be better to fall to the ground and be shot. We were surely all going to die in this place, after all; what was the point in dragging it out?

But then I thought of Danielle and something deep inside of me rallied. I couldn't leave her here to fend for herself. I was all she had in this place, the closest thing to family. How ironic that for so many years I had longed to be part of a loving family. I never could have imagined finding it in a place as terrible as this.

I looked up to the sky once more, and this time I was reminded of something Solly had once told me about there being two types of sorrow, a good and bad kind. The bad kind is when a person sits in a corner and broods over any misfortune, and the good is the sorrow a person feels at losing something. 'It is like a man who has seen his house burn to the ground,' I heard Solly's voice echoing back at me through time. 'He feels genuine grief at what he has lost, but then, if he is willing to find joy in his soul, he starts building a new house. And with every stone that is laid, his sorrow diminishes and his joy grows.'

A mist began creeping across the ground from the bogs surrounding the camp and I hugged myself to fend off the growing chill. My life as I knew it had been burned to the ground, but like the man in the story, I could choose to focus on helping Danielle and Macaroon, and anyone else who might need me too. As if celebrating my decision, the moon finally reappeared, casting its warm amber glow all around me.

21

DECEMBER 1942, AUSCHWITZ

'Once upon a time, there was a young woodcutter who lived in a deep dark forest, the kind where the trees are so old and gnarled and full of character they look like people.'

'What was his name?' Danielle asked from beside me in the bunk, her teeth chattering from the sharp December wind blowing through the wooden slats of the barracks.

'*Her* name – the woodcutter was a girl,' I replied.

'Excellent,' Macaroon murmured from the other side of Danielle.

In the past two months, we'd had several new intakes in our hut, and even though some women had died, including Hannah, who had been sent to the infirmary and never returned, it was becoming increasingly crowded. Macaroon had moved down to our bunk, which I was really glad of. The three of us were now as inseparable as sisters – or perhaps two eccentric aunts and their niece. A woman named Sophie had also started sharing our bunk. She'd only been in the camp a week and was still in a stunned state, barely saying a word. I glanced across at her, lying on the other side of Macaroon. Her eyes were shut, but I could tell from the way her eyelids were twitching that she wasn't asleep.

Macaroon started scratching her arm. 'Sorry,' she whispered. 'They're itching like crazy.' The hut wasn't just becoming overcrowded with women; the lice infestation was growing worse by the day too.

'Don't scratch, it only makes it worse, and you're making me itchy too,' Danielle urged. 'Keep telling the story, Etty, to take her mind off it.'

'The woodcutter's name was Ruth,' I continued, in a tribute to my mother, 'and she'd lived on her own in the woods ever since her parents were killed in terrible, tragic circumstances.'

'What happened to them?' Danielle asked.

'Er – her father was eaten by a wolf and her mother was eaten by a crazed piglet.' Thankfully, this elicited a giggle from Danielle and I noticed the faintest trace of a smile appear on Sophie's lips. 'Every day, Ruth would go out fishing for her dinner in the stream that ran through the forest. And every afternoon, she would chop fresh wood for the fire so that she may keep warm and cook her dinner.'

'Oh, what I would give to be by a fire now,' Macaroon sighed.

'Me too,' Danielle murmured.

'Well, if you listen to my story, you will learn how to kindle a fire of your very own any time you want.'

'Really?' Danielle shifted slightly to stare at me.

'Yes, so shh please and allow the storyteller to continue.'

'Better do as she says,' Macaroon said drily. 'You know how temperamental those creative types can be.'

'So, one day, Ruth was hard at work chopping wood when a wicked old crone named Zubata appeared.'

'Zubata.' Danielle giggled again, a sound that was sweeter than a chorus of angels to my ears.

'Yes, so named because she had the teeth of a horse,' I whispered. I'd named my tale's nemesis after one of the most senior female guards at the camp, the dreaded Aufseherin Dreschel, whom the Russian prisoners had nicknamed Zubata, meaning 'toothy one'. 'She was thin and mean and went everywhere with her vicious bloodhound, and she loved nothing more than to cause misery wherever she went.'

'What did she do to Ruth?' Danielle asked, clearly concerned.

'When she came across Ruth, she asked her what she was doing. Ruth replied that she was chopping wood for her fire. Zubata gave a sinister chuckle and put a curse upon Ruth's axe. "From now on, you won't be able to gather any more wood," she hissed, "and you won't be able to have any more fires."'

'I'm not sure I like this story,' Danielle muttered.

'Yes, it's not making my itching any better,' Macaroon agreed.

'Oh please.' I gave a dramatic sigh. 'Everyone knows that a good story involves triumph over adversity. You have to be patient: this is the adversity; the triumph is coming.'

'OK,' Danielle said.

'So the evil Zubata and her bloodthirsty hound set off through the forest in search of more lives to ruin and Ruth returned to her cottage, cold and afraid. How would she survive now she had no source of heat?'

In the bunk above ours, one of the new intakes began softly sobbing.

Danielle felt for my hand and held it tightly. 'Keep going,' she whispered.

'So Ruth sat in front of the hearth looking at the few logs she had left. If she burned them now, she'd have no fuel left for the rest of the winter, but she was so cold. "Please," she pleaded. "Tell me what to do?"'

'Who was she talking to?' Danielle asked.

'Anyone who might be listening,' I replied.

'I hope it wasn't God, because he definitely wouldn't be listening,' Macaroon said darkly. Like many others in Auschwitz, over the past few months her faith in God's ability to hear our prayers had all but disappeared. When I'd come up with the idea for my tale while working earlier, I'd been hoping it might help rekindle a little hope in her. But now I wasn't so sure. Constant tiredness and hunger were taking their toll on my imagination, but I had to keep going; I couldn't leave my audience hanging.

'And, to Ruth's surprise, she heard a voice coming from the chimney.'

'What did it say?' Danielle asked.

'It said, "If you help me out of this chimney, I'll show you how to keep a fire burning forever,"' I replied, putting on a comical, squeaky voice.

'Who was it?' Danielle questioned.

'If you let me tell the story, you'll find out!'

'Sorry.' She snuggled into me.

'"Of course," Ruth replied, and she peered up the chimney to see a tiny pixie with a long white beard and pointed ears.'

'There was a pixie in her chimney?' Macaroon said.

'Yes. This is a fairy tale, remember.'

'Of course. I'm sorry, please continue.'

'Thank you. So Ruth helped the pixie out of her chimney. "My name is Shalom," he said, brushing the soot from his long white beard.'

'But what was he doing in her chimney?' Macaroon asked.

Danielle giggled. She always enjoyed the way Macaroon and I would banter.

'"What were you doing in my chimney?" Ruth asked. "Looking for Père Noël," Shalom replied.'

'Was it Christmas?' Danielle asked and I fought the urge to scream. I somehow doubted Madame d'Aulnoy suffered from so many interruptions in her literary salon. Nevertheless, I carried on valiantly.

'"But it isn't Christmas for another week," Ruth said. "I like to be early," Shalom replied.' Thankfully, my audience seemed satisfied by this. 'So Ruth told Shalom all about the wicked Zubata's curse and he stroked his beard thoughtfully for a moment before speaking...' I paused for effect.

'What did he say?' Danielle whispered.

'He told Ruth to light the fire and then he would teach her how she could make sure it would never go out,' I replied. 'So Ruth did as she was told and lit the last of her logs.'

'And...?' Macaroon asked impatiently.

'And Shalom told her that every day Ruth would have to come and sit in front of the fire and think of something that made her happy, and that way the flames would never go out.'

'But how could happy thoughts keep a fire going?' Danielle asked.

'"But how can happy thoughts keep a fire going?" Ruth asked,' I said, taking a deep breath and praying for patience. 'Shalom gave Ruth a wise smile, his brown eyes twinkling in the glow from the flames. "Try it now and see," he said. So Ruth sat in front of the fire and she thought of the babbling brook where she caught her fish, and how the water sighing over the rocks always calmed her. And she thought of the dragonflies and the songbirds and the way the green of the trees seemed to wrap itself around her like the most soothing of blankets. And as she thought such happy thoughts, the flames in the hearth leapt higher and higher and Ruth basked in their warmth.'

'But didn't the logs burn away?' Danielle asked.

'No. Shalom bid Ruth farewell, reminding her that she needed to stoke the fire with her happy thoughts every day, then he went on his way. And, sure enough, Ruth did as she was told and the fire never went out. And she never had to chop any more wood again either, which made her even happier, as it meant she could spend more time seeking out things that made her happy, to think about to keep the fire going.'

'But I don't understand how that helps us,' Danielle said flatly.

'Whenever you think a happy thought, it makes you feel warm inside, does it not?' I replied, praying they'd see what I was getting at and that I hadn't made them long for a real fire, and made the cold and the itching feel even worse.

'I'm going to try it and see,' Macaroon said. 'I'm going to think of the day I opened my gallery; that was such a happy day.'

'Excellent,' I replied, unsure if she was being genuine or just trying to help me keep Danielle's spirits up. 'How about you, Danielle?' I held my breath and waited.

'I'm going to think about the time Xavier Fortin kissed me,' she finally replied.

'Excuse me!' I exclaimed. 'And who is Xavier Fortin?'

'The most handsome boy in my school,' she replied coyly.

'I'm going to think of the day I gave birth to my son,' Sophie murmured, making us all start with surprise. It was the first thing she'd ever said without being prompted. She opened her eyes and smiled at me. 'It was the most wonderful day of my life.'

'I can imagine,' I replied. 'It must be incredible to become a mother.'

'It truly is.' She closed her eyes again, the faintest of smiles upon her lips.

'What will you think of, Galette?' Macaroon asked.

'Think of the day you met Tomasz,' Danielle said eagerly.

I laughed. 'If you insist.' But as I closed my eyes, I thought of Solly, the inspiration for my wise pixie, Shalom, and the time he'd told me I was like a daughter to him and I felt a warm glow inside.

Danielle rolled onto her side and Macaroon and I followed

suit, snuggling together like a set of spoons in a drawer, and I pictured our happy thoughts kindling flames of hope and love inside of us. In a world where absolutely everything else had been stripped away, it was comforting to know that we still had this one thing to hold on to. We still had control over the stories we told ourselves and each other.

22

FEBRUARY 1943, AUSCHWITZ

When I first told my Happy Fire fairy tale, I had no idea how much we would come to depend upon it. If the first few months at Auschwitz had been hard, the arrival of winter took things to a new level of hardship. In spite of the biting cold, we were still expected to go outside for roll call every morning at 3.30. I started having nightmares about becoming stuck in the gluey mud, or even worse, falling over in it. If you fell over in the mud or snow, there was no hope of clean, dry clothes to change into. One of the women in our hut fell during roll call, trying to avoid being snapped at by one of the guards' dogs. Her muddy dress froze to her back that day working in the field and she died a couple of days later from hypothermia. Death and the possibility of succumbing to its long-reaching grasp was ever-present now.

Every time a new intake of prisoners arrived at the camp, the chimney would start belching its foul smoke into the leaden sky, and shortly after there would be a chorus of anguished wails, as those who had survived the selection process learned what had become of the loved ones they'd been parted from. Those of us who'd been in the camp for a few months no longer flinched at their cries – outwardly at least. A numbness seemed to have taken hold, caused partly by shock and partly by the cold. There was the overwhelming sense that everything was shrinking in on itself – that *we* were shrinking in on ourselves. But at night, Macaroon, Danielle and I would cuddle up tight on our bunk and we would take it in turn to share a happy thought to keep our fire of hope burning. Every day at work, I prayed I'd make it through to the night, when I could take refuge in the nest of stories we created. I truly believe that our nest woven from words is what kept me alive that winter, and never more so than one terrible day in February.

I had the sense that something was wrong when we were woken even earlier than usual and marched outside of the camp for roll call so that all of the women could be lined up together. As we filed onto the frozen carpet of snow and into our neat rows, the guards and their dogs barked at us to keep to our perfect formation. I'd learned long ago to escape into the world of a story during roll call as sometimes if the numbers didn't tally, we could be standing there for hours. But that morning any attempt at telling myself a story was interrupted by my mind asking anxious questions. Why had they got us up so early and made us all stand together? And why were the SS guards, snugly dressed in their warm capes and greatcoats, not making any effort to count us?

Hours passed and the sun began to rise, causing the snow to glimmer rosy gold. I could no longer feel my feet in their wooden clogs and a driving wind whipped along our lines, piercing through our threadbare clothes. I saw Danielle shivering beside me and gestured at her to switch places when the guards weren't looking, so that I was on the outside. Not that it made that much difference. I glanced down at her hands and saw that they'd turned purple.

On and on we stood there in silence, the only sound the

distant cawing of crows, a sound that became increasingly grating and sinister as more time passed.

'What's happening?' Danielle whispered.

'Shh, stay calm,' Macaroon replied from the other side of her.

'Keep stoking the fire,' I whispered, our code for thinking happy thoughts.

Sophie, who was standing on the other side of Macaroon, leaned forwards and gave me a small, grateful smile.

I heard the sound of a horse and turned to see an SS officer riding over, grasping the reins in leather-gloved hands. Oh what I would have given for a pair of gloves, or a hat, or a cape. He trotted around us and I held my breath, hoping that this was what the wait had been for and one nod from him would mean we'd be able to get on with our day. By that point even the prospect of working in the frozen fields was attractive. At least we'd be able to move and try to bring some life back into our frozen limbs. But the officer rode away, and we remained standing in our lines.

As the sun rose in the sky, the light bounced off the snow, dazzling my eyes. So many times in recent weeks I'd longed to see the sun again, but now it only brought discomfort. I shuffled from one foot to the other, trying to get some circulation going, but it was so painful.

The woman in front of me started swaying from side to side.

'Are you all right?' I whispered, leaning forward.

A second later, she went crashing to the ground. Then, a couple of minutes later, another woman collapsed. I looked round for any kind of response from the guards, but the women's bodies were left where they fell. The awful thought occurred to me that maybe this was the point of the exercise. Had we been made to stand there like thousands of neatly arranged dominoes until one by one we toppled over and froze to death? *No!* a voice cried from somewhere deep inside of me.

We couldn't die. We had to survive. I had to live to tell the world what happened here to stop it from ever happening again.

I saw a flashback of Tomasz sitting at my table on Erev Yom Kippur. He'd planted a seed of purpose in me that night and I was not going to let the Germans and their cruel games kill it, or me.

'Keep moving your feet,' I whispered to Danielle. 'Keep stoking the fire,' I whispered to Macaroon.

At midday, when the sun was at its highest, the eerie silence was broken by the low rumble of engines. I looked up to see a procession of trucks trundling past.

'Oh no!' Danielle gasped.

The backs of the trucks were laden with naked corpses, a higgledy-piggledy mess of shaven heads and thin pale limbs, jutting out at awkward angles.

'Stoke the fire!' I hissed. 'Don't look.'

I closed my eyes and tried desperately to conjure a story. *Once upon a time...*

'She's alive!' someone cried.

I opened my eyes and saw to my horror that some of the bodies on the truck passing us were moving and moaning.

'Some of the people on there are alive!' another woman cried to one of the guards.

We watched as the guard looked at the truck, then started to laugh. I'm not sure I've ever felt a hatred like I felt towards the guard in that moment. What was happening here, in this Valley of Death? Not just to us but to our captors? I understood that in every society there are people who are capable of committing despicable acts, but they are usually the smallest minority. In this hellish place, there had to be thousands of guards. How had so many of them become so evil and so quickly? How was this guard able to look at the sight of living people being transported to the crematorium and laugh?

I thought of what Solly had said about us needing to love

even harder to compensate for the Germans' hatred, but they'd killed him too. Surely even Solly would be moved to anger by now. All I knew was that in that moment it was hatred that kept me warm, that kept me determined not to fall like a domino into the snow. And determination that they should not get away with it, that I had to do everything I could to get justice. We watched in stunned silence as the trucks drove on towards the chimney. The thought that those poor people might be about to be burned alive was too much to bear. I closed my eyes tight and recalled conversations I'd had with Solly over and over again to stop my spirit from breaking.

It wasn't until the sun was sinking behind the skeletal trees in the distance that we were given the order to return to the barracks. By that point, I'd wet myself, causing the snow around my feet to turn yellow, and it was as if I'd forgotten how to use my legs, but somehow, Macaroon, Danielle and I managed to help each other keep from stumbling. I looked around for Sophie, but there was no sign of her. I reassured myself that she must be somewhere behind us. The frozen ground was littered with bodies, as if they'd been picked off one by one throughout the day by invisible snipers. Again, I was dumbfounded by the cruelty. It would have been kinder to shoot them, rather than have them die a slow, painful death in front of everyone else. The snow, which had been so pristine and white that morning was now stained with yellow and brown patches and the smell of diarrhoea hung in the frigid air. But it turned out that the Germans' sadistic game wasn't over yet. As we drew closer to the gates back into the barracks, a panicked message made its way back down the line of women. 'When you get to the gate, run!'

What did this mean? I frowned at Macaroon in confusion.

'I can barely walk,' Danielle whimpered, looking dangerously close to giving up.

'Hold hands,' I instructed, and Macaroon and I grabbed one of Danielle's hands each.

Yelps of pain echoed back from the front of the crowd and the sound of the guards yelling, '*Schnell! Schnell!*' which I knew by then meant, 'Faster! Faster!' Was this how they planned on killing the rest of us off? Getting us to embark upon some kind of crazy race.

As we drew closer to the gate, I saw the cause of the commotion. Two lines of guards and their kapo helpers with truncheons and whips at the ready had formed a tunnel of sorts for us to pass through, while they rained down blows. Any women who fell over were being yanked out by the guards.

'Get in between us,' I told Danielle as we formed a single file, Macaroon at the front and me behind. 'Don't worry, I'm right behind you,' I said.

I'm not sure where we got the strength, but somehow we made it through the hellish passageway. The blows on my frozen back stung like mad but brought the blood pulsing back through my frozen body.

When we got back into our hut, we looked around, eyes wide, like frightened rabbits. Had everyone made it back? Who was missing? Someone organised a head count.

'There are fifteen missing,' she cried.

I was so numb with shock by that point, all I could do was give thanks that Danielle and Macaroon had survived. We perched in a row on the edge of our bunk.

'Where's Sophie?' Danielle asked, hugging her stick-thin arms around her trembling body.

'I don't know,' I replied, looking around anxiously. 'I assumed she was behind us.'

'We need some helpers,' the ferret-faced kapo called, appearing in the doorway.

If I hadn't been so shell-shocked, I'd have laughed in disbelief. After everything they'd just put us through, now they wanted our help!

'We need to collect the women who've fallen,' she continued.

The women you've murdered! I wanted to yell.

I stayed firmly put, but Macaroon stood up. I looked at her questioningly.

'I want to find Sophie,' she whispered and I nodded.

As Macaroon and a couple of others went back outside, I put my arm around Danielle and pulled her to me. I was expecting her to cry, but she just stared blankly into space, which was even more worrying.

Macaroon returned a while later with a similarly vacant expression.

'Did you find her?' I asked, hoping against hope there'd been some kind of miracle.

Macaroon nodded. 'She... she died,' she stammered. 'Oh Galette, there are so many bodies. They're piling them up outside the infirmary. And the rats are...' She broke off in tears, but she didn't need to say any more.

'Come,' I said, gesturing at her to sit in between Danielle and me. 'We'll warm you up.'

Macaroon sat down between us and we rubbed her back and stroked her head. *Please don't give up*, I kept silently praying. *Please don't give up.* And as the sound of gentle sobbing filled the freezing hut, my prayer for Macaroon became a prayer for us all.

23

MARCH 1943, AUSCHWITZ

Like most of the other women in our barracks, there was a marked difference in Macaroon and Danielle after that day of death in the snow. Their eyes, the one part of their bodies that had maintained some kind of life, dimmed somehow, and their gazes became increasingly vacant. I tried so hard to spark them back to life, but it had become almost impossible to come up with hopeful stories in the light of what was going on around us. With the now omnipresent stench of death, the notion of telling an uplifting story or urging them to think happy thoughts felt tasteless and crass. To make matters even worse, our daily serving of soup had been changed from lunchtime to after the evening roll call and we were now banned from taking our precious red enamel bowls anywhere. In the Valley of Death, our bowls meant life and to not have them constantly on our person brought a fresh source of anxiety.

Then, one evening, as we prepared our aching bodies for bed, a stern-faced woman named Dora made her way down the hut to me. She wore a red triangle on her chest rather than the yellow star, which I had learned meant she was a political prisoner. Even though she was now as emaciated as the rest of us,

Dora still had a powerful presence about her; perhaps it was her perpetual glare. I hadn't had many interactions with her, but I had the feeling she didn't suffer fools gladly.

'Are you the storyteller?' she said bluntly by way of greeting.

'Excuse me?' I replied.

'Are you the one who tells stories to help people remember who they are?' she asked, as curtly as if she was asking, *Are you the one who's been putting lice in everyone's clothes?* In spite of her blunt tone, I was secretly delighted to be referred to in this way, overjoyed that in some quarters at least I was known for my purpose rather than just being seen as a number.

'Yes, she is,' Danielle piped up from her seat on the edge of our bunk. Macaroon, who was already lying down, nodded in agreement.

'I need you to help me,' Dora went on, and clearly it was an order rather than a request.

'OK,' I answered tentatively.

'One of my bunkmates is in a terrible way since what happened, you know, that day in the snow.'

I nodded. 'Aren't we all?'

'And I found out that it's her birthday today,' Dora continued. 'And I wanted to do something for her, give her some kind of gift.' She looked at me expectantly.

'Yes?'

'Could you tell her one of your stories?'

'Oh, er, yes, of course. Is there any particular type of story you'd like me to tell, anything in particular you think she'd like to hear?'

Dora looked at me as if I was crazy. 'Well, something that will give her hope again, of course.'

I looked at Macaroon and Danielle and raised my eyebrows. Macaroon gave me a sympathetic smile and I nodded to Dora.

'OK, I'll let everyone know,' Dora said.

'Everyone?' I echoed.

'Yes.' Dora turned and made her way back up the hut, limping slightly.

'But... what...?' I stuttered after her.

'All right, everyone, I have an announcement to make,' Dora called, and the chatter in the hut faded.

My stomach flipped; surely she wasn't expecting me to tell the entire hut a story, and with no notice? But apparently that was exactly what she had in mind.

'As some of you are aware, today is Nicole's birthday.' She pointed to an ashen-faced young woman, sitting on a top bunk by her. As all eyes turned to stare at Nicole, she visibly recoiled. 'And I wanted to mark the occasion by giving her some kind of gift. But what do you give the woman who has everything?' Dora said drily, raising a few laughs. 'I mean, these days diamonds and sumptuous feasts are so passé!' More laughter rippled through the hut. 'But then I heard on the grapevine that there is a storyteller amongst us – a professional storyteller, no less. Some of you may already be familiar with her.' She turned and pointed at me and all eyes followed. I felt my face flushing red. 'And rumour has it, she's been helping keep up morale with her stories.'

'She certainly has,' Macaroon called from our bunk and, to my delight and surprise, I heard a couple of the other women nearby murmur their agreement.

'So, without further ado, I would like to introduce...' She looked down the hut at me. 'I'm sorry, I don't know your name.'

'It's Etty,' I replied weakly.

'Etty,' Dora called. 'Come.' She beckoned me over. 'Gather round,' she called to the rest of the hut.

I glanced at the night-watch sitting by the door. It wasn't lights out yet, but I wasn't sure she'd approve of us all congregating like this. I was half hoping she'd order us into our bunks early and save me from the ordeal, but unfortunately she looked on, expressionless.

'Sit here, in the middle,' Dora instructed, ushering me to take a seat on the concrete bank in the middle of the hut.

I did as I was told and sat down, opposite poor Nicole, who was looking as mortified as I felt.

Help! I silently screamed, praying to Solly for inspiration. And as if answering my prayer, a memory suddenly came back to me, of a story he had told me after the Germans had confiscated my bicycle and I'd turned up at his place beside myself with grief. It had helped raise my spirits in my hour of need, so hopefully it would do the same for Nicole – and everyone else listening.

I took a deep breath and cleared my throat.

'Once upon a time,' I began, my voice wavering.

'I can't hear you,' someone called from the far end of the hut.

'Once upon a time,' I repeated, my voice stronger. I pictured Solly behind me, his gnarled hand on my shoulder. 'Once upon a time, there was a king who, despite living in a magnificent palace with a loving family, couldn't ever feel happy. All day long, his servants tried to make him joyful, cooking him feasts, bringing him the finest clothes, putting on shows, but still he remained unhappy.'

'Sounds like my husband,' Dora quipped.

'Mine too,' someone else called, causing a few chuckles.

'Obviously being in a perpetual state of misery was hardly enjoyable – least of all for his poor long-suffering wife, the queen,' I added for Dora's benefit and she nodded approvingly. 'So he decided to seek the counsel of one of his wisest sages. "No matter what I do, or eat, or buy, I can't seem to feel happy," the king told him. The sage rubbed his long moustache thoughtfully before answering. "You must find the happiest man in the kingdom and wear his shirt for an entire day," he told the king. "Then, and only then, will you be cured and find true joy."

'The king was so desperate to find happiness, he readily agreed and the next day he put on some plain clothes as a disguise and set off through his kingdom in search of the happiest man he could find. But no one he met fit the bill. Even if they appeared joyful at first, it turned out that everyone had something they weren't happy about. The king trudged on for days and days, until his legs ached and the soles of his shoes had worn thin. Finally, he arrived at a forest on the very outskirts of the kingdom. As he walked through the trees, he heard a very joyful sound indeed – the sound of a man singing. He followed the sound until he found the man in a clearing, chopping wood, singing away at the top of his voice.

'"Excuse me," the king said. "I'm looking for the happiest man in the land. You wouldn't happen to be him, would you?"

'"Why yes, I am indeed," the woodcutter replied with a beaming smile.

'"At last!" the king exclaimed. "I've been told that I need to wear your shirt for a day in order to feel happy. I wonder if you would be kind enough to lend it to me."

'"I would love to," the man replied, dancing over. "But there's just one small problem." He opened his jacket with a flourish, to reveal his bare chest. "I don't have a shirt!"

'The king stared in confusion for a moment before he realised the wisdom in the journey the sage had sent him on. The woodcutter didn't need anything to be happy. He didn't need fine food, or shows, or expensive clothes; he didn't even own a shirt! He just was happy. As the lesson sank in, the king began to laugh and laugh, and finally he experienced true joy.'

As I finished the tale, I glanced at Nicole anxiously. Her expression was blank.

'I don't understand,' someone piped up from behind me. 'How can the woodcutter just *be* happy for no reason?'

'Because he chooses to be,' I replied, my skin crawling. Did the moral of the story feel crass in the context of the camp? Had it made everyone, including the birthday girl, feel worse?

'But how can you choose to be happy when everything's been taken from you?' someone else asked, causing my spirits to sink even further.

'Of course you can,' Dora replied in her usual brusque manner. 'And you have to, don't you see?' She took Nicole's hand and in that moment I was reminded of my relationship with Danielle. For all of her rough edges, Dora clearly cared deeply for the younger woman. 'If we make our happiness dependent on other people or things, it's like... like...'

'Building a house on sand,' I offered.

'Precisely.' Dora nodded at me. 'But if we can find happiness from within ourselves – well, then we have a firm foundation.'

'But how do we find it within ourselves?' Nicole murmured. The fact that she was finally showing some interest sparked a glimmer of hope within me.

'Tell them the Happy Fire fairy tale,' Danielle said, making me jump. I'd been so preoccupied with telling the story, I hadn't seen her come and stand right beside me. I gave her a grateful smile.

'What's the Happy Fire fairy tale?' Dora asked.

I glanced over to the night-watch, but she appeared completely disinterested in what was happening, staring at the floor.

And so I began. 'Once upon a time...'

This story got a far more enthusiastic reception, the crazed piglet line raising a lot of laughs, ditto the references to Zubata. Even Nicole appeared to warm to the subject matter and when I reached the end of my tale, she told me that she was going to relive her childhood holidays in the South of France.

'My brother and I would spend all day on the beach,

building castles made of sand and hunting for crabs in the rock pools,' she said with a teary smile. 'They were the most magical times. I felt so wild, so free.'

'You can go back there and rekindle those feelings any time you like, any time you need, through reliving your memories,' I urged her. 'And no one can stop you.'

'Thank you,' she whispered.

The women all began returning to their bunks, murmuring about the memories they were going to relive and I pictured their words like tiny shooting stars blazing through the hut. As I turned to go, Dora grabbed my arm.

'Thank you,' she said, looking me straight in the eye. 'If you ever need anything, let me know.'

I nodded. Dora worked in *Kanada* – the warehouse where the Germans processed all of the belongings they stole from the new arrivals at the camp. Most of the stolen booty was sent by train to Germany, but it was an open secret that the staff who worked there were sometimes able to sneak out food, and other priceless items, such as candles or spoons.

'I mean it,' she said. She leaned closer and whispered in my ear. 'I thought I was going to lose Nicole. I thought she'd given up, but you've helped her find a source of happiness, and I can't think of a better birthday gift.' She planted a kiss on my cheek with the force of a punch.

I turned and made my way back to my bunk, murmured thanks from the women I passed ringing in my ears. I knew that what I was doing was only bringing them temporary relief. I knew that my stories wouldn't be able to stop the Germans' brutality, but the fact that I was able to do something small to help lift morale was like finding the North Star on the stormiest of nights and I was so grateful for having found this purpose to guide me.

24

MARCH 1943, AUSCHWITZ

Gradually, winter began to thaw and buttercups sprang up in the fields beyond the camp like tiny splashes of bright yellow paint. It was a sight that filled me with joy and woe in equal measure. While it was wonderful to be reminded of nature's resilience and beauty, it was heart-breaking to think that I might never live to pick another flower again. Like just about everything else, the picking of flowers was now strictly forbidden. Every day as we marched to the fields where we dug so that the Germans could keep expanding their Valley of Death, I distracted myself by drifting up and out of my feeble body with its swollen legs and bleeding gums and sore-covered skin and into the world of my imagination. The women in the block were now regularly asking me for stories so I'd spend my days trying to come up with new ideas, or remember one of the numerous stories Solly told me to recount to them later that night. It was hugely rewarding to see the effect my tales had upon my fellow hut-mates as I helped them remember that they were still the authors and heroes of their own stories, in their hearts and minds at least. But the Germans had so much power over us physically, it was hard to stay optimistic in the face of such relentless cruelty. I prayed over and over again for God to give me a sign that this wasn't all in vain, that I still had a reason to be hopeful. And one incredible day in March, when I least expected it, my prayer was answered.

The day had been anything but incredible to begin with. As we marched past the pen where the guards trained their dogs to tear at dummies wearing our blue and white striped uniform, the dreaded Aufseherin Dreschel began plucking women out of the line. Thin and plain, with buck teeth, Dreschel was the kind of woman who in any other context wouldn't have seemed menacing at all. But here, with her snarling bloodhound companion and the might of the SS behind her, she was all-powerful, and she revelled in it like no other. We knew that whenever Dreschel picked a woman out at random, we would likely never see her again. So it was a sight that instantly sent terror coursing through me.

Please don't pick them, I silently begged, as I watched Macaroon and Danielle walking in front of me. Macaroon had a sore on her foot that was causing her to limp and I was terrified that this would be enough to warrant a summons. As we drew closer, I snuck a glance at Dreschel. Oh, if only I could see her magically transported to the streets I grew up on in Marseilles, without her hound or her Nazi backers. She wouldn't survive five minutes. Hatred began burning through my fear. I saw her look at Macaroon, then glance down at her foot. *Please, please, please.*

Dreschel looked as if she was about to say something to Macaroon, but then she noticed the woman beside her and yanked her out of the line, pointing with her whip at a bulge beneath her dress. Another guard set upon the woman to reveal the cause of the protrusion – she'd tucked her precious bowl beneath her vest. Dreschel flung the bowl onto the ground, stamping it down with her heavy boots, until it was covered in mud. As she watched, helpless, the woman cried as if grieving the loss of a family member. How strange this new world was, where money and prestige meant nothing, and a simple bowl could mean the difference between life or death. Thankfully, the woman was allowed to march on, but she continued sobbing quietly.

My body almost caved in on itself in relief as Macaroon, Danielle and I passed Dreschel by. We'd survived to see another day, but for how long would our luck continue – if you could call it luck. *Please, God, give me something to be hopeful for, something to keep me strong,* I silently prayed yet again.

As we drew close to the place where we were to be digging ditches, we passed a procession of male prisoners.

Please, God, please, I continued to silently plead.

And then something made me look up. Was it God or was it fate, or was it pure coincidence? I don't know. But I looked up and my gaze locked with one of the men. Like everyone else, his stare was vacant at first, but then I noticed a flicker of recognition and a split second later, I spotted a jagged scar on the side of his face. Was it? Could it be? He was so emaciated I wasn't sure, but then he called my name.

'Etty!' A smile lit up his face and for the briefest of moments that beautiful smile was all I could see.

'Tomasz?' I gasped, as he broke out of his line and ran over to greet me. 'Tomasz!'

'Tomasz?' I heard Danielle echo, turning round to look.

One of the SS guards accompanying the men started yelling. But all I could see and think about and focus on was this miracle standing in front of me.

Tomasz grabbed my hand in his. His arms were thin and his collarbone jutted out above the collar of his striped shirt. 'I'm sorry,' he said hurriedly.

'Pardon?' was all I was able to utter. It felt like a surreal dream.

'I'm sorry, for what I did that night.'

I fixed my gaze on his and his skeletal appearance faded away. As I stared into his dark eyes, I no longer saw the heartless brute I'd imagined him to be. All I could see was the kind and loving soul who'd rescued Solly and Aurelie. 'It's OK.' I saw guards approaching in the corner of my vision but kept my gaze on him. 'I'm sorry too. For what I said to you. Solly told me...'

He tugged on my jacket, as if trying to pull me closer to him. But then the guard's hands were grabbing him and I felt a crack to the back of my head. I stumbled forwards, seeing stars, and felt arms reaching out to catch me. Danielle and Macaroon.

'Jewish whore!' one of the kapos spat at me, wielding her truncheon.

As my vision cleared, I looked over my shoulder to see Tomasz being jostled back into his row and marched on. 'Spring is coming,' he called back to me.

I didn't understand why he was saying this but I could see a beaming smile on his face and that was all I needed.

'Was that *the* Tomasz?' Danielle whispered as we continued on our way.

'Yes,' I replied, giddy from the surprise and the blow to the head.

'It was just like my story!' she exclaimed, her eyes wide.

'Yes, well, kind of.'

'What did he say to you?'

'I'll tell you later,' I replied, not wanting to dilute the moment by talking about it. I wanted some time to savour it to myself, to relive and process every second of the precious encounter.

That day, I felt a renewed strength as I dug. Tomasz was here at Auschwitz, and judging by his thin frame, he certainly wasn't boxing for any favours. Now I knew the truth about what he'd been doing at Drancy, this made me feel sad and concerned. And he'd apologised for what had happened the night we met in the Pletzl. All day long, I relived the moment, which must have only lasted a few seconds, stretching it like elastic over hours.

Thank you! I silently cried, looking up at the darkening sky. *Thank you for providing me with a moment of magic to sustain me.*

As we were marched back to the barracks that evening, I put my hands in my pockets to keep them warm and felt my fingertips brush against something soft and velvety. I took it out and saw a bright yellow buttercup. I quickly stuffed it back in my pocket before anyone saw. Where had it come from? How had it got there? I replayed the scene with Tomasz for about the thousandth time, and remembered how he'd tugged on my jacket. I'd thought he was trying to embrace me, but had he been putting the flower in my pocket? Is that why he called out 'Spring is coming'? Was he referring to the flower he'd given me? Once again, Tomasz had appeared in my life and left me with a mystery to solve, but for once the puzzle was delightful.

When we went to bed that night, Macaroon and Danielle couldn't wait to question me, and I was overjoyed to see their interest sparking life into their eyes.

'What did Tomasz say to you?' Danielle whispered as soon as the lights went out.

'Who is this mysterious Tomasz?' Macaroon asked, before whimpering in pain.

'Are you all right?' I asked.

'Yes, it's just my foot. Answer our questions.'

'Yes, answer them,' Danielle chimed in.

'He told me he was sorry,' I whispered.

'What for?' Macaroon asked.

'We had a bit of a disagreement the last time I saw him.'

'What, on Yom Kippur Eve?' Danielle asked.

'No, I saw him again after that, before Drancy.'

'I can't believe you didn't tell me!' she exclaimed. 'Why didn't you tell me?'

'I was too embarrassed.'

'Why?'

'It's too embarrassing to tell you.' My cheeks began to burn at the memory.

'So why was he apologising?' Danielle asked.

Much as it pleased me to see her curiosity sparking back to life, I couldn't help wishing she'd stop with the questioning. I didn't want the magic of what had happened that morning to be sullied by the painful memories of before.

'I suppose he was sorry that we'd fallen out,' I replied. 'But forget all that...' I paused for dramatic effect. 'I think he gave me a gift.'

'What do you mean?' Macaroon asked, shifting slightly in the bunk.

'What kind of gift?' Danielle whispered.

'A flower, look.' I took the buttercup from my pocket and held it out.

Danielle reached out and stroked the glossy yellow petals. 'Oh, this is the most romantic thing I have ever seen!' she exclaimed. 'How did he give it to you?'

'I felt him pull on my jacket, before the guard tore him away. Then, on the way back this evening, I discovered it in my pocket. He must have put it there. I don't know how else it could have got there.'

'This is even more romantic than my story about you both,' Danielle murmured.

'Is that why he shouted something about spring?' Macaroon asked.

'I think so.' I carefully tucked the flower back in my pocket. In this place where we had nothing, it felt more precious than all the gold in the world.

We fell into silence for a few moments and then I heard Danielle softly sob.

'What's wrong?' I asked, stroking her head.

'I don't want either of you to die. I want you and Tomasz to be together again.'

'Oh, thank you.' I hugged her to me, then whispered in her ear. 'I think God is keeping us alive for a reason. You and me and Macaroon.'

'Really?'

'Yes.'

'But what is the reason?'

'Maybe it is to help each other get through this,' I said, thinking of the story Solly had told me, the one I'd used in my article for *Resistance*, about the two men and the hay wagon.

'Yes, maybe.' Danielle rolled onto her side, the way she always did when she was ready for sleep, so I followed suit.

Macaroon remained lying on her back, though.

'Are you all right, Macaroon?'

'Yes, I just feel a little feverish,' she replied. 'Hopefully it will break by the morning.'

'I hope so,' I replied, concern mingling with my new-found joy.

'Galette,' she whispered.

'Yes?'

'Thank you.'

'For what?'

'For being you.'

I reached for her hand in the dark to give it a squeeze. Her palm was clammy with a cold sweat.

25

MARCH 1943, AUSCHWITZ

In the middle of the night, I was woken by the sound of Macaroon moaning. Her eyes were shut and her face was glistening. I gently placed the back of my hand on her forehead; her skin was burning up.

'Oh, Galette,' she moaned. 'Why is it so hot?'

'It's your fever,' I replied. 'Let me see if I can get you some water.'

I slipped from the bunk and down the hut to the night-watch, on her seat beside the bucket.

'Please, is there any way my friend could have some water?' I asked her. 'She has a fever.'

The night-watch was the only kapo I'd encountered who'd shown me a vague semblance of humanity, but, to my dismay, she shook her head. I don't know if seeing Tomasz had emboldened me or I was so desperate to help Macaroon, but for once I didn't humbly accept her refusal.

I looked her in the eyes in the flickering lamplight. 'I hope no one you love ever gets sick and is denied help,' I hissed before turning and walking away.

I'd just got back to our bunk when I saw the silhouette of

the night-watch marching down the hut after me. I cursed myself for being stupid enough to talk back to her. Not because I was afraid of what she might do to me, but because I needed to take care of Macaroon. I waited by my bunk to hear the punishment she was going to dole out to me. But instead, as she drew closer, she held something out to me.

'Here,' she whispered, handing me a damp cloth. 'Put this on her brow; hopefully it will bring the fever down.' Then she turned and marched away.

I stood motionless for a moment, completely taken off guard by this act of compassion. Then I got back into our bunk and placed the cloth on Macaroon's forehead.

'Oh!' she gasped, opening her eyes. 'How did you...?'

'Shh,' I whispered. 'Let's see if we can break your fever.'

'Thank you,' Macaroon murmured. 'Galette?'

'Yes?'

'Will you tell me one of your stories?'

'Of course,' I replied and, too exhausted to come up with anything spontaneous, I told her the tale Solly had told me about the rabbi helping the Christian peasant with his upturned hay wagon. When I reached the end and both men had continued on their way together, Macaroon grasped my hand.

'That day in the shower,' she murmured. 'The day we first met.'

'Yes?' I whispered.

'That was when you came across me and my upturned wagon.'

'I think it was the other way round,' I replied, remembering how Macaroon had started humming 'La Marseillaise' and explained what the German guards were saying, and how much that had helped me.

'I guess it doesn't matter,' she whispered. 'Both men in the story helped each other in the end.'

'That's true!' I agreed. 'And we're going to carry on helping each other.'

'Galette,' she whispered, her voice weak.

'Yes?'

'I think I'm dying.'

'No!' I clamped the damp cloth tighter to her head, as if it could somehow suck the fever from her body.

'My foot, it's really bad.'

'You mustn't give up,' I urged. 'Please.'

'But it wouldn't be giving up, don't you see?' She stared at me with an intensity that frightened me. 'It would be letting go,' she continued, before closing her eyes.

'But I don't want you to let go. Danielle and I – we need you.' I felt pitiful, but I couldn't bear the thought of life in the camp without Macaroon. 'You'll be better in the morning. Once your fever's gone,' I added, hoping she couldn't detect the desperation in my voice.

'Galette?'

'Yes?'

'I love you.'

'Don't say that!' I replied.

She opened her eyes and smiled. 'Don't say I love you?'

'Don't say goodbye.' I stroked her thin arm. Her skin was bumpy with sores. 'Now get some sleep, while I watch over you.'

'You need sleep too,' she said, closing her eyes.

'It's my turn to help lift your wagon,' I replied.

I remained awake for the rest of the night, stroking Macaroon's arm and keeping the damp rag pressed to her face. *Please get better, please get better, please get better*, I chanted over and over in my head, like a fraught lullaby.

When the kapos arrived for morning roll call, I was racked

with fear and concern. What would happen to Macaroon if she wasn't able to stand? Or if she wasn't fit enough for work? She would be sent to the dreaded infirmary in Block 25, and we all knew the only place that led to was the crematorium.

'We have to take care of Macaroon,' I whispered to Danielle as soon as she woke. 'She had a fever in the night; we have to help her stand up and get to roll call.'

'Of course,' she replied, rubbing her eyes.

But when I tried to rouse Macaroon, it was as if she was drunk; her speech was slurred and her eyes seemed unable to focus.

Ferret Face started making her way down the hut, dragging stragglers from their bunks by their collars and banging on bunks with her truncheon.

'Macaroon!' I hissed. 'You have to get up.'

Danielle and I grabbed an arm each and pulled her from the bunk. But as soon as Macaroon was standing, she cried out in pain and I looked down to see that her foot had turned black.

'Quick, get her socks on,' I said to Danielle.

She got them on and we somehow managed to prop Macaroon up between us just as Ferret Face arrived at our bunk.

'What's that smell?' she said, shrivelling up her nose.

I bit my lip to stop myself from saying anything.

'Stinking Jews,' she spat. 'Filthy animals.'

She had just turned to go when Macaroon stirred into life. '*Casse-toi!*' she yelled.

Ferret Face froze and Danielle and I stared at each other in horror. I didn't know if Ferret Face knew enough French to know she was being cursed at, but it was clear from the way Macaroon had yelled that it wasn't a compliment.

'What did you say?' Ferret Face turned her beady-eyed stare on Macaroon, tapping her truncheon in her hand.

'*Brûle en l'enfer!*' Macaroon shouted.

'What is she saying?' Ferret Face yelled. The other women

who'd been getting ready for roll call all froze and a terrible silence descended on the hut.

'*Salope!*' Macaroon spat and the kapo took her whip from her belt.

'She's delirious,' I said hastily. 'She doesn't know what she's saying.'

'Is that so?' Ferret Face beckoned to her fellow kapo. 'Take her to Block Twenty-Five.'

'No!' Danielle gasped and my stomach churned.

'She'll be better soon,' I said, desperately trying to salvage things.

'If you love her so much, you can take her there, both of you,' Ferret Face hissed to me and Danielle. She barked at her fellow kapo to accompany us.

I tried to protest. 'Please, she doesn't need to go there, she—'

Ferret Face slapped me on the side of my face. 'Go!'

As Danielle and I half propped, half carried Macaroon down the hut, the women all formed lines either side, bowing their heads. Their show of respect would have been touching if it didn't remind me of people watching a funeral cortège. Were Danielle and I the pall-bearers, taking our barely living friend to her imminent death? I was hardly able to breathe from the paralysing mixture of fear and sorrow.

'I'm so sorry,' I whispered in Macaroon's ear as soon as we got outside.

'Don't be.' Macaroon gazed up at me, head slumped to one side. 'I finally got to tell that bitch what I think of her; now I can die happy.'

'Don't say that!' Danielle cried, prompting the kapo walking behind us to yell at us to be quiet.

As we walked through the dark, past the endless rows of long low barracks, I longed desperately for time to stand still. Every second that passed, every step we took was a step closer to losing Macaroon.

'I told her,' Macaroon murmured, 'and it felt so damned good.'

All too soon, the ominous Block 25 came into view. At first, it seemed as if the ground beside the block was moving and I wondered if I too had become delirious, but then I realised that it was alive with rats. As we drew closer, Macaroon started humming *'La Marseillaise'* under her breath, defiant to the very end.

It's not the end, I tried convincing myself, but something in me knew that it was and having been deprived the opportunity to say a proper farewell to Solly and Marguerite, I didn't want to be left with the same regret.

'Macaroon,' I said, as we reached the door.

'Yes, Galette?'

'I love you.'

26

APRIL 1943, AUSCHWITZ

A couple of days after we took Macaroon to the infirmary, Dora whispered to me in the queue for our evening soup that she had died.

'I saw them putting her body on the lorry on my way back from *Kanada*,' she told me. 'I'm so sorry.'

I had to fight the completely unfair urge to pummel her with my fists. It was hardly her fault after all; she was only the messenger. Thankfully, Danielle wasn't in earshot. I really didn't know how she'd cope with yet another loss. I nodded tersely at Dora and took my soup back to our bunk. Yet more people had arrived the day before, so Macaroon's space had already been taken by a Polish woman who spoke no French.

That night when we lay down, I felt Macaroon's loss acutely. How would I remain positive without her wit to spark off? How would I carry on without her warmth and comradeship to keep me going? Perhaps it was because we'd spent so much time at such close quarters, but losing her truly felt like losing a limb and the pain was unbearable. Trying to find a source of comfort, I felt in my pocket for the flower Tomasz had given me. It had lost its moisture and was becoming dry and brittle. As I touched it, I remembered his voice calling, 'Spring is coming.' Was it, though? The weather might have been getting warmer, but it felt as if we were now stuck in a perpetual winter. In spite of myself, I couldn't help a sob escaping.

'Oh, Galette,' Danielle whispered, hugging me to her. 'Don't cry!'

It was the first time she'd ever used the cake nickname Macaroon had bestowed upon me and I was so touched, I cried even more.

'It's OK, we still have each other,' she whispered, planting a kiss on my cheek.

But for how long? an ominous voice echoed in my mind. I chose to ignore it and hugged her tight. 'You're a wonderful young woman, Danielle,' I whispered. 'You're so brave and strong. Your mother would be so proud of you.'

'You can call me Gateau if you like,' she whispered back. 'I think it's what Macaroon would have wanted.' She paused for a moment. 'She's dead, isn't she?'

'Yes,' I said, my voice cracking.

'Why did she have to shout at the ferret? Why couldn't she have kept those words inside her head? Then she might still be with us.'

'She told me the last night she was here that she knew she was dying. I suppose she thought she had nothing left to lose.' I thought of Macaroon yelling at Ferret Face, her old spark returning one last time. 'I think she wanted her story to have a good ending,' I said, smiling through my tears.

'What's good about dying?' Danielle replied with a sniff.

'I mean the way she yelled at Ferret Face. She ended her life in courage and truth.'

'Hmm, maybe,' Danielle muttered before rolling onto her side to go to sleep.

I stared up at the slats of the bunk above, remembering how that first day here Macaroon had leaned down to check I was

OK. Yes, hers was a story of courage and truth, and I made a silent vow to her, and to myself, that if I survived the Valley of Death, I would make sure to tell it.

That spring, a new young guard arrived at the camp. She stood out not only because she had the figure and blonde, styled hair of a Hollywood starlet but also because wherever she went, she brought a trail of her floral perfume with her. The first time I smelled her, sashaying past us during evening roll call clasping her plaited whip in her hands, I was instantly snapped from my exhausted stupor. The thought that this woman must have sat in front of her dresser, curling her hair, applying her make-up and spritzing herself with scent before coming to torment us was nauseating. According to Dora, who seemed to be the font of all knowledge, the guard's name was Irma and she was only nineteen. This made her all the more chilling. How could one so young want to do a job like this, in a place like this, and clearly revel in it? Danielle took an instant dislike to her, calling her the Icicle.

'Tell me a story where the Icicle meets a terrible end,' she whispered one night after we'd gone to bed. I was only too happy to oblige.

'Once upon a time, there was a king and queen who tragically had their kingdom stolen from them,' I began, before launching into an adaptation of Madame d'Aulnoy's fairy tale *Finette Cendron*. But in my version of the tale, Finette was renamed Daniette and her evil sisters were named Zubata and Icicle.

As I told the story of how the king and queen had to abandon their daughters because they couldn't afford to feed them, I forgot all about the lice and fleas wreaking havoc on my skin, and I forgot about the now permanent ache in my hip. It was wonderful losing myself in the world of the fairy tale, especially now I was giving it a new twist.

'Daniette's sisters, Zubata and Icicle, were mean and vain and treated her as if she was their servant,' I said as Danielle closed her eyes and snuggled in next to me.

'What did they look like?' she murmured.

'Well, Daniette was that rare creature, a natural beauty,' I replied. 'And even though the sisters starved her, it only seemed to make her more beautiful. It was as if a light shone from within her, giving her a pearly glow, just like the moon.' I noticed a smile playing on Danielle's lips. 'But as for Zubata and Icicle, well, they were the most hideous creatures. Zubata had the face of a horse – the kind of horse that has been stung by a wasp.'

Danielle giggled.

'And Icicle thought she was beautiful, but she didn't realise that true beauty is something that comes from the inside, and her insides, well, they were as ugly as a vat of slithering snakes.'

Danielle shuddered.

'One day, the evil sisters heard that the new king was throwing a ball and this greatly excited them as they thought they might be able to find themselves husbands.'

'What about Daniette?' Danielle asked.

'Her evil sisters made her stay at home and told her that they would beat her if she didn't keep it spick and span.'

'This sounds like the story *Cinderella*,' Danielle said.

'Yes, but this tale is so much better,' I replied. The popular fairy tale *Cinderella* had indeed been derived from Madame d'Aulnoy's *Finette Cendron*, but I thought the original was by far superior.

'Does Daniette have a fairy godmother?' Danielle asked.

'No, but when the sisters left her to go the ball, she found a golden key, which opened an old chest, and inside there were the most beautiful clothes imaginable.'

'Oh, tell me about them, please,' Danielle gasped. 'I would give anything to discover a chest full of beautiful clothes.'

'Perhaps you could describe them,' I suggested, eager to ignite her own imagination.

'Inside the chest there's a beautiful ball gown in pale green,' she eagerly obliged. 'And a sparkling tiara made of diamonds and emeralds.'

'Excellent, and there is also a pair of red velvet slippers embroidered with pearls,' I added.

Danielle gave another satisfied sigh.

'So, Finette— I mean, Daniette, got herself dressed and took herself off to the ball, where she introduced herself as Cendron and everyone paid court to her, including the king's son – a most handsome prince.'

'What was he like?' Danielle murmured, her eyes closed.

'Why don't you tell me?' I replied.

'He was tall, with thick dark brown hair that tumbled in curls around his face,' she whispered. I wondered if she was drawing inspiration from Xavier Fortin, the boy who had once kissed her. 'And he had a dimple in his left cheek.'

'He sounds wonderful,' I said.

'He was – *is*,' she replied, wistfully. 'What happened next?'

'Well, Prince Xavier, for that was his name, was quite enchanted by Daniette, or Cendron as he knew her, and they danced together all night – much to the disgust of the evil sisters, Zubata and Icicle.'

'Didn't they recognise her?' Danielle asked, looking concerned.

'No, her beauty was so dazzling that night it transformed her. And they'd seen her in nothing but rags for so long, she was unrecognisable in her gown.'

Danielle gave a satisfied sigh.

'But then, just as the clock was striking midnight, Daniette saw that her sisters were preparing to leave, so she rushed out without saying goodbye to the prince.'

'Did she get home in time?'

'She did, but in her hurry to go, one of her red velvet slippers fell from her foot.'

'This is just like *Cinderella*.'

'Shh! No interruptions please. Anyway, the prince found the slipper, but then he was taken ill and couldn't leave his bed.'

'What was wrong with him?'

'He was lovesick. And no doctor in the land was able to cure him, so they ordered every woman in the kingdom to come and try on the slipper. The evil sisters were overjoyed when they heard the news, both hoping that the slipper might fit them, and they might marry a prince.'

'They'd better not marry him,' Danielle hissed.

'Don't worry. Thankfully, Daniette found a horse and she managed to get to the castle before them – splashing them with mud as she rode past.'

Danielle giggled.

'And when she put on the slipper and the prince saw that it fitted, he was overjoyed, and he asked her if she'd marry him.'

'And did they live happily ever after?'

'Not so fast. Daniette refused to marry him.'

'What?' Danielle opened her eyes and frowned.

'I told you it was better than *Cinderella*.'

'How is that better?' she asked, clearly horrified. 'Why didn't she marry him?'

'Because his father was the one who had stolen the kingdom from her parents, so she demanded that he restore it to them first – then, and only then, would she marry the prince.'

'And did the king agree?'

'He did.'

'So she married the prince?'

'Yes, eventually.'

Danielle breathed a sigh of relief. 'And what became of Zubata and Icicle?'

I frowned. In the real story, the gracious Finette found husbands for them both, but I wasn't so sure this would be a satisfying ending for Danielle given the circumstances. 'They became Daniette's servants and spent the rest of their days cleaning out the castle toilets.'

Danielle giggled.

I closed my eyes, relieved that I'd helped raise her spirits for another night at least. But then I heard a stifled sob.

'What is it?' I asked. 'What's wrong? Should I have given the evil sisters an even more horrible job?'

'No, no, it isn't that,' she sobbed.

'What is it then?'

'I'm just really sad that I'll never get married.'

'What do you mean, you'll never get married?'

'Or have children.'

'Of course you will. You're still so young. You still have so much life ahead of you. This war won't go on forever,' I said firmly in spite of my own inner doubts.

'But they're killing us,' she whispered. 'And I don't even have my monthly bleed anymore – none of us do – so how will I ever be able to have a baby?'

'Oh, Danielle.' I put my arm around her and pulled her to me.

'And I look so horrible, no man would want to go near me.'

'You mustn't say these things. You don't look horrible at all.'

'Of course I do! We all do! I hate Icicle. I hate her!' she sobbed into my chest.

For a moment, I was struck dumb, unsure what I could possibly say to make her feel any better. Clearly, Icicle's beauty had had a devastating effect on Danielle, no doubt reminding her of how she herself was once a head-turning beauty. Hopelessness descended upon me, and once more I prayed to Solly for inspiration. If only he was here, I was sure he'd have something wise to say.

Be her mirror, echoed in my mind. *Tell her what you see.*

'You're only saying these things because you can't see what I see,' I said.

'What do you mean?' She sniffed.

'When I look at you, all I see is beauty.'

'You're just saying that to try to make me feel better.'

'No,' I replied firmly. 'I'm saying it because it's true. And I don't just see beauty. I see courage and wisdom and such spark.'

'You do?'

'Absolutely. You're the kind of person I would base a heroine on in one of my novels because you are so much more than just beautiful. You're funny and smart too.'

'Really?'

'Yes. There's never a dull moment when you're around, but Icicle...' I paused for effect.

'Yes?' she asked eagerly.

'She could never be a heroine.'

'Why?'

'Because she needs to bully others to feel good about herself, just like the other guards. And they're all ugly right down to their core.' I took hold of her hands and squeezed them tightly. 'From now on, I am going to be your mirror,' I said. 'And any time you are feeling low, I want you to look at me and say, "Mirror, tell me what you see," and I shall tell you gladly.' I held my breath, praying that my words might have done some good.

'Thank you,' she whispered.

I breathed a sigh of relief. 'At the moment, we are like flowers that have been deprived of sunlight and water. So yes, we are wilting and weak, but it won't always be like this.'

'What do you mean?'

'As soon as we're able to eat and drink properly again, our bodies will recover. Our hair will grow back, and our monthly bleeds will return too. That's why it's so important that we don't give up. Think of all the incredible adventures you might still have to come. You could end up married to Xavier Fortin and having ten children.'

'Etty!' she exclaimed, but I could tell she was trying not to laugh.

'Please don't give up,' I whispered, my voice wavering.

'I'll try not to,' she whispered back.

We fell silent for a moment. The Polish woman on the other side of me shifted and let out a gentle sigh.

I stared into the dark and the ache in my hip throbbed. I thought of the sores erupting all over my body and the way my breasts had deflated into loose flaps of skin. Was what I had said to Danielle true; were we really just flowers in need of water and sunlight, or had the Germans inflicted so much damage we were like the buttercup Tomasz had given me? Destined to wither and wilt and dry until we became nothing but dust?

Tomasz's words echoed in my mind: 'Spring is coming.' Could he have meant the end of the war? Had he heard a rumour that victory was in the Allies' sights? Certainly some of the latest arrivals to the camp from the trains seemed to think so. *Oh please, let it be so.*

I closed my eyes, praying for a wave of sleep to come for me, and clutching the thought that the war might finally end like a life raft.

27

MAY 1943, AUSCHWITZ

One day in early May, Dora approached me as we were queuing for the tap. It was just after four in the morning and the stars were fading and the night sky changing from black to navy. In my former life it was a sight that always filled me with excitement at the prospect of a new day ahead, but now it only signified another day in the Valley of Death.

'I was wondering if you might help me with something,' she muttered.

I was feeling nauseous from lack of sleep, so I hoped she wasn't going to ask me to tell her a story right there on the spot. 'Of course, what's wrong?'

'I – uh – I was wondering. How do you stay so... so hopeful?' She looked down at the ground as if embarrassed at having admitted a weakness, and indeed I was shocked to see the normally bullish Dora showing a sign of vulnerability. To be truthful, it unnerved me. If one of our most resilient hutmates began to unravel, what hope was there for the rest of us?

'I don't,' I answered truthfully. 'I just manage to stay optimistic more than half of the time, I suppose, even if it's only fifty-one per cent of the time. Has something happened?' I questioned.

She continued looking at the ground and sighed. 'I found something, yesterday,' she whispered. 'In *Kanada*. Something that really upset me.'

'What was it?' I whispered back, instantly feeling apprehensive at what might have upset her so.

'The belongings of someone I knew. Someone I helped – before I was arrested.'

'Helped them how?'

'Helped them escape the Germans – or at least I thought I did.'

We inched nearer to the tap.

'What do you mean?'

She looked around, then leaned closer to me. 'My husband and I, when the round-ups began, we helped Jewish people escape. We hid them in the attic above our butcher's shop. That's how I ended up in here. We got caught.'

'That's incredible.' So that's how she got the red triangle on her chest. My respect for Dora grew. 'It must have taken so much courage.'

She shrugged as if risking her life to help others was a mere trifle. 'I had to sort a suitcase yesterday and it was full of the belongings of someone I helped. I recognised her clothes – I'd given some of them to her; they'd belonged to me.' She looked distraught.

'Oh no, I'm so sorry.' It had to be bad enough sorting through the stolen possessions, especially knowing that most of the owners would have been condemned to death, but to realise that the owner was someone you knew must have been horrific.

'I'm not one to complain,' Dora said in her normal, no-nonsense manner, 'but it really... seeing that cardigan of mine, and those shoes – it threw me.'

'I'm not surprised.'

'So I was just – I wanted to know – if you had a story that could help a person who feels as if their hope is deserting them.'

Even though my tired brain felt too sluggish to string a sentence together, let alone a story, I nodded. If Dora could risk her life to save strangers then I would move heaven and earth to conjure up the right words to help her. 'Come and see me this evening, and I'll tell it to you.'

We reached the tap and she gestured at me to go first. I filled my bowl and used it to wash my face. It seemed crazy, given the circumstances and how filthy we were otherwise, but there was something about this simple act that made me feel as if all wasn't lost, as if I was still clinging to some vestige of civilisation.

As Dora filled her bowl, I turned to go. She tapped me on the shoulder and held out her water.

'What? No! I can't...'

'I want you to,' she said firmly.

I took the bowl from her and poured the water over my head. It felt so refreshing. The luxury of an extra bowlful was a precious gift indeed. I placed my hand on Dora's arm. 'Tonight, I shall tell you a story that will help you feel better, I promise.'

Of course, my mind promptly went blank and stayed that way for most of the day. I so badly wanted to help Dora, it was as if the pressure had caused my imagination to run for the hills. The truth was, I could understand why she felt her hope deserting her. Up until this point, she'd probably comforted herself with the thought that she'd managed to save others before her arrest. It must have made her feel that it had all been worth something. But to discover that one of those people at least had ended up falling into the Nazis' clutches must have been like a punch to the gut. I had to come up with something to restore her faith and make her feel better, but what? Thankfully, as we were making our way back from our day's labour, I remembered a story Solly told me when I'd been close to giving up hope over the introduction of the yellow *JUIF* badges. I only hoped it would help Dora the way it had helped me.

That night at lights-out, Dora appeared at our bunk. I'd already told Danielle that we might be having a guest and she shuffled up instantly. I got the feeling she was slightly intimidated by the blunt-speaking Dora, and I could empathise. Now it was time to tell her story, my mouth became dry and my heart rate quickened.

'I'm going to tell you a Jewish fable,' I said quietly as she settled in beside me. At least then if she didn't like it, she wouldn't be able to blame my storytelling abilities.

'I love fables,' Danielle murmured.

'Hmm,' Dora muttered. 'I find them slightly childish.'

Trying to ignore her lack of enthusiasm, I said a quick prayer to Solly and began.

'Once upon a time, there was a very poor man – although he was only poor financially – in every other way he was rich indeed.'

'How do you mean?' Danielle asked.

'Well, not only had he been blessed with a very intelligent wife, but they had also been blessed with four kind, talented and beautiful daughters.'

'What were their names?' Danielle asked, prompting me to inwardly groan. I wasn't sure if Dora would be able to tolerate her endless questions. Plus the daughters' names hadn't featured in the original fable, so I needed to do some quick thinking.

'Their names were Hope, Faith, Love and... and Patience,' I replied.

Dora gave a little grunt. I wasn't sure if it was of appreciation or derision. I carried on, regardless.

'The moment the oldest daughter came of age—'

'Which one was the oldest?' Danielle interrupted.

'Patience,' I replied, praying I'd be patient enough to get to the end of the fable without gagging her.

'Anyway, as I was saying, as soon as Patience came of age, matchmakers began knocking on their door, offering suggestions of suitors – all fine young men, Torah scholars no less.'

'I think I'd rather marry a Hollywood actor,' Danielle muttered. 'I'm not sure a Torah scholar would be all that much fun.'

'Back in the time when this fable is set, I'm sure Torah scholars were the equivalent of Hollywood stars,' I replied. 'Anyway, it was all in vain, because as soon as the matchmakers found out that the father had no money to offer as a dowry, they told him they wouldn't be able to help his daughters get married after all.'

'What, even though the daughters were kind and talented and beautiful?' Danielle shifted onto her elbow and stared at me indignantly, as if I myself had been one of the matchmakers.

'It's just the way things were back then,' I replied, 'but it really isn't important in the grand scheme of the story.'

'I'd say it was very important,' Danielle huffed.

'So what happened next?' Dora piped up.

'Thank you for asking,' I replied, nudging Danielle in the ribs.

She sighed and lay back down.

'Next, the man went to see his friends and neighbours and begged them to help and give him some money, but none of them were able, as they were living in poverty too.'

'Well, this is a cheery tale,' Dora muttered.

I was starting to feel as if I had a pair of woodpeckers chipping away either side of my head, what with her muttering in one ear and Danielle questioning in the other. I swallowed hard, trying to suppress the wave of exhaustion suddenly threatening to overwhelm me.

'As the man made his way home, he was so overcome with

worry and sorrow for his daughters, he didn't notice he'd taken a wrong turning,' I pressed on. 'And he was so tired from travelling so far, he decided to sit down and take a rest beneath a tree.' I paused, half expecting Danielle to ask what kind of tree, but both my woodpeckers mercifully remained silent. 'He'd only been resting for a couple of minutes when he heard a man calling to him. "Excuse me, what do you think you're doing? You're trespassing on private property."'

'Who was it?' Danielle asked.

'The man opened his eyes with a start and saw to his horror that he'd somehow wandered into the grounds of the local lord, and to make matters even worse, it was the lord himself who'd apprehended him. "I'm so sorry, Your Lordship," the man cried. "I've had a very difficult day and I was in a need of a rest and your tree looked so inviting, I just wanted to sit for a while and lean against its trunk and absorb some of its strength. I'll be on my way." But as the man began scrambling to his feet, the lord gestured at him to stay. "I can see from the lines on your brow that you have indeed been suffering," he said. "Please, tell me the cause of your troubles. Perhaps I'll be able to help you."'

'Clearly he wasn't a German,' Dora remarked wryly, causing Danielle to giggle.

'Clearly,' I replied before carrying on. 'So the man told him about his wonderful daughters and how he felt he'd let them down by not being able to provide a dowry for them, and the lord listened sympathetically. Once the man reached the end of his tale, the lord took a leather purse full of coins from his pocket. "Please, take this," he said, handing the man the purse, "and let your daughters be married and your family be happy." As the man began protesting that it was far too generous, the lord shook his head. "I'm an old man and I have all the money I need. It would fill my heart with joy to know that I have helped you and your family, and that is worth all the money in the world to me."'

'Definitely not a German,' Dora muttered.

'The poor man stumbled home,' I continued, 'dazed from this remarkable turn of events, and it wasn't long before news of his good fortune spread throughout the village. Two of the villagers who heard the tale thought that it sounded like an excellent way to make some easy money and decided to try their luck. So they set off for the lord's estate and sat down beneath one of the trees. "Who knew it could be this easy to get rich," one of them sniggered to the other as they leaned against the trunk. A moment later, the lord appeared and asked them what they were doing. "Oh master, please show us your mercy," one of the men cried. "We were feeling so poor and hopeless that we decided to lean against your tree to try to absorb some of its strength." The lord frowned at them and shook his head. "You're nothing but a pair of charlatans," he bellowed. "Get up and get off my property!"'

'But why did he say that to them and not to the first man?' Danielle asked.

'*That* is about to be revealed,' I replied. 'As the men got up to leave, one of them asked the lord, "Why were you so friendly and understanding to our friend who came here, but when we told you a similar story you refused to believe us?" "It's very simple," the lord replied. "When a man is truly alone, he has no choice but to turn to a tree for support. But there are two of you. You can be each other's support. That told me that you weren't quite as desperate as you were pretending to be." Acknowledging that he was absolutely right, the men shrugged and set off for home.' I looked at Dora. 'And the moral of the story is, as long as you have a friend to support you, you have something to be grateful for and a reason to feel hope.' I held my breath, hoping that the message of the fable would warm her heart the way it had mine when Solly had told it to me. 'You have a friend in me,' I added. 'And you can lean on me any time.'

'And me,' Danielle piped up.

There was a moment's silence and then Dora coughed, or was it a sob? I couldn't be sure. 'Thank you,' she said gruffly. 'Thank you.' She sat up, but before returning to her own bunk, she placed one of her calloused hands upon my cheek. 'I appreciate you,' she whispered, before making her way up the darkened hut. The fable had worked. I thought of Solly and how I'd been able to lean on him yet again, like the oldest and strongest of trees, and how this in turn meant that others could lean on me, and my eyes filled with grateful tears.

JUNE 1943, AUSCHWITZ

As spring warmed into summer, typhus began tearing through the camp with renewed vigour, so much so that even the Germans weren't able to escape it, with the chief doctor, the wife of the camp commander and Dreschel all falling victim to the disease. The thought of our principal torturess, Zubata, suffering from the fever, diarrhoea and stomach cramps that had plagued so many of us that year was, I have to admit, a satisfying one, and I found myself wishing on more than one occasion that it might claim her life. I wasn't proud of the fact that I found it so easy to wish someone dead and I was certain that if Solly had still been alive he would have had something to say about it, but one thing I'd learned by then was that living with the constant threat of death changes you. How could it fail to?

In the light of the Germans falling victim to the epidemic, the camp commander announced that he would oversee the next delousing himself and rid the camp of lice once and for all. Long iron troughs of water reeking of gas were set up between the barracks and on the morning of the delousing, we were told that there would be no work that day. Instead, we were ordered to strip naked and bring our clothes outside to be disinfected. As we shuffled outside, we were greeted by the sight of a row of men wearing gas masks standing by the troughs. Our *Block-alteste* yelled at us to drop our clothes in front of the stinking vats. Danielle instantly flinched.

'It's all right,' I whispered. 'Just imagine what it will be like to have a camp with no lice.'

She nodded, grim-faced, and we dropped our clothes by the vats, keeping our gaze on the ground to try to pretend the masked men weren't able to see our naked bodies. As they started gathering our clothes and throwing them into the vats, we were taken to wait for our own delousing in the bathhouse, as always being made to stand in rows of five. I glanced ahead of me at the surreal sight of hundreds of hunched, naked women, their skeletal torsos snowy white in contrast with their arms and the bottoms of their legs, which were tanned from working outside in the sun. Lank folds of skin were the only remaining evidence of their former curves, their former selves. It was a sobering sight, so I did what I always did when sorrow threatened to engulf me: I reached for a thought of something happier, and remembered my encounter with Tomasz. But any joy I felt was short-lived.

'Oh no!' I gasped.

'What is it?' Danielle asked from beside me.

'The buttercup – I left it in my jacket pocket.'

'No!' Danielle cried.

How could I have been so stupid? For months I'd been so careful to remove the flower every Sunday when our clothes were disinfected and tuck it beneath my pillow. Why had I forgotten this time? Hunger and exhaustion were causing my brain to slow down as well as my body.

'Hopefully it will still be there,' Danielle said, linking her hand in mine.

'But you saw those vats. You saw the way the men were pummelling the clothes.' The flower had become so dry and brittle, I was certain there'd be nothing left of it.

After an interminable wait, it was finally our turn to file in for our 'bath' and to have our hair disinfected. As soon as it was done, we hurried back to the troughs. This time I didn't care about the men in their gas masks seeing my naked body; all I cared about was finding my precious flower, or whatever was left of it. Even if there was only a solitary petal. But we returned to the troughs to even more bad news – the deloused clothes had all been dumped into one huge, stinking pile. As we approached, the fumes from the gas were overwhelming. I tried to find my jacket, but it was impossible.

'Just take anything,' a woman beside me cried, gasping for breath.

Unable to stand the smell and the burning sensation in our eyes and lungs, we did as she said, picking out wet clothes and running back to our barracks, blinking and gasping for breath. As we all began waving our clothes in the air in a vain attempt to dry them and shake off the dying lice, I felt as if my heart was breaking. It was ridiculous really, to be so heartbroken over a flower. But over the months, it had been such a symbol of hope for me to cling to, and a connection to Tomasz, knowing that his fingers had once held the buttercup too. Some nights when I touched the flower, I'd imagine that we were holding hands through it. Now, that connection had gone, and because of my own stupidity.

'Are you all right?' Danielle asked as she scrambled into her new set of rags.

I nodded, unable to speak for fear that I might start crying and never stop.

'The flower will never die in your memory,' she said softly, taking hold of my hand. 'And neither will your meetings with

Tomasz. That's what I tell myself about Maman, anyway,' she added, looking down at the ground. And in that moment I felt so much love and gratitude for this girl who had experienced so much horror and loss, my broken heart seemed to glue itself back together.

29

SEPTEMBER 1943, AUSCHWITZ

As the months went by, a new game was invented to pass the time in the evenings and during the endless roll calls, a game called 'Would you rather...?' It basically involved someone posing a question designed to test our longings. Would you rather eat a delicious steak or wear a long fur coat? Would you rather watch a movie featuring your favourite actor or take a luxurious lavender bath? We'd all moan with a bittersweet mixture of yearning and delight as we weighed up the options.

'Would you rather have a box of the richest chocolates or a good night's sleep in a warm bed?' Dora asked, one morning during roll call in September. There was a chill in the air and a low mist clung to the camp, obscuring the base of the watchtowers. We'd been standing in our rows of five for over an hour while the guards counted and re-counted us – dragging the sick and the dying from the barracks to lie on the ground beside us so that their precious numbers would tally up.

'A warm bed,' most people answered.

'Really, not the chocolate?' Dora, who was standing to the left of me, looked perplexed. 'I think I miss chocolate more than my husband.'

A few of us started to laugh. Ever since I'd told Dora the fable about the poor man and the tree, she'd returned to her normal unflappable self and I was hugely grateful for it.

'Silence!' a woman's voice barked from behind us.

I caught a waft of floral perfume and my blood froze. It was the Icicle. As always, her blonde hair had been styled into neat rolls at the nape of her neck beneath her hat and her grey jacket was belted tightly at the waist, emphasising her hourglass figure. She was holding her whip in one hand and a dog on the leash in the other. Like Zubata, she'd taken to parading through the camp with dogs, and the rumour was she deliberately kept them hungry so they'd be more prone to attack the prisoners.

'What is funny?' she asked, fixing her pale blue eyes on Dora.

'Nothing,' Dora muttered.

Without a word of warning, Icicle brought her whip back and cracked Dora across the face, causing her to career sideways into me. I quickly reached out to catch her. The dog started snarling and frothing at the mouth, baring its long, sharp fangs. Dora righted herself, clutching her mouth, blood trickling between her fingers. Icicle continued to stare at her, as if contemplating whether or not to hit her again. Then she raised her whip to summon a couple of nearby kapos instead.

'Take her away,' she said coolly.

'No! Stop!' Dora cried as they each grabbed an arm and started pulling her away.

My mouth went so dry, I was unable to swallow. Every fibre of my being wanted to launch myself at them to try to save Dora, but I knew from bitter experience that this would be futile and only result in me being taken away to be killed too, and then what would happen to Danielle? I'd never felt so powerless.

'Stop! Please!' Dora cried as she was dragged away, causing the dog to bark and growl, tugging on the leash.

I glanced at Danielle standing to my right and noticed a dark patch of urine spreading on the ground by her feet. *Please, God, don't let Icicle notice!*

'There is to be no laughing,' Icicle called, mercifully moving on down the line. 'The next person I catch laughing, I won't be so kind to. I'll let the dog kill them instead.'

Instead of what? I imagined the same thought hanging over all of our heads. How was Dora going to meet her end?

Then, to make things even worse, the band who saw the men off to work every day started to play and strains of a jaunting, rousing melody drifted through the mist, as if taunting us.

That day, we walked to the fields in total silence and we worked in total silence. My hope felt like the last of the brittle autumn leaves, barely clinging to the tree. When we returned to the barracks that evening, flames were hungrily leaping from the chimney in the distance and the smell was fouler than ever. We returned to our hut to find a batch of new women there, fresh off the train; one of them had already taken Dora's space in her bunk, as if she had never existed.

'I hate Icicle! I hate her!' Danielle muttered as soon as we'd gone to bed.

'Shh,' I whispered, stroking her stubbly head. 'We mustn't think about her. We have to think of happier things.' Although, truth be told, I'd thought of nothing but Dora all day.

'Like what?' Danielle hissed. 'There are no happier things.' She rolled onto her side, sighing heavily.

I lay in the dark, trying but failing to find some words of consolation. How had it come to this? That a woman could make a harmless joke and pay for it with her life? And how could another woman, still just a teenager, take her life so casually, as if it were nothing, as if she was snuffing out a louse she'd found on her skirt? Now I understood why 'Where is God?' had become such a common refrain here in the barracks. Man might have created this situation, but why wasn't God doing anything to save us?

Please, God, give us a sign that you're still there, I silently implored.

The next morning, Icicle was at roll call again. This time as she strolled past us with her huge bloodhound, she had a shiny red apple in her hand instead of her whip. She stood before us and held the apple out in front of her, causing it to gleam as it caught the rising sun. Then she sank her perfect white teeth into the fruit, causing a collective intake of breath from the rows of starving women. It had been so long since any of us had seen any fruit, let alone such a perfect specimen. I wanted to moan with longing as the juice erupted onto her ruby painted lips. Oh, to experience the clean, crisp tang of an apple again. Oh, to eat something other than the putrid slops they fed us. Oh, how I wanted to launch myself upon that evil woman and shake some humanity back into her.

She licked her lips, then held the apple out again. Her dog began snarling and straining on the leash.

'Are you hungry, Jewish swine? Would you like to taste my apple?' She threw back her head and let out a sickly laugh, then she placed the apple on the ground and ordered her dog to sit beside it. 'Help yourself, why don't you. It really is delicious,' she said with a smirk before walking away.

One of the women in the front row right by the apple let out a moan of longing.

Don't do it! I silently willed, certain that the dog would have been trained to attack anyone who came close.

The woman took a step towards the apple. The dog growled.

'Don't look,' I hissed to Danielle. 'Close your eyes.'

Thankfully, she did as I asked. The woman reached for the

apple and the dog leapt, clamping its jaw to her arm. Her screams of agony pierced the air.

'Oh!' Danielle cried.

'Shh, it's OK. Keep your eyes closed.' I linked my little finger with hers while the dog tore at the woman's arm.

Icicle stopped and turned, a terrible smile on her face as she watched.

Call off your dog! I wanted to yell, but just like the day before when Dora was taken, I remained mute. We all did. We all stood there while the woman was savaged. I don't think I've ever felt so appalled. Not just at Icicle, but at myself for being so completely and utterly impotent.

Finally, Icicle called off her beast.

'None of you will have breakfast today as a punishment for her greed,' she said, looking down at the woman writhing in pain on the floor before kicking her in the stomach with her booted foot. I was consumed with rage, but with no way to express it, I felt like I might implode.

We filed back into the hut in stunned silence. Danielle was shaking violently.

'We mustn't give up,' I told her as we stood crammed together beside our bunks. 'Remember what I told you. If we give up, she wins.'

Danielle looked at me and shook her head. 'She's already won.'

'Well, I never imagined you would be a quitter,' I said. It was a high-risk strategy as I really didn't want to make Danielle feel even worse. I crossed my fingers and prayed for a sign of her old spark.

'I'm not a quitter,' she bit back, much to my relief.

'That's excellent news because I need your help.'

'With what?'

'Working out a way we can get our revenge on Icicle.'

She gasped. 'But she'll have you killed.'

'Not if we outwit her. And we will outwit her, because she's no match for our intelligence.'

Danielle sighed and shook her head.

That day, as we toiled on our latest project, helping build a road as part of the extension to the camp, I thought long and hard about how I could possibly get revenge on Icicle and help boost Danielle and the others' morale. Dora had been excellent at keeping people's spirits up with her firm attitude and her funny jokes. Her loss was being felt acutely. Could I use the power of storytelling to get revenge and help cheer the others up? I really had no other tools at my disposal. In spite of being weak from no breakfast, the sparks firing from my imagination kept me going as I dug and hauled slabs of stone. It felt good planning something. It slightly eased my feelings of powerlessness and guilt.

Once we'd all settled in our bunks that night, I said a silent prayer to Solly to send me some of his wisdom and, heart pounding, I began to speak – loud enough for the other women in the nearby bunks to hear me.

'Once upon a time, there was a place called Pitchipoi,' I began and I heard someone above give a wry laugh. Danielle turned onto her side to face me. 'Pitchipoi was a very strange place,' I continued, praying my plan would work. 'Its name made it sound like a magical kingdom, full of fun and joy.'

'Huh!' someone further along the hut commented. 'We should be so lucky.'

'The truth is, it *was* a magical kingdom,' I said, praying this didn't prompt a chorus of boos. 'It's just that the magic wasn't where you expected it to be.'

'What do you mean?' a woman asked from the bunk above.

'Well, when you think of a magical kingdom, you imagine magical creatures, such as unicorns, dragons and fairy godmothers. But Pitchipoi was different because it gave the ordinary people who were brought there magical powers. Indeed, when you first arrived you had to walk through a gate that said: "Imagination makes one free".'

I held my breath, aware that I was risking completely alienating my audience before my story had properly begun. We all knew by now that the sign above the entrance to Auschwitz said 'work makes one free'. But no one said a word, so I continued.

'Of course no one really understood what that sign meant when they first saw it, and when they encountered the creatures that lived in Pitchipoi, they could be forgiven for thinking that the place was far from magic.'

Murmurs of agreement rang out from the nearby bunks.

'Tell us about the creatures,' Danielle, my wonderful assistant, said, clearly realising what I was trying to do.

'Well, they were some of the most horrifying monsters the fairy tale world had ever seen – in fact, they were so monstrous even the legendary storytellers Charles Perrault and the Brothers Grimm refused to feature them in their tales.'

To my huge relief, I heard a couple of sniggers at this, so I kept going.

'First there was a beast named Zubata – who had the face of a horse and the personality of a bowl of cold gruel.'

More laughter rang out as people realised who I was talking about.

'And there was another beast called the Ferret who loved her truncheon so much, she named it Walter and slept with it every night, lying next to her on her pillow. But don't worry, she married it in a ceremony on a gondola in Venice, so theirs was not a sinful union.'

This raised more laughter and I pictured sparks like fireflies, lighting the dark.

'But the worst of the monsters who lived in Pitchipoi was Princess Ice Heart, who, as her name implies, had a heart chiselled from the coldest glacier in the Antarctic. She wasn't actually a princess at all; she was actually a snakelike creature with black skin and red eyes. But every morning she would spritz herself in a magic potion that reeked of flowers and it would give her the appearance of a Hollywood movie star. But if you looked closely enough in a certain light, you could see the black scales of her real skin glinting beneath.'

'So how did the people who came to Pitchipoi get their magical powers?' Danielle asked, and for once I was grateful for one of her interruptions.

'Thank you for asking.' I found her hand in the dark and gave it a squeeze of gratitude. 'The monsters in Pitchipoi fed upon people's fear so they did everything they could to prevent them from finding their magic. They starved them half to death, they refused to call them by their names, they would brutally beat them and even set their bloodthirsty hounds upon them, but the one thing they couldn't do was take away people's imaginations, unless, of course, the people let them.'

I held my breath for a moment, aware that I might be on dangerous ground again. But the women listening remained silent.

'And once the people who were brought to Pitchipoi realised this, they realised they had magic powers. I mean, how incredible is it that a person can be starved and beaten and tortured and yet the monsters still can't get inside their heads and their hearts and control their thoughts and dreams?'

'I'd hardly call that freedom,' someone muttered from the bunk above.

'But our imagination is always free,' I replied, hoping I wasn't about to lose my audience. I was acutely aware that what I was trying to convey could be construed as silly or even insensitive in the face of all that was being done to us, but I still believed that it was our only possible source of strength and hope. 'And this is where the magic really begins, because you can travel wherever you want to on the wings of your imagination. Let me give you an example,' I added hastily. 'Once upon a time, there was a woman named Galette – and yes, she'd been named after a cake, but that's a whole other story – who was brought to Pitchipoi and the monsters tried with all their might to break her. But Galette had realised that her imagination gave her magical powers and so, no matter what the monsters put her through, she was able to escape any time she needed. Sometimes she escaped into happy memories of her past. Other times, she escaped into hopeful dreams of the future. And sometimes she would entertain herself with fantasies of Princess Ice Heart and her monstrous pals meeting a terrible end.'

'I do that most days too,' someone said, prompting murmurs of agreement.

'And even though telling herself stories seemed like such an insignificant thing to do in the face of the horrors of the monsters of Pitchipoi, Galette realised that her mind was the one place where she could still achieve victory over them.'

Once again, I held my breath and waited. I heard someone sigh, but the others remained silent.

'So, are we supposed to live forever only in our imagination?' someone asked.

'What if we want to live in the real world?' said another. 'And go back to our real lives.'

'Yes,' another muttered, and my heart sank.

'We will one day,' Danielle said quietly. 'But, until then, our imaginations can help keep us strong.'

I gave her hand another grateful squeeze.

'Maybe,' someone said from the bunk next to ours.

Silence fell, broken only by the rattling cough of someone at the other end of the hut. I felt disappointed that my story hadn't elicited a more enthusiastic response, but it had reached Danielle, and that meant the world to me.

She snuggled up to me. 'Thank you, Galette,' she whispered in my ear.

'I think I'm going to let my imagination take me to Paris tonight,' someone from the bunk above said.

'I'm going to the opera,' someone else said with a laugh.

And then, one by one, the women announced where they'd be travelling to on the wings of their imagination.

I closed my eyes and breathed a sigh of relief. My story appeared to have worked, but for how long would I be able to keep kindling their faltering hope? I pushed the fear from my mind and focused on taking a flight of fancy to the pre-war dance halls of Pigalle instead.

30

YOM KIPPUR, OCTOBER 1943, AUSCHWITZ

By the time Yom Kippur came around again, the wings of the imagination game, inspired by my tale, had spread through our hut like wildfire – like the typhus, which had returned with a vengeance along with the constant stream of new transports arriving at the camp. The game was a welcome distraction and became a regular nightly pastime in our bunks before going to sleep. There was always someone willing to share where they wanted to travel to that night, or where they'd travelled to that day, while their body had been toiling away. On Erev Yom Kippur, I announced that I would be travelling back to the eve of Yom Kippur three years previously, and shared the story of how Tomasz and I met, which Danielle loved, of course.

Thankfully, this time the guards didn't torment us with delicious food – in fact the offering was even more putrid than normal, the bread as hard as a rock and the 'coffee' ice cold.

After roll call, we were told that we were being sent on a new job. I didn't pay much attention to this, feeling certain it would be just another marshland with the same old stones and ditches and the same old mud clinging to our feet like glue. But, to my delight, we were marched into the forest. I'd seen the forest from afar many times before, but now I was finally getting to walk among the trees I'd gazed at so longingly. And, joy of joy, I was able to hear the rustle of the wind combing through the leaves, and inhale the sweet scent of pine, such a welcome relief from the stench of the camp.

The fact that it was Yom Kippur only made it all the more special, for, surrounded by the beauty of nature, it suddenly became easier to believe that God did exist and he hadn't abandoned us, at least, not completely. The soft sound of the birdsong was like the most moving rendition of Kol Nidre, every note bringing life to my weary body.

Once we reached the heart of the forest, we were ordered to carry rocks needed to form the bed for a new road. Where the road was leading, I had no idea. I felt so drunk on nature and light-headed from hunger, I was numbed from the physical toil and as I worked, I prayed for the dead – for Solly, and Marguerite and Macaroon and Dora and all the other souls I'd seen perish since arriving at the camp. It had become so commonplace to see dead bodies now, stacked outside the barracks every morning for roll call, or lying where they'd fallen by the end of the day, I'd had to become like a horse wearing a pair of blinkers, trying to avoid taking in the full horror. But now, as I prayed, a sadness came over me. This was the second Yom Kippur I'd spent in Auschwitz; would I live to see another? It seemed unlikely. But I pushed that thought from my mind and focused on remembering the loved ones I'd lost.

When we returned to the camp, we were made to kneel for evening roll call – the latest new directive designed to try to break us physically and mentally. That night, we were ordered to keep our arms raised as well, to exert even more strain on our broken bodies. As my knees began trembling from the exertion, my father came into my mind and for once I didn't try to push him out. Before I came to Auschwitz, he'd been a monster who haunted my nightmares, but now, in contrast to the guards, he seemed more pitiful than menacing and I was struck again by the strange irony that so much of what I went through as a child had ended up standing me in good stead for the treatment I received in the camp. I wasn't exactly ready to thank my father, but what was the point in holding on to my anger towards him in the light of everything else I had to face?

As I watched wisps of smoke drifting over from the crematory, a random memory from my eighth birthday came back to me. Madame Bellamy had gifted me with a doll with brown wavy hair as glossy as horse chestnuts, rose-pink cheeks and bright blue glass eyes. It had been love at first sight and my new baby, Rosebud, and I were instantly inseparable. That evening, my father had wanted to talk to me, but I'd been preoccupied putting my new baby to bed in a cot I'd made from an old cardboard box. The next thing I knew, he'd taken Rosebud and thrown her at the wall with such force that one of her glass eyes had smashed to smithereens. I'd been devastated, but then to my shock, my father had fallen to his knees and started sobbing too. 'I'm so sorry,' he'd cried over and over. I'd crept up to him, assuming he was apologising to me, but then I heard him crying my dead mother's name. 'Ruth, I'm so sorry!'

As I relived the memory, there on my knees in the middle of the camp, I wondered, was he apologising to my mother because he blamed himself for her death as well as me? Maybe he only blamed me as a way of absolving himself of his own guilt. Maybe I wasn't really to blame at all. Neither of us were. I felt something in me shift, a protective guard around my heart loosen. I raised my aching arms higher, reaching for God in a Yom Kippur prayer, and whispered the words, 'Papa, I forgive you.'

Winter arrived, bringing with it yet more disease. Every day, a new pile of corpses would appear on the snow-covered ground outside the barracks, their contorted limbs and faces frozen forever in the moment death took them. And every day, the bodies would be loaded onto carts and trundled off to the crematory to be turned into the choking smoke that hung over the camp, and we would have to breathe in the remains of the women we had worked and lain beside just the day before. Seeing those bodies each day made one question play over and over in my mind, and I'm sure in the minds of the others: *How long until I join them? How long until I'm just smoke and ashes too?* Those of us who had been there for over a year were seen as having some kind of secret to immortality, but it only made the pressure worse – surely we more than anyone were now living on borrowed time. Surely one day soon our luck would run out. But, instead, Danielle and I had an unexpected upturn in fortune – we were ordered to go and work in the new *Kanada.*

Of course, like everything else in Auschwitz, any good fortune was due to someone else's misfortune. The Germans had needed to build a new warehouse complex to store and sort the belongings they'd stolen from the new arrivals because there were now so many transports arriving at the camp. *Kanada* II had been built in the women's camp and consisted of three rows of ten barracks, with a T-shaped disinfection room at the front. It was situated next door to a crematory, to make stealing from the Germans' victims as effortless as possible. Even though I'd been there for over a year and shouldn't have been surprised at what they were capable of, the fact that the Germans could have used their precious imaginations to conjure something so grotesquely efficient horrified and bewildered me.

Becoming a *Kanada Kommando* was considered a privilege and made Danielle and I both the victims of envy and the subject of popularity. We now had access to food and clothes and shoes, and even though it was strictly forbidden to take things from the warehouse, people did, sparking a fierce bartering system within the barracks.

The first day we reported to work, we had to walk past a group of male prisoners who were unloading a truck full of suitcases and other possessions. Instantly, my heart rate quickened – what if Tomasz was now working here too? But there was no sign of that tell-tale jagged scar on any of their thin faces, much to my disappointment.

As we drew level with the truck, a young man on the back threw a couple of cases onto the ground without looking and one of them struck Danielle's leg, causing her to yelp in pain.

'I'm so sorry!' he called in French, jumping onto the ground and removing his striped cap and holding it to his chest. Like us, he had a yellow star sewn to his chest. 'Are you all right?'

'Yes, I'm fine,' Danielle replied, looking down at the ground, her pale face blushing.

I looked back at the man. Like the rest of us, his painfully thin frame made him appear older from a distance, but up close he didn't look much older than Danielle.

'What's your name?' he said softly.

'Danielle,' she replied.

One of the kapos herding our work party yelled at us to keep going.

'Nice to meet you, Danielle,' the boy called after us. 'I'm Pierre.'

Once inside the barracks we'd been assigned to, we were given our orders and got to work. I was itching to talk to Danielle about her encounter with the boy, hopeful that it might have cheered her up. But as soon as I started opening cases and sorting through people's belongings, a deep sorrow engulfed me. All I could think about was the person these items belonged to. Had they been instructed to walk to the right, or were they now going up in smoke in the building next door?

And what if, like Dora, I happened upon the belongings of someone I used to know?

With every case I unpacked, unwelcome stories began writing themselves in my head, and characters began to emerge. Who was the woman who once wore these clothes now tangled together in a higgledy-piggledy jumble? Was this pink dress with the white daisy pattern her favourite? Where had she worn it? Where was she from? The language on the labels bore clues. The worst were the shoes, imprinted with the feet of those they'd been stolen from – the hollow dips caused by bunions, the scuffs on the heels and the toes. Traces of a journey that was to end in the worst way imaginable. How could they have ever known when they bought these shoes where they'd end up walking them to? And yet I was struck by a wave of longing every time I handled a pair of comfortable, well-made shoes that looked as if they'd be my perfect fit. It was like being trapped in a horrible version of *Finette Cendron* – if the red velvet slipper fitted, it would mean relief from my torturous, ill-fitting clogs, but stealing these shoes would make me no better than the Germans.

I glanced at Danielle, who was working to the right of me. She was holding a pair of tiny blue, buckled children's shoes and tears were streaming down her face.

'Don't think about it,' I whispered. 'Think of something else. Think of Xavier. Make up a story about him in your head.'

She wiped her tears and nodded, but I felt little relief. The only way to survive in this place and stop yourself from going crazy was to force yourself to not think, to not care, to become desensitised to the horror of it all. But if we didn't think and didn't care, would we end up just as heartless as our captors? It was a terrible dilemma, a choice between our sanity and our principles.

· · ·

That night when Danielle and I were standing by our bunk trying to kill the lice on our blanket, I broached the subject of Pierre.

'So, it looks as if you've gained an admirer in Pierre,' I whispered.

Danielle frowned and shook her head. 'I don't think so. He was just apologising for hitting me with the case.'

'Hmm, I'm not so sure – I saw the way he was looking at you.'

'Really?' She looked at me hopefully.

'Absolutely. And the way he took off his hat so respectfully. He seemed like the perfect gentleman.'

'Are you just saying this to try to make me happy?'

'No!' I slammed my bowl down on the blanket to kill a louse. 'Well, yes, but I'm not lying; I'm merely reporting what happened.'

'Hmm,' she said, but a smile played on her lips.

'Maybe you'll see him again.'

'Maybe, but what difference would it make? It's not as if we're allowed to get to know each other.'

I wasn't sure how to respond to this. She was right and it was probably foolish of me to encourage her to get her hopes up.

We clambered into our bunk, trying not to jostle the women already there – an impossible task – and settled down into our space. Although it would normally be horrible to be so crowded, I was grateful for any warmth our close proximity generated.

'Perhaps you could get to know him in your imagination?' I suggested.

She sighed.

'Remember what you said to me, about our imaginations keeping us strong?'

To my relief, she nodded.

'And what I said about our imaginations setting us free.'

'Yes,' she whispered.

'Let your imagination set you free to meet Pierre. I bet he's thinking about you too, somewhere in the camp.'

'Do you think?' Now she seemed genuinely engaged.

'Of course. I can see him now, lying in his bunk, wondering about the beautiful young woman he met this morning, and hoping he'll meet her again.'

Danielle closed her eyes. 'Thank you, Etty,' she murmured.

'You're welcome.'

I shut my eyes and pictured the two of them drifting up and out of their bodies, into the worlds of their imagination, where anything was possible and the Nazis didn't exist.

Over the next few days, Danielle and I became immune to the horrors of *Kanada*, the way we'd had to become immune to so much else. I still drew the line at smuggling anything out for myself, but I did smuggle a spoon out for one of my bunkmates, a Polish woman named Aleksandra, who'd lost hers. I hoped that whoever the spoon originally belonged to wouldn't have minded it being stolen for this purpose. Surely it was better than it ending up in Germany. Thankfully, Danielle remained strong but every time she came across a child's belongings, she'd become tearful.

'Do you think the owner is crying for this?' she whispered to me one day, taking a rag doll from a suitcase. The doll had clearly been well loved: its woollen hair was tangled and its painted-on face was fading. I pictured the ghost of a child hugging the doll tightly. Another story I didn't want to create.

I shrugged, unable to find any words that could possibly make things better.

'I hate them!' Danielle hissed. 'I hate them for killing the children!'

'Shh.' I glanced around, anxious that a truncheon-wielding kapo might hear her.

Danielle put the doll on a pile with the other toys we'd found.

Clearly, the latest transport to come in had been a rich one. Every other case I went through seemed to contain beautiful clothes from the best Parisian boutiques. As I placed a blue satin slip onto the pile of underwear, I thought of the woman it belonged to and how she'd chosen to bring it with her, how she'd folded it so neatly and tucked it so carefully into the bottom corner of the case. Perhaps it held happy memories. I pictured a lover undressing her, his fingertips caressing the satin. The thought that mine should be the next fingers to touch the slip was an eerie connection that sent a chill right through me. Her case also contained a velvety box of jewellery and a fur stole, all things that would have afforded her a certain status in her previous life but were completely worthless here.

I hope you're still alive, I prayed as I filed her belongings into the appropriate piles, a silent refrain I'd taken to repeating over all of the possessions I handled. It was the only way I could make the job vaguely bearable.

At the end of our first week in *Kanada*, Danielle and I were shuffling into the complex, our feet numb from the cold, when a truck pulled up and Pierre jumped out. When he saw Danielle, his face broke into a beautiful smile of recognition.

'Hello again,' he said softly.

'Hello,' she replied shyly.

'I was hoping I'd see you,' he said, looking equally bashful.

My heart lifted at the sight of such a sweet and innocent moment of connection. What a miracle it was to witness such a thing in that abhorrent place.

Danielle remained tongue-tied and we kept filing onwards.

'She was too,' I called over my shoulder as we walked past.

'Why did you say that?' she exclaimed as soon as we were out of earshot, her face flushed.

'Well, someone had to say something.'

'But you should never tell a boy you like them; they might think you're loose.'

'Have our surroundings somehow escaped you?' I muttered as we hurried inside the barracks. 'This is not the time or the place to be coy.'

As I said it, I was cast back to the night I first met Tomasz, and how our situation had compelled me to be honest about my feelings. Then I thought of the second time I met him and cringed. Perhaps it wasn't a good idea to wear your heart on your sleeve, even in a war.

'I suppose so,' Danielle grudgingly agreed. As we took up our posts, she gave a small smile. 'He said he'd been thinking about me.'

'I know!'

'Do you think he likes me?'

'Of course.'

The smile on her face grew, lighting the room like the most brilliant of sunrises.

'Do you promise me you won't ignore him the next time he speaks to you?' I encouraged.

'If there is a next time.' Her smile faded.

'Oh, I think there will be. I think that you two meeting was *bashert*.'

'What does that mean?'

'You were fated to meet.' Obviously I couldn't be certain about that fact, but it was worth saying it to see the excitement in her eyes.

I'm not sure if it was the power of both our wishful thinking, but we did indeed see Pierre again the following week. This time, he was bringing some belongings into our barracks. I spotted him first and nudged Danielle to get her attention. He put the pile of cases down and walked over to us, putting his hand in his jacket pocket.

'I have a present for you,' he whispered as he drew level with Danielle and with a magician's sleight of hand he slipped something from his pocket to hers. 'For Chanukah. I know it's only one, but maybe you could light it for each of the eight days,' he added before continuing on his way.

Danielle remained frozen rigid, her eyes wide as saucers.

'What is it?' I hissed. 'What did he give you?'

She glanced down into her pocket. 'A candle,' she replied, her eyes glassy with tears.

Candles were frequently smuggled out of *Kanada* and they were a valuable currency in the camp, but the fact that Pierre had given it to her so that she might celebrate the festival of light made it an even more beautiful and thoughtful gift, albeit dangerous.

'Let me take it for you; I don't want you getting caught,' I said, coming close so she could slip it into my pocket.

Later that night when we were in our bunk and had lit the candle, Danielle gazed into the flame and sighed. 'Wasn't it the most romantic thing?'

'It really was.'

'I couldn't believe it when he said he had a gift for me. I shall remember that moment for as long as I live.'

We both fell silent and I wondered if her words had prompted the same subsequent thought – *but for how long will that be?* I tried to push it from my mind. Tonight was the first night of Chanukah and I was determined to stay positive.

'I should blow it out. Save it for the other nights,' Danielle said before extinguishing the flame.

Racking coughs echoed through the hut and amongst them I heard Danielle begin to sob.

'Oh no, what's wrong?' I said, putting my arm round her.

'What if Pierre and I never get the chance to get married and have two children named Charlotte and Leo?' she cried. 'It's what I've been dreaming of, ever since you told me to meet him in my imagination,' she explained. 'In my imagination, we've got married and started a family already.'

'Wowie, you have been busy,' I replied, trying to lift her spirits, but as I pictured her wistful imaginings hovering over our bunk every night – a constellation of hope in the darkness – I had to fight the onset of tears.

'What if we don't have enough time?' she said before letting out another sob.

I had a sudden memory of Solly and our last conversation when we were getting off the train, when he told me that love wasn't measured by a clock. I'd been too bewildered and exhausted to properly understand what he meant back then, but if my time in Auschwitz had taught me anything, it was that love was measured purely and solely by the heart.

'I want to give you a present, for Chanukah,' I whispered, wiping the tears from her face.

'A present?'

'Yes. Unfortunately, Chanukah gelt is a little hard to come by this year, but I would love to give you a story as a gift.'

'That's the greatest gift of all!' she exclaimed.

'I'm very glad to hear it,' I replied, wanting to laugh as I thought back to when we had first met and how distinctly unimpressed she'd been by my storytelling credentials. 'Once upon a time, there were two souls who were destined to meet—'

'Why? Why were they destined to meet?' she asked eagerly.

'Listen, if I am giving you this story as a gift, I would greatly appreciate it if you would give me the gift of not interrupting me,' I said mock sternly.

Danielle giggled. 'I won't, I'm sorry.'

'Thank you. So, as I was saying, there were two souls who were destined to meet.'

'How do you know when souls are destined to meet, though?'

'For goodness' sake!'

'I'm sorry. I just really want to know.'

'Well, if you listen to the story, you might just learn.'

'OK.'

'The business of destiny works something like this,' I said, trying to buy some thinking time. 'It's a giant magical tapestry, and everyone's lives are separate threads running through it. For the pattern to be perfect, certain threads have to intertwine. Sometimes they intertwine just once or twice, and sometimes the threads run together for years, but it's all part of the divine pattern and all threads are equally important.'

'I like that,' Danielle murmured.

'Good.' I planted a kiss on top of her head. 'Anyway, the two souls my story is about were named Danielle and Pierre and in the tapestry of life they were the brightest, silkiest threads and—'

'What colour?'

'Pardon?'

'What colour threads were they?'

'Danielle was deep gold and Pierre was shimmering silver,' I replied, praying for patience.

'Could I be silver? I prefer silver.' She giggled.

'Danielle, who could be a bit demanding, it has to be said, was shimmering silver and Pierre was deep gold. OK?'

'Yes, thank you.'

'So, in a bid to make sure their paths, or rather, their threads crossed, Destiny made sure that they were both born in France.'

'How do you know he was born in France?'

'I don't; I was just assuming. I mean, he has a French name and he speaks French fluently.'

'Yes, of course. Please continue.'

'Thank you! Now, some people are destined to meet so that they might live a long life together, but the trouble with this kind of destiny is that it can end up being a bit tiresome.'

'What do you mean?'

'Well, familiarity can breed contempt and people who have been together forever can get bored of one another, or even worse, they start to bicker over every little thing – the colours of their threads begin to clash,' I added, really warming to the tapestry metaphor.

'My parents were a bit like that,' Danielle said.

'Right, well, Danielle and Pierre weren't destined to bicker and get bored of one another,' I continued. 'They were destined for far greater things than that.'

'Like what? Sorry, I didn't mean to interrupt.' She clamped her hand over her mouth.

'They were destined to be...' I paused both for dramatic effect and to give myself time to think of a powerful enough phrase. 'They were destined to become each other's Chanukah candles.'

'What does that mean?'

'To bring each other light in their darkest moment and to remind each other of the possibility of miracles. For was there any greater miracle than Danielle and Pierre meeting and falling in love in a place like Auschwitz?' I continued, rather proud that I'd been able to work the theme of Chanukah into the story.

'I'm not sure we've fallen in love,' Danielle murmured, but I could detect a smile in her voice. 'We haven't exactly had enough time for that.'

'Love isn't measured by a clock, my dear,' I said, saying a silent prayer of thanks to Solly for coming to my aid yet again.

'What do you mean?'

'It's measured by the heart,' I replied. 'You can know

someone a whole lifetime and they never affect your heart as much as another person might in just one meeting. How did your heart feel today, when Pierre gave you the candle?'

'Incredible,' Danielle replied.

'I rest my case.'

'So how does their story end?' she asked eagerly.

'It ends with them creating a beautiful addition to life's tapestry,' I replied cryptically. 'For who could argue with the beauty of their meeting, and the fact that they were able to create light in such circumstances. Every time there is such a miracle, it lights up the tapestry of life like the brightest of shooting stars.' I prayed this would be a satisfying ending for her, for how could I promise her any more?

'Thank you,' she said with a sigh. 'I really hope I make a beautiful addition to life's tapestry.'

'You already have,' I replied, hugging her tight. If only she knew what a beautiful addition she'd made to my own life, bringing me purpose and meaning and the greatest gift of all, a true feeling of family.

31

FEBRUARY 1944, AUSCHWITZ

That winter as the camp became covered in a thick shroud of snow, bringing with it a strange muffled quiet, it became increasingly hard to keep despair at bay. Were we destined to remain hidden away forever until one by one the epidemics sweeping the camp took us and we dropped to the floor and were carted away, and the camp became as lifeless as the skeletal trees on the horizon? But for every body that fell, there seemed to be at least two more being brought in on the transports to replace it. Perhaps the Germans wouldn't stop until they'd killed every Jew and Romani and political prisoner and homosexual on the planet. What a dull and hateful place the world would become if it were solely populated by their precious Aryan, alcoholic race – for every SS guard seemed to reek of alcohol those days. Were they drinking to celebrate the success of their master plan, or did they need to be drunk to carry out their atrocities? It was hard to tell.

Danielle and her budding romance with Pierre provided the only light and warmth during those cold months, although their encounters were few and far between – in real life, that is.

In the stories I told her every night, they'd adventured all over the world together.

Then, one cold February day as I prepared to go through yet another suitcase in *Kanada*, I was jolted from my despondent stupor. There, staring up at me from a tangle of clothes, was a copy of my first Aurelie novel. Seeing this symbol of my previous life, my previous self, sent a lightning bolt of recognition surging through me. I carefully disentangled the novel from a sweater sleeve and held it in front of me. It had clearly been very well read; the cover was faded and scuffed around the edges and the spine was cracked. As I looked at the illustration of Aurelie on the front cover, it was like finding a photograph of a long-lost friend. It had been so long since I'd heard my beloved character's voice in my mind, so long since our lives had run in tandem.

I traced my finger over the Paris skyline in the background of the image. What I wouldn't give to see Sacré-Coeur or the Eiffel Tower again. In spite of everything the French authorities had done to me, homesickness pierced me to the very core of my being. Fingers trembling, I opened the front cover and saw a handwritten dedication in elegant looping script. *To Annette, happy birthday dear friend, all my love, Sara.*

I flicked through the yellowing pages, stopping abruptly as I noticed a section that had been underlined in pencil. What had I written that Annette had deemed important enough to highlight in this way? I quickly checked that no guards were on the prowl and began to read.

> *There are moments when I feel as insignificant and over-whelmed as an ant about to be crushed by the trampling feet of the city, but in those moments I remind myself that I'd rather be crushed pursuing my passion than die a slow painful death curdling in disappointment. And what could be more disap-*

pointing than never having found the courage to answer the call of your dreams?

As I read the words, *my* words, it was as if they were sucking me back through time and space, to the tiny attic room I'd rented when I had first arrived in Paris. And there I was sitting at the rickety table beneath the dingy skylight, hunched over the second-hand typewriter I'd found in a flea market, answering the call of my dream to write. I had no idea back then if my Adventures of Aurelie would ever amount to anything. Those words I wrote for her were my own thoughts, my own feelings, as I spent my days cleaning the dance halls of Pigalle for a pittance and my nights spilling my heart onto the page. Running away to Paris had felt hugely overwhelming, but I had kept going, kept dreaming. I never would have guessed when I first wrote those words that they'd end up reaching so many readers and bringing me such success. Clearly they'd meant something to Annette too, for her to highlight them.

I looked back into the suitcase. Her clothes weren't from expensive boutiques, but they were quirky and colourful and showed an original sense of flair and style. I felt around beneath them and pulled out a gold lipstick case. The lipstick inside was dusky pink and had been worn into a sharp point. I pictured Annette's hand holding it, just as mine was now, and I felt a deep connection to this woman I would never meet, and who could very well already be dead. Although our threads in life's tapestry had only met for a moment, she'd given me the most beautiful of gifts.

Checking no guards were looking, I quickly tore the underlined page from the book and stuffed it into my pocket. Annette hadn't just reminded me of who I used to be, she'd reminded me that the books I wrote had helped people, and perhaps one day I'd be able to do that again. As I gazed down into her case, I made a silent vow that if I ever made it out of Auschwitz and was able to write about what happened, I'd be sure to include her story.

Finally, the snow thawed and the disease subsided, as did the new transports to the camp. What did this mean? Danielle and I would ponder at night in our bunk. Could we allow ourselves to feel any kind of hope? On Sunday afternoons, our only time off, the women's orchestra began playing concerts in the disinfecting barracks. These concerts were so popular, the crowd would spill outside, cramming as close as possible to hear the wondrous sounds. I'd forgotten how much I loved music, and how I used to have a radio in every room of my apartment so I could dance and sing the day away. Thinking of my life in Paris was like reading a book about a fictional character – it was hard to believe I had once had such freedom. But whenever the pain of loss started to become overwhelming, I'd feel for the page from my novel in my pocket and I'd remind myself of the importance of never giving up.

Sometimes, the orchestra would play a piece that brought back a specific memory, the way music is prone to do, and then it was a battle to keep the tears from my eyes. But other times, when the music was new to me, it helped me to daydream. The soaring violin would paint a picture in my mind of a lark; the full warm tone of the clarinet for some reason reminded me of a glass of red wine. One Sunday during a cello solo, I was reminded of Tomasz's voice as he sang Kol Nidre, and it was so evocative, it was as if I'd been transported right back to the dining room and I could see him sitting there in his tablecloth shawl. I wondered if he was still alive, if I'd ever see him again, and once more I had to blink away the onset of tears. Yes, those Sunday concerts were a bittersweet thing.

Then, in early spring, a flurry of activity broke out. Danielle and I were relieved of our duties as *Kanada Kommandos* and sent to work with the rest of the women in our hut in an empty sector of our camp that was adjacent to the men's camp. As we toiled away making new roads, we saw huge teams of men building a set of barracks and furnishing them with newly constructed bunks. Another fresh development throughout March and April had been the extension of the railroad right into the women's camp and by the end of April a dense wall of trees and bushes had been planted all around the crematories, so that only the roofs and chimneystacks remained visible. It reminded me a little of the fairy tale *Sleeping Beauty*, where the fairy casts a spell to make a forest of trees and brambles grow up around the castle. But in the fairy tale the forest was there to protect the sleeping princess. In Auschwitz, it was there to disguise a place of death, although thankfully the only people being taken there at that point had died of natural causes. I'd always loved trees before, but when I looked at the wall of weeping willows and oaks and birches surrounding the crematories, I couldn't help but shiver.

Then, one night at the start of May, we were jolted awake by a piercing scream.

'What is it? What's happening?' Danielle cried beside me.

I heard what sounded like the hiss of steam and then a voice shouting, '*Los! Aufgehen!*' A few women started stumbling from their bunks in confusion, but then the door burst open and the *Blockalteste* appeared.

'Stay where you are!' she bellowed. 'No one is to leave.'

'It sounded like a train,' I whispered to Danielle.

'But I thought they'd only laid the tracks into the women's camp to give the prisoners something to do,' she replied.

That's what we had all thought that strange, quiet spring. My body tensed as I wondered if we'd been lulled into a false sense of security. What if the new barracks and the new railway hadn't been constructed to keep us occupied but to prepare the camp for yet more waves of transports? What if, instead of slowing down their operations, the Nazis were speeding them up?

The next morning, we were sent to work in a different direction and forbidden from using the toilets on the north side of the camp. Anything, it seemed, to prevent us from seeing the new railroad station. The weather that day was deceptively beautiful, the May sun casting a warm, buttery glow. But I found it impossible to get warm. Something sinister was afoot, we all knew it, and we were all subdued as we made our way to work.

Sure enough, as we toiled away, a horrible familiar stench grew heavy in the air, and two columns of dense smoke began pouring from the chimneys of the nearest crematories. That evening at roll call, flames shot from the chimneys, as if setting the darkening sky on fire. How could we have been so stupid? How could we have entertained the prospect that the worst was over? I thought to myself as I tried not to breathe in the cloying stench. It seemed that the worst, in fact, had only just begun.

After a few days, the SS guards, who were clearly preoccupied by the size of the new transports, seemed to forget about us and we were free to wander wherever we wished – within the confines of the electric fences, of course. On the Sunday afternoon, Danielle and I walked down to the new railroad station in the heart of the women's camp and saw a sight that instantly filled me with dread. People, so many people, filing along the wide road that we had helped build towards the flaming chimneystacks, piles of their belongings left on the station platform. I vowed there and then that if I was asked to return to work at *Kanada*, I would refuse. It was hard enough sorting through the belongings of people I'd never seen, but now it would be impossible. Now I'd seen the women in their smart dresses, the men in their suits. Now I'd seen the children looking around curiously, as they clung to their toys. Now I'd heard the babies crying.

We soon discovered that the trains full of people arriving in the camp every night were from Hungary and they'd brought so much with them, even us prisoners were allowed to benefit from the spoils. Pieces of salted pork started appearing in our daily soup ration – the first time I discovered one was like finding a jewel – and we began receiving rations of Hungarian cheese and sausage at supper. I wish I could say that my principles led me to refuse the plundered food, but unfortunately my hunger was too all-consuming.

Sure enough, more *Kanada Kommandos* were hastily recruited to try to deal with the task of processing so many possessions. I didn't have to worry about refusing the role; there were plenty of volunteers. Danielle, however, was presented with a moral dilemma.

'I miss seeing Pierre,' she told me one day as we broke for lunch. 'Wouldn't you want to work there if it meant you might see Tomasz?'

I pondered this for a moment before realising that, yes, I probably would. And besides, Danielle's happiness was the most important thing to me.

'I think you should do it,' I said.

'Will you do it too?' she asked eagerly.

I shook my head. And so, for the first time since we had arrived at the camp, Danielle and I were separated – during the day at least. At first, it seemed like a good thing – my heart always lifted when I'd see her arriving back for evening roll call. Her eyes were so expressive, I could tell almost immediately if that day had brought a sighting of Pierre as they would be gleaming with excitement. Most days, though, they were downcast.

'What is happening to the children?' she whispered to me one night. 'I see so many toys. And today there was a perambulator and there was still a tiny dip in the pillow from the baby's head.'

I held her to me as she began to cry. 'You mustn't think about it. You have to think about other things. Think about Pierre. Would you like me to tell you a story?'

To my dismay, she shook her head. 'I just want to sleep.'

I lay awake that night cursing my decision to leave her to work there on her own. Perhaps I could offer my services in the morning. Danielle's happiness was far more important than my stupid principles.

In the distance, I heard the shriek of a train whistle and the strains of the women's orchestra as they began to play. They'd been ordered to play every night now, I assumed to try to drown out the cries of the new arrivals. How did the musicians do it? I wondered. How did they play those upbeat tempos, knowing they were providing the soundtrack to a death march? I guess, like all of us, they had learned to block the horror out in the name of survival.

The next morning when I enquired, the *Blockalteste* told me in no uncertain terms that my services at *Kanada* weren't needed and I was to remain part of the work party assigned to digging ditches. All day long as I dug, I worried about Danielle and what state of mind I'd find her in when I returned. But, to my delight, I got back to find her eyes sparkling with joy.

'Oh Etty, you will never guess what happened,' she gasped as we queued for our evening rations.

'I think I probably can,' I replied. 'Does it, or rather *he*, begin with the letter P?'

'Yes!' she exclaimed. 'I saw him today and he told me that he can't stop thinking about me *and...*'

'There's more?' I asked, my heart filling with relief.

'Yes! He said that when we get out of here we are to meet.'

'How?' I asked curiously.

'We agreed to both go to the Eiffel Tower on the first Sunday of the month, once we're back in Paris. That way, if one of us gets back before the other we can keep trying until we're both there. Isn't it the most romantic thing ever?'

'It really is.' As I replied, I wished with all of my heart and soul that their dream would come true. I was also hugely grateful that Danielle's spirits had been raised. Hopefully this plan of theirs would keep her going now, in spite of everything else that was happening.

Then, one happy day in June, Danielle brought news I could never have dared hope for.

'Something truly incredible has happened,' she whispered to me during evening roll call.

My first thought was that she'd managed to see Pierre again and he'd proposed marriage, but then I noticed other poorly suppressed bursts of excitement breaking out amongst our rows of five.

'You'll never guess what Pierre told me,' she whispered.

'Did he declare his undying love for you?'

'No!' She stifled a giggle, then, as soon as the nearest kapo had turned their back, she leaned closer. 'The Allies have landed in France.'

I was so happy to hear those words, my legs almost buckled from the relief. Could it be true?

'How does he know?' I hissed.

'He heard it from someone who works in the German hospital. They heard it on the radio. Isn't it the best news ever?'

'It is. It is!' I gazed up into the sky, beyond the foul smoke billowing from the chimneys, fixing my gaze upon a star, and I prayed with all my might that the Allies would find victory, that they would push our occupiers out of France and liberate our country and that Danielle and Pierre would be reunited beneath the Eiffel Tower.

32

AUGUST 1944, AUSCHWITZ

'Once upon a time there was an army named Hate, made up of horse-heads and people so poisonous they caused the air to curdle and the birds to wail,' I began. It was a hot August night and all the French women in the nearby bunks were listening avidly. 'This army was led by a hateful leader named Monsieur Moustache...' Several of the women giggled, a sound so rare, it was even sweeter than a symphony from the women's orchestra. 'Monsieur Moustache believed that he could take over the entire world. He thought that he could murder anyone who stood in his way, but he hadn't estimated the strength and bravery of his opposition, an army named Hope.'

For the first time since I'd arrived at Auschwitz, I'd started telling stories rooted in truth rather than fantasy. Rumours of the Allied advances both from the east and the west now buzzed through the camp on a daily basis, and there could be no doubting they were true as we could hear the distant rattle of guns and the slow rhythmic thud of detonations as the Russians moved into Poland. Even better, Allied planes had started flying over the camp, en route to their bombing raids, prompting the wail of sirens and the joyous sight of our German captors scrambling for cover in the ditches we were digging. Of course, we prisoners weren't allowed to take cover, but I don't think any of us really cared. The closest the Allied bombs came to us was when they attacked a German factory on the outskirts of the camp and we were giddy from this change in fortunes. Finally we could dare to dream that we might not be forgotten about and it instilled a new desire to live in all but those previously driven mad by despair.

In an attempt to build upon this burgeoning hope, I had taken to telling nightly stories to my bunkmates on the theme of victory, all featuring loosely disguised guards from the camp meeting a variety of terrible ends. I'm not sure if Solly would have approved, but by that point I was unable to contain my desire for retribution, even if it was only fictional.

As I reached the end of my latest tale, in which the Dreschel-inspired character drowned in a vat of our so-called soup and Irma Grese, known in my tales as Ice Heart, choked on an apple, the women began sharing their fantasies of how we would leave the camp.

'I'm going to be rescued by a tall Russian soldier,' a woman named Colette declared. 'His name will be Vlad and he will have the body of an Adonis and the heart of a lion.'

Next to me, Danielle giggled. Clearly Colette had been spending some time playing the Wings of Imagination game.

'Pfft! I'm going to be rescuing myself,' a long-faced woman named Suzanne announced. 'But not before giving those Germans a taste of their own medicine. They'll have worse in store than choking to death on an apple if I have anything to do with it.'

As the conversation moved on to dreams of revenge, Danielle snuggled into me.

'I think Pierre and Tomasz are going to come and find us and we'll all leave the camp together,' she said quietly.

'That would be lovely,' I said, but privately I couldn't help feeling a sense of trepidation. The Germans had shown time and again how cruel and ruthless they could be – surely they wouldn't go down without a fight and free us so easily.

Sure enough, before long, a strange reversal in the transports to the camp started occurring and our captors began using their trains to take women from Auschwitz to Germany. Every day, a new batch of women would be selected, taken to the bathhouse, where they were issued with grey dresses, and any meagre possessions they might have accrued were confiscated once again.

'We can't get sent to Germany,' Danielle said to me one night after half of our barracks mates had gone. 'Not now freedom is so close.' She clutched my hands. 'What if one of us is chosen to go but not the other. Oh Etty, I think I shall die of a broken heart if that happens!'

'If you are chosen, then I'll demand to come with you,' I replied. 'I'll stow away on the train if I have to.'

'And I would do the same,' Danielle said, her voice wavering.

'No!' I replied firmly. 'You must stay here, I insist.'

'But...'

'What?'

'I can't imagine being without you.'

'I can't imagine it either,' I replied, squeezing her thin hands.

She fell silent for a moment and I thought maybe she was going to sleep.

'Etty?' she whispered.

'Yes.'

'Can I ask you something?'

'Of course, anything.'

'When this is over – if we get out of here – can we... can we be each other's family?'

'Oh, Danielle, of course. I would be honoured to be your family. I always wanted an annoying little sister,' I added, trying to lighten the mood.

She elbowed me in the ribs. 'I'm not annoying!'

'No – only when you interrupt my stories with your thousands of questions.'

She laughed. 'That makes me your curious little sister.'

'Yes, I guess it does.' To hear her say those words made my heart burst with love.

There was another beat of silence and then...

'Etty?'

'Yes.'

'Do you remember that story you told me about me and Pierre being destined to meet?'

'I do.'

'Well, I think that you and I were destined to meet too, as part of life's tapestry.' She sounded tired now, her words slowing.

'I don't just think that; I know that,' I said, hugging her to me. And as her breathing slackened, I thought back to the day we first met and marvelled that it should have come to this, that in spite of all of the loss and the fear and the pain, we should have forged a bond as strong as blood. What a blessing.

My eyes filled with tears. For so long, I'd wondered what my life would have been like if my mother had lived and I'd been able to experience her love. Little did I realise that one day I'd experience a love as fierce and powerful as a lioness has for her cub – but as the giver rather than the receiver. To me, it felt just as good.

. . .

The next day, a new transport arrived at the camp from Italy. Several of the women were sent to our hut, including a woman named Lucia, who ended up next to Danielle and me in our bunk. That first night she didn't stop sobbing. She spoke some French and was able to tell us that her two little girls had been taken from her at the station and sent to another part of the camp, along with all the other children. Her words filled me with an icy dread.

'I'm sure you'll see them soon,' I told her, but inside all I could think was, had the Italian children all been sent to their deaths?

'I can't stop thinking about the children,' Danielle whispered in my ear as we settled down to sleep. 'What if the mothers never see them again?' It dawned on me that it must be bringing back painful memories of her own separation from Marguerite and I felt for her hand beneath the blanket.

'They will; we have to keep faith,' I whispered.

Perfectly on cue, the air-raid sirens began to wail.

'*Licht aus! Licht aus!*' came the command from outside, ordering the lights on the barbed-wire fence to go out. Then began the rat-a-tat-tat of the German anti-aircraft fire and the tapping as fragments of the shells fell like the sweetest rain upon the roof.

'See, it won't be long now until we're liberated,' I whispered and I felt Danielle nod beside me.

Thankfully, we learned, the Italian children had not been killed. They'd been taken to another area of the camp, which seemed almost as cruel as their mothers were forbidden from seeing them. On the first Sunday afternoon after she arrived, Lucia asked Danielle and me if we would go with her to help her try to see her children.

'Surely there is something I can do to get them to allow me,' she said, looking at me hopefully.

Not wanting to dash her hopes, I nodded, and Danielle was even more optimistic.

'Together, we will persuade the guards,' she said determinedly.

And so the three of us set off to the fenced-off section of the camp where the children had been sent.

'Oh they look so small,' Danielle murmured as we saw the children wandering about their barracks, listless and dazed.

How could they be kept there without their parents? What was this doing to them? They all looked so subdued and none of them were playing.

'*Bambine!*' Lucia cried, running to the fence.

Two little girls who'd been walking hand in hand stopped and stared over. An instant later, they were running for the fence, crying out for their mother.

'Oh, Angelina! Isabella!' Lucia gasped.

I breathed a sigh of relief. They were alive at least.

The youngest of the girls, who looked to be about three, threw her hands up to Lucia, as if expecting her to be able to reach over the fence and scoop her up. The older daughter, who was about seven, crossed her arms tightly, not saying a word. There was something about the withdrawn and shuttered nature of her pose that reminded me of myself at that age, and it broke my heart even more than her younger sister's tears.

Lucia turned to me and started speaking in a stream of Italian. I could tell she was pleading for my help, but what could I do?

The sound of the weekly women's concert drifted over on the hot breeze. A jaunty melody completely at odds with the pain of Lucia's situation.

'We need to do something. We need to help her,' Danielle said. 'Let's go and ask the guards if they'll let her in.'

'OK.' I took hold of Lucia's hand. 'Come.'

We made our way over to the gate, with the little girls following us on the other side of the fence, and Lucia calling encouraging things to them.

But when we reached the gate, my heart instantly sank. Scowling and surly, the SS guard on duty didn't look as if he had an ounce of compassion in him. He also reeked of alcohol.

'Please, can this mother see her children?' I said to him in broken German.

He looked at me and smirked, then turned his piggy bloodshot eyes upon Lucia, who had started pleading in Italian.

'*Nein!*' he shouted, taking his truncheon from his belt. '*Nein!*'

But Lucia wouldn't be silenced, and even worse, she grabbed him by the lapels of his jacket. Then she fell to her knees, sobbing and begging. The music from the orchestra reached a cheery crescendo, a soundtrack so discordant, it seemed to tear at my eardrums.

'No!' I cried as the guard pulled his truncheon back and cracked it across her head.

As Lucia slumped to the ground, her youngest daughter began to scream.

'Oh no, oh no,' Danielle began muttering.

Thankfully, Lucia stirred back into life, although clearly dazed.

'Go back to your barracks!' the guard yelled.

Finally, the jaunty music finished, to a burst of applause.

Completely oblivious to what had just happened, a female guard appeared from inside the children's barracks and opened the gate. Quick as a flash, Lucia's youngest daughter shot past her and flung herself at her mother.

'Oh, Angelina! *Bambina!*' Lucia exclaimed.

The male guard's face flushed an almost purple shade of red

and his voice raised an octave as he began screaming a torrent of abuse.

Ignoring him, Lucia rocked her daughter back and forth. On the other side of the fence, the older girl started to cry.

'Get back! Get back!' the male guard screamed, taking his gun from his belt.

'No!' I cried. And then everything slowed, each second stretching as if to magnify the horror about to unfold.

The guard lowered his arm, pointing his gun at Lucia's lap, where her child sat hugging her tightly.

'No!' I cried again, taking a step towards them. But then Danielle appeared in front of me, blocking my way.

The orchestra began playing a fresh piece. The guard cocked his rifle.

'No!' I screamed again, but I seemed to be moving even slower than everything else.

A shot rang out. Followed by a cry. I saw the female guard's mouth drop open in shock. How could he have shot the child? Did he really have such little humanity? I heard Lucia begin to wail. Then I heard the baby's cry. I heard the baby's cry! Could she by some miracle still be alive? And then, finally, my gaze found Danielle. She was on the ground. Why was she on the ground? And she was clutching her stomach, a crimson stain flowering on her flimsy dress. Finally, time regained its natural pace and my brain caught up with the terrible train of events. She'd been shot. Danielle had been shot. She must have leapt into the line of fire to protect the baby.

'Danielle!' I cried, ignoring the guard's yells and collapsing onto my knees beside her. 'Danielle.'

Her eyes were closed.

'Danielle, please!' My eyes filled with tears. I blinked them away furiously. 'Please. Can you hear me?'

Her eyelids fluttered open. 'Etty?'

'Yes, it's all right. We're going to get you help.' I looked over my shoulder to a gathering crowd of women. 'Get help! Someone get help!' I looked back at Danielle. Her face was white as snow and the stain on her dress was growing larger.

'Etty,' she gasped. 'Did I save the baby?'

'Yes, my love, you did. Now we're going to save you.' I looked up at the female guard. 'Please, get a doctor. Please I beg of you!'

She looked to the male guard and he shook his head before returning to his post at the gate. I wanted to strangle him but there was no way on earth I could leave Danielle.

'Etty, I feel really cold,' Danielle whispered.

'It's all right. I'll keep you warm.' I held her to me, the way I'd done so many times since arriving in that hellish place. I felt something wet on my hands and realised to my horror that it was the blood seeping through her dress. 'I'll keep you warm.'

The haunting sound of an oboe filled the air. High above, a raven cawed.

'Etty, I'm scared,' she whispered.

'It's OK, I'm with you. I'm always with you.' I held her even tighter. 'I'm always with you.' I glanced over my shoulder. 'Please, someone, do something!'

Her breathing became shallow. 'Am I dying?'

'No,' I said, unable to keep myself from sobbing.

And then all other sounds faded.

'I saved the baby?' She looked up at me hopefully.

'Yes, yes you did.'

She sighed and gave the faintest smile as her eyes fluttered closed. 'My story had a good ending.'

'The very best,' I sobbed, and I felt her body go limp.

33

AUGUST 1944, AUSCHWITZ

Hands – I felt hands touching me. Some stroking. Some gently tugging.

'You need to let go,' someone said.

But if I let go, it really would be over. Danielle really would be dead. And then those monsters would leave her outside the barracks overnight, to be slung onto the cart of death the next day. No. That was not going to happen. I was not going to allow it. My shock began to fade and I looked down at her beautiful heart-shaped face. 'My family', she'd called me; we'd promised, and as her family, I was going to lay her to rest. And if they killed me, we might at least be together again. And I might be reunited with Solly, Macaroon and Marguerite. There was nothing, *nothing*, left here for me now.

'I am taking her.' My voice sounded unfamiliar, harsh and shrill. I slowly shifted into a kneeling position. 'I am taking her,' I said again, louder.

The hands touching me fell away. I placed my arms beneath Danielle's frail body and slowly lifted her. She was light as a feather. As I stood, I saw that the gathering crowd had grown even larger. The women at the bathhouse concert must have heard the gunshot. The kapo who was night-watch in our hut came hurrying over.

'What are you doing?' she asked, looking shocked. 'What has happened?'

What has happened? Those three words, that one sentence, sparked a hysterical desire within me to laugh. *What has happened to make a man want to shoot an innocent child? What has happened to make people create this Valley of Death at the end of the line? At the end of the world. At the end of humanity.*

'That bastard killed her,' someone shouted in French.

The female guard said something to the night-watch in German.

'I'm taking her to the crematory,' I said, a strange calm descending upon me. Nothing mattered in that moment apart from giving Danielle the dignity she deserved in death.

The guard began to object.

'You've already killed her,' I interrupted, 'and you can kill me too afterwards if you want to. But I am doing this.'

Someone behind me started a slow clap, and another joined in, and another. And then, in what felt like a perfect act of divine timing, the air-raid siren began to wail.

The guards exchanged glances and then, like the cowards they were, they fled for shelter. The night-watch looked me in the eyes and gave me an almost imperceptible nod before turning and walking away.

I looked down at Danielle, my curious little sister, she who so loved to interrupt me with her endless questions. *I didn't mean to say you were annoying*, I wanted to cry. *I meant to say that I loved you.* 'I love you!' I gasped, tears splashing from my eyes onto her face. She looked so peaceful, in spite of the deadly crimson bloom on her dress. She looked so young and so free from stress.

I started walking in the direction of the crematory, along the road that I had helped build, the road to death. In the distance, I heard the gentle hum of planes, and in the corner of my vision, I saw figures starting to walk alongside me, either side of the road. Ragged figures in dirty dresses. But when I looked across to meet their gaze, all I could see was love flowing back at me. And then I heard someone begin to softly sing '*La Marseillaise*', and then another and another. And my tears flowed so heavily, my vision blurred. Somehow, the road to death was being transformed into an avenue of love. The song grew louder until it almost drowned out the sirens and the hum in the air turned into a roar.

As I reached the wall of trees surrounding the crematory, carrying my own Sleeping Beauty, a squadron of Allied planes flew over, leaving trails of white in the bright blue sky. Could they see me? I wondered. Did they know what was happening down here? Surely if they did, they would bomb the place.

The rattle of anti-aircraft fire began as I continued walking the path that so many others had to their deaths. Aware that I didn't have much time left, I slowed my pace and looked down at Danielle. There were so many things I wanted to say to her, so many conversations yet to be had that now never could, so I said the only thing that really matters in the end.

'I love you.'

'What are you doing?' A man's voice rang out and I looked up to see a *Sonderkommando* – one of the Jewish prisoners made to work in the crematories. He hurried over and looked at the bloodstain on Danielle's dress. 'What happened to her?'

'What do you think? Please, I beg of you, can she have a dignified end?'

The man glanced over his shoulder, but thanks to the air-raid warning, there were no guards about. 'Yes, give her to me.'

I held Danielle for a moment more before passing her to

him, then stroked her cold face and kissed her forehead one last time.

'I'm sorry,' he said.

'She was a wonderful person,' I replied, the closest I would get to giving her a eulogy. Not that I'd ever be able to find the words big enough or beautiful enough to express what Danielle had come to mean to me.

'Was she your sister?' he asked.

'Yes, yes she was.' I turned and walked away, pain piercing every cell of my body.

As I left, I heard the man begin saying the Kaddish in a voice so full of tenderness, it made me want to weep.

Another squadron of planes flew overhead and my sorrow deepened. Danielle and I had survived so much and we were surely so close to liberation. Why, oh why, couldn't she have lived to see it? Why, oh why, did that monster have to murder her?

The women were still waiting in silence when I got back to the road, and as I returned to the barracks, they folded in behind me in a silent procession. Fragments of anti-aircraft fire rained down around us, but no one cried out or ran for cover. Somehow I made it back to our hut, but as soon as I reached our bunk, my heart splintered. Danielle and I had managed to create a cocoon of warmth there, but now the bunk seemed as cold and claustrophobic as a coffin.

As I lay down, Lucia appeared, standing in front of the bunk, her head level with mine. She started speaking passionately in Italian. Then she paused and said in broken French, 'I never forget, your friend, she save my daughter.'

I nodded, completely unable to speak for the rage building inside of me. A rage I couldn't direct at the ones who were truly guilty and so it flowed to her instead. *Why did you have to ask us to help you?* I wanted to yell at her. *Why couldn't you have just gone to the children's camp by yourself?* It was completely unfair, but I was overwhelmed by the loss now engulfing me. I rolled away from her onto my side and closed my eyes, wanting to shut out the entire world. For it was a world that meant nothing without my beloved Danielle in it. My beloved Danielle Courageux. My beloved Danielle Très Belle.

34

1944, AUSCHWITZ

Once upon a time, the world became such a terrible place that stories ceased to exist. All of the letters in all of the alphabets refused to come together to form the words necessary to speak of such horrors, and the storytellers became obsolete...

35

YOM KIPPUR, SEPTEMBER 1944, AUSCHWITZ

'Once upon a time, there were two young French women who were inseparable...'

As my bunkmate Colette began to speak, I was jolted from my depressed stupor. It had been several days since Danielle was killed, days I'd spent in a haze of grief and indifference, somehow stumbling through the routine of roll call to work, to roll call to sleep. I'd spoken barely a word to anyone in that time, much less told one of my stories, but now it seemed that my bunkmate had taken over the mantle and her words were seeping into my consciousness even though I longed for oblivion.

'These two young women were the perfect example of female friendship,' Colette continued. 'In fact, you could search the entire world and not find a better example.'

I heard someone in the bunk below murmur in agreement.

'No matter what hardships befell them, their love never failed; in fact, it only became stronger and more beautiful, like a diamond forged in the most intense heat.'

I kept my eyes closed, but they began filling with tears.

'The older of the friends was a very special woman, a kind

and caring woman, and a marvellous teller of stories,' she went on. 'And any time her younger friend felt sad or scared, she would do her utmost to help her with one of her tales. But what she might not have realised was that other people were listening to those tales too. Not out of nosiness,' she quickly added, 'but due to their somewhat unusual sleeping arrangements.'

'Like matches in a box,' someone from the bunks next to ours added, prompting a wry laugh.

'So every night, when the older woman was helping her young friend, she was also inadvertently helping many others too.'

I froze. Was she saying what I thought she was? Obviously I knew the women were familiar with the stories I'd told the whole hut, but had they heard the stories I'd told Danielle privately? And had those stories helped them too?

'Night after night, the storyteller of Auschwitz would tell her young friend tales to help her believe in love and wonder and the power of her imagination. And night after night, the other women close by would be transported into the world of her stories and apply their lessons to their own lives. It was as if the storyteller had magical powers and was able to reach deep inside the other women's hearts and minds and show them a strength they didn't know they possessed.'

'Yes!' someone exclaimed in agreement and I felt my eyes become warm with tears.

'But then tragedy struck,' Colette continued. 'The younger of the two friends was brutally murdered, and the storyteller became so paralysed with grief, she was no longer able to speak. And oh, how the women who'd listened to her stories shared her pain, and oh, how they longed to do something to help her, the way she had helped them.'

'Yes, yes,' someone else said, and the tears spilled from my closed eyes and onto my cheeks.

'After a while, they realised that maybe the best gift they

could give her was to show her how much she had helped them. And how much she was still loved, and needed.' Colette's voice began to crack. 'We love you, Etty.'

'Yes!'

'Yes, we do.'

I opened my eyes, my tears spilling onto my face, unsure if I was really awake or in a dream. But my bunkmates were all there, and they were all looking at me, and most of them were crying too.

'Please don't give up,' Colette said.

'We need you,' Suzanne added.

And that one word 'need' struck a chord deep inside of me. I looked at them all gazing at me so intently and finally I was able to speak.

'Thank you.'

36

WINTER 1944, AUSCHWITZ

As summer faded into autumn and autumn paled into winter, we began living for the radio communiqués bringing news of Allied victories and German defeats. The emancipation of Paris, the Warsaw uprising, all brought great cheer. Trainloads of Poles arrived, then trainloads of Poles departed for Germany, just like the chill October mist rolling in and out of the camp. The siren signalling escape attempts started to wail even more frequently than the air-raid siren, and every time I heard it, I prayed for the brave soul's safety. I could no longer imagine what it must feel like to want to survive so badly you'd be prepared to risk being shot or having the dogs set upon you. That night in the barracks when my bunkmates had told me they needed me had stopped me from giving up completely. And since then a cold tight ball of determination had formed in the pit of my stomach and kept me going. If I made it out of Auschwitz alive, I would let the world know about the evil that had happened here – and the love that had prevailed in spite of it all. I would light up the world with my tales of Solly, Marguerite, Macaroon and Danielle. But beyond that I no longer burned with dreams of my future. I no longer cared what happened to me. I had no other plans or desires.

And then, one day in early December, we were arranged in our rows yet again, and I was prodded with a baton and told to join a line I assumed was destined for the crematorium. *So this it*, I thought to myself, *finally, I am going to die*, and I can honestly say that I felt no panic. But it turned out that life was having one more joke with me – it turned out that my line was destined for the train. And so I found myself once more being rounded onto a cattle truck.

'Where are they sending us?'

'It has to be Germany to make munitions.'

'Don't they know they're going to lose the war?'

The air was filled with speculative chatter. But all I could think about was the last time I was herded into a cattle truck, and my fellow musketeers, Solly, Marguerite and Danielle. Why had only I been spared? Why couldn't they still be here? I felt lost without them.

After a couple of days, the train stopped and we were ordered off. We were in the middle of nowhere and an icy wind tore through our clothes, biting right down to the bone. As I breathed in, I was sure I could smell the sea. One thing I could mercifully not smell was the stench of death that had hung over the camp.

We were ordered to march for a few miles through a forest before arriving at another camp – Bergen-Belsen. Thankfully, there was still no stench of death, or a macabre fairy-tale chimney looming over a wall of trees. We were housed in tents and grouped together according to nationality. It felt comforting to be in our mini France, a taster of what life might be like if we were able to return to the new, free France. But every time I felt the slightest dash of hope, it was tempered with a feeling of guilt that my fellow musketeers would never be able to experience

such freedom again, and back I would sink into gloom and indifference.

In February, hundreds more women arrived from
Auschwitz, but they had been made to march all the way and
were like walking corpses. They told us they'd been forced to
leave before the Russians arrived to liberate the camp. Unfortunately, the worst of the guards came with them, bringing their
incessant roll calls and their thirst for killing, even as they faced
defeat.

Once again, I felt certain that death had come for me, but
once again, life had other ideas, and along with my fellow
Frenchwomen, I was put on another train, bound for an
airplane factory in a place called Raguhn. Once there, we were
placed on an assembly line making plane motors in a surreal
exercise in utter futility. Allied bombs rained down all around,
and yet the Germans still couldn't accept defeat. It would have
been infuriating if I hadn't felt so numb.

Then one day we were loaded onto yet another train, this
one bound for Leipzig. It soon became apparent that some of
the others on board had typhus. And when we were kept locked
in the freight car for days on end, it seemed that this was how
the Germans intended to kill us. They would keep us there
until the disease had taken us all and the car had become a
mausoleum. By the time the train juddered to a halt, there was a
pile of dead bodies by the car door. But still I remained alive;
still death refused to relieve me of my misery. Danielle's death
had left a gaping hole where my heart used to be and, combined
with my physical exhaustion, I felt like a husk of a human being.
As I heard the sound of the bolt on the car door being slid open,
it reminded me of the time I'd heard that same sound on arrival
at Auschwitz.

I stared at the door, my skin prickling with goosebumps as it
slowly creaked open. Surely death was now only moments
away. I felt certain our German guards would shoot those of us

still clinging to life. But as my eyes adjusted to the daylight streaming in, I saw a cluster of soldiers in khaki uniforms rather than grey. I'm not sure who looked more stunned, them or us. I heard one of them cry something in shock and although I didn't immediately recognise the language he was speaking, I knew it wasn't German. They weren't German! This instantly jolted some life back into me.

'Russians!' the woman slumped next to me rasped.

The Russians were on our side.

I shifted into a more upright position. How had this happened? How had a German train delivered us to the Allies? Could it really be true or was it yet another cruel trick?

Once the soldiers had carefully helped us off the car, we learned that as our train had crawled along, the German guards had abandoned it one by one, and we were in a newly liberated ghetto in Czechoslovakia. It took quite some time for this to sink in and we all stared at each other in stunned silence.

After gratefully receiving some water and dry bread, and finally accepting that what had happened wasn't some kind of bizarre hallucination, a group of us decided to walk into Prague, concluding that we'd have more hope of making it back home from there. I barely remember anything from that walk other than my aching feet and weary limbs. It's a miracle that we were able to walk at all, but I guess our newfound freedom made for a potent fuel. Once we reached Prague, we were directed to a repatriation camp. Repatriation: the return of someone to their own country. But could France ever feel like my own country again? After all, wasn't it France that had sent me to an almost certain death? Who knew what I was going to find there. More train rides followed, but this time we were in carriages with seats rather than cattle trucks.

A couple of days later, we arrived in Paris. Hundreds of us swarmed onto the platform at Gare d'Orsay, many still wearing the striped uniform of the camps they'd been liberated from. It was impossible not to notice the wide eyes of the staff who ushered us onto the buses waiting outside the station, their expressions full of horror and concern. But where were we being taken? For a terrible moment, I thought we might be being sent back to Drancy, but our driver reassured us that we were in fact going to a hotel.

In what felt like the most surreal of dreams, we pulled up on the boulevard Raspail outside one of the grandest hotels in Paris, the Lutetia. The street was full of people holding hand-made signs. At first, I thought they were there to welcome us. But as I shuffled off the bus, I saw that names were written on the signs and the people's faces were full of angst.

'Have you seen my son?' a woman cried as she shoved her sign in my face. 'Do you know if he's still alive?'

I shook my head and focused on the ground until I made it through the huge revolving door and into the hotel. It had been so long since I'd seen such grandeur, I felt as if I'd been winded.

As I gazed up at the ornate ceiling and the huge Art Deco chandelier, a woman started spraying a white powder at me. 'To treat lice,' she said apologetically.

I nodded numbly.

Once we were deloused, we were sent for showers, proper showers, with warm water and soap, checked over by nurses and given a clean set of clothes. When I was issued with repatriation papers, I wanted to burn them on the spot. *If you hadn't deserted us, denied us, sent us to our deaths, the people I love would still be alive*, I wanted to yell at the poor helpless clerk who'd issued me with the documents.

I returned to my apartment the following day with a lock-smith in tow as I obviously no longer had a key. As he opened the door, I felt sick with fear. Would the Germans have plundered everything? Would I have nothing left? But, to my surprise, my belongings were still there. It was only when the locksmith had gone that I started to see evidence of intruders.

An ashtray overflowing with cigar butts, a wine glass with a ghostly lipstick imprint on the rim. When I saw that my bed had new linen, I stared at it in horror. Who had been living here while I'd been in Auschwitz? What had happened here while I was gone?

As I paced around the rooms, it was like being in a stranger's home, just as looking at myself in the bathroom mirror felt like staring at a stranger's body. Who was this unfamiliar person with her jagged hair and jutting hips? Everywhere I looked on my body, there were reminders of the Germans' barbarity, from the saggy folds that used to be my breasts, to the scars on my skin where the lice had feasted. And, of course, that terrible tattoo. The scars might fade and my hair might grow back, but I would never, ever be able to escape the number branded on my arm. Not that I cared. How could I give a jot about anything when I'd seen the ones I loved murdered? I felt terrible that I should have survived when they'd all perished.

I glanced down at the bathtub and thought of the night almost five years previously when I'd drawn a bath for Tomasz. I contemplated lying in that bathtub, taking a knife to my wrists, and waiting for the life to drain from me. But then Tomasz's words of so long ago came back to me. 'You have to write about this, about what they're doing to us.' And I remembered the vow I'd made lying in my bunk after Danielle's death. I had to write one last story, about what happened, and about Danielle and Marguerite and Macaroon and Tomasz and Solly. And how their love brought me joy and hope in the darkest of moments. And then they might live on, in the hearts and imaginations of all those who read their story. Once I'd finished it, I would deliver my manuscript to Anton and I would beg him, if need be, to publish it. Surely he owed me. Then, after the deal was signed and I was certain the book would be published, I would finally be ready for death to take me too, for there was nothing left there for me.

. . .

For the next month, my life took on a routine not too dissimilar from the one at Auschwitz. Unable to go anywhere near the bed, I slept on the floor beside my desk. I'd wake at four and after a cup of tea and a meagre breakfast, I would sit down to write for hours on end. Bringing Solly, Marguerite, Danielle and Macaroon back to life through my words was a magical experience. I felt their souls all around me and speaking through me. Even writing about their deaths brought some solace, as I was finally able to properly grieve. When I wrote about Danielle's death, I was barely able to breathe, but as the tears streamed down my face, I felt some release. I was no longer consumed by guilt for surviving when they hadn't because my survival now had a purpose; it was going to keep them alive in my book, and then, of course, I was going to join them.

37

SEPTEMBER 1945, PARIS

In mid-September, I typed the words *The End*. I took the final page from the typewriter and hugged the manuscript to my chest. The pages felt alive with the spirits of my friends. I said a prayer of thanks to each of them, then prepared to leave. I'd contacted Anton the week before and told him I was working on a new book. I don't know if it was guilt, but he was only too keen to offer me a new publishing deal and invited me to join him for lunch at Café de la Paix.

It was a beautiful day, the sky a vivid shade of blue with feather-like wisps of cloud lazily drifting by. It struck me that it was the first time I'd noticed the weather since returning to Paris. I'd barely been out of my apartment, my entire focus having been on my writing. I found Anton at his usual table on the terrace, clad in a sea-green velvet jacket and sipping on a glass of wine.

As I approached, he glanced at me without a flicker of recognition before doing a dramatic double-take.

'Etty? Etty!' he cried, getting to his feet. 'My God, it is so good to see you.'

As he flung his arms around me, I stood rigid in his embrace.

The smell of cologne and cigarettes was so familiar and yet it belonged to a life that no longer existed for me.

'I can't tell you how overjoyed I was to receive your call,' he continued, stepping back and gazing at me. 'I was so worried.' I saw him take in my short hair and thin frame. 'Are you all right?'

I nodded, urging myself not to cry, to stay strong. 'How are you?' I asked in what I hoped was a breezy tone.

'Oh, you know, a lot better now that the Germans have been defeated.'

It must have been so nice for people like Anton, I thought to myself wistfully, who were able to feel that the Germans *had* been defeated, who didn't look in the mirror every day and see their victory stamped all over their body. How could we be expected to rejoice and move on, we who had been through so much, lost so much, and were still plagued by the horrors they'd inflicted upon us?

'Yes, indeed,' I said simply, sitting down at the table.

'Let me get you something to eat.' Anton gestured to a waiter. 'How about a bowl of your favourite onion soup – you'll be pleased to hear they've put the beef stock back in.'

I looked at him blankly before remembering our last lunch and my ridiculous outrage over the soup. It seemed so crazy now, in the context of years of starvation in Auschwitz. How could I have complained about such a trivial thing?

The waiter came over and Anton ordered two bowls of soup. 'And after the soup we shall have sausage casserole,' he announced. I nodded, although I still didn't have the stomach for larger meals. 'So, tell me about this book of yours,' he said as soon as the waiter had gone. 'I'm so delighted you've written another Aurelie adventure. Is it the one you told me about, at our last lunch before...' He broke off, looking embarrassed. 'I'm so, so sorry for what happened that day.'

'It's OK. You weren't allowed to publish me. I understand.' I took the manuscript from my purse. 'This book, it... it isn't an

Aurelie story, it's a true story, about what happened to me, during the war.' I placed the manuscript in front of him and closed my eyes, unable to bear it if he turned me down again and I was unable to fulfil my promise to Tomasz or honour the memory of my friends.

'Oh.' He sounded surprised, but was he disappointed also?

I risked opening my eyes a fraction. He was staring down at the manuscript.

'I had to write it,' I said. 'The world has to know what happened to us, so that it will never happen again.'

To my relief, he nodded.

'Were you sent to one of the camps?' he asked quietly.

I nodded. 'Auschwitz.'

'And is it true what they're saying? About the mass murders and the gas chambers?'

I nodded again.

'Oh Etty. I'm so sorry.' He placed his hands on top of mine. They felt so warm and strong that for a moment I almost came undone. 'I would be honoured to publish your book,' he said, meeting my gaze, and I saw that his eyes were glassy with tears. 'Honoured.'

'Thank you!' I cried. 'Thank you!' And then my own tears came, and they wouldn't stop.

Anton was good to his word. He read my manuscript that same day and when I called in to his office a couple of days later as instructed, he had a publishing contract waiting for me.

'Will you write another Aurelie novel now?' he asked me hopefully as I signed the contract.

'Maybe,' I replied. 'But I'll be going away for a while first.'

'Of course. I imagine you want to be with your family and friends.'

I nodded. If only he knew how true this was.

I decided to walk back via the Latin Quarter, Anton's mention of friends reminding me of Bruno. What if he'd managed to escape the Germans' clutches? What if I found him behind the counter of Once Upon a Time? The thought of seeing him again sent the faintest pulse of hope through me. But when I reached the bistro, I found the doors and windows boarded up and the Once Upon a Time sign painted over in black. Another story abruptly brought to an end.

I returned to my apartment and waited until darkness fell, holding my Aurelie doll and thinking of the day I first met Tomasz and how the threads of our lives had interwoven so fleetingly and yet so powerfully. 'Thank you,' I whispered, as I once again thought of him urging me to use my storytelling for good. 'Thank you,' I whispered as I thought about the day he'd given me the buttercup. Much as it pained me, I was certain that he must have died. So few people seemed to have made it home from the camps. Even those who had survived until the end mostly perished on the death marches the Germans sent them on.

At two o'clock in the morning, I decided that it was time. Taking my doll with me, like a child with her comforter, I left the apartment and went down to the bridge. The bridge where I'd first met Tomasz. The poignancy of the memory pierced right through me. A huge silver moon hung in the sky, causing the river to shimmer like silk. It was so beautiful, but I was so tired. All I wanted was to sleep forever.

Checking no one was coming, I hoisted myself up onto the ledge.

'*Don't do it*,' I felt Aurelie whispering to me from some-where deep inside my subconscious. It was the first time I'd heard her voice in years, but she no longer held any sway over me.

I propped the doll on the ledge and gazed down into the water, shuffled forwards, ready to drop.

'Etty! Etty! No!'

I glanced over my shoulder with a start, but there was no one there. I looked back at the water and again I heard a voice calling to me, telling me no. Was it Tomasz? Or was it Solly?

Now there seemed to be a chorus of voices. 'Don't do it, don't give up,' they were saying. 'We want you to live!'

Tears stung my eyes, obscuring my vision, but for a moment I thought I could see them, my musketeers, standing in a line behind me, in the moonlight, on the bridge. Tomasz, Solly, Marguerite, Macaroon and my beloved Danielle.

'We want you to live!' they were crying over and over again. 'We don't want your story to end!'

EPILOGUE

SHAKESPEARE & COMPANY BOOKSTORE, PARIS, 1946

'So, as you can see, I didn't die that night,' I said, smiling at the audience as I placed the book on my lap.

Spontaneous applause rang around the bookstore, warming my heart.

'And we are very glad of that!' Anton boomed from his seat in the front row.

My book had been out for a few months now and had taken France by storm. This was the last promotional event I was doing in Paris before travelling to London to launch the English edition.

'Thank you so much for your reading, Etty,' the owner of the store and our host for the evening said. 'Does anyone have any questions?'

A woman in the audience raised her hand. 'How do you feel now? Would you say you've healed at all from your experiences in the war?'

'I'm not sure it's possible to heal from something like that,' I replied. 'I think it's more about learning to live with the wounds, to live with the losses, and to keep trying to find sparks of goodness to release, as my dear friend Solly would say.'

'I love Solly!' a young woman exclaimed and it made my heart so happy to hear her speak as if she'd known him, as if he was still alive. And of course, in some sense he was, both in my book and in my heart.

'I love him very much too,' I said.

'What about Tomasz?' a man in the second row asked. 'Did you ever find out if he survived?'

I shook my head. 'I tried finding him here in Paris, but he never returned, so I can only assume that he must have perished.' I felt a stab of pain as I uttered the words.

'I always think it's foolish to make assumptions.' A man spoke from the back of the store, his face obscured in the low lamplight.

'Maybe,' I replied. 'But I think in this case it's safe to do so. So few people made it back from Auschwitz.'

'But some did,' the man said quietly.

'True, but I wasn't able to find him. And trust me, I really tried.'

'I loved how honest you were about Tomasz in the book,' the store owner said. 'And how you admitted you'd been wrong about him.'

'Thank you. I was wrong about him.'

'Yes, you were,' the man at the back piped up again.

I shot an anxious glance at Anton. One of the perils of book signings was that you couldn't control who turned up or the things they might say, but I was in no mood for any kind of provocation on this particular subject.

'OK, I'm afraid that's all we have time for tonight,' Anton said, taking my cue and getting to his feet. 'Thank you so much for coming, everyone. If you'd like Etty to sign your book, just bring it up to her at the table.'

I took a sip of water and began signing. It appeared that everyone present had bought a copy and as yet another book came sliding across the table towards me, I rubbed my aching wrist.

'Who shall I sign it for?' I asked without looking up.

'Tomasz. Tomasz Zolanvari,' a man's voice replied, causing my heart to skip a beat.

I took a moment. Took a breath, not daring to look up for fear that it was some kind of terrible prank. The strange man at the back perhaps. Finally, I found the courage to look. And there he was, smiling down at me, that familiar jagged scar on his cheek, that cleft in his chin. His frame had filled out again and his hair was longer, but his face was more lined than before and there were shadows beneath his eyes.

'You... you're alive!' I gasped.

'Apparently.' He shook his head and gave a sigh. 'Maybe one day you'll stop making wrongful assumptions about me.'

'You're the man at the back. You're alive. You're...' I stammered as I stumbled to my feet. He'd clearly hung back to be the last in the queue and the store had emptied. Anton was deep in conversation with the owner by the door. 'But... but where have you been?'

'Poland. I had to find out who was left of my family.' His smile faded. 'And then I came looking for you. But you no longer live in your apartment.'

'I had to move out. I couldn't stay there,' I replied. 'I have a new place now, in Montparnasse.'

'I see.' He smiled and shook his head. 'I thought you were dead. So imagine my surprise when I saw posters about your book popping up all over Paris. It was an excellent read, by the way,' he added.

'You've read it?' I felt a mixture of shock and embarrassment, thinking of all I'd written about him.

'Oh yes. It was very moving, and hopefully it will shock the world into never allowing such evil to happen again. But I feel I should clear up the mysteries I left you with.'

I winced as he repeated my words back to me. 'Oh yes?'

'Yes. Do you remember the night we met in the Pletzl, and how I behaved after we kissed?'

'How could I forget?'

'It wasn't because kissing you was *like drinking poison*.'

Again, I winced to hear my words.

'It was the opposite. It was because it felt so good. And that in turn made me feel very guilty.'

'Because you were in a relationship with the bookmark woman,' I burst out.

'Who?' He frowned.

'The woman in the photo that you kept in your book,' I said, thankful for the dimness of the lamplight to hide my blushes.

'Yes. But Marie and I weren't still in a relationship when you and I met.'

'Oh, I see.' Although, truthfully, I didn't see at all. My head was spinning from so many shock developments.

'She was dead,' he said softly, looking down at the table. 'She was the person I killed.'

'What?' I stared at him in shock.

'Not with my bare hands, but I might as well have.'

'I don't understand.'

'We were engaged to be married. Then, one night, we had a terrible argument. A stupid argument, over nothing, and she stormed out, and I let her go. I didn't stop her. And she was hit by a car as she ran across the road. I guess she was so upset from our argument that she didn't look properly. She died instantly.' He finally met my gaze. 'I never thought I'd feel like that for another woman until...' He cleared his throat. 'Meeting you really confused me, and it made me feel so guilty. I didn't believe I deserved to have such feelings ever again.'

'I understand,' I said quietly, thinking of the guilt I'd felt after Danielle died. 'But you weren't to blame. All couples have arguments. She was killed by the car, not you.' I felt a surge of relief at finally learning the truth about Tomasz.

'I know,' he replied. 'I realised that when I read about your father and mother in your book. And then when I read the ending, it was as if it freed me too. For so long I was drowning in guilt, but I think Marie would want me to live, and to love again. Especially after everything that's happened.'

We looked at each other for a moment.

'Perhaps, if you like, I could walk you home,' he said softly.

I nodded, my eyes filling with tears. 'I would like that very much indeed.'

A LETTER FROM SIOBHAN

Dear reader,

Thank you so much for choosing to read *The Storyteller of Auschwitz*. If you want to be kept up to date with all my latest releases, just sign up at the following link. Your email address will never be shared and you can unsubscribe at any time.

www.bookouture.com/siobhan-curham

A couple of years ago, when I was doing research for my World War Two novel *The Paris Network*, I came across the story of the novelist Irène Némirovsky. Némirovsky had been a bestselling novelist in France before the war, but once the Germans began their occupation, Jewish authors were no longer allowed to be published there. Némirovsky and her family fled Paris and in 1941 she began secretly writing a novel called *Suite Française*, inspired by what was happening in France. Tragically, Irène was arrested by the French police in July 1942 and deported to Auschwitz, where she died the following month. Thankfully, Irène's two young daughters were saved by their governess, and they spent the rest of the war in hiding.

Before they fled the family home, Irène's daughter, Denise, grabbed Irène's large, leatherbound notebook to take as a memento of her mother. For many years after the war, she couldn't bring herself to read the contents of the notebook, assuming it was her mother's personal diary and feeling it would be too painful. When she did finally read it – needing a magnifying glass to decipher the tiny writing inside – she discovered that it was in fact the manuscript for a masterpiece of a novel about life in Occupied France. *Suite Française* was finally published sixty-four years after Irène's death. If you haven't read the novel, I highly recommend it. To me, it's all the more moving, knowing the circumstances in which it was written. After I read about Irène Némirovsky's story, I couldn't get it out of my head. As a novelist myself, it felt impossible to imagine what it must have been like to be told that your publisher could no longer publish your work because you were Jewish. I was hugely inspired by the fact that she continued to write, and it made perfect sense to me; to a novelist, writing feels as essential as breathing, and not having a book deal is not going to stop that.

Then I read Etty Hillesum's diary and letters. Hillesum died in Auschwitz in 1943 at the age of twenty-nine and she is often referred to as the adult Anne Frank. Just like Frank, she was a wonderful writer and an extraordinary woman, who was able to find and express hope in the very darkest of times. Her diaries, written during 1941 and 1942 in wartime Amsterdam, chart an incredible spiritual journey. And even when Hillesum was sent to the Westerbork transit camp, she was determined to be the 'thinking heart' of the barracks, to help others find meaning and hope and inner peace.

The third writer who inspired this novel was Dr Viktor Frankl and more specifically his book *Man's Search for Meaning*, which my dad bought for me many years ago and helped me through a very difficult time in my life. Frankl was a psychiatrist who also ended up being deported to Auschwitz. Although he survived the death camp, his wife, parents and brother all perished. After the war, Frankl wrote about his experience in Auschwitz and his observation that although the prisoners had everything stripped away from them, they were left with one final freedom – the freedom to choose their attitude towards their circumstances. Frankl concluded that those who were able to find some kind of meaning in their suffering were able to continue to grow in spite of everything. Or as Nietzsche put it: 'He who has a *why* to live can bear with almost any *how*.'

Némirovsky, Hillesum, Frankl – each of these writers added a vital *what if* to the starting point of this novel. What if a bestselling French author lost her publishing deal because she was Jewish, and ended up being deported to Auschwitz? And what if she decided that she wasn't going to be beaten, that she would use her storytelling skills to help encourage and inspire her fellow prisoners to find purpose and meaning? And so the character of Claudette Weil was born.

Although *The Storyteller of Auschwitz* is a work of fiction, it is heavily rooted in fact. Prior to writing the book, I spent months immersing myself in true accounts of life in the camp. So while the characters and their stories are fictional, all of the background detail about the camp is real. Events such as that terrible day in February 1943 in the snow really happened, as did the scene featuring the guard and the apple, and the delicious soup served on Yom Kippur to try to tempt people to break their fast. I also came across an example of a Jewish boxer who was made to fight for the Germans in exchange for extra food, under the threat that they'd kill his family if he didn't obey them.

I've written over forty books in my twenty-three-year career as an author, but none of them have felt anywhere near as important as this one. When I was about twelve years old, my mum showed me a book about the Holocaust. There was a series of photographs in the book, one of which was of a mass grave full of the dead and emaciated corpses of Auschwitz prisoners. It was the first time I'd seen ever seen a dead body and I will never forget the horror of that image, which is exactly why my mum showed it to me. I remember her saying to me, 'We must never forget that this happened, so that we can prevent it from happening again.' At the time, it seemed impossible to imagine that the Holocaust could ever be repeated, and I struggled to understand how Hitler had managed to do what he did. In more recent years, however, due to a combination of current world events and my extensive research into World War Two, I've started to see how it all begins, and that has really troubled me.

Writing this novel is my small attempt to extend the sentiment conveyed to me all those years ago by my mother: we must never forget that the Holocaust happened so that we can prevent it from happening again. I also wanted *The Storyteller of Auschwitz* to be a tribute to the power of storytelling as an act of resistance, inspiration and remembrance, and with that in mind, I hope you have also found something to inspire you within these pages.

Siobhan

siobhancurham.com

 facebook.com/Siobhan-Curham-Author

 twitter.com/SiobhanCurham

instagram.com/SiobhanCurham

ACKNOWLEDGMENTS

First and foremost, MASSIVE thanks to Kelsie Marsden, for being such a wonderful editor. What a special gift it was to work with you on this novel; I'll never forget it. And, as always, huge thanks to the whole team at Bookouture, Sarah Hardy, Kim Nash, Noelle Holten, Ruth Tross, Alex Crow, Alex Holmes and Alba Proko, to name but a few. Much love and thanks as always to Jane Willis at United Agents for all of your support. And to Mara Bergman for being my sensitivity reader, and for all of the support you've given to me and my books over the years.

I'm also hugely indebted to all of the people who took the time to review my other historical novels, *An American in Paris*, *Beyond This Broken Sky*, *The Paris Network* and *The Secret Keeper*, on their blogs, Goodreads, NetGalley and Amazon. There are way too many of you to mention here, and I'd hate to accidentally miss someone out, but please know that I read and deeply appreciate every review, and all of the work you do to support authors and the book industry.

I'm not sure I'd have been able to write *The Storyteller of Auschwitz* if I didn't have the parents that I do. The fact that they first met at an anti-Apartheid meeting (organised by my dad) says it all really. I'm so grateful to them for instilling the need to speak out against hatred and oppression in me from a very early age. And I have to admit that the character of Solly is loosely based on my dad, and many of the Jewish beliefs and fables shared by Solly in the book were actually shared with me by my dad over the years. So a huge and heartfelt thank you to Anne Cumming and Michael Curham.

I'm extremely grateful to the friends and family members who have been so supportive of my historical fiction. Special thanks to Alice Curham, Steve O'Toole, Lacey Jennen, Gina Ervin, Amy Fawcett, Charles Delaney, Carolyn Miller, Thea Bennett, Linda Lloyd Sara Starbuck, Pearl Bates, Marie Hermet, Thea Bennett, Caz McDonagh, Sass Pankhurst, Linda Newman, Diane Sack Pulsone, Jan Silverman, Patricia Jacobs, Mavis Pachter, Mike Davidson, Liz Brooks, Fil Carson, Jackie Stanbridge, Pete Haynes and Abe Gibson.

And last but by no means least, THANK YOU to all of the readers who've taken the time to send me such lovely messages about my World War Two novels. Writing can be a lonely business, so it means the world to me to hear how much my books have meant to you.